Praise for Carole Nelson D

P9-CLR-508

Cat in a Gol...

"[A] superb series. . . . A fabulous novel. . . . Midnight Louie alone [turns] this novel into a gourmet treat."

—*Affaire de Couer*

"Carole Nelson Douglas provides lovable Louie with several believable anthropomorphic traits that make him seem like a feline with a human brain inside. . . . This entire series is unique and refreshing and highly recommended for someone who enjoys a different type of mystery." —Amazon.com

Cat on a Hyacinth Hunt

"Turn those summertime blues into cool, cool jazz as Midnight Louie trips the light fantastic one more time as sleuth extraordinaire—defender of truth, justice, and the American way. . . . As always, Ms. Douglas dishes up a crackerjack mystery superbly developed and resolved. But even better, she provides a depth of ambiance and a keen insight to the soul. Each of her books is a treasured "keeper" for her ever-increasing, totally devoted audience."

—*Romantic Times*

"*Cat on a Hyacinth Hunt* is the ninth entry in the Midnight Louie cat series and surprisingly the book retains the fresh and exciting perspective of its forerunners. The mystery remains first-rate while the romantic triangle (or is that rectangle with Louie being the other corner) has become more complex and interesting. The brilliantly talented Carole Nelson Douglas has set in motion story line twists leading the series in a new direction that is sure to surprise yet please Louie's biggest fans."

—*Midwest Book Review*

Cat in a Flamingo Fedora

"Douglas leads her readers on a merry chase before neatly drawing these disparate threads together. Midnight Louie's fans will be delighted." —*Publishers Weekly*

"It is always a joy to be reunited with that adorable tomcat, Midnight Louie, whose thoughts, deeds, and devotion make the feline seem more human than most Homo sapiens."

—*Affaire de Couer*

By Carole Nelson Douglas from Tom Doherty Associates

FICTION
Marilyn: Shades of Blonde (editor)

MYSTERY

IRENE ADLER ADVENTURES:
Good Night, Mr. Holmes
Good Morning, Irene
Irene at Large
Irene's Last Waltz

MIDNIGHT LOUIE MYSTERIES:
Catnap
Pussyfoot
Cat on a Blue Monday
Cat in a Crimson Haze
Cat in a Diamond Dazzle
Cat with an Emerald Eye
Cat in a Flamingo Fedora
Cat in a Golden Garland
Cat on a Hyacinth Hunt
Midnight Louie's Pet Detectives (editor)

HISTORICAL ROMANCE
*Amberleigh**
*Lady Rogue**
Fair Wind, Fiery Star

SCIENCE FICTION
*Probe**
*Counterprobe**

FANTASY

TALISWOMAN:
Cup of Clay
Seed upon the Wind

SWORD AND CIRCLET:
Keepers of Edanvant
Heir of Rengarth
Seven of Swords

*also mystery

Cat in a Golden Garland

A MIDNIGHT LOUIE MYSTERY

Carole Nelson Douglas

A Tom Doherty Associates Book

New York

CAT IN A GOLDEN GARLAND

Copyright © 1997 by Carole Nelson Douglas

A Forge Book
Published by Tom Doherty Associates, Inc.
175 Fifth Avenue
New York, NY 10010

Forge® is a registered trademark of Tom Doherty Associates, Inc.

ISBN: 0-812-53036-5
Library of Congress Card Catalog Number: 97-20790

First edition: November 1997
First mass market edition: December 1998

Printed in the United States of America

0 9 8 7 6 5 4 3 2 1

For all of Midnight Louie's "rabid" readers and fans,
who offer good homes to cats and books,
encouragement, expert advice on occasion,
and always fascinating cat tales of their own

Contents

viii • Contents

This Star Is Not in the Sky

Have you ever noticed that those who practice the mantic arts are not happy unless they are telling you about it?

In fact, they are happiest when they are telling you about *you*. Whether you want to hear it or not. *Especially* when you most particularly do *not* want to hear it.

This is my very situation with Karma, our landlady's more than somewhat strange resident cat. I do not deny that Karma has a certain "talent," I simply am not sure that it is psychic. True, our recent Halloween adventure at the haunted-house attraction did seem to produce a presence that could have been Karma. Still, I am not ready to agree that the will-o'-the-wisp of light that I saw on those occasions was some incendiary projection of a Birman cat with pretensions to prognostication.

I have been thinking long and deep on the situation (that is what I am really doing whenever I appear to be "resting") and I have concluded that the dancing dollop of candle power I saw could have as easily been a spark from the pipe of the English gent who turned up in the Ghost Parade. That Doyly dude in tweeds and overgrown eyebrows with the checkered cap. The British do like their patterns. Their preferences in that direction even run to calico and tiger-stripe cats. I of course am like Jackie O when it comes to fashion taste: I never wear patterns. Being born with a superb coat of shiny black hair that needs only an occasional shake and the lightest of licks now and then is another advantage. In case my moniker of Midnight Louie has not tipped you off or you have been in Tibet for the first half of the nineties, my appearance is a symphony in subtle black, with the white in my whiskers and the truly elegant green of my eyes keeping the rich simplicity of my daily garb from being a tad dull. Not that an undercover operator like myself would not stoop even to dullness to guarantee a low profile when I am investigating a case.

But I am off duty now for the holidays, and enjoying the simple life: loafing about the Circle Ritz apartment I share with my little doll, Miss Temple Barr. Not that she is any good at loafing; she is too young, in human years, to appreciate the pursuit. No, she is all bustle on her three-inch shivs—those high heels she prongs around on. I must admit that she is a bit deflated since the death of Darren Cooke. It was ruled a suicide, but I can tell that Miss Temple is not happy with that likelihood. I can only describe her as moping. In fact, she is so unnaturally sober and quiet these days that I would welcome a nocturnal admission of Mr. Mystifying Max. He is a magician whether he works at it or no, and likes to make surprise appearances, usually in the dead of night.

Ordinarily, I do not cotton to interlopers, and Mr. Max Kinsella is a territorial guy on top of it. I doubt that we would get along if forced to associate for any period of time. Miss Temple Barr is my roomie now, since Mr. Mystifying ran off like a scalded alley cat with no notice or explanation a year ago. What you leave is mine, if I want it. And I have nothing to complain about in the accommodations Miss Temple Barr has put at my disposal. The bathroom window is always ajar, a narrow, burglarproof invitation to the open road. (Though with Las Vegas's growing resident population and almost fifty mil of tourists ankling through day in and day out, open roads are pretty hard to find around town.) My bowl is always piled high with the latest tempting garnishes to the plain Jane Free-to-be-Feline health food lurking— untouched—beneath. And I have an emergency facility under the bathroom sink should I care to get clay litter under my nails, instead of the sandy desert dirt of Las Vegas.

Since I am recuperating from some minor surgery incurred in my last case, I am not minded to hop out the window for a night on the town. (Luckily, thanks to a bizarre twist of fate and despite extreme attempts to pare me down to the size of these petty, ultra politically correct times, I am still the same larger-than-life macho dude you know and love.) And Miss Temple Barr is out for the evening. I hope that she is out with Mr. Matt Devine. Him I could put up with, if he did not hog the covers. Unfortunately, I do not believe that even Miss Temple has explored Mr. Matt's sleeping habits. These humans are annoyingly slow with their mating rituals!

I understand the need for maturity and caution nowadays, as felines are subject to AIDS also, but I could give Mr. Matt Devine a tip or two about courting the female of any species. First, you show up and refuse to go away. Then you put up with the customary repeated brush-offs. Persistence is the name of the dating game. Finally, you wait until she is not looking and jump her, sinking your fangs into her neck . . . well, maybe human dudes can forget the fangs unless the lady is partial to vampires. I must admit that it is all over in a few seconds, which is why we feline dudes try again . . . and again . . . and again. Persistence wins lady fair every time, although she may yowl and slap your face when it is all over. Dames!

I am musing on the dating game when I hear one of the several French doors to the patio rattling. We are on the second floor and safe from all but the most agile cat burglar. Still, I am home alone and all my senses go on alert. In my invalid condition I am not ready for fisticuffs. Might pull out my stitches in a delicate area.

So I wait and watch, ready to make some really nasty noises if an unauthorized party breaks in. I am not worried that it might be Mr. Max Kinsella; he never announces his imminent arrival with any vulgar noises. Actually, we have a lot in common when you come to think of it—black hair, a way with the ladies, slightly felonious intent and a possessive nature—which is probably why I cannot stand the guy.

While I wait I speculate on who, or what, might be broaching my retreat. This is how to keep an active mind even when the body is in full sloth. I have ruled out: the seasonal overnight delivery service with Christmas presents for Miss Temple; the pizza guy; the big ole palm tree outside dropping one of its leaves with an anticlimactic shudder like a stripper doffing her last pastie.

Now I hear a not inconsiderable weight launched at the door. Or kicking the door. The force was applied very low to the ground. A door-stomping burglar. This could be serious. Guys with no regard for the delicate fretwork of a fifties-vintage glass-and-wood French door would do anything, including stomping the petals off the begonias on poor Miss Temple's patio. I recall when my little doll was assaulted in a parking garage by some thugs the size of Godzilla. Are they paying my lovely mistress a midnight call? They will get more Midnight than they planned on.

I snick out all four sets of shivs, hearing the satisfying rip of surgically sharp nails into the canvas covering of Miss Temple's sofa. My recuperation has meant that I have not been wearing my feline edge down to a dull nub with street wanderings. I am twenty pounds of thorny, snarling, growling pussycat, and if I am not quite as formidable as Kahlúa, the magician's panther, I am a close second. I prepare to leap high when the door is broached, and go for the eyes.

Finally the door pops ajar. I know how rickety those old locks are from my own surreptitious comings and goings.

I leap into the air like a heavyweight butterfly, prepared to sting like a manta ray, a big black winged shape at one with the darkness, yet darker still than night, and out for blood . . . the Hooded Claw!

It is an imposing attack, and it is launched at empty air. Nothing. *Nada* to a Chihuahua. Nil. The Big Nothing. Nowhere.

I twist to make sure I land shiv-first, and snap my switchblades to "safety." I return to earth like a sack of potatoes with bunions.

On top of the intruder.

Which is pale and soft like some huge spider-creature.

And which has blue eyes.

Uh-oh.

And which is hissing and cursing me in some very ripe language.

"Louie, you obnoxious unbeliever!" she finishes up. "Why did you not help me open the door? I have ruined my best nails trying to break in."

I roll away as fast as a dude in my delicate condition can manage it. "I thought you could just sort of . . . leak in, like mist or daylight."

"Only under special circumstances, like psychic emergencies. And the stars are not right. All Hallows' Eve is long past."

"I can read a calendar all by myself, Karma. So what brings you out of your hidey-hole in the penthouse suite?"

Her blue eyes blink and water at the faint nightlights Miss Temple leaves around the place for my nocturnal convenience, though I think it is mostly for her own peace of mind.

"You do this all the time?" the Birman babe asks, in tones that are either admiring or disbelieving. "Fighting the plant life and the railing and then . . . leaping to the lower balcony. Oh, it was too awful. And however shall I get back up again? Miss Electra Lark will be so shocked to find me missing."

"If you are missing, how is she going to find you? Do not worry, I will escort your Psychic Self back up. You should avoid the physical world like the plague, and stick to the hoodoo-voodoo stuff, doll. Your coat is a mess and you look a little wobbly on the pins. You definitely are not dressed for breaking and entering."

She shakes out her café-au-lait fur coat, then smooths her white gloves and gaiters into apple-pie order before deigning to answer me.

"If you knew how difficult it was for me to leave my refuge and find you . . . gratitude is not one of your virtues, Louis."

"Cut out the 'Louis' stuff. You are trying to make me sound like an uptown cat when I have always been a downtown cat. My name is Louie as in King Louie the Umpteenth and in Crab Louie and in the rock 'n' roll classic song 'Louie, Louie.' "

"The various kings of France called 'Louie' spelled

their names 'Louis.' The French merely drop the last consonant when pronouncing the name."

"No wonder the French beheaded their kings! Poor old Louie the Sixteenth! If the French are that care- less about dropping the terminal *s* on a classy moniker like Louie, what difference will chopping off a reigning monarch's head make? At least they had the pronunciation right, and in my book that is a lot more important than getting the spelling perfect."

"Getting the spelling right is very important in ar- cane matters," she retorts with a sniff, one of those effete little purebred sniffs that implies access to a gourmet brand of catnip. "And that is why I braved the awful out-of-doors and performed a most dangerous balancing act to come down and tell you my latest news hot off the crystal ball."

I shake my head. A five-week-old kitten could make its way down two floors at an old building like the Circle Ritz, which drips with "architectural details"— stepping stones to my breed—like a black marble Christmas tree decorated in bric-a-brac.

"I cruise the Internet with Miss Temple myself," I put in with a yawn. "That is where all the real action is these days. So what tricks is Miss Electra Lark's big green-glass globe up to?"

Karma settles onto her haunches, tucking her forefeet under like a yogi, or a swami or some Ori- ental pundit from Siam. (I understand that we are supposed to say "Asian" nowadays, but "Oriental" has a ring to it I cannot give up, and I do not see why political correctness must edit the language of words that make a nice singsong yowl in the conversation. Certainly my usage has ruffled the ineffable Karma's fur, for the pale hair-tips seem to glow in an unseen aura.)

"I am channeling a new ancient. Ever since my psychic exposure, through you, to the forces at the doomed Houdini séance, someone impossibly old has been trying to come through."

I shrug, and her enormous blue eyes whip to my twitching shoulder blades. Blazing out from the dark brown that masks her face, them there eyes are pretty potent.

"I have finally found out who I am dealing with," she announces. "Someone incredibly old. Unfathomably powerful."

"Bob Dole?" I quip, the recent election having been decided by a landslide for Socks Clinton, a personal buddy of mine, on account of I saved him from running away from the will of the people and abdicating his First Cat status. And he was the First Cat in the White House in a long, long time. It sets my mind at ease to know that Bill Clinton's ear is purred into nightly by the *real* power behind the presidency— Socks himself. Hillary is just there as a front-woman to take all the flack.

Karma waits for me to stop grinning, then says, "Bast."

"No need to swear at a little political humor," I say.

"Bastet," she adds, using the ancient deity's full, formal name.

"Sssst!" I hiss. "You do not wish to take that particular honcho's name in vain. Or honchette, I guess I should say. I have met the lady, and this is one goddess you do not wish to hiss off."

"I know. Bast and I have had many conversations about you."

"Me? What is there to talk about, except my ancient lineage that goes back all the way to the Pharaohs? Through the maternal line, of course."

"Bast was most pleased to hear that you have re-formed your alley-cat ways. The choice may not have been free but at least the neutering operation was."

"Listen. There is nothing neutered about any part of me. I did not have your usual back-alley procedure, you know. This was a VIP-level operation in every respect. This doctor dude has worked on Schwarzenegger and Stallone. I have not lost a thing. Not one thing! And not even two. It was all done with lasers and lipo. You want to see my scars?"

She shuts those blue-lightning eyes for a weary moment. I suppose that when your soul is older than the Hollywood hills, the concerns of ordinary beings are paltry things. But then, my concerns are never paltry, B.O. or A.O. (Before Operation or After Operation).

"So you have been rendered sterile but remain virile. Interesting, but hardly the coming thing. I understand you still leave your odorous 'marks' around the place, still get into immature fisticuffs and still play the Romeo. You will have to undergo many more lives before you can progress to another level of development."

"I do not want to progress! I want to stay right where I am, doing what I am doing. Eating, drinking and making whoopee."

"I am afraid that this is exactly what you will not be able to do for the immediate future. That is why I am here, to warn you."

She shakes her sagacious Birman head. For the first time I notice a tiny gold ring against the brown of one eartip, and I admit I get the shivers. The last cats I have seen so decorated were mummified models wrapped up in gauze so tight that they resemble two-thousand-year-old bowling pins.

Her head tilts so the earring catches and ricochets back the night-light glow. "A mark of favor from Bastet. Poor Electra is quite confused about when she took me to the mall for a piercing. Mine, unlike yours, was a psychic procedure, and performed by the goddess herself with her own Sacred Fang."

I swallow. I am glad that I am not in Bastet's favor, if she is going to staple-gun my ears for the privilege.

Besides, I do not wear any sissy earrings. I even disdain a simple leather collar, and certainly those new, Day-Glo jobbies that are elasticized like a brassiere or something. Supposed to be a safety feature, but I personally think they are designed to make a normal dude look like an idiot.

"So what is going to happen to me? Nothing like knowing the future to give a person a nasty sense of impending doom."

"Oh, it may not be doom in store for you, Louie. Merely a sudden, long trip to a far, alien place more strange than any you have seen before."

"I am going to be kidnapped by extraterrestrials? Those bug-eyed grasshopper guys who haven't heard about needle safety regulations? They might mess with my altered state. No way. Besides, the only saucers I like are filled with brandy Alexanders, not grasshoppers."

"Such an imagination." Karma almost smiles, save I have never seen a cat smile yet. Maybe grin a little when no one is watching. "But you have been earmarked for a great role in the affairs of the day."

I do not like that "earmarked" idea and feel one of mine twitch. Ever since my involuntary surgery, various extremities have developed nervous tics. I know, I know. Nothing was lost. But it was close. If Miss Savannah Ashleigh had not been so dumb as to take me to her personal surgeon, I could be singing falsetto with the rest of the "retired" boys in the band right now.

"Do not growl, Louie." Karma stretches her limousine legs, then arches her back and rises. She is big enough to tower over me. "Change is not necessarily loss, but opportunity. See that you take advantage of the ones soon to come your way. Now. Can you see me up to my room?"

She makes it sound like a little gentlemanly escort duty, but it is more like baby-sitting. Turns out this babe is afraid of heights, and going up is a lot worse than coming down. Our return is supposed to be discreet, but that is hard to achieve when it takes an occasional claw-prod in the posterior to keep her moving up the façade of the Circle Ritz, which has suddenly become as black and slick and smooth as a frozen lava wall. But she bites back any yowls of protest at my herding technique and I finally goad her over the patio railing into Miss Electra Lark's territory again.

"Even Bast's psychic surgery was kinder than your ministrations, Louie. Was such rudeness necessary?"

"Rule One in Advanced Climbing Technique: keep moving or drop dead."

With that blunt summary I leave her.

Bast's earring winks at me as I turn to head back down.

Maybe the goddess—a pretty hip chick two thousand years ago, after all—is wondering if I am fully recovered from my operation.

Chapter 1

An Offer Not to Be Refused

"Don't move! Just listen. You've got to get an agent, pronto!"

Temple listened to the voice on the phone, still numb from the import of the previous call, one made to her, not like this one that she had made immediately afterward.

"It's such short notice, though," Temple answered the urgency on the line's other end. "I'd been thinking about visiting you for the holidays—"

"Don't think. You can hire someone to do that for you. This could be very, very big."

"Not at one hundred and fifty a day."

"That was last week. This is . . . this week. From what you said they said, this is a whole new ball game."

"I hate ball games. I hate that expression. Could you try something less clichéd?"

"You're concentrating on trivia because the Big Picture is too new to take in. Look. I must know Someone who knows Someone. This is New York City, after all. Everybody's a specialist. Let me call around and get you a reference. Then we can talk housing arrangements."

"Yes, but I don't see—"

"Yes, but. You don't see. That's the problem. Just hang up. Sit tight and let Aunty Kit handle it. I'd love to see you for Christmas, sweetie, but I'd much rather see you with a decent contract in your hand. Cheerio."

Temple couldn't tell if her aunt was under the influence of a food craving or simply wishing her good-bye. But she did as instructed, she hung up and looked at Midnight Louie, who had actually exchanged his comfy sofa for the hard kitchen countertop when the call had come half an hour ago.

"Looks like we'll be seeing Kris Kringle at Macy's this year, Louie. You know, *Miracle on Thirty-fourth Street* Macy's. Except they might not let you in. Oh, golly, I hope Aunt Kit knows what she's doing. If she blows this deal . . . but she's a novelist and she used to be an actress, and they both use agents, so I guess she's my nearest expert, besides being a contact in Manhattan. Just think, Louie! You and me, living it up for the holidays in New York, New York."

I yawn. I have interrupted my nap, after all, to rush over and eavesdrop. The first call was a lot more interesting, because it was mainly all about me.

"Poor fella! You're so pooped from your medical nightmare, and now I'm supposed to whisk you off to New York and all the performance pressure, in pursuit of mythical beasts: cruel chimeras of Fame and Fortune. I wonder if we need another agent to look after your interests alone? Like in messy divorce cases. You are going to be a 'party of the first part,' after all."

I got a late-breaking headline, doll. I have always been the Party of the First Part, especially now that I still have all my parts—by some miracle and a dopey blonde's mistake. And they call *us* dumb beasts!

"I do not know." Miss Temple kicks off her magenta suede high heels so I can read the label. Some dudette named Nicole Miller. It is nice to see the little dolls coming up in the world nowadays and becoming majorettes of industry and design.

She wiggles her toes, a gesture I can appreciate, and I do not even wear shoes, much less skyscraper shoes. I wonder if she will take her designer stilts to New York, New York. It is an either-way call: heads she wears 'em and is not fit to flee a mugger, and tails she does not, and is therefore unarmed with a sharp instrument when attacked in Broadway daylight.

"Will any hotels let you in? Maybe the Algonquin. It has always had a 'house cat,' after all, along with a house tie for errant gentlemen in too-casual attire. Kit says we could stay with her, but I hate to impose."

Say, this Indian joint is my kind of place. I am always dressed in formal black. As for staying with Miss Temple's aunt, one Miss Kit Carlson, that is okay with me. Impose, impose! I am the only "house cat" on any premises I choose to honor with my presence.

She sighs. "I would consult Matt, but he has left for work, and Electra is officiating at a wedding downstairs . . . why does good fortune always strike when all your friends are AWOL?"

I am here. She must have heard me because she starts stroking my ears. I wonder if I am destined for the Mr. Clean earring. Well, all the rock stars have them. I suppose I could have something tasteful. Like a sterling-silver carp. Or eighteen-karat gold, if I am a star.

She jumps so high when the phone rings again right in front of us that I nearly leap off the countertop. Get a grip, girl! If you are going to be a big-time manager, you will have to be as cool as Ice T.

"Hello? Yes, I heard from your account exec and I'm giving it serious thought. Of course I have to consider all the ramifications—That is a lot of money, but I need to discuss it in person. Oh? On your tab? And the cat? Well, he has to fly too. Only in the cabin. I won't have him in the cargo area. All those horror stories—"

Cargo area? What does the geek on the other end of the line think I am, chopped liver? I would not confine Miss Savannah Ashleigh to a cargo area, and after what she had done to me, that is a severe indictment indeed of cargo areas.

"I'll call you as soon as I know something definite. Yes, I realize it's eight P.M. in New York. You work awfully late there, don't you? Oh, everyone does. We work hard in Las Vegas, too, only we get done three hours earlier. I'll call tomorrow. Yes, it has to be tomorrow."

She holds her hand over the receiver and finally asks me something. "Who can Kit dig up at eight on a Friday night?"

Beats me. Elvis, maybe. Or an out-of-work vampire. Now that's an agent after my own heart, a genuine bloodsucker.

Miss Temple hangs up and continues what she thinks is a monologue. "Oh, Louie! What a strange turn of events. You, a corporate mascot. I wonder if they know what they're letting themselves in for?"

Temple stared at the phone. Like a watched pot that never boils, a watched phone never rings. Public relations rule number one. Public relations rule number two: never work with children or animals; they're too unpredictable and they'll steal every scene.

But that was all right if scene-stealing was the name of the game, and Louie was a natural.

"I wonder if they know your proclivities for crime?" she asked her only audience.

My proclivities for crime? The only proclivities for crime that I have in these latter domestic days of my lives are *your* habits of tripping over dead bodies. Maybe if you gave up high heels you would trip over bodies a lot less.

"Maybe my strange affinity for murder only works in Las Vegas. Maybe in New York everything will be differ-

ent. I sure get a high-pressure feeling from that vice president. I thought *this* town thrived on hype—"

The phone trills again. I cannot take this Grand
Central switchboard act. I leave Miss Temple to her
fate and jump down to inspect my Free-to-be-Feline
bowl. Still pretty uninspiring. The couch calls.

"Yes!" Temple was relieved to hear her aunt's haunt-
ingly husky voice. It was like eavesdropping on an aural
doppelgänger. Temple cleared her throat, though it never
helped to banish the frog from her voice. Why it should
work by proxy, she didn't know.

"Got someone," Kit said. "Does this sort of thing all the
time."

"What sort of agent?"

"An odd sort. Not an actor's agent. More like a personal-
appearance agent."

"Is this person working for me, or Louie?"

"You. You're the only one who can sign a contract. Pre-
sumably you own the cat, not vice versa."

"Have you ever kept a cat?"

"No."

"Then you don't know how wrong you are. But I assume
Louie will press his paw on the dotted line if I make him
do it. The trip to New York will be the test. If he doesn't
like traveling, it's no deal. I'm not going to cart a twenty-
pound feline protestor around."

"This could be a major opportunity for you as well as
the cat, Temple. Quince tells me big money should be in
it. You could become like . . . Shari Lewis and Lamb
Chop."

"Louie's no Lamb Chop. If I want to make like he's a
hand puppet, he'll probably eat my hand."

"Are you saying the animal is vicious?"

"I'm saying he's determined; there's a difference. He
was a street cat for Lord knows how long. He went his own
way and still does to some extent. At least Savannah Ashleigh has made sure that he won't father any inconvenient

kittens, but he'll still be interested in any available girl-cats he comes across."

Any? I think from the other room. Does she believe that I exercise no discretion in these matters? What does she take me for, an alley cat?

At this point Miss Temple launches into a dramatic description of my recent kidnapping and stint as an involuntary subject of a mad plastic surgeon. I doze off, having heard this story before, in person.

I know all the important stuff anyway. We will fly to New York City. We might stay at a tony hotel, or we might stay at the aunt-doll's digs. Miss Temple will take me places to see people neither of us know, who will give us lots of money. We will have an agent. We will be big shots. We will have to watch our hindquarters. So what is new?

Chapter 2

Sofa, So Good

"When do you leave for New York?" Matt asked Temple.

The December sunshine refracted from the pool as they passed it on the way to the Circle Ritz's minuscule parking area.

"Day after tomorrow."

He stopped dead. "And this can't wait? Don't you have better things to do?"

She had stopped too, and stood jingling her key ring, which dangled a lot of hardware besides keys to jingle: police whistle, pocket flashlight, pepper spray. For a small woman, Temple's accessories were usually king-size.

"Can't wait," she explained. "It's my Christmas present to you, and I won't be here for Christmas."

"Believe me, I can get along without this at least until the New Year."

"But I can't! What do you get the man who has nothing?"

"Nothing."

"You don't get off that easy. Come on. This'll be fun."

He doubted it, but once Temple made up her mind about something insignificant, she was as hard to stop as a Sherman tank. On significant matters, she was as two-minded as anybody else.

Matt followed the muted click of her high heels over the asphalt, the winter sun surprisingly warm on his sweatered back.

"You drive," Temple suggested, digging in her tote bag for the actual keys to the car. "I'll navigate."

"You're the expert."

He was glad to get into the Storm, small as it was, to adjust the seat, shut the door, take the wheel, after an exclusive stint on the Hesketh Vampire.

A motorcycle was an antisocial vehicle, he had found. You rode alone, even with a passenger behind you. A car was not only weatherproof, but a portable parlor as well.

"I know you probably hate this," Temple was commenting, "but it's a good lesson in everyday life." She flourished a fist of scrunched Yellow Pages torn from her phone book. "The best route would be The Bee's Knees first, then hit Leopard Alley. We can save Indigo Albino for last, or even swing past the Goodwill and Saint Vincent de Paul's."

"Sounds like a list of speakeasies." He started the car, amused. The expedition rather intrigued him, this innocuous hunt so unlike the genuine track-down on his mind.

"Just aim me toward the right part of town," he told Temple.

"That's the problem. Most of these shops aren't in the 'right' part of town, but in the iffy side. Rents are cheaper."

She directed him north to Charleston Boulevard, away from the Strip. Matt liked tooling around town on weekday noons, when everything was less crowded. It reminded him of Saturdays off from school when he was a kid, when his mother took him shopping in downtown Chicago for clothes.

And that reminded him of less pleasant plans.

"Some of this stuff"—Temple was studying her battle

plan marked in ballpoint pen—"is pretty wild. Or far gone. But gems are still out there. A lot of it is fifties or sixties; you may not like that."

"I don't know what I like yet."

"Really?"

Matt shrugged, floating the Storm through a left turn. No sideways slippage, like on the Vampire. No charge of excitement either. Matt could finally tell the difference, but didn't know which he liked better. Yet.

"What was the house you grew up in like?" Temple asked next.

"Built in the nineteen twenties. Our neighborhood was brick and stucco two-story, two-family places crowded together. Two-flats, they called them: small, dark rooms; small, mostly dirt yards, because that's where the kids all played."

"We had one of those bland blond fifties ramblers, one-story, everything rectolinear, like a railroad car. That's why I love the Circle Ritz. No room is square!"

"Our furniture was forties stuff. Saw tons of it in the rectories later, only that was rich parishioners' mahogany hand-me-downs. Every rectory looked like a set for *The Bells of St. Mary's.*"

"Missed that one. A movie?"

"Forties movie with Bing Crosby as a priest and Ingrid Bergman as a nun." He hummed a bit of the title song.

"Wow. A real golden oldie. And old Ingrid running off to have an out-of-wedlock child, too."

"That was later. Here's Burnham. Where do I park?"

"Anywhere along here."

The lot was sand and stones. Matt had glimpsed a psychedelic sign and display window out front, both radiating color and clutter.

"I'd never set foot in a place like this in a million years," he said as they left the car.

"Good. Stretching your boundaries already. Honest, no illegal drugs and naughty adult toys sold here. Just funky old stuff."

He still felt he wouldn't want Lieutenant Molina catching him going into this place. They wove past unmatched pieces of furniture set up outside the shop, Temple stopping to squint seriously at a wicker rocking chair. "Be nice on the patio, maybe."

Inside was more of the same. Matt studied the chrome glitter of vintage appliances, the bright secondary colors of orange and turquoise dishes, the wire-framed chairs. Suitable for furnishing a clown academy, maybe, but not for his mostly empty five-room apartment.

"Oooh. That's a nice dinette set."

Temple zeroed in on a chrome and gray table surrounded by four chairs pneumatically upholstered in silver-flecked gray plastic.

"Great condition." She ran her hand over the plump plastic, her silver-blue nail polish making her hands seem armed in stainless steel.

Dinette sets gave Matt the willies, for some reason. "I'm not about to start serving guests."

"No, but the odd neighbor might drop in."

"Very odd, if she frequents this place."

"You've got to look past the bizarre stuff to the treasures."

"Sounds like a motto for visiting the risqué establishments along Flamingo Road and Paradise."

But Temple was already engrossed in exclaiming over a chrome thingamajiggy with attractive pierced panels on either side. With a razor-tipped fingernail she demonstrated that the panels flipped down. "Twenties toaster. Will clean up like new. Twelve bucks. Sold." She picked it up. "Rule number one: if you see anything you like, hang on to it."

"What for?"

"You're eyeing my treasured toaster dubiously."

"It can't still function."

"No, but it'll make a great letter-holder. 'In' mail on one side, 'Out' on the other."

"Never would have thought of that."

"That's why you have rooms full of nothing."

"I don't think twenties toasters are on my 'most urgent acquisition' list."

"You don't even have a list. Just look. See if anything catches your eye. Don't worry about what it used to do. Just think how you could use it now."

His hands slid into his pants pockets as he wandered the crowded floor. Maybe if he didn't touch anything, he wouldn't have to buy anything.

Temple streaked from area to area like a butterfly cruising honeysuckle vines. She had to touch, lift, tilt, study a dozen pieces. And then she was paging through the clothing racks. Except for the somber shadows of old tuxedos and worn leather jackets, the racks were a kaleidoscope of women's clothing. Weird women's clothing. Or maybe that was a redundancy.

Matt found himself staring down at a fifties-model black telephone, its brown cords trailing like rat tails. Funny. He'd forgotten the old phone number in Chicago, before the exchange was altered when phone usage exploded in the sixties. They'd had a word as an exchange, not three little numbers. Exchanges back then had sounded classy. Very British. Very WASP. Madison, not Mahoney. Kent, not Kaplan. Wentworth, not Waschevski. Emerson, not Effinger.

"A phone?" Temple's voice was so close it startled him. "You work on phones all night and now you moon over one in a vintage store?"

"Hadn't seen one like this in a long time."

"What a difference three years make," Temple mused. "I was born after everything went from black and white to color—appliances, sheets, telephones and even television."

Matt smiled. "We didn't keep up with the latest trends on Sofia Street. Black and white, and a few good shades of gray, were good enough for St. Stanislaus parish."

"No wonder you have virtually nothing in your apartment. Come on. Except for the toaster, this place is a bust."

"But . . . I haven't looked at everything."

"I have."

Temple swept out, toaster in the crook of her arm, along with a small yellow paper, the receipt.

"What's next?" Matt asked when he was behind the wheel of the car and the toaster was stashed on the backseat. "Leopard Lane?"

"Alley," she corrected. " 'Lane' is far too upscale for a vintage store. The name should be a little tawdry. Leopard Alley. It's only twelve blocks away. Take a right at the next corner."

Leopard Alley lived up to its name. It was inside an aging strip shopping center that had been converted to an antiques mall. The interior was a maze of cubicles allotted to various dealers. In one booth glassware dominated; in another, kitchen and garage tools.

Leopard Alley announced its imminence with a painted canvas path of faux leopard spots.

"Look at that footstool! Isn't that wild?"

Matt regarded the wrought-iron stool upholstered in fuzzy fake leopard skin. Wild, and not his style. At least he was learning something on this expedition. Perhaps he was hopelessly addicted to Rectory Rococo. Something convoluted and diocesan in Ash Wednesday mahogany, reeking of incense and parish politics.

"Oh! What do you think of this?"

Temple had donned a leopard-skin pillbox hat from the fifties, that sat as uneasily upon her springy red hair as Bob Dylan's "mattress on a bottle of wine."

"Not your color," Matt said.

"I guess I'm not built for exotic." She lifted a long black plastic cigarette holder dotted with rhinestones. "Thirty-eight dollars! Give me a break."

"Louie would look like the king of the jungle on this pillow," Matt pointed out.

She studied the huge furry leopard-pattern pillow. "Yeah. Poor Louie. He doesn't know he's in for a major dislocation."

"It's a long time away from home."

"Not so long, ten days. I added the holidays so I could

see my aunt. Louie will only be on call for business for three or four days. You'd think this could wait until after New Year's, but apparently when they're hot to trot in advertising, they don't waste a millisecond."

"You'll have a great time."

"But you're not having one now." Temple eyed the pillbox. "You sure I shouldn't invest in this piece of nostalgia? It's only eighteen dollars."

"When would you wear it?"

"I don't know. Maybe for Halloween."

She replaced it on the time-battered bald head of the mannequin bust that wore a matching stole. "I'll think about it. Maybe, if it's still here when I get back . . ."

"What's next on the list?"

"Indigo Albino might be too . . . kicky for your taste. Tell you what, I'll take you to lunch at the Monte Carlo as a Christmas present, and on the way we can stop by the Goodwill. You never know."

"Antique-hunters are eternal optimists, like detectives. I can see where you got your sleuthing instincts."

"Well, you're passing out class pictures of Cliff Effinger all over Vegas. Is it cockeyed optimism or dogged footwork? Anything turn up on that, by the way?"

"Nothing," said Matt the pessimist. "Yet," added the optimist that Temple brought out in him.

"Hey, this Effinger dude could be hanging at the Goodwill," she suggested playfully as they returned to the car. "You did say that he was dressed like a seventies midnight cowboy."

"More like a midlife-crisis cowboy. Okay, a prelunch gander at the Goodwill. I'm beginning to see that hunting anything is ninety percent persistence and ten percent damn foolishness."

"Damn foolishness is the best kind. You owe yourself a little."

Matt mulled the alien concept of owing himself anything but angst as they drove to the Goodwill building, a low, bland bunker of green-painted cinderblocks with a few dusty display windows near the entrance.

Inside, it was a warehouse crowded with racks of wilted clothes on twisted wire hangers, homemade shelves of abandoned dishes and household whatzits and a weary odor of must, stale cigarette smoke and dust.

Temple's pale eyebrows rose. "Never been here. I didn't know they had a rack of vintage clothes."

She was off like a racehorse interbred with a bloodhound.

Matt felt a benign, avuncular amusement as he watched her page expertly through the sorry castoffs looking for buried treasure. Men hunted furred and feathered creatures in the woods, and then killed them. Women hunted inanimate things, expressing the same instinct in a bloodless way. Men proved their virility with limp, frail legs and dead antlers on a car hood; women announced their femity with a fake leopard-skin pelt draping a footstool.

Matt strolled the naked concrete floor through cluttered aisles, watching the people here as if they were in a casino. Many Hispanics, mostly women, a lot of children in tow. Fussing, sharp Spanish reprimands, whining. They needed these fifty-cent jars and two-dollar baby rompers. By the register, a woman was checking out. Some dirty beige acrylic gloves for the Las Vegas "winter," a few navy-blue towels in still-good shape, a child's plastic toy in Crayola colors. A small pile of children's clothes.

She had a one dollar bill on the counter, and was doling out coins from her purse for the rest. Her face was the pinched, unlearned mask of Depression-era photographs. The poor could wax fat or lean on malnutrition, depending on their metabolisms, and this wizened mother had thinned with want.

"Twenty-five cents?" She gazed at a child's orange jacket, then counted out pennies. Meticulous. One. Two. Three. Right down to the last penny, which was coming fast.

"I guess I'll leave the rest," she said, shutting the worn wallet.

The woman at the register knew better than to argue with the face of the bottomed-out. Or to extend the too-obvious magic wand of charity. This charity cost. Not much, but enough for self-respect.

"Here." Matt extended a ten-dollar bill to the cashier. "Merry Christmas."

"Oh." The woman wanted to say no. Her eyes rested on the toy pushed away at the last moment.

The cashier rang up the abandoned goods with swift efficiency, before the woman could protest.

"Thank you." She barely looked at him. She barely spoke aloud.

He said nothing more, because it would be too little, and too much.

And he accepted the change the cashier solemnly counted into his hand. Offering it to the woman would have been insulting.

So little had been needed of the ten. Two dollars and thirty-five cents.

The woman snapped the coin section of her wallet shut, gathered up the recycled brown grocery-store bag, and left, with one more murmured "thanks" over her shoulder vaguely in Matt's direction.

"That was nice." Temple stood beside him, chastened. "I never even noticed her."

" 'Tis the season."

He shrugged to avoid the eyes of the clerk, as she avoided his. Face-to-face charity was always as delicately negotiated as international treaties. It did not "blesseth he that giveth and he that taketh," as Shakespeare promised that mercy would via Portia the Wise, the "Daniel come to judgment" in female guise and guile. It embarrassed them both.

Temple took his arm. "I'm sorry I took you out on this wild-goose chase. I just wanted to help you get *something* for that empty apartment of yours."

"Why?"

"Nest instincts. Maybe I just wanted to make sure you're staying."

"Oh, I'm stuck here—not at the Circle Ritz, per se, but in the real world. At least they tell me it's real."

"It is." Temple's eyes narrowed with the vigilance of the huntress. She skittered away toward the far wall, through a weary, grazing herd of melamine end tables and crooked lamps and dirty lamp shades.

"Oh, God!" she said.

And to his embarrassment, he paid attention and followed her.

"Will you look at that."

"That" was apparently a long, long sofa, an overstatement in curves, upholstered in red fabric, that stretched perhaps eight feet along a wall.

"Real suede," Temple pronounced, stroking the surface to verify the diagnosis. "This is custom. From the fifties. Can you imagine custom-ordering an eight-foot sofa?"

"No. I can honestly say that I absolutely cannot imagine ordering an eight-foot sofa."

"How much do they want for it?" She was patting along the sinuous length, looking for tags. "Aha." She held up a card on a string from behind the back. Her voice lowered. Matt had to come closer to hear. "Only three-twenty. This thing costed thousands when it was made! And it's in perfect condition. You can tell granddaddy died and they pulled it out of the den after forty years of placid use."

She squeezed behind the sofa and began trying to push it away from the wall.

"Temple."

"Heavy." Temple was not usually one to state the obvious. "Can you push out the opposite end? I want to see the backside, because of course it's made to sit in the middle of the room . . . good, good—ah, something happened here, but . . . you could lay something over the back. A leopard skin or something with a little kitsch. Or have just this section recovered. Look at these seams. Perfect. This is hand-sewn." Temple straightened, fire in her slate-gray eyes. "Matt. You've got to get it."

"Three hundred dollars, I don't think so."

"That's nothing! You could buy junk at the warehouse furniture stores for that amount. This is the real thing. It's a classic. Pure design, pure materials, almost unused. You'd never find this in a million years."

"Especially if I weren't looking for it."

"It's made for the Circle Ritz. Don't you get it? It's in the period and it's of an equal quality."

Temple raced over to the cashier. Matt, bemused, followed.

"That sofa over there. Yes, the big red one. When did it come in? Two months ago? And where did it come from? Uh-huh. Oh, sure."

Matt heard the masterful inflections of mere curiosity in her comments as she wheedled every detail available about the huge sofa from the clerk, all the while acting as if her interest was merely . . . academic.

"Such an interesting piece," she finished up. "Too bad it's so *big*. I mean, where would you put it if you didn't have some huge recreation room in the basement, and so few houses here have basements . . . it sure is something, though."

She ambled back to study it, Matt her obedient servant coming up behind. He understood that an entire scenario was being enacted here.

Temple grabbed his sweater sleeve as soon as they were out of earshot. "You could offer two-ninety for it. Easy. I'd hate to go lower, and lose all chance of negotiating."

"*You* could offer two-ninety, Temple. You're obviously in love with the piece. You should have it."

"But my place is built around that stupid hide-a-bed sofa. It's hemmed in with furniture and accessories. Your place is a blank slate. Matt, you could build a whole room around this wonderful piece. Imagine it sitting on that lovely old parquet, warming as burgundy wine. It would save you buying a love seat and two chairs and this and that. Hey, you could sleep someone over on it."

He eyed the slow but definite curves. "If they had scoliosis. How would we get it moved out of here anyway?"

"Electra's a landlady. She must know dozens of reliable outfits that move stuff. Couldn't cost more than . . . fifty bucks."

"I'm on the third floor—"

Temple shook her head impatiently. "This is a once-in-a-lifetime find, trust me. You need to put something in your living room. With this as an anchor, the job's three-quarters done. You have to get this, or you're absolutely crazy!"

"I'm absolutely crazy," he said deadpan.

Her face fell, but even in defeat a new argument was marshaling in the back of her mind. He saved her the trouble.

"But I'm going to get it, okay? Sold by the lady in the leopard-skin pillbox hat. Almost."

"You know, maybe we should swing by afterward and get that—"

He took her elbow and hustled her to the checkout table.

"I'll take the sofa. The one the size of Godzilla's grandmother, but first I have to see about arranging to have it picked up."

The clerk was in seventh heaven. "We have a list. Check, credit card or cash?"

"How about half now and half on pickup?" He pulled out his new Discover card.

The clerk snapped it up like a 'gator grabbing a guppy.

Beside him, Temple writhed in swallowed agony. "Matt, you didn't *deal,*" she whispered when the clerk was absorbed by punching in numbers.

"It's already a good deal, so you swore. Besides, it's almost Christmas. Consider it a donation."

"Donations are donations. Dealing is dealing. You could have always sent them the donation later. Paying sticker price like a rube ruins it for everyone else."

"I'm getting it, right? Aren't you happy?"

She took a deep breath. "I'm ecstatic. It really is . . . wonderful. It deserves a good home. I'm so glad you got it."

"It's not a living thing, Temple. It doesn't know it'll be the star of the Circle Ritz."

"Yes it does," she answered fiercely. "Yes it does."

Chapter 3

Escape from New York—Please!

Temple sat in her aisle airline seat, as queasy as Midnight Louie probably was feeling right now.

Louie was invisible. All Temple could see was his new airline-approved Kit-Karrier, tucked under the seat ahead. Temple herself was all too visible in the getup she decided was necessary for this hasty jaunt to New York. Looking down in disenchantment, she saw clunky, well-padded high-top tennis shoes. Black leggings. (She expected to be doing a lot of bending over to tend to Louie. And black wouldn't show cat hair. Much.) A loose, almost knee-length sweater over a heavy turtleneck. All black, so as not to show Midnight Louie hair.

Her usual tote bag was stowed overhead. Her valuables—wallet, ID, credit cards and the directions to Kit's place on Cornelia Street, plus sundries—were crammed into a weensy boxy patent-leather purse, also black, that made Temple feel like an eight-year-old showing off her new Easter bag. She loathed impractical purses almost as much as she despised practical shoes. Inconsistency, she believed, is the hallmark of a discriminating mind.

But . . . anything for Louie.

At least he was being quiet. Ominously quiet. Too-angry-to-spit quiet. Wait until he saw the new CatAboard Seat Temple had purchased at the pet store before they left. It even came with one of those despised diamond-shaped yellow signs first used to announce "Baby on Board," now adapted for anything portable, including "Cat on Board." Temple had tried to peel it off, but the glue proved too tough and too disfiguring. She had considered covering the noxious sign with a real "Baby on Board" badge. She figured she might get more respect in transit, but doubted it. Especially when she shoved the carrier under the seat. Pride of portage didn't count for anything any more. Not even "My Cat is an Honor Student."

"How about 'My Cat is a Star'?" she bent down to ask Louie in a whisper.

The businessman in the adjoining seat flashed a look that was half annoyance and half alarm. He had arrived after she and Louie were installed, and had whipped out a lap-top computer as soon as the pilot announced passengers could get plugged in and turned on.

Everybody talked to their underseat luggage, Temple told herself with a haughty shrug. Mr. Laptop was cluck-ing away on the small keyboard, grim and concentrated.

Since her feet seldom reached any floor, Temple usually propped them on her underseat bag. But the lightweight Kit-Karrier was too flimsy to support a pair of massive high-tops. She wrestled her paperback book from under the carrier strap and sighed. This was a four-hour flight, with nothing to munch on but an air-swollen bag or two of pret-zels as dry and appetizing as matchsticks.

She opened the guide to New York City and began reading.

More than three droning hours later, Laptop Man had ab-sconded to the rear restrooms. Temple shook her wristwatch, moved the dial ahead three hours and wriggled her legs. Landing soon. She lifted the middle armrest in the tandem seats, then cozied up to the window and raised the shade Laptop Man had kept drawn tight all through the flight. It was sixish in Manhattan, winter twilight time when the sun takes its own sweet time in setting. The whole visible world basked in a bruised burnt-orange afterglow.

She caught her breath. Below the plane was the East River, a glitter of beaten-copper ripples in the dying light. Manhattan landmarks strove to stab the pale sky in the twilight's last gleaming. The Statue of Liberty, a tiny dot in the black water, flashed the slow-moving plane overhead, the lit torch flaming like a match head. Temple could just make out the wakes of tiny boats wrinkling the water like irons gone amok.

The World Trade Center's twin towers, wrapped in glass, reflected the sunset in a plaid of windows lit from within and without. Dozens of other modern building-block towers also resembled glitter-wrapped packages under some cosmic Christmas tree. Accidental autumn warmth sparkled everywhere like gold foil. The sun's tangerine lightning galvanized the Empire State Building's familiar spire. The Chrysler Building's graceful fluted cap shone as silver leaf turned gold. From up here, the Chrysler Building was undeniably much lower than the Empire State Building. Temple had pictured them as nonidentical twins, matched in size if not style. Now she saw that the Chrysler Building was a squirt. An illusion about New York City shattered already, and she hadn't even landed!

The plane, an ocean liner of the air, dropped altitude at a dignified rate.

"Excuse me."

She looked up to find Laptop Man standing beside her empty seat, managing to look both impassive and annoyed. Oops.

Temple scrambled back to her seat and out into the narrow aisle to let him enter.

He replaced the retracted armrest as if reinstalling a security system, glanced out the window at the shimmering scene, then snapped down the shade. Under the reading light's singularly narrow, yellow stare, he jotted figures onto a notepad.

Temple preferred a taciturn traveling partner. With landing imminent, she felt like a marathoner about to enter a race. Mentally, she ran the rush to retrieve her bags and the dash for the terminal, then the rapid, long walk to the baggage area, with a ladies' room stop for her (and Louie too). Then she would have to wrestle her huge bag off the luggage return and get out to the cab area without being waylaid by a gypsy cab driver. Kit had warned her against those con men. Then would come a traffic-choked entry into downtown Manhattan during rush hour. Lord, she hoped she got one of the few cab drivers who still spoke English so she could tell him where to go.

After that came seeing Kit, meeting all the ad agency people and the pet-food company executives . . .

Temple leaned her head against the seat, concentrating for a moment on what she had left behind instead of speculating on what lay ahead.

She'd told Electra Lark, her landlady, first. Gone for ten days over Christmas. Back by New Year's. Left Kit's address and phone/fax number. Asked Electra to make sure that Matt Devine wasn't alone for Christmas . . . Then she had called good neighbor Matt, who still seemed stunned that she would fly off like this, on such short notice. He had promised to keep an eye on her place. She had debated calling Max Kinsella, but he was prone to drop in on her without warning, and she didn't want him to think she'd been kidnapped by the thugs who were after him for mysterious reasons he refused to explain. She'd left a message on his answering machine, which still answered in the dead Gandolph the Great's voice, wondering where he'd gone. Max the magician was like that: there and not there at the same time.

Then she'd told Van von Rhine and Nicky Fontana at the Crystal Phoenix Hotel and Casino, the closest thing she had to a regular employer. They thought the reason for the trip was a blast and told her to have a good time.

I will, Temple told herself.

Temple's seat back was hit from behind, suddenly.

"Oh!" She sat forward with a start.

The plane was landing. The pilot had just applied the brakes, and Temple found an irresistible force plastering her against the upholstery. Just landing.

"You must have dozed off," her seatmate finally commented. "We're here."

As soon as the seat-belt-sign light deadened, people jumped up. Temple was among them, in the rat race of the present and future, lugging, tussling, jockeying for position, inching forward, tote bag slung over one shoulder, book and handbag stowed inside, Louie's carrier held before her with both hands, so he wouldn't jostle against the seats bracketing the narrow aisle. Better bruises on her legs than a howling dervish on her hands.

Louie gave one piercing yowl as they exited the plane. The flight attendant smiled indulgently, no less than he would have done at seeing the last of a bawling two-year-old.

Temple huffed up the exit ramp into the terminal. Laptop Man had been right behind her. Now, with only a briefcase and a small bag to carry, he sprinted ahead. Temple studied the faces that flowed past her, recognizing no one. And no one recognized her.

The entry-into-New-York-City scenario unreeled as her mind had played it.

Except for an unforeseen circumstance. In the women's

restroom she attracted a circle of admirers when she heaved Louie's Kit-Karrier to the baby-diaper-changing shelf and brought him out for water and a snack. He drank the water, sniffed disdainfully at the Free-to-be-Feline and looked put-upon for the admiring ladies.

"What a handsome animal! Do you travel with him often?"

"This is the first time. If it works out, who knows? Say, could one of you watch him for a sec while I, you know—"

"Sure," said several voices.

Temple hastened to a cubicle, uneasy about leaving Louie even with his own groupies.

When she returned and pulled the CatAboard Seat out of her tote bag, they oohed with interest. Temple wriggled into the contraption and latched it shut over her chest and stomach.

"The idea is," she explained, panting, to the bemused audience, "he rides up front in this carrier, I fold away the airplane carrier and now have both hands free for the rest of my luggage."

"Marvelous," said a glossy blond career woman who at first glance had looked too cold to care.

"Like with a baby," added a Hispanic woman with grandmotherly certitude. "Much better to carry the weight in the front."

A rawboned woman with a Swedish accent actually lifted Louie into the bag. Temple winced as his weight pulled on the shoulder and waist straps. She felt like she was en route to the booby hatch, and was properly trussed up for the journey. But the *Forbes* woman put her expensive eelskin briefcase on the baby platform to tighten the drawstring around Louie's neck.

In the mirror Temple looked like a demon-possessed mountain climber. The nylon CatAboard looked like a backpack in reverse whose disembodied head had made a one-hundred-eighty-degree rotation.

The Hispanic woman chuckled.

A college girl with a glossy brown braid down her back grinned. "He looks pretty disgruntled with just his head sticking out."

"Disgruntled I can handle." Temple was still reeling from the unaccustomed weight up front that pulled her off balance. Must be what being pregnant felt like.

She thanked the fan club and reentered the slipstream of jostling people in the concourse outside.

Of course she—or Louie, rather . . . or rather Louie's disembodied head—drew the kind of constant comment that becomes harder and harder to accept gracefully.

By the time they were bumping along in the back of a cab that smelled like the cockpit of a World War II troop transport plane, or what Temple thought such a locale would smell like, she was too exhausted to make sure the driver was taking the approved route: the tunnel, not the bridge. Temple didn't know which tunnel was preferable to which bridge, but Kit had sternly instructed her to recite this secret phrase, and so she did. If it cost her an arm and a leg, heck, her extremities were going numb anyway! And this was all on the advertising-agency tab.

The driver and the drive into Manhattan were as expected: curt, fast and jerky. Temple fought nausea from long, idling waits in carbon-dioxide-clogged air while the engine trembled before vaulting forward with a snort.

The driver broke a long silence finally to growl something that sounded like Kit's address followed by a question mark.

"Yes. Cornelia Street."

More lurching down side streets, wheel-well to wheel-well with parked trucks. Temple's eyes closed at every imminent collision, which meant she spent the last leg of the journey in almost total darkness. She could have been diverted to New Jersey and would have never known the difference. Then the cab stopped in a dark, narrow street.

"This is it?" Temple wondered aloud.

No comment. But the driver was looking impatiently over his shoulder at the choked tide of cars, cabs and trucks.

"Couldn't you pull up to the curb? There's an empty space."

His head shook vehemently. "Out here."

"I'll need a receipt," she called through the smudged Plexiglas between them.

She could read the meter, but not the name on the driver ID card, just a vowel-laden string of foreign syllables.

She paid and tipped him, struggled out with Louie's significant weight shifting wildly against her stomach . . . he kicked her! Yup, just like being pregnant. Which she might never be able to be now, not unless aliens kidnapped her to accomplish it. She could barely tilt herself out of the low backseat. The driver had thoughtfully used the internal lever to loosen the trunk latch for Temple.

Temple trotted around the huge yellow cab, amazed to see no blatant scrapes, reached in to heave her monster bag over the high trunk liftover. Horns performed a hoarse hallelujah chorus around her, probably *at* her. Temple gritted her teeth. Let them honk! She hated luggage. She hated New York. She slammed the huge lid shut so hard it startled Louie into a loud growl.

"Shut up!" she told him through her teeth. "People will think my stomach is growling."

As if the people milling past on the sidewalk had time to think of anything besides where they were going and how fast.

At least the big suitcase had rollers. Temple finally wrestled it to the walk, hooked her tote bag on for the ride and began scanning the building fronts for an address.

She was aware of a carpet of crushed refuse on the

sidewalk, of men who could only be described as "loungers" leaning against the buildings and closely watching her struggles, of narrow doorways that seemed to be numberless, of cramped shop fronts that looked crowded and jumbled and sleazy. Was this even the right street?

Temple hoofed it to a corner, people colliding with the bag she towed behind her, and searched for street signs. Standing and looking was not a safe activity in New York City, she decided, taking shelter against a wall herself near the entrance to a drugstore.

She finally went in, waited in line, and asked about the address.

The female clerk didn't even look up, so she missed seeing Louie on his maiden voyage as a floating head. "Block down. The other side. Left."

A block! Why had the cabbie dumped her and Louie a block and a half away? And on the wrong side of the street? Couldn't he count? Read? "New York, New York," she muttered as she dragged herself and the luggage back into the mob.

Nobody noticed.

She could have been carrying the decapitated head of Alfredo Garcia and no one would notice, she thought grimly. She could be mugged, murdered, taken by aliens and nobody would notice. Except the men hovering by the buildings, watching the passing women and shouting nasty things they fortunately couldn't quite hear. No one shouted anything remotely nasty at Temple. Being pregnant with a cat was not altogether a bad thing, she decided.

By that time she'd gone too far, and had to retrace her steps, cross at a green light a street that everyone else had already crossed on the previous red light. Finally, squinting in the dark at absent or illegible numbers, she found the right one. But could this narrow, dingy entrance possibly house a respectable apartment building?

By the time she'd entered and found the small elevator and wondered at the wire crisscrossing the glass in its small window, and had gone up to the proper floor, she was ready to walk all the way back to Las Vegas, *en famille*.

She rang the doorbell. This had better be the right place!

Chapter 4

A Ticket to Ride

Some may be wondering at my saintly conduct during the trials and tribulations of my transport to New York City. Is it possible that they take Midnight Louie for a prima donna of some kind?

But no; I am the most laid-back and genial of dudes. Why should I object to being cooped for several hours within a purple nylon Kat-Karrier with sexy peek-a-boo black mesh ventilation areas, much resembling the fishnet stockings on the legs of certain damsels of an exhibitionist nature?

Should I take umbrage at my public transfer to the purple nylon CatAboard Seat in a ladies' room of a major metropolitan airport?

Does any of this detract from my macho dignity?

Not at all.

Purple, after all, is the color of royalty, and we all know just how royally I am descended. My great-great-great-etcetera grandma (Oh, mighty Bastet; I bow to your female feline superiority) was Pharaoh's

favorite gumshoe. Or perhaps it was gum-sandal.
And sometimes footstool. They also serve who only
sit and accept weight.

And at least these portable devices are modern
and lightweight. There is nothing worse to rattle
around in than the plastic shell of an old-fashioned
carrier with a steel grille. The newfangled products at
least use zippers (and those who have followed my
adventures know that my way with a zipper is almost
as smooth and sassy as my way with females—
of any species). The amusing and inventive Cat-
Aboard Seat even offers the prisoner—I mean the
passenger—a view. If said passenger is not inadvertently throttled by the neck-area drawstring. Also in
this front-tote device, I am kept close to the heart and
best interests of my little doll, Miss Temple Barr.

Did she think no one saw the nasty dudes ogling
her from the building walls? Had one ruffian dared to
approach, I would have huffed and puffed my way
loose of the drawstring (or, if unable to burst free fast
enough, bitten anything tender within reach).

Besides, one other fact explains my extreme docil-
ity in being dragged from pillar to post at forty thousand feet high and six hundred miles an hour fast: I
like to travel. I got around quite a bit before deciding
to honor Miss Temple with my cohabitation.

I have even been to the previous Inauguration in
Washington Dee Cee, where I saved the president-
elect from an embarrassing moment involving a sax-
ophone and a hidden stash of grass as in illegal
tender, aka marijuana. In fact, if there is any justice
in the world, I should be invited as a special guest at
the next Inauguration. So I have flown before, and not
on catnip. Hence my calm demeanor during this
whole expedition. I understand that one's dignity suf-
fers dearly going from one place to another. Just look
at Miss Temple Barr as she stands here huffing and
perspiring in front of a pretty nondescript door on the

eighth floor of a nondescript building in lower Manhattan.

She is a mess. I, however, travel well. I do not even have a hangnail. I can hardly wait to get out and about to explore what some have named Baghdad-on-the-Hudson, the Big Apple, the Naked City. None of these nicknames makes any more sense than what my kind call it: the Mother of all Hairballs.

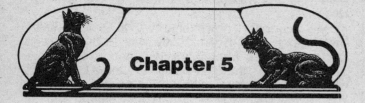

Chapter 5

Ho! Ho! Ho!

The door opened at last.

Temple braced herself for a stranger, for a snarling New York City apartment-building superintendent, the legendary "Super" of sitcoms. She would have been prepared for one of Santa's errant elves, for who-knows-what, but anything other than her aunt Kit. This had not been her day and there was no reason for the evening to start playing into her expectations.

She retained her cool when Santa Claus himself stood there, white beard and long curled hair flowing, wearing nothing but red long johns that matched his cherry-red button nose, and Rudolph's, for that matter.

A stubby crystal tumbler of amber liquid in one hand might explain the red nose.

"You must be Temple Darling!" he exclaimed in a deep baritone that belonged to a Don Giovanni at the Metropolitan Opera.

He was also as thin as a cat's whisker. Did Santa have a secret eating disorder? Bulimia might explain how he dealt with having to consume all those cookies on Christmas Eve.

Temple Darling was uncharacteristically speechless. Clearly, she was expected. Clearly, this was not her aunt.

"Come in, Little Merry Christmas!"

Santa stood aside, a grand welcoming gesture perilously tilting the glass and its eighty-proof contents. "And bring your little cat too," he added with a cackle that was far from jolly. "Oops, sorry! Just did the matinee witch at the Children's Museum. Wrong part."

Wrong place, Temple thought.

But she was unwilling to lug a single thing, especially Midnight Louie, anywhere else for a while. Besides, they knew her name here.

Coming in surprised her.

The polished oak floors were glossy enough to see your underwear in, if you were wearing skirts, and neither she nor skinny old Saint Nick were.

High, white and handsome walls intersected at unexpected angles, creating the feeling of an ultramodern maze, or a blank theater set.

"Kit Darling," Santa called over his red shoulder to the Great Unknown beyond the current cliff of albino wall. "Mother and Child are here, seeking a room for the night. No guy, and no donkey, unless I'm to be dragooned into the part. Probably the ass." He slugged down a fat finger of booze in one gulp that made his Adam's apple prance.

"Must whip up the reindeer and run, Temple Darling. Got to do the whole boring nine yards: boots, belt, hot red felt fat-suit, everything. Not to mention the Mae West underneath for the proper avoirdupois. But anything for the kiddies and an honest buck."

He vanished around one white wall at the same moment her aunt, Kit Carlson, rounded the other wall like an ingenue in a Sardou farce.

"Did our Father Christmas pull his vanishing act? I wanted to introduce you formally. How are you, Kit?"

Kit, draped in a caftan of a far more sophisticated cut

and color than an Electra Lark muumuu, swooped open her arms in the proper pose for a ballet third position. The resulting butterfly effect wrapped Temple in a cocoon of muted earth-tone silk and some spicy, expensive and thoroughly decadent perfume.

"He'll pop off in a couple of minutes. He has a Macy's gig tonight, and I let him change here. I'll introduce you later, when he comes back."

"I didn't know Santa Claus made return engagements. And should he have Cutty Sark on his breath for the kiddies?"

Kit laughed. "One lowball to help face everything from pathetic Tiny Tims to greedy little monsters will hardly ruin Santa's reputation. Besides, he'll use a mouthwash chaser. Leave your luggage here by the door. You look like you've been lugging it long enough. Rudy can take it to your room after he gets back."

"Rudy?"

"Seasonal, isn't it? One of those outré coincidences that happen so often in a city this large. Come on. Sit down. Kick your shoes off. Unfasten your cat. Hello, Louie! Holding up, are we?" Kit laughingly surveyed the carrying device.

"Temple, I'm sorry, but you look like a candidate for a freak show, going to a job interview with your cat-headed Siamese twin attached."

Louie responded to Kit's greeting with a long drawn-out meow of disapproval.

"He is not Siamese anything," Temple translated more accurately than she could know.

"Sorry." Kit's husky voice had gone small and wee. She beckoned them around the white wall, and Temple went. An ajar door on the right tantalized with a slice of a powder room with black fixtures and malachite-design wall paper. Potpourri scent teased through the opening.

Midnight Louie sneezed.

The hall was really a kind of gallery. Uncurtained windows on the left offered a broad sill trailing pink camellias and poinsettias. On the right they passed an open kitchen done in butcher block counter tops, white appliances and stainless steel everything else, and undoubtably as efficent as a Danish Jack the Ripper.

All along the hall, faint reflections in the night-dark windows followed them like ghostly Siamese twins.

These unshrouded canvases of glass, blackened by the night beyond so it was impossible to see out, but acting as display windows into the apartment's well-lit warmth, unnerved Temple. They violated her cautious Midwestern sense of privacy, even safety. Anybody could look in and see every detail as easily as a child spying into the secret world of a snow dome.

"Doesn't New York City sell blinds or curtains?"

"Temple," Kit chided, "we're eight floors up. Plus, even all those distant office towers are closed for the night."

"So you assume."

Kit stopped, her caftan an autumnal flutter around her slight form. She was an older (and one would hope, wiser) edition of Temple herself, down to the slightly foggy voice, the oversize eyeglasses and her petite size.

"Temple. Trust me. I know New York. You're not in Las Vegas now. Everything is not a peep show. The sad fact is that damn few people in Manhattan have the time, inclination or elemental curiosity to pry into other people's lives, much less their windows. We are hives of worker bees, each on our own buzzing mission, with no time to sightsee. So relax."

Temple made a face behind her when her aunt resumed walking. Kit's assessment sounded depressingly true. Only rank newcomers—tourists was the demeaning description—would be as curious, or as cautious as she.

Then the white wall on their right ended with a column and a brick wall. Before them, the wide, welcoming main room narrowed to a point as sharp as a pencil's.

And the focal point framed by the converging window-walls from both sides of the apartment was Manhattan glittering in all its towering Christmas glory, the illuminated lightning-rod tips of the Empire State and Chrysler Buildings as thin and elegant as lit candles on a birthday cake.

Only it wasn't Temple's birthday, and getting here had been no piece of cake.

"This feels like we're on the prow of a ship," Temple began, "but—"

"Goodness, Temple! You live in a round building in Las Vegas and think nothing of it. Don't be so square. This building is shaped like a flatiron."

"The guidebook said the Flatiron Building was uptown from here—"

"*It* is. We're in the Village. But the building is similarly shaped, although smaller."

Temple edged into the unusual space, feeling doubly watched by the windows streaking to meet in a vanishing point of midnight cityscape just thirty feet in front of her.

"The view is magnificent."

"Too magnificent to cover with curtains or blinds. I'm glad you like it. I bought this place dirt cheap in the mid-eighties, before Reagan-era greed really got prices going skyscraper-high."

"Dirt cheap?" Despite the tawdry street-level neighborhood, Temple couldn't believe that any domicile in Manhattan was cheap.

"A hundred and thirty thousand." Kit shrugged. "Now close your jaw, take off your cat and coat, and sit down for a while."

"That was mondo money over ten years ago."

"I'd written a lot of historical romances by then, and the place has at least tripled in value since. I guess when it comes to retirement plans, you could say I'm sitting on it."

Kit plunked down on the black leather tufted sofa that faced straight into the nexus of New York, New York. "Can you really get out of that straitjacket solo? Do you need help?"

"No. I just unfasten these side latches, open the sack

drawstring, pull Louie out and then gracefully shrug out of the, uh, straps."

The pulling out of Louie and ungraceful shrug that divested Temple of all encumbrances took three minutes.

"Let me get you a drink." Kit jumped up.

"I worry about Louie's claws on this leather—"

"Don't. I've had Russian wolfhounds on that couch. Louie is a fine example of a gentleman compared to them, I'm sure."

Kit returned with brandy in small snifters, sharing a tray of crackers and various spreads that looked gooey and foreign.

"Bye, Darlings!" a short, jolly fat man's voice shouted from the foyer.

"Knock 'em dead!" Kit hollered back, lifting her glass in a toasting gesture.

"Isn't he going to be dealing with hopeful little children expecting comfort and joy?"

"It's only one of those black-humor theatrical expressions, like 'break a leg.' " Kit looked Temple up and down from over the rim of her glass. "Are you in mourning? Did one of the Divine Mr. M's kick off since I was in Las Vegas? Tell me it isn't so!"

"I wore black traveling to *minimize* cat hairs."

"You look like you're dressed for an expedition to Machu Pichu high in the Peruvian Andes. No high heels, however, a wise move."

"I brought 'em along, so I can change off when I arrive where I'm going."

"Which is Madison Avenue. We're not right on top of it, but you can always catch a bus uptown if the cabs are all busy. I don't recommend the subway, even in running shoes. A lot of women use it, but they're residents stripped down for battle. You're going to be handicapped by toting a feline passenger around."

"I know. I know." Temple sipped some brandy. She was no judge of fine-anything alcoholic, but whatever the brand, blend or vintage, the liquor melted away the day's anxiety like a velvet blowtorch.

"We can have dinner out around here, or in, if I dive into my astounding selection of deli take-withs."

"Here is fine. I'm worn out. And I have a nine A.M. appointment at Colby, Janos and Renaldi tomorrow. Louie and I do," she corrected as he paused in settling beside her on the couch to place a forefoot on her thigh, claws lightly extended. "I imagine he's tired too. I didn't have time to tell you about the recent Atrocity."

"Oooh. An Atrocity and a fresh one too! As if the newspapers didn't run enough news of that ilk on a daily basis. I'll sprint back to the microwave and warm up something starchy while you kick off those tennis shoes with the glandular problem and prepare to tell your tale. I don't suppose we can call it an 'Old Wives' Tale'?" she caroled from the kitchen.

"More like a 'New Knives' Tale.' Or 'Tail' as in attached to the rear end of an animal."

"Not Louie's end?"

"Indeed. And almost unattached."

"Oh, dear." Kit peered intently around the kitchen wall to inspect Louie's extremities. "He looks all there. Oh. He hasn't lost something invisible? Did you have him fixed?"

"I didn't have to." Temple explained how the cat was kidnapped by an enraged Savannah Ashleigh, certain that Louie was the Unfortunate part of the Condition that afflicted her purebred Persian, Yvette.

Kit was scurrying back on her velvet holiday mules to see Temple's full performance as the infuriated aging starlet playing Cruella de Vil.

" 'And furthermore,' she told 'the finest plastic surgeon in Las Vegas,' and she oughta know, 'I want this beast fixed so that he will never leopardize a female cat's breeding potential again!' "

"She ought to have been thinking of a jaguar. She abducted your cat just to have him neutered? Without your knowledge and against your will? Incredible. And she took Louie to a plastic surgeon?"

"I'm afraid Savannah was running on her Energizer bunny batteries again, instead of the usual brain power. Actually, it turned out fine. The dazed doctor performed a vasectomy on Louie. That was the only 'neutering' procedure he knew anything about. And he threw in a free tummy tuck."

"Oooh!" Kit's eyes momentarily turned envy-green as she admired the lounging ex-tomcat. "You couldn't get me an appointment for something similar? I don't need surgical contraception at my age, but I sure could use all the tucking I can get."

"You look trim as a paper cutter, Auntie dear, act twice as sharp and look half your age."

Kit almost purred in time with Louie. "Children are so sweet . . . when they're all grown up. And if you expect me to confess my age after all that buttering up, forget it, Niece."

"I wouldn't dream of asking. Besides, my mother is sixty-seven or -eight, so—"

"Never mind. I can tell you that I was a wisp of forty-nine not nearly as long ago as it seems. What a demented bimbo!" Kit had returned to the subject of Savannah Ashleigh. "How anyone would let *that* attempt to act is the biggest mystery of all."

"No, the biggest mystery about Savannah Ashleigh is what she'll do when she finds out what I did."

"And that is?"

Temple coddled the brandy snifter in both her hands, as if warming them at a private fire. "I filed suit against her. In small-claims court."

"In Las Vegas?"

"That's where the crime took place."

"But . . . isn't there an antiroaming cat law there? Wouldn't Louie be in the wrong just for being available for catnapping?"

"The issue is the willful alteration of a cat she knew was

not hers. And, besides, Louie was wrongfully accused of parenthood."

"He didn't do the wild thing with the nubile Yvette?"

"Not long enough to produce four yellow-striped off-spring. I understand that kitty litters can result from more than one tomcat, but a black sire would always produce at least one black cat."

"Who do we know that is yellow-striped?"

Temple allowed a smug expression on her face as she stroked Louie's satin-furred ears. "Maurice."

"Maurice? Chevalier is dead. I think. Yvette's name is the right nationality to appeal, but the species is wrong, even for a Frenchman."

"Haven't you seen those Yummy Tum-tum-tummy ads on TV? The big yellow cat that comes running?"

"Not often. Oh. That's Maurice? The British pronounce it 'Morris,' you know."

"Well, over here we pronounce it 'Maurice,' as in *Father of the Bride.*"

"Then that's the cat that Louie bounced to get the commercial job that's brought you both to New York to visit the ad agency? I'd say Yvette's indiscretion was lucky for all concerned."

"I sure hope so. This has come up so fast I haven't had time to consider if a show-business career is the best thing for Louie and me. I'd have to be away from home, traveling, and Louie's no lightweight."

"But he's obviously star material. Look at him lolling on black leather as if to the limo born! You can't deny the thespian talent. Louie deserves his time in the spotlight."

Chapter 6

Phantom of the Wedding Chapel

Just because it seemed so perversely inappropriate, Matt played the theme from *The Phantom of the Opera* on the small Hammond organ.

At three in the morning five days before Christmas, the Lover's Knot wedding chapel was deserted except for the attentive, soft-sculpture presence of its constant "congregation." Not that the Christmas holidays weren't a popular time to get married; they were. So popular that Electra had to schedule weddings for the holiday period and used her new drive-by service for the overflow.

Like Santa, she'd taken on a few seasonal "elves" to help with the nuptial overload, and had even inked in time off for herself.

Oddly, Matt had never cared much for performing weddings. Despite the picture-perfect look to the grand day, behind-the-scenes involvement revealed all the familial cracks in the united front produced as lavishly as a Broadway show for one day of pomp and circumstance.

The high cost of contemporary weddings, even modest ones, only upped the stakes.

Beyond the in-law tensions, the money squeeze and open warfare over who should pay for what, beyond tiffs about who was in the wedding party, the bridesmaids' dresses, the music or the flowers, Matt most hated the hypocrisy so common nowadays.

The Charade, he called it privately and contemptuously. This was the prewedding dissolution of a common household, when bride and groom who had been cohabiting, as the sociologists called it, for months, or even years, established separate addresses for the few weeks before the wedding . . . before they showed up at the rectory, parents in tow, to discuss the ceremonial details.

Matt was supposed to counsel them, ignoring the unspoken awkwardness of the true situation. He was supposed to publicly endorse a fruitful union, and privately assume that of course they would not resort to artificial means of contraception . . . when they had been using such means for months, or years. Now, though, in his office, they would be born-again virgins, presumed innocent of unworldly ways, baptized in the church's desperate desire to pretend that mores were what they had used to be.

Older priests, proud to be known as die-hard conservatives, used the prenuptial period as an opportunity to thunder like Moses come down from his mountain with his shalt-nots carved in stone: "You will," the priests would force eager-to-wed couples to agree, "be open to all the children that God gives you."

Obviously, they had not been open to possible children while living together, and would not gladly accept the possible nine or twelve now, not with college costs sky-high, and women planning on careers. But they pretended conformity, needing the communal blessing. Words were as crooked as runes, begging interpretation. "As God gives us (despite contraception)."

So everyone on both sides of the unspoken equation lied to each other, or to themselves.

Matt didn't blame the couples or the families. They believed in the vows and the sacrament. They also believed in the ideal of a lasting marriage, so much so that "trial runs" had become almost universal.

He just hated to see marriages launched so dishonestly. In prenuptial conferences, he avoided flat pronouncements, instead encouraging the couple to be mature, considerate, aware of the seriousness of a lifetime commitment.

And Matt had to admit that twenty-something couples who had lived together (as everybody in the parish knew) were better prepared for the realities of life together than the old-model ignorant teenage lovers rushing to the altar to formalize their untried mutual infatuation.

Mixed feelings like these had forced him to reevaluate his vocation. They weren't the only reasons, but they remained with him, months after his priesthood had become past tense.

His attention came back to his playing. His fingers had slipped into the familiar chords of "Silent Night, Holy Night," that most placid of Christmas carols.

He smiled, and glided into "Jesu Bambino," one of his favorites.

He played by heart, in the near darkness, his fingers finding the familiar chords as they read the oversize Braille of the ivory and ebony keys.

Overhead lights switched on in a crashing chord of utter illumination, flooding the blinding, wedding-white walls and furnishings. Matt blinked, feeling the equivalent of an optical migraine.

"I thought I heard the Phantom playing." Electra's voice was a bit breathless. "I expected a blank white half-mask, at least, or—even better—a hideous visage. You're quite a nice surprise."

She wore one of her eternal muumuus that bloomed like hibiscus against a white stucco wall.

"Maybe I do have a mask on. I came down to search for the Lost Chord, not operatic revenge, and not for a pretty soprano to dominate."

Electra smiled, plopping down on the butt end of a pure-white pew, next to a Madonna-as-Evita clone in a mothball-scented pair of politically incorrect silver foxes that looked inutterably sad drooping over a fashionable shoulder.

"Quite a repertoire you've got there, Matt. What are you playing now? It's catchy."

"Now? I don't know. Your arrival shocked me out of the 'Jesu Bambino.' "

"Yeay-zoo what?"

Matt's smile broadened, but his hands kept cajoling the keys. "This is a melody Temple asked about once. She thought it was a wedding march."

"Kind of is, at that, although I run canned music now. The organ is for atmosphere or media opportunities if celebs drop by. Everybody wants speed, not mood. So what's the tune?"

"I'm embroidering it pretty freely, but the bones are Bob Dylan's 'Love Minus Zero—No Limit'."

"Bob Dylan? Hey, that's my era, not yours. You were barely born in the folkie heyday. How'd you hear about him?"

"I'm not sure how anyone finds word- and mind-benders like Bob Dylan and Gerard Manley Hopkins, but we do."

"Who's this studly Hopkins fellow? A folkie?"

Matt laughed. "A monk. English. Late nineteenth, early twentieth century. Wrote poetry with an invented style, something he called sprung rhythm."

"Honey, I got something you could call sprung rhythm in my back, but I take pills for it." She sighed and braced her hands on her flower-trellised knees. "I could use a different wedding march, in case I ever decide to marry again. Don't want to hear the same old tunes that marched me to disaster before."

"You've been married more than once?"

"Oh, yeah." Electra sounded nostalgic. "See, I'm from the Liz Taylor generation. Think you're in love and want to sleep with a guy? Marry him. You can always get divorced. And we did. Liz and me, I mean. Not from each other."

"Serial divorce. I don't know if that's admirable or insane."

"I'm betting you'd say 'insane.' You strike me as a pretty straight arrow for these times."

"You don't know how right you are. I'm so straight I'm not sure the earth *isn't* flat, because otherwise people would be slipping and falling off, wouldn't they?"

"Maybe the earth is round, but people *need* to slip and fall once in a while. You never know what you find down the rabbit hole. Like that Max Kinsella. You never know where he'll turn up next."

"So I've noticed."

"I remember when those two first moved in." Electra grinned nostalgically. "All that energy and expectation. They were the cutest couple. You could tell they were waiting for their second AIDS tests. Temple was checking the lobby mailboxes for an envelope from up north twice a day. And then one day . . . well, I didn't see hide nor hair of them for days on end. Oh, sorry. Guess tales of Love's Young Dream aren't going to cheer you up."

Matt had segued into a funeral march without even noticing. "I was just thinking, none of the old songs celebrate getting your 'papers' certifying that you are plague-free."

"AIDS is a plague, isn't it? That sexual free lunch I saw all around me when I was just a little too old-fashioned to take advantage of it; I felt like such a square. That's what we called being a straight arrow in my day. Me and my marriages. And now it's all over, the sexual free-for-all. Or it should be. People want safety and longevity in relationships."

She nodded in time to Matt's increasingly upbeat dirge.

"Do you have children from any of your marriages?"

"Oh, sure. Adult children, although sometimes I'm not so certain about that. They move, I move. I write, they call. Now they wanta E-mail me. Can you imagine?"

He nodded, not in time to the soft organ chords. "I'd have a computer if I could afford one."

Electra shook her head. "To me, E-mail is like safe sex. Something's not quite all there."

"I suppose a couple, once they've established that each of them is disease-free, has quite a stake in the relationship, even if they're not married."

"I hope it makes 'em think that way, if they're sensible."

"Have you seen marriage rates go up, since AIDS, I mean?"

Electra was startled. "Gee. I don't usually think like a pollster. And I've haven't been here with my little wedding chapel since the Ice Age, lad. I just opened it five years ago, so I have no basis for comparison. I see a bunch of folks who shouldn't get married going right ahead and doing it, though. But what the hell? I shouldn't have a few times and I did."

"I grew up Catholic." Matt paused to consider if he really did grow up. "Anyway, staying married mattered a lot. Divorce was anathema."

"Oh. Catholic. What's 'anathema'?"

"Seriously forbidden, almost blasphemous."

"Honestly, Matt! Those big, bad words. A lot to heap on a child."

"They're a lot to heap on an adult."

"So you really expect to get married once, and that's it? Is that why you're still single? Waiting for a sure thing?"

"I don't know that I expect to get married, but if I did, I'd have to think that."

"Everybody thinks that, when they're on a hormone high. But that's just Nature making sure more people get born to ride the real-life roller coaster and then check out. That's a pretty big gamble: to think you'll get married and stay married forever."

"That's what I'd have to do."

"Hey, I don't knock anybody's religion, but to this old broad, that's either admirable . . . or insane."

"Maybe the admirable is often insane."

"You got it! We drive ourselves crazy trying to live up to other people's concepts of how we should live. That's why I don't take marriage seriously. It's a party that often turns into a funeral, but more often into pure habit. So I had five husbands, so what?"

"Electra . . . five?"

"Hey, Liz had eight or something. I've changed a lot in the last forty-some years. Wasn't always a plus-size. Wasn't always a real-estate magnate and prominent justice of the peace either."

"That's why you spray your hair all those colors, isn't it?"

"Sure. Punk Senior Citizen. Hey, if you can't go wild in some little area that's all your own, what's the point of being here?"

Matt stopped playing. He let his hands fall to his knees. "Maybe that's my problem. I don't have a wild little area."

"Your problem is you're a nice young man who thinks too much." She rose, came behind him and wrapped her arms around his neck in a bear hug. "Why don't you plan on coming up to my place for Christmas Day? I don't cook the whole turkey and stuff, or stuffing, but I scramble some goodies together, and a couple of my 'adult children' are coming. You'll dig my daughter the herpetologist. She's not too much older than you—"

"I don't want to—"

"Intrude! Go ahead, Matt dear. You need to intrude more. Walk right in. Break down a few doors if you have to. Come as you are. Leave as you want to be. Smile. And sing something for me before I go back to bed. You do sing?"

"I used to, but not exactly pop tunes."

Maybe he should say he's into Latin rhythms, Matt thought, realizing that Electra had improved his mood. Hmm. Latin rhythms with hymns. Church music is seldom heard elsewhere, unless a monk's choir becomes an international novelty act for a half note on the endless scale of media fads.

Churches are made for music like vases are made for flowers. His mind and fingers revisited some of his favorites. Attending high mass at a major cathedral, high, heavenly voices filling the eaves. Visiting the small wooden playhouse of a neighboring black Baptist church on Sunday, where the Gospel choir can clap their way into high heaven. He'd always gone on these informal ecumenical expeditions in Roman collar. So blond amid all that black, he understood the isolation of oppositeness.

Afterward, the congregation spurned the polite distance toward line-crossers that you found in white urban churches. They beamed and called him "Reverend." "Fine day, Reverend," they'd said, nodding on the way out.

The minister would pump his hand at the simple single doorway, cheered by a visit from a brother clergyman. Matt would say, "Fine sermon, Reverend. Great choir." "Thank you, Father. Thank you very much," the other Reverend would say, meaning it.

Matt didn't visit non-Catholic churches now. He felt he had no right. No instant brotherhood wherever he went.

His hands finally found something secular Electra would know. "Hey, Mr. Tambourine Man," mellow and made for the organ. He found his voice again, not intoning measured responses but searching old, mysterious words for new meanings and emotions.

Electra's arms tightened on his neck when he was finished. "Terrific, hon. You should sing more often."

She bent to give him a motherly kiss good night, then left him to the dark and the melancholy organ notes.

Matt always welcomed spontaneous affection, but found it startling. Affection was something left unsaid rather than demonstrated in his life. But Electra, with her five husbands and earthy attitude, was too outgoing to skirt his reticence, or even notice it. Affection. Matt liked it.

And then his willful hands were playing Bob Dylan's "Spanish Harlem Incident," a romantic song the title belied, as Dylan's titles often denied any romantic contents of lyric or melody. Somehow the flamenco-dancing, fortune-telling gypsy girl the songwriter celebrated reminded Matt of Temple. Or maybe he just identified with the singer longing to warm himself at the errant flame of the eternal female.

Dylan's songs about male-female relationships could be bitter, or cynical, or playful. And even Biblical. His moving "Sara" was a wail of Job to his lost wife as they separated. Matt wondered if the recording field was capable of supporting constancy. Then he wondered if that would matter more than the changes Electra mentioned.

Break down doors, huh? Suppose Matt started doing that? How many new doors would Max Kinsella materialize to stop him? How many doors had Matt himself slammed shut over the years to barricade himself against chance, and change?

An Elevated Experience

Strapped into Midnight Louie's carrier, with Louie in it, Temple set forth early Thursday morning to catch a cab to Colby, Janos and Renaldi.

With her various burdens, flat-footed boots and bulky down-stuffed jacket, she felt (and probably looked) like a Sherpa guide en route to an assault on Mount Everest.

Catching a cab was enough of a challenge. The first step was crossing the street. She had to flag down a cab pointed in the right direction: uptown. The next step was spotting a free vehicle. In the gray December daylight, telling whether the milky light topping each cab like a button on a beanie was off or on was a toss-up. The greatest challenge, though, was luring the empty cab to her.

Apparently neither she nor Louie had cab magic. She watched seasoned New Yorkers arrive Johnny-come-lately on the block she had been firmly planted on for minutes, then spy, call and snag cabs that by right of being there first should have been hers, dammit!

What did she have to do? Throw herself and Louie into

mid-traffic? Actually, that finally worked, although some rude drivers made a point of swerving away at the last minute and trying for a world's record horn-honk.

But at last she had trapped one of the wily Yellows. She collapsed into the backseat on her tailbone, feeling relief if not comfort. The only position she could take in a cab with Louie weighing her down was the slightly reclining one of a partially upended turtle. At least it kept her too low to see out of the window, which meant that she didn't have to witness the thousand close shaves that New York cabs are heir to.

The address she gave the driver had gone down smoothly. Madison Avenue was a major street that caused cabbies no gray hairs, and Kit had said the building Temple wanted was in the "Larry block," so named after a long-standing, celebrated watering hole called Larry's on one corner. In a what seemed like a wink, the cab jerked up short and stopped.

Temple struggled upright to glimpse the meter, before pulling out the right amount of money. Then she had to wrench the door open and tumble out. Louie growled softly during all the maneuvers; her exiting position resembled a jackknife in gym class, and his boyish girth was the only part of the equation that could give.

Safely upright and on the sidewalk again, Temple adjusted the straps on the twenty-one-pound carrier-with-cat, pushed up her jacket sleeve and slid down her glove to bare enough of her wrist to check the time. Fifteen minutes early. She'd have to stroll the rest of the way to avoid arriving embarrassingly early.

A search of the building's stone facade revealed the very numbers she sought, their tall aluminum dignity mimicking the skyscraper.

Temple joined the people scurrying through the chrome revolving doors into an echoing lobby as busy as all outdoors.

"Does everybody know where they're going?" Temple muttered to Louie. His head was twisted so his big green eyes could study her soulfully. He produced a silent meow of protest to her transportation arrangements so far.

Temple had memorized the office number: 3288. She threaded through the humorless crowds, hunting for the elevators. For a while, it looked as if there weren't any. Only when she had penetrated the building's interior to an alarming degree, worried about exiting shortly on the opposite street, did she spot briefcase-bearers hurtling around a corner like zombies caught in a speed warp.

Temple scrambled to follow. In a few steps she had entered a granite-paved narrows between two opposite banks of the most gorgeous examples of Art Deco elevator-door metalwork that she had ever seen. Shangri-La-La land.

Naturally, she came to a dead stop to gawk.

Naturally, no one else would stop dead here even to view the dead, were anyone so unlucky as to be laid out before them. If Temple didn't get moving, *she* would be laid out beneath them.

Clutching cat and tote bag, she headed for a pair of elevator doors opening like the beaten-gold temple doors in a Cecil B. DeMille Bible epic. Just in front of them, she stopped dead again. Must be a death wish. People parted behind her like an angry Red Sea and flooded the elevator car.

Temple jumped back just in time to keep Louie from being ground to death in the closing jaws of classic Art Deco style.

Temple edged away from the next wave of people clogging up behind her. She stared at a set of tall, elegant numbers, these arranged in a semicircle, with an ornate golden hand lazily gliding past them: one to twenty-two.

Not thirty-two. Was this the wrong building? The wrong address? She turned and studied the numbers above the five other golden doors. The same numerals: one to twenty-two. She dislodged her clothing, feeling unbearably hot in the crowded lobby, to examine her wristwatch. Now she was only six minutes early.

Holy cowabunga! Holy Howdy Doody! Now what was

she going to do? Find someone who had to stand still in this mess, that's what, and answer a simple, heartfelt question: where's the thirty-second floor? What on God's green earth is wrong with people in Gotham City? Hasn't anyone ever noticed that half of this building is missing in action?

Temple turned against the crowd's lemminglike rush to the elevators. No one even noticed her literal figurehead, the face of Midnight Louie eyeing each and every one of them. Struggling upsteam, she craned her neck to see over the mob, a fruitless effort in the best of situations.

There must be a newsstand somewhere. A shoeshine stand. A fruit stand. A stolen goods stand. She'd even ask Frankenstein's *grandmother* if she were here selling something, like Tickle me, Igor dolls!

In despair, Temple noticed that she had steered back between the flanking elevator doors. This must indeed be a circle of Dante's Hell.

"Louie, we're going to be late for a very important date! What do we do?"

He knew what to do. He twisted, snapping at the drawstring that hemmed his head in. The effort, though futile, didn't do Temple's precarious balance any good.

She stared glumly at the heavenly Art Deco elevator doors and their frustrating lofty numbers. The only thing missing was the legend, "Abandon hope, all ye who enter here."

She could almost see those fatal words etched in living flames above the floor pointer.

Which now read . . . twenty-three to forty-six.

She accelerated forward like a New Yorker–born and squeezed herself onto the next departing car. Louie's head protruded past the dark slit between elevator and shaft.

"Baby on board," Temple caroled loudly, backing shamelessly into whoever was behind her. In this mob, who could see what really was in her carrier? From behind, Louie looked like a black-haired baby, nice little Italian baby, maybe, future Al Pacino of cat-food commercials . . . who's to know?

She didn't notice a mass making-way, but as the doors slid shut, Louie's white whiskers bent at their pressure, then sprang to full width again after the doors had shut.

Oops, Temple thought. How to reach the distant control panel to punch in her floor? No way in this sardine factory. No way to lift an arm to check a watch either. Crammed jacket to jacket and boot heel to boot toe with a phalanx of native New Yorkers, Temple resigned herself to shooting past the thirty-second floor and catching it on the way down.

No way would she be on time for their appointment.

Her luck finally turned. Someone else wanted the same floor, for the doors cracked their gleaming twenty-four-carat smile and the mob shifted, and someone behind her elbowed his or her way out. Temple let the natural riptide action pull her and Louie out after the dear departing one. She could kiss him/her!

Actually . . . no, Temple reconsidered as the elevator doors shut behind her, stranding her in an almost-empty hall. She would rather kiss a Tickle me, Igor doll.

The man was Nosferatu in a trench coat, cadaverously thin with blue veins mottling his temples and a Grim Reaper look on his face that did nothing to relieve the initial impression.

Temple let him go ahead, feeling she'd be trailing a hearse otherwise. More gilt numbers cast narrow shadows on the grass-cloth-covered hall walls. Probably the plaster was old and cracked, and grass cloth made an elegant camouflage.

She noted that the number she sought was well within the awesome range indicated to the left, 3262–3298. She would have to tread in the creepy gentleman's footsteps, after all.

"He'd probably be scared white if *you* crossed his path, Louie," she whispered to the patient cat. Carrying an animal up close and personal like this encouraged conversation, however one-sided. This was the way eccentrics were made, Temple thought, the pathetic folks who wander the streets discoursing with fire plugs and such. One day in New York City, and to this she was reduced!

Just outside the double frosted-glass doors labeled Colby, Janos and Renaldi, Temple battled her outerwear for a condemned woman's glimpse of the time.

One minute to 10 A.M. Well, she certainly wasn't embarrassingly early ... .

She walked in. A small foyer, crowded with the usual people, awaited her. Incurious eyes looked up from magazines like *Advertising Age,* then dropped to the slick pages again. She marched up to the receptionist's desk, where a chic young black woman in beautifully sculpted dreadlocks drummed her mandarin fingernails on the desktop while she cradled a phone receiver on her shoulder.

She looked up and actually noticed the cat. When she hung up, unsuccessful in reaching her party, Temple announced, "Temple Barr and Midnight Louie to see Kendall Renaldi."

Much to the astonishment of everyone in the room, with the possible exception of Midnight Louie, Esquire, they were shown right in.

Chapter 8

A Killer Xmas Present

By late afternoon, the gray collar of concrete surrounding the Circle Ritz pool like a homely pewter bezel hoarding an aquamarine had warmed in the December sunlight. At least the blue plastic exercise mats strewn over the surface didn't quite freeze-burn the soles of Matt's bare feet.

The fifties-vintage pool was more decorative than functional these days. Thirty feet the long way cramped exercise fanatics. Devout suntanners still thrived in Las Vegas, gauging by the dusky leatherwork on many faces. They would disdain the old-fashioned tables and chairs, not one a lounge model.

Matt gazed at the deserted site, unable to concentrate today.

He jerked the tie of his roomy white cotton gi tighter, as if deceiving himself about finally getting down to a serious workout. He really should do this at Jack Ree's gym during what passed for winter months in this climate. He had started with tai chi, which looked like shadowboxing to Westerners. And he had stopped when he realized whose shadow he was boxing.

The shadow wasn't very tall in person, but in absence it stretched into a long, thin tether of memory. It ended in flame, like a match. Like red hair. Temple was out of town for the holidays, gone for Christmas, and that irritated him for some reason.

Come on! he coached himself, not sure if the voice he imitated was Jack Ree's or Kyle Menninger's back in Chicago. Or Frank Bucek's in seminary.

Matt hurled into a machine-gun burst of lunges and positions, punctuated by the ritual yells, his irritation striking its real target at last: himself. His sense of being stalled. Because Temple was gone, a niggling reason that shamed him. Because he couldn't find the always shadowy figure of his stepfather that he had pursued through Las Vegas like Francis Thompson's Hound of Heaven. That was a more legitimate reason that didn't shame him as it ought to.

Moving through the martial-arts positions, he felt more like a hunting hound and less like a moping water spaniel. Sometimes his anger took him; he always performed better when it did. Yet anger was the least desirable quality in a martial-arts exercise. The art came in the control, in the seemingly artless control, of oneself, and thereby of others around oneself. That was the paradox so beloved of philosophers and religious leaders the world and ages over: to give up the self is to gain for oneself.

"Impressive force."

Was the voice a mere echo of a past master in his head?

Matt had been so concentrated, body and soul, that he couldn't tell momentarily if he had heard a real voice. Wasn't that how those beautifully dangerous Old Testament angels had appeared to the poor humans chosen by God to marry a certain woman to sire a certain son, or later to sacrifice that son on a mountaintop? Or to send their daughters into the streets to be raped.

He turned slowly, knees bent to spring in any direction, at any enemy, even an invisible one such as delusion.

He saw an angel, maybe, but no Old Testament émigrée. Matt straightened, feeling a stranger had caught him enacting one of his fierce internal fantasies.

"Do you teach?" She approached him with harsh, measured steps like a flamenco dancer just warming up.

He shook his head.

"The woman inside—housekeeper, I think—said I could find you here."

"You were looking for me?"

"You sound like no one ever does."

"I guess I more often do the looking."

He was looking now. He had seen women more beautiful, but none more arresting. Beauty's remote perfection repelled him, if anything. She didn't need it. The only thing medium about her was her height. Her Snow White coloring invited fairy-tale comparison: coal-black hair with a hard sheen that seemed lacquered, but wasn't. Skin white as department-store-window snow. Lips black-red, like a cherry split by its own ripeness, and not nearly as natural. Her eyes were the only compromised feature in her face, a changeable blue-green color that recalled the "aqua" eyes Temple raved about in Midnight Louie's lady friend, the Persian cat Yvette.

This visitor obviously expected all action to stop while her bold palette of features was assessed. Her cool eyes returned the favor, but revealed no conclusions, or even presumptions.

What she wore was a frame, no more. Matt was learning Temple's character-reading through accessories. A simple, expensive pantsuit in an exquisite shade of jade green underlined her unusual eyes. He was aware of pointy-toed, low-heeled boots or oxfords that gleamed with a halo of excessive cost. And though Lieutenant Molina might wear this rigorously gender-neutral suit, in this case Matt saw/sensed that it only added intrigue to a men's-magazine figure. She might be ten or fifteen pounds heavier than the ideal woman her height, but that was only another unfair advantage she had over her sex; an inescapable lushness lurked beneath the suit's severe lines.

She didn't speak until she was close enough to extend her left hand, but not for an introduction. Something was in it.

He reached for the expected business card, then froze. She held out one of the laminated sketches of his stepfather he had been plastering all over Las Vegas casinos for the past month. On the back he'd typed estimated height, weight and whereabouts, as well as his own name and phone number. But not his Circle Ritz address.

"Friend of yours?" she asked.

"Not exactly. Friend of yours?"

"Not exactly. But he's bought me a drink or two when he's won for a while, or just wants to feel like a winner. He doesn't stay a winner very long, because he never stops playing. I work at one of the Strip casinos." She had seen and answered the question that was forming in his mind, and maybe his mouth and eyes.

"It's true." She laughed, as if the questions and reactions were always the same, and always in the same order. "I don't talk or dress like one of the sleazy sisterhood men expect to find working in a casino."

"I have no expectations," he said abruptly.

She studied him, her smile something she put on easily, like a jade-green pantsuit. "I guess you don't. You're not what I expected. And do you even expect to find him?"

"Not really."

"Still, you look."

He shrugged. " 'A man's reach . . .' "

She laughed, extending her right hand. "Kitty O'Connor."

A heavy square ring impressed his fingers. He stared at the culprit, a huge emerald-cut aquamarine embedded in a rope-of-gold setting, as her pale hand withdrew.

Ambidextrous, he thought, with the attention to detail a counselor brought to bear on all new personalities. *Unusual in a woman. Wonder which hand she writes with.*

She considered the homemade wanted poster again. "I've seen him, should see him again."

"And?"

"And what?"

"I didn't mention a reward."

"I didn't ask for one, did I?"

"I thought you might expect one."

"You don't expect anything, why should I?"

"Maybe you're more optimistic than I am."

"Don't bet on it."

Kitty's cool smile turned unexpectedly mischievous. He found himself grinning back, and resented the manipulation. "If you don't want anything," he suggested, "you might as well tell me where he's turned up."

"Oh, darlin'. I just said I didn't want a reward. I didn't say I didn't want anything."

She took a slow turn around the five exercise mats, a tour that would have honored sensitively placed sculptures in a Japanese garden.

The "oh, darlin' " had that sleazy saloon sound Matt would expect from a woman who worked at a casino, but her speaking voice implied a foreign tinge. Maybe something as incongruous as finishing school, maybe just the theater.

He realized late that her tour of the mats had become a turn around Matt, singular. He turned to confront her, meeting a gaze of such candid calculation that the sun-warmed afternoon blanched as if now aware it had come out without a coat in the dead of winter.

"I'm not an Iscariot," she said, her smile and eyes as chill as blue aquavit, that thin Nordic firewater so strong it's served in tiny narrow glasses like test tubes.

A Finnish-descent monsignor had held a New Year's gala: innocent rounds of northland hors d'oeuvres alternating with blue aftershave bursts of potent aquavit. Certainly helped the oily sardine sandwiches go down.

"Iscariot," he repeated. "An odd expression. Most people just call him Judas."

"I don't turn anybody—even a deluded old drunk—over to parties unknown until I'm satisfied as to why he's wanted."

"He isn't wanted, that's the irony. Only I want him, and I hate his guts."

Matt was beginning to find secular overstatement as effective as sudden anger on the exercise mats. It wasn't how he'd been taught to fight, but he'd never been taught to fight anyone but himself. He sensed that she required struggle, this furiously self-contained woman. She needed to regard him as a possible opponent for some reason, and he had to reassure her that he was up to her mettle, whatever that was.

She could be a professional seductress. The lurid thought almost made Matt flush, not a good thing in this game of hidden moves.

"What a great little hideaway." Now she was studying the apartment building as avidly as she had gauged him. "Nouveau Trendy."

"Electra, the lady you took for housekeeper, owns it, by the way."

"And the tacky wedding chapel out front?"

"And the wedding chapel out front."

"Oh, come now. You're not going to defend pink and blue neon bows. Really."

"You have no idea what I'd defend. I'm standing on royal-blue oversize place mats."

"Yes. Dreadful color, for that material, at least. But I bet it keeps your feet warm."

He nodded, tempted to bring her back to the subject, but resisting it. Women liked to shop. To see everything, and test-drive most of it. She hadn't pinched the produce yet.

"If I'm going to turn a man over to you, I've got to know your . . . credentials. I can't have something . . . unjust on my conscience."

"I can understand that."

"Can you really?"

"You sound incredulous, but I do understand."

"Why are you looking for this Effinger man? You're not a policeman—"

"I could always grow a mustache."

She smiled at that, the unspoken facial badge of many young patrol officers, especially of fair-haired Anglo officers.

"You can't pass as an urban cowboy," she objected. "You're not from these parts."

"How did you know?"

"I'd say Illinois. Chicago. The South Side. Out in the boonies. An immigrant community originally. I hear voices in your voice. A foreign trace. Don't look so startled, Mr. Devine. The name is Anglo-Saxon, but the voice says . . . German?"

"Polish," he corrected unhappily.

"Should have said my first guess! Effinger could be a German name."

"I don't know the man's national origins, and I don't care. No blood relation, if that's what you're really getting at."

"Sorry. I'm being circuitous again, aren't I?"

The word "circuitous" evoked her slow tour around him. Matt realized that he was the object of her interest for some reason, and that her interest was usually, if not always, somehow sexual.

He was used to straightforward women: nuns until now; now Temple the wayward public relations specialist, who always told the truth as best she knew it; Carmen Molina, the homicide detective who allowed no gender nonsense to compromise her professionalism or her single-parenthood.

Kitty O'Connor was different. She played games, and she liked to win them. She was always testing, especially strangers, especially strange men.

As a priest, he'd encountered lonely women, parishioners even, who were tantalized by the untouchable, who swooned over Mr. Spock of *Star Trek* or another woman's husband or even the friendly neighborhood Catholic priest.

He'd come to recognize the type instantly, and to ignore its temptations no matter how attractively packaged.

Compared to those sad, delusional groupies, decent women with compulsively self-destructive hankerings, Kitty was a pro. She knew something he was desperate to know (and she knew it). To gain her confidence, he would have to play on her field with her terms. He would have to tease, to flirt back. Not exactly taught in seminary.

He thought of Max Kinsella, the Mystifying Max, blast him! Temple had said he was good with women. The magician. Max always acted as if he had a secret, and maybe it was about you. Always acted as if he knew more than you did. Maybe that had something to do with it.

"I can't tell you why I'm looking for Effinger. The information isn't mine to give."

She nodded, looking more interested. "Can you tell me a reason in general?"

"Family business," he said curtly. He gave up the words with a wrench of self-disgust. It wasn't anybody's business but his. *"I am about my Father's business."* Not in this instance, although maybe his real father, his genetic father, would want this unworthy replacement dealt with too.

Perhaps his emotions as much as his words reassured her, because she understood what he meant.

"Family business is hell, isn't it?"

He nodded, relieved. "And Purgatory thrown in for good measure."

"But once dealt with, it's the Heaven of a job well done, a job that needed doing."

Their eyes were steady on each other now, as if they spoke the same unspoken language, with the slightly "foreign" accents of their lone, cautious outsider voices. Foreign to what?

"This means a lot to you."

He didn't need to answer the obvious.

She put her hands on her hips, sweeping the open jacket to either side, emphasizing the hourglass of her figure almost as a weapon. She reminded him of an Old West gunfighter with her pointy-toed boots in a wide-legged stance, her challenging eyes that were only green now and hard as laser light.

"What would you do, if you found him?"

The pass/fail question. He had nothing to fall back upon but his own bitter truth. "I don't know. Kill him, maybe."

She was impassive. If she chose to shoot him down now, she would never help him, even if she was the only soul in Nevada who knew the creep's whereabouts.

"The Gilded Lily. You'll have to look it up in the Yellow Pages under 'Dives.' Try about nine P.M. He likes to start in the bar."

The capitulation left him breathless, confused. "You work there?"

"Not as of tonight. You might give me a day or two before you come calling. Don't want to dash off the very day Mr. Effinger might have a big fall."

Like Max Kinsella at the Goliath and the first casino dead man.

Matt felt a dizzying sense of déjà vu. He almost felt like Max, or a waxwork imitation of Max. He managed a knowing smile, a nice trick when he knew nothing.

"And if I want to find you again? Tell you what happened?" he asked.

"I'll know." She had turned and was leaving.

He realized that she carried nothing—no purse, no sunglasses. Maybe she had been a visitation . . . from somewhere.

Hard heels clicked the concrete. Beneath Matt's feet, the blue plastic felt damp. He had grown no mustache but his upper lip had materialized a dewy pencil-thin line of sweat.

"I'll find you," she threw behind her in farewell.

She sounded happy. No . . . content.

He wondered . . . what a priest could . . . should never wonder.

His hands were as cold as his feet were hot. He made fists to warm his fingers in the waning afternoon light. Nine P.M. Not a good time. He'd have to take time off, or change his schedule. Maybe change his schedule. Then he'd have an alibi.

Dear God, why had he let her glimpse his naked vengeance? And, worse, why had that one factor, or failing, put whatever fears she had to rest? He hoped he never found out, never saw her again.

He doubted that he'd be that lucky.

Chapter 9

Cat in a Gray Flannel Suite

Despite the cavernous lobby downstairs, the offices were a maze of cubbyholes arranged along a wall of windows that looked out on other windows, in which small moving figures of worker bees could be glimpsed buzzing soundlessly in a concrete hive.

A tall tawny-haired woman younger than Temple was waiting beyond the foyer door to greet her.

"I'm Kendall Renaldi, and I see you have something to get off your chest."

"I have twenty *pounds* of something to get off my chest."

"So this is Midnight Louie. Love that name."

"He came with it. I probably would have called him 'Blackie' or something totally unoriginal."

"I doubt that, judging from the materials you sent us. You're in the same game as we are."

"Well, we're kissing cousins, anyway," Temple demurred, flattered to have been symbolically accepted on

Madison Avenue, the pinnacle of advertising, promotion and public relations.

"We are if you work the hours we do," Kendall added, rolling her eyes. "You can unload Louie in my office."

"What I'd most like to do is lose the outerwear for a while. It's best if I keep Louie close to my heart where he can't get into trouble."

"But he's so big, and you're so small. If we did tour you, we'd have to send a handler along."

"That's why I bought the baby-bag for cats. It's supposed to balance the weight. If only I could find a 'Papoose on Board' decal.

" 'Don't Kitty Litter' would be a nice touch too."

"If Louie's going to be a media cat, I suppose he'll have lots of messages to bear, poor baby."

Once inside Kendall's office door, Temple demonstrated getting out of the carrier's waist and shoulder straps. "It's really simple if you get the hang of it."

" 'Hang of it' is right. I'd really get hung up in all that harnessry."

"Try it," Temple suggested. "Somebody has to hold Louie while I undress anyway."

She slung her tote bag down on the paper-piled chair beside a small desk mounded by an avalanche of paperwork. Kendall's office was one in name only, Temple noticed as she struggled out of her down jacket and mukluks and put them on the . . . the—

"There's a hook on the back of the door," Kendall suggested.

Temple hung up what she could, then straightened the short fuchsia wool skimp dress she wore (very sixties) and rummaged in the tote for her shoe bag. She leaned against the desk edge while pulling on black suede chunky heels. Presto, from Nanook of the North to something a bit more citified.

Kendall had managed to buckle Louie on sideways,

despite risking her long, manicurist-abetted, bronze-enameled fingernails. She shrugged, but eyed Temple with approval. "Thank goodness the male ad execs didn't see you in that marshmallow outfit. They would have ruled you out as too fat to go on TV no matter what you looked like underneath."

"Decisions are made that fast around here?"

"Decisions are made like lightning. Good thing I was a rock-climber in college and learned to think on my feet and hands. That's why we're moving on this over the holidays. You do know that you and Louie are not the only candidates."

Temple did not know, and did not like hearing about it now, but she kept a polite smile on her face and said nothing.

"Maurice is still under consideration, and we do have a film pro who's anxious to take this on, although it's a bit awkward with what happened with her cat."

"Film pro?" *This is Christmas,* Temple implored (and possibly, in her heart, threatened) whatever gods may be. *Don't do this to me!*

All this way, and it was a beauty contest.

"Don't worry. I've seen her, and you'll do fine. But, ummm . . ."

Kendall's narrowed hazel eyes stared at Temple.

"Yes?" Temple asked anxiously. Gosh, did she have a snag in her smile or something? A run in her fingernail polish? Her hose had to be all right because they were opaque black, so as not to show black cat hairs.

"It might be to your advantage to meet everybody without an addition of twenty ugly pounds. You're so petite, why hide it? Why don't I tote Louie in this getup, and prove even a dunce can don a cat carrier? You know, the manufacturer might be interested in offering the carriers as a premium."

Temple nodded. She was beginning to understand the corporate culture at Colby, Janos and Renaldi. Every-

thing had an angle. Everyone was always thinking.
Something positive. Something negative. She hadn't
been under this kind of magnifying glass since high
school gym class, when they'd been subjected to a
harridan who was part marine drill sergeant and part
Marquis de Sade. Everyone had a use. Everyone had no
excuse.

She eyed Midnight Louie, who eyed her right back.

Act sharp, she told him mentally. *This place may look
disorganized, but so do shark tanks when the itty-bitty
fishes school past.*

Louie blinked in that solemn way cats have. He was all
eyes, and all ears. He acted as if he understood every word,
but cats don't read minds. Do they?

Temple appreciated Kendall's concern, but wondered
why she was its beneficiary. Right now she was being
shepherded toward the inner offices, being briefed on who
was who in the firm's hierarchy.

Usually a quick study, Temple was befuddled by the ros-
ter of Colby, Janos and Renaldi. Apparently all were
founders or scions of same. This was a family company,
by all appearances, but the family was not necessarily all
happy.

Kendall opened the unmarked walnut door before them,
and Temple waltzed confidently through, pretending to
make a stage entrance as Joan Crawford.

She was glad she had chosen to come in six feet tall,
because she walked right into a set change as drastic as
from rural Kansas to downtown Oz. Temple faced a
huge multimedia conference room muted with upholstered gray-flannel walls. It was filled to the giant,
built-in film and TV screens with men in, yes, Brooks
Brothers suits. Here and there Temple glimpsed patterned
suspenders as a racy, individual touch. One man even
wore a bow tie. None cultivated mustaches or other
facial hair. The women in the room, few but fierce,
were Stepford wives: impeccably groomed clones wear-

ing the latest version of the corporate woman's power suit.

Except for one woman. Temple's rival. The film performer, and Louie's blond bête noire . . .

Savannah Ashleigh.

Chapter 10

Cacaphoney

A long, shocked silence that slowly became a long, hostile silence prevailed while those previously acquainted sized each other up. Unfortunately, only two people present were previously acquainted, and it hadn't been a success.

The shivers at Temple's nape eased once she realized that Savannah Ashleigh had arrived for this key East Coast conference in full Hollywood Babe regalia.

A television spokesperson must be neat, clean, thrifty, brave and conventionally attired at all times. Savannah's champagne-colored leather jumpsuit with brass studs interlarded with festive, cashew-size red rhinestones might work for a Country Western singer, or a reincarnation of Elvis, but it did nothing for a cat-food rep. Not to mention what cat claws would do to that butter-soft Rodeo Drive hide on camera, either the leather jumpsuit's, or Savannah's.

And the shoes! For once Temple was conservatively shod in closed-toe suede pumps. Savannah Ashleigh's feet, however, were a playground of metallic leather and clear plastic straps on four-inch heels. Even at their highest, Temple thought from her new, lofty prominence of sub-dued taste, her own high heels never surpassed three inches.

It was also obvious that Miss Ashleigh had been a fashion victim in too many B movies of late, as well as in too many plastic surgeons' offices.

She wore a shoulder-dusting clatter of earrings, an over-populated gold charm bracelet and several large cocktail rings of dubious ancestry. All that armament would chime against microphones and rattle on paper and batter the on-set furniture.

Temple knew her fashion style was a happy-go-lucky hybrid of her theatrical and television-news backgrounds, and the one immutable, her petite frame. In casual clothes she looked like a thirteen-year-old, hardly a serious spokes-woman for a television news program. So on camera she'd resorted to stylish suits and very little jewelry. Jane Pauley used attractive pins as a riveting signature: very visible but also very out-of-the-way when hands and head had to lit-erally be plugged into a national network.

As for Temple's shoe-thing, it had always been there, like her freckles, from her earliest years. And female TV reporters, invariably shot from the waist up, sometimes ex-pressed their real off-screen personality in footwear. Tem-ple remembered a pioneer Twin Cities female reporter whose legendary pair of hot-pink pumps were never seen on screen, but were well-known and discussed witnesses to numerous juicy trials and other utterly serious news-making events.

So Temple straightened her shoulders and prepared to go head-to-head with Savannah Ashleigh. If she felt in-timidated by competing against a semi–movie star, she need only glance at the actress's lips. Miss Ashleigh's plas-tic surgeon had taken the suggestion Temple had impishly planted in retaliation for Savannah's altering Midnight Louie's personal plumbing only weeks ago.

The Ashleigh lips were so collagen-inflated that they could pass for the Goodyear Blimp. *Too, too, too much, dahling,* Temple thought cattily. *Hopefully, you now lithp!*

What Savannah Ashleigh thought she was not actress enough to keep off her face. Dismay and shock jousted with fury. Apparently neither woman had been advised that this was to be a gladiator event, not a job interview.

"*Et tu,* advertising?" Temple murmured.

Kendall had the grace to color.

Meanwhile, Midnight Louie had assessed the room and its occupants from his royal-purple perch on the person of Miss Renaldi. He finished with a final sweep of his head from corner to corner, and then released a low, loud meow with a nice vibrato of sheer rage under it.

"He does 'talk,' as advertised," a florid-faced man at the table replied.

"I'm afraid Louie has been confined to carrier for most of two days," Temple said. "He's feeling a trifle cramped."

The red-faced man patted the long wood-veneer conference table.

"Then let him out. Here. Let's take a look at this wildcat."

"Here? Now?"

The others apparently heeded the man who spoke, for heads nodded all around the table.

Kendall leaned close to Temple. "Brent Colby, Junior."

Temple nodded and accompanied Kendall to a break in the chairs. In a moment the carrier straps were loosened and Louie himself was about to be loosed upon the eminences of advertising.

"Be good," Temple whispered as he tumbled out of the bag and rolled upright.

Oh, he was good. Very good.

First he stretched, starting at his front legs until his belly polished the conference table, then reversing the motion until he stretched out one back leg after another, his tail sketching a perfectly executed *S* in the air. This introductory maneuver elicited polite applause.

Then he sat, glanced around to ensure their full attention, and began fastidiously grooming a paw.

"Mick Jagger," murmured one advertising scion to another, an apparent compliment to the length and agility of Louie's tongue.

Louie flicked the commentator a glance, then yawned very slowly to display an extraordinary array of teeth.

"More like *Jaws,*" said a neat, dark-haired man with a permanent five-o'clock shadow as well as worry lines in his forehead.

"Victor Janos, Junior," Kendall whispered to Temple. She hastily pointed out the other figures at the table. Tony Renaldi was tall, dark and lean, quite handsome, but maybe Temple was biased. She was surprised by how many junior Colbys, Janoses and Renaldis populated the table, either founders or offspring. Apparently keeping it in the families was a priority among the high-level executives with the advertising firm.

Meanwhile, Louie worked his feline magic up and down the table, doing the Las Vegas Strip strut. Savannah Ashleigh was not too dumb to know when she was being upstaged. She fidgeted on her leather-upholstered conference chair until her clinging pantsuit squeaked.

"I really think Maurice has superior stage presence," she put in at the moment Louie appeared to be mesmerizing the entire group.

"Maurice." The name rolled off the tongue of the firm's president like a stale breath mint. "Perhaps he's been overexposed."

"Would you call Tom Cruise 'overexposed'?" a man leaning against a gray-flannel wall put in. Maurice had acquired another handler, a crew-cut-haired man with the arms of a staff sergeant and the blunt red hair and freckles of a Tom Sawyer gone to beefy and unimaginative middle age.

"It's true that Maurice is established as a film personality," began an advertising guy, a still-perky youngster with a very discreet ear stud that glimmered like the Mark Cross automatic pencil parked behind the opposite ear.

A number two yellow pencil wasn't good enough for a copywriter at Colby, Janos and Renaldi? Temple wondered. She did some of her best thinking while doodling with disposable felt-tip Flairs.

Louie had taken advantage of the distraction to rise and stroll regally around the conference table, pausing frequently to ingratiate himself with the seated executives.

Before one, he sat to inhale the aroma from a ceramic mug.

"Hey, he wants my coffee!"

Louie moved on to stop before the head man himself. His lifted forefoot patted approvingly at a tiny tack on the boss's dull navy rep tie. It was shaped like the Empire State Building.

"We're about to get one of those in Las Vegas," Temple noted.

"I doubt he's into the tie tack. He likes my old school tie!" The boss looked flattered. "Sorry, cat. You'll have to put in four years to earn one of these."

Too much for Louie. He ambled toward the table's opposite side to toy with one woman's expensive pen (he was an equal-opportunity brownnoser), then to chew experimentally at the edge of a man's notebook. He strolled back to rub his chin on Colby junior's Rolex band, with impeccable taste, of course, in both executives and watch brands.

Kendall thought his conduct worth another sotto voce comment. "Temple, your cat sure knows who to cozy up to. Did you bribe the bosses' dry cleaners to put sardines in their breast pockets?"

"Say, what a dynamite idea! Grease their palms with fish oil. No, Louie just has It."

"Just what does Louie have? That's a serious question. How would we position his personality?"

Temple considered. "Mystery and distance. Yet an in-your-face charm when he wants to use it. He can be very affectionate in private, and aloof as a Dalai Lama at other times. He comes and goes as he pleases, shows up where and when he's least expected. Sometimes I think he reads minds. At other times, I think he's just a con man at heart."

Temple realized that her description also matched a certain missing-in-action magician of her acquaintance.

"He's the eternal male," she finished. "Fancy-free, but capable of being domestic when least expected. He's every man you knew who walked away, and every man you'd give your eyeteeth to have back."

"Wow. Is this a tomcat or a model for Lounge Lizard aftershave? Guess Louie doesn't shave, huh?"

"Oh, he's had quite a few close shaves, but they were purely metaphorical."

"That's right. He's been involved in real crimes, hasn't he? And so have you."

Temple nodded cautiously. She wasn't so keen on her crime-solving past now that she knew a murderer and had let said murderer go free.

"What a great double angle. You can discuss safety for cats and owners. Everybody loves personal-safety issues nowadays."

Speaking of personal safety, Temple glanced back to Louie's stage, the conference table. He had been working his way around to Savannah Ashleigh's spot. Temple didn't trust Louie to restrain himself with the woman who had abducted him with intention to neuter.

But Louie did enjoy a particular affinity for Savannah Ashleigh's cat Yvette, the shaded silver Persian who advertised Free-to-be-Feline, a feline health food that the portly Midnight Louie would not touch with so much as a whisker tip.

If Yvette were anywhere near her mistress, Louie might forgo revenge for a romantic reunion.

Temple looked high and low, but couldn't spy Yvette's pink canvas carrier, although Maurice was captive on the sidelines, looking fiercely lionlike in a cat carrier with a wire grille.

"I thought this was a done deal," Temple told Kendall,

trying not to whine. "Now I find out there's competition not only for my role, but Louie's."

"Nothing's certain in advertising but the uncertainty. Three weeks ago, the Allpetco account was firmly in the pocket of Sloan Van Eck and Associates. Now we get a swipe at it, and Christmas or not, peons labor overtime alongside the brass to make sure we meet the deadline with our best shot."

"Swipe. Deadline. Shot. Sounds . . . murderous."

"Advertising *is* murder." Kendall's statement sounded unnervingly sober. "We work twenty-hour days, sometimes, on a major account. Deadlines, and doing our darnedest until we drop. But we have fun too." She grinned. "Successfully selling your idea, yourself and your client's product is an incredible high."

Keeping an eye on the table, Temple saw Louie approach Savannah Ashleigh. He came to a full stop, lofted his tail and waved it like a scepter of office. Then, slowly, deliberately, he turned to show her his business end. The very spot she had intended to irrevocably alter.

Temple could swear he shook his fanny at her before mincing in a manly fashion back down the shining lemon-waxed walnut to Mr. Big, whom he honored with a purring rub on the outstretched hand.

"He likes you best, B.C.," said a junior executive identified by a nonnavy suit.

The boss chucked Louie under the jet-black chin. "He knows who's Santa Claus around here at Christmas bonus time. All right. Let's see Maurice in the flesh."

Temple took advantage of the changeover to retrieve Louie's carrier, and approach the table to claim Louie.

"Have a chair." A man stood to pull back the heavy arm-chair he'd been occupying.

Temple hesitated, then took it, establishing Louie in his carrier on her lap. That would prevent any sudden lunges at Maurice, whom Louie did not appear to care for one tiny bit.

But Louie was on supernaturally good behavior, almost

as if he understood what was at stake. Still, Temple could feel his big body tremble with excitement when Maurice vaulted from the open carrier atop the conference table.

"Yellow photographs better than black," the handler noted as Maurice strutted his stuff.

Tony Renaldi doodled on his personalized notepad. "Film technology today can overcome that old shibboleth. We need a charismatic cat here, whatever the color."

"And a dashing one. Kevin Costner in fur," Colby added.

"One who makes the ongoing romance with the À La Cat feline fatale credible," a young woman said, upping the ante from the sidelines.

Brent Colby, Jr., frowned into the half-glasses resting on his nose like an odd see-through bug. His regular features, softening with middle age, were hard to read. "Not too credible. Makes the damn cat too hard to handle. Animal rights people find tomcats politically incorrect."

"Ahem." The handler cleared his throat. "I'm sure that we're all aware that somehow Maurice slipped past the scissors." He smiled nervously. "A little play on words: slipped past the censors."

Savannah Ashleigh ground leather on her chair, crossing and uncrossing her legs.

"Are you saying that the rape of my darling Yvette was just a little slip of the tongue? Actually, of something a lot worse than a tongue! My adorable girl's bloodlines have been wasted on a worthless litter. I'm told that the publicity in the tabloids about her litter of little yellow . . . bastards has the cat-food manufacturer reconsidering her spokescat role."

"Now, Miss Ashleigh." Brent Colby was obviously the tone-setter at the firm. "We'll talk to the representatives of Allpetco tomorrow, all of us, and iron out any little differences. How are Yvette and the little, er, children doing?"

"Yvette is shattered, but tries her best to be a good mother. She refused to travel without the miserable little half-breeds, so they are all back at my hotel room. I can bring her out on her own, though her coat is sadly dulled by the strains of motherhood. A lawsuit is in preparation." Savannah glowered under white-blond brows at Maurice and his handler.

"There is," Victor Janos put in suddenly, "a morals clause in her contract. We don't know if the company will wish to invoke it."

"She was raped!" came Savannah's soprano wail. "While my attention was misdirected to that green-eyed Lothario Midnight Louie—even the name would make a careful parent suspicious!—that yellow-bellied molester in prison stripes was sneaking up on my undefended baby, who is, by the way, underage for recommended breeding. So if there is a morals clause in Maurice's contract, as there should be unless sexism is at work here and another suit is in order, he should be liable for losing his job too."

"He was not the one pictured in the *Las Vegas Scoop* with the unsanctioned offspring," Janos said. "And the photo was reprinted in *Vegas Voyeur,* then went national in the *Animal Inkquirer* and *National Noses.* When it hit the *human* tabloids, the kitties were really snoot-deep in some pretty unpalatable litter."

Savannah sunk lower and lower into a despondent pose with every journal cited. "Those are all gossip-mill rags!"

"What about the photographic evidence?"

"A rotten paparazzo broke into my private Malibu grounds and used a long-range lens to photograph Yvette *in famille* while I was busy sunbathing in the nude. Who could imagine that some pervert was photographing *her* at such a time?"

While male eyes glazed at the scene Savannah portrayed, Temple thought it was time to remind them of her own clothed presence. And Louie's advantages.

"Obviously, Midnight Louie is free of any tabloid taint," she said. "He could not have sired the kittens in question. I am willing to have all and any DNA tests recommended, and, in fact, due to a false and premature accusation of fatherhood, Midnight Louie is not quite a tomcat any more. He was forcibly altered at the behest of Miss Ashleigh."

"No!" Men all up and down the conference table blanched in synchronization.

"Yes!" Temple stood as if making a speech, as indeed she was. "But . . . thanks to a small confusion on Miss Ashleigh's part in spiriting Louie to a plastic surgeon, he is now the proud possessor of a vasectomy. In case you gentlemen don't know the results of such a procedure on a cat, this means that he has lost none of his masculine charm—and dare I say swagger—but may exercise it with responsibility to all and malice toward none. Except, perhaps, toward Miss Savannah Ashleigh, the mastermind of back-alley neuterings."

Damp brows the table over were dabbed by Bill Blass silk squares.

"Then Midnight Louie is . . . intact as a male, but politically correct as a progenitor?" Tony Renaldi asked, one fine Italian hand smoothing the wings of dove-gray at his temples.

"Exactly."

"Interesting. Might it start a trend?"

"I don't think so." Maurice's handler stood away from the fabric walls, erect for battle. "Maurice has been fixed the old-fashioned way since this unfortunate incident. Had Miss Ashleigh kept her cat kenneled as professional animal trainers recommend in the high-tension circumstances of a commercial film shoot, no doubt Yvette would still be as pure as the driven Dreft today. But she didn't, and all the world saw the result."

Louie hunkered down on Temple's lap, and hid his face in his tucked paws. Was he guilty about something? she wondered. But he didn't accost Yvette. He liked her, all right, but theirs was a platonic relationship, wasn't it? At least none of the contested kittens had come out with a spot of black on it, and were, in fact, all long-haired yellow stripes.

"So Maurice is neutered now, as he was not before?" Victor Janos looked as stern as a Salem judge.

"As he should have been all along, but it was overlooked," the handler answered. "Most trainers don't spend their time examining rear ends. And he came from a shelter, so we assumed—"

Savannah also had risen to plead her case. "As a matter of fact, I had Maurice's early history investigated by a private detective in my employ. My private dick found the original intake papers on this so-called Maurice, and they were very revealing."

"How so?"

"He was accepted into the shelter as one 'Maurine, a fixed female.' "

This revelation caused another stir up and down the conference table. Being a Hollywoodite, Savannah clearly did not realize the sensation that any suggestion of a sex change might have on Middle America. She plunged on as carelessly as her cleavage.

"Clearly, the shelter made an error."

Now she was playing a lady lawyer on TV. Carrie Mason. Wonder if she carries a hatchet in her briefcase? Temple thought.

"An error that those who acquired Maurice, and turned him loose as a media cat, never adequately looked into. Did you?" Savannah asked the handler. "You admit that you never looked. How could you be sure?"

"Despite the intake error," the handler returned, "we were assured that Maurine was now a fixed 'he,' but we didn't know until the unfortunate birth that he had a small congenital defect. An undescended testicle. The busy shelter vet noted a testicular anomaly, but must have assumed that what was only hidden, was actually missing in action. And since animal training does not involve that kind of probing touchy-feely—"

"Too bad that rape does!" Savannah was furious.

Brent Colby, Jr., was not amused. "Lady. Gentleman. This discussion is becoming, ah, heated. Perhaps we should adjourn for the day, since all parties have met and made their cases on this unfortunate matter. Colby, Janos and Renaldi invites all of you, cats included whatever their state of, er, gender, to attend our annual Christmas party here tomorrow night. No gifts required, save that of your presence. Santa Claus will be the usual guest of honor, with tokens for employees and guests. Thank you all so very much for coming. Now, my children. Take up thy cats, and walk."

"What a smooth brush-off, huh, Louie?" Temple asked as she stroked him awake. "Makes you feel as slick as satin when you've really been handed the back of a boar-bristle brush. Santa and sacks of presents tomorrow night. Tomorrow, more cat spats."

Louie yawned hugely, then stared unblinking at the departing admen and women.

"Come on." Kendall had materialized at Temple's shoulder. "I'll get you two swathed and swaddled for the cold. I hope you can get out, Temple, for some New York fun tonight."

Temple smiled at the departing executives, then skedaddled before she'd have to acknowledge Savannah Ashleigh, who was still arguing with Maurice's handler.

"What do you think?" Temple asked Kendall under her breath as they hurried down the narrow maze to her office.

"Louie is a hunk and you've got that breathy-voiced witch beat by an Epsom Downs mile."

Temple appreciated Kendall being such a quick study. "Any advice for tomorrow?"

"Same time, same act, only with the client present. Just be yourselves and let us figure out the packaging."

"Speaking of packaging, what's with the Christmas party? Surely that's a company affair; we visiting cat people aren't needed."

"Ah, don't tell anybody, but the boss man loves to play Santa, and the bigger the audience, the better. Plus, he believes that people show their true colors under pressure. Maybe animals, too."

Chapter 11

Red, Red Whine

"And then she said—"

Temple perched on the rolled rim of Kit's leather couch and crossed her legs somewhere near the hip. Her diction was the overarticulated prattle of the amateur actor. "Are you saying that the rape of my darling Yvette was just a little slip of the tongue? Actually, of something a lot worse than a tongue!"

Temple's laughter after delivering this line almost tumbled her sideways into Midnight Louie, who was disguising himself by sprawling on the camouflaging black leather upholstery as if to the Naugahyde born.

Kit finally finished laughing. "Do you think the Tramp of Savannah has a prayer at getting your spokesperson job?"

"Thanks for the loyalty of that 'your,' but advertising is just theater in a multimedia guise. Anything's fair, and anything's possible. Savannah's self-parodying ways may be just the shtick the client and the agency settle on."

"Great! Another 'test' in Santa guise. Will Louie get a lump of coal in his cat-sack if he's not good? And is something solid really going to come out of this? It seems so . . . hasty."

"That's when advertising really gets cooking—on the run. Yeah, we're gonna snag that account, by hook or by crook, and we'll do it best by coming up with the most attractive package of cat and human. I kind of doubt it'll be Savannah Ashleigh and Midnight Louie, or Temple Barr and Maurice."

"But . . . . if it is?"

"Everybody had better learn to live with it, and each other. Or the deal dies right there in front of us all."

"I can't believe they'd want that floozie, as we used to say before World War Two, to flog their products."

Temple dug in her tote bag. "Want to see a family portrait of my new maybe-bosses? They put together this jazzy booklet on the company."

Kit's burnt-auburn eyebrows rose as she fanned through the heavy glossy pages. "Spent a fortune. Looks like an annual stockholders' report for a two-hundred-dollar-a-share company."

"I wouldn't know, Auntie, the only 'stock' I've got is Louie, but I do know that this brochure showcases their graphic capabilities as well as the staff."

"Smart. An uptown audition book. What's this in the back? A family tree?"

"That's their real angle. 'Three generations of advertising-industry excitement.' They're so family-oriented that with that Italian name in their letterhead I should be reporting them to the FBI."

"Snitch, huh? Remind me not to trust you with my cannoli recipe." Kit flipped to a new page and frowned. "Looks like the family of man is running the place, though. I haven't seen such a collection of prosperous middle-aged white men since I attended an audition for the revival of *How to Succeed in Business Without Really Trying*. Talk about an aging script showing its sexism . . . These guys could really go for a Central Casting bimbo like Savannah Ashleigh. Better tease your hair tomorrow and wear violet lipstick."

"Well, yeah, it does look like the typical middle-aged WASP operation, but then look at the firm's melting-pot names, and that family tree listing all the women, and the intermarriages. Even divorced in-laws seem to stick with the company."

"Profit is thicker than blood?"

Temple reclaimed the brochure, fanned through it again, then tucked it back into her tote bag. "Don't want to forget this. Might need to do a quick review in the ladies' room tomorrow. And I have to bring along a change of clothes for the Christmas party tomorrow night. No way am I going to tote Midnight Louie and all his stuff back and forth during rush hour."

Temple absently stroked Louie's solid girth. "Umph. Between toting His Majesty all over Manhattan and the tension of those meetings all afternoon, my shoulders feel like Atlas is standing on them, with the world only a little blue bonbon on the top."

"Poor baby! I forgot how rough improvising can be. If you were trying out for a real play, you wouldn't have to make up your own lines over and over again. Try this."

Kit, attired in one of her elegant floor-length at-home caftans that were the antithesis of Electra Lark's blowsy muumuus that only reached the most unflatteringly wide part of the calf, bent over to fiddle with something under the couch.

A moment later she straightened, a weird small appliance in her hands.

Temple ducked defensively. "Don't tell me. You're an alien spy, and all that's left of my brain waves has been sucked into that demonic machine for E-mailing to Rigel Three. Good luck, traitor! All that's on my mind now is natural nutrition and the ash content of cat food."

"Relax. It's just a shiatsu machine. Put it behind your head like a pillow, turn it on and your sore muscles are being kneaded by the twin bouncing balls."

"Ooh. Weird feeling!"

"Hang in there. It'll feel good in a second. And you can reverse the action."

"First we rub the left brain, then we rub the right brain . . . Yeah, that does feel better. Maybe Louie would like to try it."

"He's as relaxed as a rubber glove. Cats don't sweat the small stuff."

"Cats don't sweat, period. No sweat glands. That's why dogs and cats pant in severe heat; they release all the poisonous stuff via their tongues."

"And don't people, my dear? Especially nasty critics.

You *are* an animal expert! Bet Savannah Ashleigh doesn't know that. Here's an ottoman for your feet. We might as well stay in for a deli dinner. I want to hear all about what's been happening in your life since I saw you. I'll get a bottle of wine to start us off."

"On dinner? Or on catching up?"

Kit was already invisible around the corner. "I hope you don't mind a decent screw top, Temple. These small, arthritic hands can't manage impediments like corks."

"I know what you mean about impossible corks." Temple raised her voice to carry around the corner. Kit's apartment, like her own, encouraged shouting from room to room. "That's one thing I miss since Max has been gone."

Her aunt's head popped around the corner like a disembodied talking mop. "That's *all*?"

"I was speaking of minor advantages."

"Here." Kit scurried into the main room, two wine glasses filled within an inch of their brims. "I know, full glasses are gauche, but I loathe hopping up and down to refill glasses that could have held a decent amount to begin with."

Kit curled into the couch's tapestry pillows that turned a corner into a comfy curve, her slippered feet tucked under the hem of her caftan.

Temple suddenly noticed the soft brittle rhythm of a CD echoing off the hard windowpanes like insect wings beating a mass retreat. Temple recognized swing music from the forties, the mellow, jazzy jounce of the Big Bands.

"If only you had a fireplace." Temple sighed, rolling her head so the machine's circling cue balls massaged a different hot spot.

Kit gestured to the illuminated city panorama. "Consider it cold fire."

"I do love this place. I could write here. I mean, write something wonderful, maybe even fiction, gazing out the windows on Manhattan, its great, unseen engine churning industrious cogs beneath the city's imposing architectural mantle . . ."

"Maybe I overfilled our glasses, after all. The wine is supposed to be red, but not florid. Don't glamorize cosmopolitan life. I pay a mortgage like everyone else. The super's never there when you need him or her, a self-protective woman needs to wear running shoes on the subway and sometimes we have garbage strikes, which in a city like this means it piles up on the curbs."

"No alleys with little cans for everybody, huh?"

"No alleys. And writing fiction for a living sometimes feels like you're in a dead-end alley and there's a garbage strike on all around you. The publishing business is addicted to turmoil and the outlook is always bleaker than last year somehow."

"Still, you can't say you haven't achieved something."

Kit nodded and sipped. "But I'm not what I came here for."

"An actress?"

"That game is even worse than writing. At least nobody can *can* me because I gain ten pounds."

"But you don't gain ten pounds."

"And that hasn't been easy, even with the edge of good genes. The years have a way of turning on you and all your dietary sins, and sticking out a tongue. Before you know it, you've gained ten pounds, and then another, if you're not careful."

"That's what I was afraid of. I'm seeing the weight issue front and center at the advertising agency. They're even looking a little askance at Louie."

"Of course, looking askance is the only way you can see *all* of him." Kit, hands held up like a moving frame, mimed a camera pan of the cat in question. "What a lug! A full yard stretched out from claw to shining claw, with his front feet flopping over the couch edge. Such a gigolo at heart!"

"Careful what you say. If anyone heard, the agency might invoke Louie's morals clause."

"Morals clause! For a cat? Claws I can buy. Morals? No."

Temple nodded soberly, quite an achievement considering that her glass was half empty already. She hadn't realized that she had been stressed out enough to chugalug a fine vintage screw-top like this.

"Same clause actors and athletes have to sign when they become national spokespersons, Auntie. If even a *cat* gets bad press, it could terminate the contract."

"If you sign up with these people, will there be a morals clause in your contract too?"

"I suppose so, although I'm not famous enough to be pilloried in public." Temple smiled wickedly. "But Savannah Ashleigh is. Her cat Yvette's already in hot water for an unplanned pregnancy."

"By a cat?"

"The father of the quadruplets is rumored to be Yvette's last leading man, previous to Louie."

"No! Stop the presses. CATS SHACK UP IN LAS VEGAS LOVE NEST. I can see the headline now."

After they stopped laughing, and Temple restrained the sleeping Louie from sliding right off the sofa, Kit retreated to the kitchen, returning with the wine bottle and a coaster.

"I'm beat too. Baby-sitting Rudy last night wasn't a piece of cake."

"The guy who played Santa needed baby-sitting?"

"Not exactly. But not too long ago he was a street person. It's easy to slide back into that life. That's why me and a few old acting friends try to keep him gainfully employed."

"Boy, acting must be worse than publishing, if you've got out-of-work thespians panhandling."

"It's not just that. Rudy's a Vietnam vet, and sometimes the nightmares come back. I mean, he won't hurt anybody, and never kids, but we have to keep him focused, especially around the holidays. Playing Santa seems therapeutic. I guess that's what Rudy did with the kids in Vietnam. Looking after them helped him forget the horrors of war. My pal Mitch got him an elf gig at a kids' party, and he's got more for the holidays."

"Vietnam! Kit, that was ages ago. I'm surprised he's not in retirement."

She looked amused. "Temple, darling, Vietnam was still going strong when you were in diapers. Just because you don't remember it doesn't mean it happened before your lifetime."

"No, but it seems like such ancient history. International terrorism has become the preferred conflict of the eighties and nineties."

Temple held her glass with both hands as Kit leaned forward to refill it.

"You seem so hip," she explained to her aunt, "compared to Mom. I guess it's hard to realize how old you are."

"Thank you. I think. I'm several years younger than your mom, and I'd like to believe that living in a cosmopolitan city has polished off some of the hayseed hulls."

"Kit, I didn't mean to insult you. I was actually thinking about international terrorists."

"Commendable."

"Fighting them isn't such a bad thing, is it?"

"No, but how do we do it?"

"Not us. Someone. Maybe someone who has to do it clandestinely."

"Speaking of clandestine, let's forget terrorists and focus closer to home. You're edgier than when I saw you in Las Vegas, and when I last saw you in Las Vegas, you were almost the second victim of a murderer."

"Ooh, yeah. And then Max himself *almost* strangled me for getting into that onstage *pas de deux* with a murderer."

"Max is it now?"

"Sometimes."

"Hmm. That what's making you edgier?"

"I'm not edgier. I'm . . . just burned out from my last case."

"Your last case."

"The Darren Cooke murder."

"I saw the *Times* obituary, but the death was ruled a suicide."

Temple shook her head mournfully.

"The official version is suicide," Kit tried again, "but murder is still suspected?"

Temple's solemn head shook again.

"Temple, for heaven's sake! I'll think you have palsy soon. Well?"

"The official version is suicide. The case is closed. That's all there is."

"But—?"

Temple shrugged gingerly. The shiatsu machine had done its work well. It still buzzed off target, slipping down the couch back.

"But the officials don't know what I know," Temple admitted.

"Which is?"

"*Cherchez la femme.*"

"Your French accent gets comedic when you drink."

"Don't laugh. *La femme* could be *cherchez*-ing me now, because I know too much."

"So. You're looking over your shoulder for a female killer. And that's why you're edgy."

"Maybe. If I *am* edgy. I'm not sure I endorse your diagnosis."

"What about the divine Mr. Devine?"

"Matt? He's not edgy. *Au contraire.* Although he did sound a bit hyper for him when he called me after I got in."

"He called you. I've been wondering about that. Are you two—?"

"Oh, stop making that matchmaker wiggle with your hand, as if my love life could go either way with either guy. It's all at a standstill. Them, me, it. We are all stuck in the mud. Up to our fenders in snowdrifts or sand dunes or self-delusion. Mired."

"I can think of worse men to be mired with."

"How do you know?"

"I've been mired with them. The worse men, that is."

"It's so . . . serious nowadays. With AIDS. Max and I have a tremendous investment in our relationship. Almost two years of monogamy, if you count our six months in Minnesota waiting out the AIDS tests, and the six-month honeymoon in Las Vegas and then another six months of separation."

"Two years? Tremendous?"

"It is! If you want to be real and don't want to take risks."

"And while he was mysteriously away?"

"He says he was faithful. I know I was."

"You believe him?"

Temple stared into the wine's garnet depths. A wine with body seemed thick, like blood. Certainly thicker than water. The wine left a viscous slick on the glass if you tilted the container, then leveled it again. Playing with your drink was always a sign of indecision.

"I don't know what to believe about Max Kinsella nowadays, even what he tells me himself. But fidelity? That I believe. I'd stake my life on it."

"Temple, you're being seriously inconsistent!"

She shrugged. *"C'est la vie."*

"How do you know Max is that reliable?"

"Because I never even *considered* telling those creeps who were beating me where he was, and wouldn't have, even if I had known, and I'm no . . . Joan of Arc. There are some betrayals neither of us is ready to make yet."

"This is not logical."

"No, that's how I can be so sure. But just about that."

"What about Matt Devine?"

"Oooh, worse conundrum even than Max."

"Temple, you're obsessing over this stuff. This stalking woman, and the two men in your life. You're young. Go with your heart."

"You can't nowadays, Kit. You don't know. You didn't grow up in the age of AIDS, when you knew all about it by junior high school. Half the men in the U.S. who die between the ages of twenty-five and forty-four die of AIDS. Think of how many 'eligible' guys are exposed, and are out feeling immortal, exposing new partners. Just because you're from an older generation who's pretty much out of it—"

"Oops. Beg your pardon. I'm not entirely out of it. I have hopes, even at my advanced age, which you'll see when you get there."

"*If* I get there."

"I had no idea you kids were taking this so seriously."

"This one is. That's why I'm hamstrung. Reason says stay with Max, where we've both invested ourselves. But there's so much he's hidden from me . . . and Matt—"

"Matt you don't know well enough to trust when he reports his safety record." Kit nodded sagely.

"That's just the trouble. I *do* know his background all too well."

"And he got around pretty thoroughly. Well, that's natural with his looks—"

Temple laughed bitterly.

"That laugh would do so well in *Private Lives*," Kit, the casting director, said. "But you're not brittle enough to play Amanda yet," her aunt added. "Wait till you're thirty-five."

"You don't understand."

"Maybe not. But I understand more than you think about all this." Kit leaned over to refill her glass.

Perhaps they were getting a bit sloshed, Temple thought, but it was just us girls . . . we girls? And Midnight Louie, and he didn't seem to be listening to a darn thing they said.

"Just how damn old do you think I am?" Kit's eyes were schoolteacher-stern over her incongruously kicky metallic-framed half-glasses.

"Mom's nearly seventy." Temple idly rotated her ankle until one bedroom slipper lived up to its name and floated to the floor. When she felt Kit had been held in suspense long enough, she added, "You've got to be sixty-something."

"That's right. And that's not the end of the world for the libido either. Sixty doesn't look so bad once you've managed to get there. And I didn't get here the same way your mother did. I'm not your mother, Temple, but I'm going to give you a crash course in Life 101A."

Temple swallowed, but not wine. Somehow she'd irritated her aunt, without meaning to. Now here came the lecture that was one of the few perquisites of age.

"You know I left Minnesota for New York to become an actress. Just nod or shake your head, and I'll fill in. You don't have to say a thing. This is my monologue. Well. Here I am in the Big City, my Midwestern cheeks rosy, my miniskirt not nearly as short as the ones on the streets of New York, my hair blowin' in the wind and long enough to touch the bottom of my miniskirt."

Kit took in the tribute of Temple's widened eyes and settled back into her pillows, her foggy-bottom voice growing more reflective.

"It was the sixties, the age of rebellion and rabble-rousing. Make love, not war. A revolutionary concept, and my own generation's invention. We appeared nude in *Hair*. Some of us burned flags. Some of us burned pot. Some of us burned the candle at both ends, usually ours. Can you imagine what it was like to plunge into this sociopolitical-sexual insurrection away from home? The city was our circus, our arena, our life. We were young and we were going to star on Off-Broadway and drink ouzo at four in the morning and walk alone at midnight through Central Park and smoke dope in front of a TV camera and make love with whoever we felt like. So we did."

"We? You mean the generation, not you personally."

"Do I?"

"I mean, Aunt Kit, you weren't, uh, promiscuous?"

"Not in my own mind. I was in the forefront of a revolution, a happy campaigner. I was smashing taboos, stamping out repression, having fun."

"You couldn't have had that kind of fun! You were from the Midwest."

"Honey. Big-time repression brings big-time rebellion. It isn't a coincidence that the Times Square area with the most underage hookers was known in the seventies and eighties as the 'Minnesota Strip.' "

"I heard about that. I mean, in high school. But I didn't really believe it."

"Nobody believes reality. That's why there are— *ta-dah!*—actors."

Temple frowned and sipped judiciously from her glass, thinking that it was about time she sipped judiciously.

"But women then weren't that careless—"

"You know Garrison Keillor's hallmark description of Lake Wobegon?"

"Lake Wobegon! That name is such a priceless satire— 'where the women are strong and the men are good-looking . . .' "

Kit shook her head. "The women in my day were never strong. They were just well controlled."

"You're saying you were—"

"Taken for a revolutionary ride. Used. Again. I was too busy being an artiste to get into the protest movements more than superficially, but when women started waking up from the sexual revolution and took a look at what they did during the civil-rights and Vietnam-protest wars, Mommy, it was manning the coffee and mimeograph machines—a primitive sixties duplicating device, kid— worshiping at the feet of the male gurus who made the speeches and smoked the dope, and scrubbing the floors with their backs. Why do you think women's lib was the last liberal movement of the trio to come along?"

"I didn't think about any of this. They never taught it in school, except very generally."

"These are not things that are taught in school."

"But now you're writing historical romance novels. Isn't that a tad unliberated?"

"Maybe. Maybe not. What women do is always labeled unimportant unless it's in imitation of what men do. Then it's labeled ball-busting."

"Kit, you shock me."

"It's the wine talking. Want some more?"

"Umm . . . just a little. I think I see what you're saying. Thanks to AIDS, women have a chance to say no to exploitation."

"If they'll take it. And I don't think being scared too silly to live is an answer either."

"Then what is?"

"Women making sure that sex is safe. I do respect the longevity of your arrangement with Max. But it wasn't a marriage, Temple. He left, you're free to love again."

"Nothing's ever really free." Temple looked at her glass, surprised that it had refilled almost to the brim. She sipped it down to below the spill level. "Kit, I probably wouldn't tell you this without having had the wine . . ."

"Yes?" Kit looked politely out of focus at the couch's other end.

"And I'm only telling you because you live on the other side of the country and you'll probably never visit Las Vegas again, or meet any of the principals."

"Principals? Are you talking like a lawyer, Temple?"

"I'm hedging like a lawyer, because I'm about to break a confidence, and I wouldn't do it, except I don't know what to think and I could use some advice from someone who doesn't know anybody who's involved . . . personally, that is. Except for me, of course."

"Of course," Kit assured her in far too well enunciated syllables.

Temple had committed the impossible and didn't notice. "You see, the reason Matt's such a dicey romantic partner—"

"Yes?"

"—is he's a priest. Or was until very recently."

"Priest. *The Power and the Glory* kind, not the pleasant chap in England with the collar and the manse and the wife and kiddies?"

"You always go to plays. Yes, the Graham Greene Catholic kind, only he doesn't drink. Except socially a little. And not as much as this," Temple added, squinting at the contents of her glass because the claret color looked so much richer a little out of focus.

"Or do anything, if I've got the religion right." Kit carefully set her wine glass on the cocktail table and put her hands on her akimbo knees. In the long caftan, she resembled an Eastern guru a bit, and Yoda from *Star Wars* a bit. The hiccup was just a small distraction.

"You are telling me that the man is a virgin."

Temple nodded.

"And looks like that?"

Temple nodded.

"Wait a minute! He is heterosexual?"

Temple nodded.

"But he never—?"

Temple nodded.

Kit leaned back and sighed. "How can you be sure of all the aforesaids?"

"I've been around a little, in my modest postsixties way."

"Then grab him."

"It's not so simple, Kit, as you were just reminding me a while ago. What brought him to this position has to be dealt with. Then, he's still Catholic, and if you think about what that religion doesn't let you do . . . if I married Matt I could have fifteen kids! Easy."

"That's right. No birth control." Kit leaned forward. "You could be sterile."

"I think the word for women is 'infertile,' and I wouldn't bet on it."

"He could be infertile."

"I think you mean sterile. And I wouldn't bet on that either."

"Does he want fifteen kids?"

"I don't think so, but he'd have to abandon his entire faith, not just the priesthood, to have anything like a normal sex life. So all is not gold that glitters."

" 'All that glisters is not gold,' " Kit corrected her absently.

Temple recognized the corrected quote from *The Merchant of Venus . . . Venice!*

"All right." Kit grew stern when she drank. "Basics. Who do you love?"

"I loved Max madly . . . until he left without a word."

"And, and . . ." Kit's left hand flopped in circles, but no name came. "And the other guy?"

"I like him tremendously. I respect him." Kit's face was growing grim. "And I'm madly attracted to him."

"Hmmm. If I were to cut one in half, which would you prefer?"

"That old Solomon trick doesn't work with *two* objects of affection, Kit. Do you want me to make some coffee?"

"And ruin our wonderful session of girl talk? No way. Let's see. If Max came home to stay and wanted to get married and didn't want to have fifteen kids, could you be happy with him?"

"Probably, but—"

"Then it appears to me that what Matt needs is right in this room."

"I beg your pardon? I thought I was happily married to Max, who no more will roam?"

"You are. But I have the perfect solution to Matt's problems."

"You do?"

"Sure. Me."

"You?"

"Too old to get preggers, dear. Just what the poor lad needs. Nice experienced menopausal lady with ambition. Not too over the hill. I even look a little like you. What more could he want?"

Temple picked up her fallen bedroom slipper and heaved it at Kit.

Unfortunately, it hit Midnight Louie, who started awake and tore off the couch and across the cocktail table, which overturned Kit's carefully placed glass, which spilled its red, red wine all over Kit's handsome area rug, which Kit and Temple spent the next half hour soaking and soaping in this vale of tears.

Whether they were tears of rue or tears of laughter only the wine remembers.

Louie had retreated someplace secret and invisible where cats go when people are too below them to notice.

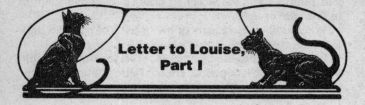

Being the Meditations of Midnight Louie in New York City

Ancient history is only interesting when it is one's own. I cannot tell you how many son-of-a son-of-a's have strutted their hour upon the stage of life during the thirty-something years my two little dolls had under discussion recently.

I mean, when I say I go way back, I go way back to Egyptian times, but only thanks to the intervention of countless generations between then and now.

It is so unfair. My species is superior in many ways, but has definitely been short-sheeted in the longevity department. There are even some spiders that live as long as our eldest examples, big hairy black spiders too, like tarantulas. There are birds even, who outlive us by decades. I refer to the parrot family, which not only hangs around obnoxiously long, but are prized for their aping of human speech. This does not mean that they have the brains to shell a peanut, only an ear for idiocy and the knack of repeating it, which is how some very respectable human careers got started, if you pause to think about it.

But I am in a sober mood after lying about absorbing the *sturm und drang* Miss Temple Barr and Miss Kit Carlson are slinging and sloshing around. Perhaps the Christmas season produces reflections of a nostalgic and familial nature.

Me, I thought the point of the holiday was getting time off work, a chance to collect lots of presents and an excuse to eat oneself into a stupor. And look at me, I have been uprooted and transported to a city so big that I must be carted about from pillar to post for my own physical and sanitary safety . . . I am engaged in the most crucial competition of my new-born performing career . . . and I am not offered so much as a saucer of wine sauce after my long hard day at the office.

So I slink off when the opportunity arises, which it does pretty soon after Miss Kit uncorks her shockingly mediocre bottle of wine. I retreat to Miss Temple's and my room, which, in addition to the presence of a nice queen-size bed for the both of us, features a computer setup by the window.

Despite myself, I am in a reflective mood, so I hop up to inspect the keyboard. It is the usual expanse of letters and numbers interspersed by arcane keys bearing such titles as "Pig Up", "Pig Down" and "Esc," which must be short for escalator and "Alt," which must be short for Altitude, because there are a bunch of F keys with numbers next to them, like F7 et cetera, and I believe those are designations of fighter planes or some such.

Many are the mysteries of the computer, but I do not sweat the small stuff. I know my ABCs and I know where the turn-on buttons are.

In this case the critter is only dozing on low power,

so I give the big round mouse ball a bat or two, and the screen—a tasteful arrangement of flying toasters that I am tempted to have some fun with—is replaced by an image I well recognize: lines of words.

This is my mode, although I do not use the excessive number of exclamation points I see before me. Miss Kit Carlson's newest novel must be stalled in the middle of either an action scene or a sex scene. Only sex and violence merit this plethora of exclamations, in my experience, vicarious as it may be when it comes to human variations of such basic instincts.

So I paw the keys until the smeary or smoochy stuff is off the screen and I have a fresh expanse of gray.

It is hard to get up to writing speed on a foreign keyboard, but I soon get the hang of it and my agile pads are pounding out whatever crosses my mind, which is a letter to my ingrate offspring, Midnight Louise.

"Dear Daughter," I begin.

Well, it is alliterary-ative, but I am not sure I want to give the chit a legal claim on my worldly goods, especially now that I am on the brink of a media career breakthrough. Midnight Louise is likely to take a mile when she is offered an inch.

"Dear Miss Midnight Louise,"

No. Sounds submissive.

"Dear Distant Relative,"

Too cool for Christmas.

"Dear Girlie,"

That will get me four sharp ones across the nose.

"To whom it may concern,"

There, a nice lawyerly approach, no admissions, no obligations.

"I am here in the nation's most impressive metropolis for the holidays, and thought I should ~~kill~~ occupy some time by sending a post card without a picture. You know what I look like and you can always look up New York City in the library if you want pictures.

"Now that 'tis the season for reconciliation and all that mush, it has occurred to me that perhaps we do not understand each other. You do not seem fully impressed by my new (involuntary, it is true) state of reproductive restraint, and still seem to blame me for your presence on this planet.

"Frankly, I agree that the planet might be better off without you, but times change and even a surly, accusatory offspring who has snared her own (possibly) daddy's old job has a role in the overall plan, no doubt.

"I know that you are bitter because you believe that I deserted you and the other litter lice, not to mention your mama, at a bad time. What makes you think that I even knew you were a mote on the Mojave desert's vast sandbox under the sky?

"Your mama could have kept the advent of you and your siblings hush-hush, you know, for reasons of her own, such as not wanting to tie down such a magnificent specimen of feline free spirit as myself. Perhaps she saw that I was destined for greater things than wiping snotty little noses with these talented mitts.

"Whatever the reason, I have now had sufficient time to figure out who your mama was, and I think it is her you should ask a few key questions of. Like is she sure just who your daddy is? Not that I cast any aspersions her way (though I believe that there was a touch of Persian in her ancestry; I always was partial to a female who does not shave her legs). But you know that life on the streets does not encourage the exchange of visitors' cards in these matters. You may have been barking up the wrong dude all this time. Also, why do you not track down your dear old mama and ask her how it is that she seems to have vanished from your life? Perhaps you put too much stake in mere blood kin. In my experience as a master crime-solver, I have seen that the family that stays together, *slays together. There is something to be said for an early and independent lifestyle, such as you and I have had.*

"I mention these things only because I have nothing better to do at the moment, and I wish you would get off my case. I am a normal dude. I just went my way and did my thing, and I think you owe me a little more respect, especially now that I am no longer in a position to produce disgruntled offspring like yourself. The buck stops here. You do not see me carping about my missing parents.

"So, in the spirit of the season, I wish you no ingrown claws or whiskers in the coming year, and a little mercy toward your fellow creatures, especially us poor reviled guys, who may be better than you think.

"Sincerely, your maybe-relative,

Midnight Louie, Esq."

Then I save the whole thing under the file name of "spitfire."

Chapter 12

Unwelcome Matt

Visitors to Las Vegas would find it hard to believe, but some of the city's zillion casinos weren't rip-roaring success stories.

The Gilded Lily was one of these lower nightlife-forms. The minute Matt entered he heard the telltale sluggish ring of too few coins hitting slots. True, it was only Thursday night. Luckily, his regular night off coincided with the first day that fit Kitty O'Connor's time line.

The dark interior struck him as underlit to save on electric bills, not as intriguingly dim on purpose. The low lighting also disguised a worn carpet, he discovered, tripping on a tear in the busy pattern underfoot. Curious and curiouser.

People moved as slowly as the money inside this *Twilight Zone* gambling den. Cocktail waitresses cruised like airliners in a holding pattern: aimless, lumbering, remote in the skimpy crimson uniforms so common to their calling. Matt couldn't envision the woman who had visited him masquerading in one of these saloon-girl getups: limp red satin ruffles edging drooping hems and framing sagging shoulders. Nothing about Kitty O'Connor had drooped or sagged, least of all her attitude.

"Drink?" One of the red satin girls had blocked his path with a tray of smudged gas-station glasses.

She hadn't really looked at him; instead she eyed the half-empty casino for more candidates, customers who had entered, then paused to reconsider.

Under one of the few bleary overhead lights, the drinks showed their true watered-down colors through the dingy glasses: these freebies were straw-colored hybrid freaks, a thimbleful of scotch to six fingers of soda, probably flat.

"No, thanks," he said with no regrets. "But maybe you could check out this ID. You ever see this guy in here? Last name is Effinger, first, Cliff."

"Honey, in Las Vegas the only names that count are on the games of chance, and you see everybody everywhere at some point. Jerry Lewis even came in here once. 'Course, it was years ago, before he had his big Broadway revival and this place hit the skids. No, I don't remember this here guy, but I don't look much anymore, you know? And I guess I don't have to."

She glanced up finally, as her restless eyes stopped their weary evasions.

"Whatever name he uses, that guy's your typical low-rent loser. They all look alike. You, though—"

"Kitty been in lately?" He didn't expect her to know that name. Now that he'd seen the place, he couldn't see Kitty O'Connor working here, not even long enough to earn thirty pieces of silver.

"She quit."

"She did?"

"Don't sound so surprised. We'd all quit if we could get jobs at anyplace other than this dump."

But he was surprised, so taken aback that he forgot to resent the sudden speculation in her tired eyes. She was maybe forty-one passing for forty-eight, with the underfed, slightly bucktoothed look of a lot of not-quite-pretty women who end up slinging hash and dipping at the knees to place paper cocktail napkins on damp tabletops while avoiding pinches and worse.

He was thinking of moving on, when he realized he'd never get anywhere at the private-investigation game if he didn't play the cards he had. If she thought he was the best-looking customer who'd come in a blue moon, so be it. Amen. Use it, brother, use it.

"I don't know if they allow you to sit down, but I'd buy you a drink if—"

"Listen. They let us do anything that sells booze or poker chips." She sashayed ahead of him to the almost-empty lounge area, ruffles swaying.

Barrel chairs upholstered in dirty-orange crushed velvet sat at inhospitable angles to each other, pulled away from tables as if all the Gilded Lily's customers had decamped in a mass panic not long before.

"Verle." She threw herself into the chair nearest a table. Crossed legs showed off fishnet hose with one visible hole. She worried a pack of cigarettes from under a once-puffed red satin sleeve. "Got a match? Hey, I don't mean personally, honey. Obviously no one in this place, and a lotta other ones, can't even come close to you. I mean, can you light my fire?" By now, an unlit filtered cigarette was attached to her lips like an albino leech.

Matches, Matt noted. Something no investigator of the back alleys of life should be without. That and a strong stomach for rotgut.

He shook his head, but she was already beckoning the waiter. Or an albino leech seller. Matt smiled. If Temple could see him now.

"Ge-orge," Verle wheedled. "You still got that Zippo lighter of yours outa hock? Hit me. Thanks." She sank back into a contrail of her own fresh smoke, coughing. "The usual, and see what Pretty Boy Floyd is having."

"Black Russian," Matt said quickly. Whatever brand passed for vodka at the place, they couldn't fake Kahlúa.

He hoped. He also hoped that the coffee liqueur would overpower any untoward tastes.

"You work here for long, Verle?" Matt asked pleasantly.

"Six years, off and on. I come and I go."

"Did Kitty come and go?"

"Nah. She was here for a few months, then she quit suddenly. You know her?"

"Not well. I heard about her, you know?"

"Yeah, well, she's gone, Little Boy Blue."

"Too bad." Matt had pulled out his wallet and now fingered the greasy sketch of Cliff Effinger. "I heard she might know something about this guy."

"What if she did? She's been gone eight months or so now. She's not the one who could tell you about this Effinger guy, if he was here lately."

Verle had picked up the portrait like a card dealt to her in a game, maybe even a lucky card. Her lukewarm brown eyes flicked at his.

"You want to find this guy bad?"

"I'm looking, aren't I?"

"You're not a cop. You a private dick?"

He shook his head.

"I didn't think so. This isn't your scene, is it?"

He shrugged, spread his fingers, wondered if he should search for a lie, realizing that he had no good story ready. And Kitty? She had left too long ago to be the woman at the Circle Ritz. Kitty was a good name for a lot of women in Las Vegas.

When George returned, Verle grabbed the drinks from the tray before he could set them down. Matt paid, and handsomely. He had seen George's glance narrow at the tiny image of Effinger face-up on the table. Verle, he figured, had done him all the good she could, but now he was stuck for at least half an hour, easing her out of his way without hurting her feelings. He supposed Sam Spade would just smash her cigarette into her buckteeth and leave.

Verle puckered her lips into a wrinkled O to exhale a

blast of blue smoke. "God, you are a breath of fresh air in this place. What's your name?"

"Matt."

"Matt. Good name. I get taken for Pearl a lot. Now I ask, do I look like a Pearl to you?"

He eyed her dry, bleached tangerine hair, her long artificial nails covered in a milky-blue polish that had chipped along the thick, uneven edges.

"Not a Pearl. Maybe an Opal."

"Oooh, an Opal. I like that. Fire opal, maybe." She waggled the cigarette, now sporting a half-inch of ash, between her long fingers.

Matt turned Effinger's face toward himself. "Maybe somebody else saw him."

"Sure. I got a distracting job. Some people just sit and wait on their ashcan all day." She glanced over a satin-edged shoulder at George behind the bar. "How many women bartenders you see in this town?"

"I'm not the best person to ask. I usually work nights."

"So do I, sugar. I do some of my best work nights. Or used to." Her drill-sergeant nails played "Taps" on the tabletop. "Anyway, there's more dough in tending bar, at least the tips. I saw what you handed George, and I'm the one who's talking to you."

Matt felt mild panic. He couldn't just throw some bills at her, but she was definitely hinting she wanted consideration. What to do? He sipped the Black Russian that was more black than Russian, and more coffee than vodka. It didn't even taste like a Red Russian.

"It's pretty important that I find this guy. Family matters."

"You mean people still have those?"

"Families? Yeah. Sure. You can't get rid of relatives, you know."

"Oh, I can. And if I were you, I'd get rid of this Effinger fellow too." A long, ragged nail tapped his nose. "Trouble, if you want my guess. I can see his kind coming a mile away. Wants some celebration honey when he wins, which is pretty unlikely, and even then his cash dries up as soon as you've let him check out your chips, if you know what I mean." She snorted in a strangely ladylike way. "But you don't. You're way out of your league here. Forget it. Forget Cliffie-boy. And forget Miss Kitty . . . oh, yeah, I can see she made quite an impression on you, probably belly to belly at some jamboree or other. You don't want that drink? Leave it, hon. I'll drink it for you."

She waved him away with fingers as flaccid as her tired ruffles.

He left a five on the table anyway as he reclaimed Effinger's likeness. "Cigarette money," he mumbled, retreating to the bar.

George held court behind a mirrored circular hulk that winked like a carousel from Hell. Gold streaks through the mirror tiles reminded Matt more of varicose veins than a mother lode of glamour. Stacked cocktail glasses and bottles of booze reflected fragments of the tawdry scene, including himself as he sat on a barstool.

"You got away faster than most," George said, jerking a head to Verle at her table, now stuffing his five-dollar bill up her sleeve. At least she didn't use a garter.

"I'm here on business. I'm looking for this guy."

"Yeah, I seen him here. Recognized him right away. You're not the law, and I can't see you working for broken-down dames like that, so you're not a PI."

"I'm a relative." Matt lowered his eyes to the sketch to hide his self-disgust at the admission. Maybe someday his mother would explain herself.

"Daddy dearest?" George's damp linen towel stopped swiping at rinsed glasses.

"No, but my mother sure would like to know where he is."

"Uh-huh. The old lost stepdaddy routine. Hey, I say something wrong?"

"No. I was just startled. We don't use that expression where I come from. Yup, he's my stepfather."

"Your ma as good-looking as you?"

"She used to be, I guess."

"Yeah. Take some advice. Get out of here. Forget this guy. He's been trouble for someone all his life. Why you, now? Huh? I see a lot from behind these walls of booze and lousy tips. You don't want to find this guy. Nobody wants to find this guy but a landlord he owes or a loan shark whose pearly whites need a little exercise."

Matt smiled at the mention of "Pearl" again.

"But if you gotta be a asshole"—George leaned close, his breath ripe with onion—"ask the bartender at the Brass Rail down the street. Ole Cliff has developed a pattern in his old age. Moves on down the line, casinowise, every couple of weeks. He was here, but not no more. Try the Brass Rail behind the Goliath."

"Thanks." Matt fished for a twenty of thanksgiving, but George slapped the damp dishtowel over his hand resting on the bar.

"You paid enough in here. Just watch you don't get hurt when you find the guy. I sure got sick of his ugly face; maybe you can rearrange it." George's smile somehow morphed into a snarl. "Don't plead innocent with me. That might work on the half-hazed ladies, but not on me. You're out for blood, not money, and I'm glad to point you on down the road, so I don't get a mess on my pristine Formica slate bartop here. Besides, that Effinger guy stiffed me on one boilermaker too many."

"He drinks boilermakers?"

"Say, you're pretty fast for an amateur. Yeah, that's the best way to ask for a guy at a bar, by what he drinks, not by his face or his handle. That's all we remember, what they drink and what they leave us."

Matt took the hint and left another twenty behind. A bargain, given the going price for professional counseling these days.

"Down the street" was far enough to take the motorcycle.

Any map of the Las Vegas Strip looked checkerboard-simple. Just a few main roads, a few major intersections.

Only when you stood on the spot, you realized that the blocks between intersections were made for seven-league boots and three-story-tall MGM Grand hotel lions.

Matt always had a moment of anxiety when returning to the Hesketh Vampire in the parking lot. One time, he expected, it would be gone. It was bright as polished sterling, obviously rare. It begged to be stolen. But it wasn't, this one more time. He was always torn about following anti-crime tips and parking under a light. The light might give away a thief trying to hot-wire it, but it also would spotlight something worth stealing.

He settled for the solution the morally compromised so often take. He had it a little bit of both ways: near enough a light to be seen, not too near to flash like heat lightning.

The helmet and the motorcycle roar in his ears, the rush of cold night air, did nothing to tamp down his loose thoughts. Only flashing by the soon-to-open site of New York–New York did that: Temple was coping with the real thing this Christmas, right now. She was moving on up, to the Big Time, on a whisker and a hair and a hank of tail.

He was heading deeper into the lower depths. The Brass Rail was stuffed between a strip joint and something sleazier that offered wares Matt couldn't quite determine. Strip joints always kept their windows boarded up, as if passersby would try to peek for free. He couldn't imagine cozying up to those grimy windows and doors or even to the nerveless naked skins of the women behind them.

Entering the seamy Brass Rail seemed like a refuge. He ignored the lackluster gaming tables and chimefree slot machines to head for the bar at the back. Another slow night in Silver City.

Matt sat on a barstool without hesitation.

"What can I get you?" The guy who slouched over was young, with thick curly hair and a mustache out of the previous century.

"Boilermaker."

"Bad night?"

"No, George up the way just said you did a good business in boilermakers." Matt listened to himself, amazed. He was learning.

"George sent you, huh? How is old George?"

"Fine as he ever gets, I guess. He gave me some good advice, though."

The guy was moving all the time they talked, wiping off the ledge, pulling out the whiskey and the beer. "I hope you were properly grateful."

Matt nodded. The shot glass filled up to the brim. The beer glass barely foamed. Both containers hit the bartop in tandem, slopping a little of this and a little of that over their rims.

Matt suddenly realized he didn't know which one to drink first. He must have seen this on television at least a dozen times: was it beer/booze, or booze/beer? His newfound pride in exploring the darker side of night-life evaporated.

So he reached for his wallet and pulled out a twenty and the sketch of Cliff Effinger.

"George thought you might know this guy. If you do, there's another one of this guy—" He tapped . . . General Grant on the bow tie! Shhhhoot. He'd pulled out one of the two fifties that he used at the grocery store. Too late to retract. "There's a twin of him if you can tell me where the other guy is." Might as well go for the sixty-four-thousand-dollar question at this point.

"I like your brand, bud. Grant's always been good enough for me. Don't know this geezer's name, and I couldn't tell you if he's right- or left-handed, but I do happen to know where he hangs out. Signed an IOU right at this bar on the back of a Blue Mermaid Motel rate card. I'd know that piss-ant ugly shade of aqua-blue anywhere."

"When was this?"

The bartender eased both Grants off the slick bar into some out-of-sight cache. "Couple nights ago. Better hurry. People who pay less well than you have been lookin' for him too."

"What do you mean 'pay less well'?"

"I mean their money is all in their knuckles, knocking on your door. You pay, they stop. They don't ask after guys like this, they tell you to spill your own guts before they do it for you."

"Did you tell them what you told me?"

"They didn't ask hard enough yet, but they'll get there."

Matt nodded and stood.

"Don't you want your drink?"

"Nope. Lost my taste for it."

"Don't worry. It's on the house."

Matt left, wishing he'd had a swig of something. A hundred dollars, when he could probably have bought the information for forty or fifty. Stupid move. Or . . . maybe smart. Maybe big enough to shake something loose from that guy. He'd decided to tell what he knew before someone came along and made him do it for free, hadn't he?

Matt inhaled the crisp night air, ignoring the lowlifes slouching at doors on either side of the Brass Rail. The Blue Mermaid. He roughly knew where it was. Downtown. Not far from the police department. Temple had told him all about it, raving about the huge plaster mermaid figure that had reared its sinuous curves over the motel since the thirties. Next thing he'd get for his living room would be a big blue mermaid to lounge on his huge red sofa. Right.

Tacky place, he thought next. She hadn't said a lot, but he'd read that between the spurts of her enthusiasm for the blue mermaid figure, for the wacky artist Domingo and his million flamingos. The place had stunk, even if it had an artsy mermaid for a hat.

Matt walked down the side street to the Goliath lot, where he had parked the Vampire in a halfway point between light and darkness. He remembered standing outside the Araby Motel at the Strip's opposite end near McCarran Airport not many months ago, watching a door that Cliff Effinger might exit, or enter. Guard duty had put him into a kind of temporal trance that night. He couldn't say how long he had stood there, or if he'd slept standing up, like a horse, or had dreamed, like a dope fiend. The past and its buried emotions always took him by the throat like a watchdog and choked until he couldn't tell real from false, present from past, right from wrong.

What would he do when he finally found Effinger?

He had no idea. He had never even stopped to wonder what Effinger would do when he saw Matt again.

Chapter 13

Auditions Can Be Murder

Temple would never have thought it possible for the huge conference room at Colby, Janos and Renaldi to look crowded, but today it did. Five new faces sat around the large oval table, and one of them was feline.

And the tension level felt even higher, perhaps because "The Client" was present.

Actually, the four new humans present were from Allpetco, but the advertising agency personnel referred to them in singular form as "The Client." Temple found that as absurd as referring to the Marx Brothers en masse as "The Comic."

The Client was officially the company itself, so Temple supposed it made sense, but the frequently used phrase kept reminding her of the John Grisham book and movie. She kept looking over her shoulder for rogue lawyers.

"The Client wants to watch you and the other candidates do their stuff on camera," Kendall had said the moment Temple reported to her office, dress bag, tote bag and bagged Midnight Louie hanging off different parts of her person.

"The Client? I didn't realize we'd have an audience."

"Now that you've had a day to get used to the surroundings, everyone should be relaxed. The client makes the decision, we just present the possibilities. Want me to hang that dress bag on my door?"

"What would we do without backs of doors?" Temple had wondered as her bag vanished onto a hook behind the open door.

So now Temple again made a dramatic entrance to the conference room, Midnight Louie in his purple sack fastened to her chest like some protective life vest.

By now she had affixed names and faces to the agency people. It was easy once you understood the family, and ethnic trees. Colbys were medium in every respect—height, coloring, vocal tones. Placid, happy, humming WASPs like Kendall, despite her Italian last name, for Temple had discovered in the agency brochure that Kendall was Brent Colby's daughter.

Janoses were intensely brown in coloring and choleric in temperament, Middle European to the toes of their sensibly sturdy wing-tip shoes. Renaldis were either as tall and elegant as Respighi pines or, conversely, as round and black as olives, both species intense in a deceptively laid-back way.

Stereotypes didn't hold across all members of a particular family, but they helped Temple grasp the essential character of each of the three "tribes" she must deal with.

"The Client." Now that was no neat familial or ethnic union. The Client was one man and three women. She had no idea what position these four had with the company. She hoped someone would explain that to her before the day had much advanced, but no one seemed inclined to, although introductions had been made, too hastily to take root. In the meantime, Temple would do as she had always done when meeting new people: assume that they were fair-minded, intelligent and friendly until they proved themselves otherwise.

Temple the TV news reporter had used that basic technique with everyone from multimillionaires to homeless transients, man or woman, adult or child. Cynical reporters—and she had discovered that not only was the stereotype true, but that there were far too many of them for the good of truly unbiased reporting because cynicism cuts both ways—ended up not respecting certain stories and certain people. They also ended up getting lousy stories, and missing many good ones that way.

Call her a cockeyed optimist, but Temple had learned early that overestimating yourself and underestimating other people was the worst mistake you could make in professional matters. Or personal ones.

Her musings stopped. Midnight Louie's whole body had stiffened against her. This feline alarm was as startling as a dog's sudden bark. If Louie had been a dog, heaven forbid, he would have been a pointer at that moment.

Temple followed the direction of his glassy, fixed gaze, and saw that everyone in the room (except her, of course, who had been insight-gathering) was staring in the same direction. Was something wrong?

She steeled herself to view the usual dead body. What was new? Death by staple gun, perhaps, this time. Caffeine poisoning. Nicotine fit. This was New York. What she saw instead was a new furry face in the room.

This animal was indeed remarkable. A beautiful dark-blond Persian cat sat full-length on the table, like a demure, fluffy sphinx, her long golden forelegs casually crossed.

Her earth-toned coat was a mélange of dark, foxy red-gold down the back and incredibly full tail, then caramel on the long, flowing sides. Cream frosted her dainty chin and luxuriant bib. Her green eyes gleamed mossy, like agates in an old-gold frame, and her nose was the same rich brick-red as the paler twin's: Yvette.

One was sun, the other moon.

And Midnight Louie was mooning at the sun!

Temple shook his carrier, trying to break the golden cat's spell. No such luck. Louie wasn't the only one struck to stone. No one spoke, or stirred, for at least a full minute.

"Magnificent," Brent Colby, Jr., declared, reaching out his Rolex-banded wrist to stroke the creature's head as if touching a golden object.

"Fabulous doming." One of the women from the foursome known as "The Client" spoke with a hush in her voice.

Temple had heard that expression before about purebred Persians. What the heck was doming, besides a furry forehead? And who cared anyway? Louie didn't need doming; he had brains and initiative. Or he had used to have them. Temple twisted her neck around, trying to catch Louie's bright emerald eye. No use. He was as transfixed as the rest of them.

"This is very good," a low voice commented into her left ear.

Temple turned on Kendall, suppressing a snarl.

"What's good?" Temple asked with resentful stage-mother vehemence. "That gilded lily taking the spotlight from Louie?"

"She's golden. He's black. Maurice, if you recall, is yellow-striped."

It took half a minute for Temple's old television instincts to kick in. "Maurice too closely matches the color of this one. Louie doesn't."

Kendall nodded, never dislodging a scissor-snipped strand of her Fifty-seventh Street haircut.

And then Savannah Ashleigh clip-clopped over on her platform heels. "Isn't she divine? Solange is Yvette's sister."

Temple wasn't going to put up with misrepresentation. "How can she be? Aren't purebreds supposed to all be the same color and have the same markings, give or take minor variations? Yvette is a shaded silver Persian. And this is . . . a horse of quite a different color, though the darker markings are the same."

Savannah sighed dramatically, doing much to reinforce Dr. Mendel's shoring-up and -out operations on her bust. "I don't understand it myself. Something to do with genetics. But I think Solange is a missing link. A throwback. A recess of Jean." Savannah frowned at her last expression. "I don't know what Jean has to do with it. Maybe she was an important breeder who took frequent time-outs."

The moment Savannah had begun speaking in her pneumatic voice, overemphasizing her esses until she sounded like an oversexed air hose, everyone's attention had reverted to Solange.

The woman from Allpetco rolled her eyes at Savannah's interpretation of "recessive gene," but went on talking as if she had never been interrupted.

"I'm by no means an 'important breeder' like Jean, yet I do know that the shaded silver Persian is basically a white cat with brown tabby markings: black tipping the hairs. Of course, early shaded-silver litters threw up some kittens with brown tabby coloring. Those poor 'throwbacks' were brushed off and sold as pets. Eventually, some breeders recognized that, once in a harvest moon, an anomaly shines through human concerns about controlling color and breeding true, and deserves its own spotlight. Thus you have shaded golden Persians like Solange. Some people breed them exclusively, and now we all recognize that it is truly impossible to say which is the lovelier shaded Persian, the silver or the gold. It's not uncommon for silver litters to produce golden siblings. Although"—here she frowned—"it is exceedingly odd for a shaded silver like Yvette to produce what are essentially 'red,' which can be yellow or orange, tabby kittens."

Savannah stirred. "Are you saying that the lousy Maurice can't be the father of Yvette's babies? Oh. It must be a *virgin* birth, then. This changes everything. This means *good* tabloid coverage. Yvette is redeemed!"

"I'm afraid not. Before I'd buy spontaneous regeneration, I would suspect a tarnish spot on the mother, which would mean that Yvette is actually a shaded tortoiseshell."

"Yvette? My sterling silver sweetums?" Savannah waxed highly indignant again. "A tortie? Look at her! A symphony in platinum. There is nothing red about her but her little red nose and tongue."

The woman smiled tolerantly. "To carry the red strain, she would only need two red hairs somewhere, anywhere, on her body. Perhaps between a toe—"

Savannah shrieked. The notion of Yvette secreting unauthorized foreign-colored hair was too unspeakable to address further.

Besides, advertising agency personnel had no interest splitting cat hairs and paternity issues.

"Getting back to practicalities," young Andrew Janos interjected. "This blond cat . . . er, red cat . . . er, sister Solange, she has no performing experience, though?"

"No," Savannah admitted, still pouting at the latest assault on her darling Yvette's reputation.

"And we know," said a young adwoman in a navy Anne Klein II suit, "that Yvette and Midnight Louie work together like . . . sugar and spice, sweet and sour, cream and Kahlúa." She seemed ready to go on forever, oxymoronically speaking.

"It's too early for lunch," Kendall interjected with smooth good humor, "but *you* must be hungry already. Maybe we should see how the boy-cats react to this girl-cat. Has Maurice met Solange?"

"Only a hissing acquaintance," Savannah put in cattily.

"I see," said Kendall, well pleased by Maurice's ill manners. "Shall we let Louie take a good look at her?"

She supported the weight of his carrier while Temple loosened her bonds and shrugged out of the contraption. All eyes were on her and Louie. She felt like Houdini performing an escape.

Only . . . as she let Kendall hold the carrier and loosened the neck drawstring to give Louie a little more freedom of movement . . . he took a lot more freedom of movement . . . by leaping to the ground, leaving the bag behind as Kendall's tightened grip helped him squeeze out like a large boneless black furry lump of Silly Putty . . . and then Louie bounded over the sleek industrial carpeting while women squealed and brave men frowned and ordered: "Stop him!" But no one did because he was atop the conference table and nose-to-nose with the Divine Solange before Temple could race after and corral him before he did something foolish.

Louie bent his head to touch noses with Solange, then he paced toward her rear as they sniffed tails. He returned again to touch his matte-black nose to her deep dull-red one. Solange's whiskers, black and spidery, mingled with Louie's striking white facial vibrissae.

It didn't take an advertising genius to see that this was kitty chemistry at first sight.

A plaintive mew issued from the pink canvas carrier that everyone had forgotten about on the floor. Temple, having stopped at the table edge to let nature take its course, cast the carrier a sympathetic glance.

"This is great," the senior male member of The Client said, nodding sagely. "Film it."

So Andrew Janos picked up his camcorder and filmed.

Another mew emerged from the pink carrier, but this time not even Temple noticed.

If only, Temple thought about four hours later, sitting in the dark around the conference table, they had confined the day's filming to Louie and Solange.

But, no, they had to reshoot Temple and Savannah, various cats in hand, in endless mock interviews. After this orgy of amateur filming (and interviewing, in Temple's opinion), invisible minions were sent for trays of coffee-to-go in giant Styrofoam cups and two pizzas that arrived cold and congealing. Not even Louie, connoisseur of alley bonanzas, would touch the cold circles of oven-curled pepperoni sausage floating pools of hardened grease like miniature terra-cotta birdbaths filled with frozen ice water.

Besides, Temple was too nervous to eat by now, and one

more cup of black, syrupy coffee would have her on the ceiling.

Before her queasy eyes, the film ran, paused, retracked, fast-forwarded and moved frame by frame at the request of various experts in the room: the agency creative directors, the agency senior members, the agency young turks, the agency gofers . . . The Client's lead member, The Client's one-minded female triumvirate who always disagreed with the lead member . . . Maurice's handler the animal-behavior expert, Savannah Ashleigh the actress, whose bubbly monologue pointing out her own strong points often continued into Temple's segments, where she found only flaws.

Temple no longer felt very civil. She had noticed when she held him on camera that Louie's claws, both fore and aft, were slightly extended at all times by the later sessions. In fact, Savannah Ashleigh had complained of this long and loudly during her last tandem "interview" with Louie, and had writhed in her chair in considerable pain apparently . . . or under the misconception that the writhing human female form can sell cat food.

Now if Solange had writhed . . . but Solange was a lady to her gilded toes. Poor Yvette seemed listless and diminished her few times on camera—what ragged-out new mother could compete with that corona of sun-bright fur shining in the spotlights?

Maurice was brought out, but, next to Solange's sable-blond aurora borealis, his American short-hair yellow stripes looked like a cheap suit bought in Times Square.

Louie was gracious to both ladies of the feline persuasion, a lamb when with Temple, and a lion when with Savannah. But he never crossed the line to out-and-out misbehavior.

Although Savannah accused him during one film session of "leaking" on her best Ultrasuede skirt, no spot could be found, even by the agency art director, who examined it thoroughly. The group conclusion was that the warmth of Louie's considerable weight had felt like a "leak" to her.

Temple feared that Savannah's running critique of Temple's failings had struck home and mentally agonized over how to compensate for them:

Savannah's Slams	Temple's Fixes
Toothpick legs	Calf-length skirts
Bony ankles	Boots
Squints at camera	Glasses (no, contact lenses)
A Midwestern accent	A French accent
Red hair	A blond wig
Speaks too fast	A molasses mouthwash
Waves hands too much	Handcuffs

Of course, by the time Temple had actually corrected all the supposed flaws Savannah had mentioned, she would be unrecognizable and quite literally unspeakable.

The replay session ended with actual film of the recent Las Vegas commercials done at Gangster's casino and surrounding attractions. Temple was not in these segments, so could settle down to watch Louie's shenanigans with unselfconscious pleasure. Among the chorus line of pastel zoot-suited gangsters in lime-green and flamingo-pink fedoras, his nimble black form stood out like a flea on a tie-dyed cat. He certainly could cavort down onstage stairways faster than Marilyn Miller at full tap, swim harder than a sinking hamster on an exercise wheel in the Mirage's volcano pool, and leap over Gangster's thirties-vintage car seats with a single bound, she thought proudly.

Finally the room's peripheral down lights came on and the huge built-in television screen went black for the last time.

"Most instructive," said the lead client, whose first name was Gerald.

The foursome now wore sticky name labels pasted to their left chests. Temple wondered why people always affixed such labels right where their hands would rest over their hearts when reciting the Pledge of Allegiance in school.

She was too exhausted to worry about what the verdict was, and suspected that none of them would know until Monday.

Chapter 14

"...A Creature Was Stirring"

Nothing is more annoying than home movies. Even if you happen to be one of the stars.

Luckily, I have established myself as a free spirit, thanks to Miss Temple's innovative carrier. I never thought I would come to appreciate that embarrassing sling of purple nylon straps attached to a drawstring baggie, or looking like a couch potato. It simply does not befit a media star in the making.

However, it is a snap to get in and out of when no one is looking. And no one is looking when they can see the likes of myself on the silver screen. (All right, it is a black screen until it is turned on. But my personal style is silver screen. Just give me a cravat and a pencil-thin mustache and I would be Ronald Colman. All right. I have a pencil-thin mustache already. It just does not show to good advantage amidst all this hair.)

I must say that the Sublime Solange does show to

good advantage on camera. The Divine Yvette is most cast down by this reversal of fortune. I, however, have obligations to the entire project and cannot show favoritism. Besides, has she never seen *A Star Is Born*? As one goes up, another may go down. I hope that this is not the case between Miss Savannah Ashleigh and my little doll. I do all I can to provoke Miss Ashleigh to unleash her most vixenish characteristics.

But she is so relentlessly competitive that I fear she has done Miss Temple irreparable harm.

Then, again, perhaps my little doll should consider toning down her hair color. And her figure is not of the Rubenesque proportions the Sublime Solange illustrates so well. I am not too sure who this Rubens was. Perhaps he invented the sandwich of that name, which I understand can really pile on the pounds, containing as it does so many healthful items from the four major human food groups: fatty protein (corned beef), salty vegetable (sauerkraut), fatty dressing (Thousand Island), bread (which is for the birds), and fat fat (whatever else you put on it).

Now that I am as good as a spokescat on matters nutritional, I believe I should not hold back in criticizing the human diet. Nutrition, after all, is a cross-species issue.

But a dude can only take so much self-adulation, so I paw open the conference door so narrowly that no one notices, and slip out into the well-lit hall. I am never at ease until I know the lay of whatever landscape I inhabit. I begin to sniff around discreetly.

What I notice first off is that this is not a place that welcomes any but human visitors. The only interesting scents I detect are Miss Temple's shoes, the airborne essence of three felines, two of them female, and it does not take a genius to figure out that these individuals are all present and accounted for and in the conference room.

So I amble down the hall, hearing the halfhearted buzz of distant employees whose immediate supervisors are otherwise and otherwhere occupied. Since I know what areas are sure to be mostly unoccupied, I head to the back and the windows. Sure enough. The hallways widen, the carpet thickens, the piped-in Muzak gets tonier.

I nudge open a wide door of some exotic wood and find myself in a handsome outer office. I push onward and inward to forbidden territory. The dude's desk is the size of a Ping-Pong table, but much classier. The wood-paneled walls smell of lemon wax, which does nothing for my taste buds. I am not a citrus kind of guy and thank Bast that I was not born in Florida. I can just see my old man lolling on some boat called the *Bastet Royal Flush,* snagging marlin and sailfish with one mitt while dolls in thong collars come calling with sickening regularity. My old man is more than somewhat old-fashioned.

I, however, embrace the coming millennium. I am all for high technology and cyberspace cruising. I have been known to tap-dance on a keyboard or two in my day. So I hop atop the desk and take a gander at the screen. I have glimpsed screens with glowing letters the color of my eyes, and Miss Temple had a Karma-blue background on her computer screen, with white letters. But then she got a new one and it all comes up plain old black on white, which is not a bad combination once you think of it. And this is the kind of screen I see here with rows of black letters.

Now I can read the writing on the wall, and this office has the same boring bank of wooden plaques with gold lettering and framed certificates as the other executive offices. Why does having a big office make dudes think they must tack up every piece of paper they ever collected in life?

Me, if I had an office like this, I might go for trophy specimens. Like a gopher. Or maybe that record-quality blue and white koi I snagged from under Chef Song's meat cleaver at the Crystal Phoenix when I first blew into town. There are a few rats I could display, but why upset the visitors?

And of course I would have framed photos of all the glamorous tootsies in my life, feline and human.

And could I curl up on this emerald carpet and make a pretty picture! In fact, I am considering artfully allowing the Big Boss—Brent Colby, Jr.—to catch me in just such an irresistible circumstance when I hear voices down the hall and must vacate the locale lickety-split.

The other back offices are nice, but not as big. After a hurried scramble, I manage to zip into a maintenance closet someone has thoughtfully left ajar. I am hoping nobody sees me who might return me to the matinee of tedium down the hall.

I manage to paw the door almost shut, so it is coal-cellar dark within, except for a pinstripe of light. The voices are coming closer, which is the only reason I can understand what they are saying. Both speak in cautious whispers, so I cannot tell whose voices I hear, or even what gender they are.

"Will they not miss you in the conference room meeting?" I hear one voice ask.

"Not in the dark," is the sardonic answer. "You sure that no one saw you come in today either?"

"Not even a mouse," says the other person with a chuckle. "As you suggested, it is going to be a big surprise. I can hardly wait for the unveiling afterward, when the others figure out who I really am. Will that blow them away!"

"Please! That phrase might bring back some bad memories."

"All my memories are bad ones, which is why it is

so great we ran into each other again. Nothin' like old friends gettin' together and talking over old times. I bet some of us have forgotten more than we remember. Except me. I may not have a pot to piss in, 'scuse that phrase, but my memory's A-one. Hey, I even recognized you first. Imagine that, running into each other by coincidence in a great big city like New York. I bet that now that has happened, you will be seeing me again. And again. That is the way it goes. And I, uh, appreciate your doing something extra special for the Christmas kitty. You were always a big spender . . . especially when the money was not yours."

"Whatever, whatever. We do not want your cover blown now. Better duck out of sight for the duration. Then you can hit the scene on cue. Got a glow-in-the-dark watch?"

"Hell, I think *I* still glow in the dark from the old days. Orange. Okay, I am outa here. See you later. I can hardly wait to see the others' expressions, afterwards."

"I guess you could say you are bringing them some extra holiday presence."

"Presence, spelled like presence? Pretty good. You were always clever. Well, why should I not give 'em the Christmas surprise of their lives? I am supposed to be a jolly old soul."

At that point, somebody laughs, not a nice laugh at all.

I sigh in my closet, waiting for the parting rustles to subside. That is when I realize that I have been so intent on hearing this conversation (for I am nothing if not curious, to a fault), that I have been derelict in scouting out my refuge.

In fact, I realize that the background sound that was making my ears twitch now and then in annoyance was not the distant drone of some heating unit, but was a soft, rhythmic subsonic hiss like . . . breathing.

Whoops! I am not alone. Something is in here. With me. In the dark. Making not a peep, like it does not wish to be detected either.

Too bad I do not have one of those bowser-quality snouts that can scent anything from garbage to Garbo at fifty feet. My sniffer is pretty sharp on a certain range of odors, mostly animal and vegetable, but I am not a tracker by profession. If I cannot tell *who* is my closet-mate, I am also not sure *what* is confined with me.

I hear the rustle of motion behind me. The odors of turpentine and lemon oil clothe the intruder in a miasma of mystery. This could be a tiny little Manhattan house mouse, for all I know, or Jurassic Alligator.

I am trying to decide if it is worth my while to find out which when an aluminum pail comes sweeping down over me like a bell, doubling the darkness and caging me with an overbearing scent of Mr. Clean.

I loathe any kind of involuntary confinement, so I bolt out from under the descending metal prison at the last instant. I head for the spaghetti-thin line of light where the door do-si-dos with the doorjamb. In my haste, I manage to go dancing in the dark with one of those old-fashioned string dust mops that is all cotton-twist tendrils dripping oil and allergens. I am about to sneeze, and the floppy mop part is hanging over my head like a wig.

I hate being in the dark.

So I lose the dust mop and bust the door open without looking back to see what creature is stirring behind me. I also loose a big sneeze as I head back toward the home movies, where I *know* what I'm keeping company with in the dark, feeling as if a herd of demonic reindeer were behind me. Down the hall, I dart into the first ajar door, under the mistaken impression I will be greeted by my own lovely mug up close and personal on a big-screen TV.

Have I taken a wrong turn!

I am in a conference room, all right, but every light in the place is blazing and a lot more that do not normally belong here, even though this is New York City and they do a lot of things that are not normal here all year long. Some people think that my hometown is a bit unreal, but they have never explored the outer limits of this toddling town, let me tell you.

Anyway, what to my wondering eyes should appear, but a sleigh and eight tiny reindeer?

They are hanging high on the wall, just under the ceiling, and Rudolph's nose is blinking like a big red stoplight. (I wonder if Rudolph is any relation to that chef, Ruben?) Beneath this poster paint stands this awesome 3-D chimney, all red brick and dripping cottony snow from the top as if it had the sniffles.

I think fondly of the chimney through which I made my dramatic but sooty entrance at the Halloween séance to revive Houdini. Perhaps I can manage such a trick tonight. That would impress Solange, the ad people and The Client. Maybe even Miss Temple, but I doubt it. She does not seem to be surprised by anything I do any more.

Just call me the Mystifying Mr. Midnight.

I trot over to investigate the scene of my next transportation triumph.

I pass a real live Christmas tree in one corner, smelling like pine room deodorizer. It is decked with golden garlands and little glass . . . well, I will be a monkey's uncle, but only if one of my relatives has gotten into something kinky! Tiny glass cats hang all over the tree, dangling from golden cords around their translucent necks. I edge over to investigate, and recognize statues of Bast, upright, with her front legs straight as columns and a twenty-four-carat gilt ring glimmering in one ear. I shiver a hair. Actually, several hairs. I could stand a little less Bast in my life of late.

But I am immediately distracted by a swath of wrapped presents under the tree. Dozens and dozens. Here and there I scent the real smell of Christmas . . . exotic, imported catnip!

I can hardly restrain myself from snicking out my shivs and tearing into that primo stuff.

But I am applying for a job here. It would be best not to display any addictive habits until the position is in the bag. Or I am.

My eyes narrow. I know that rat Maurice has been waiting to make his move on me. I wonder if I can turn the tables on him before he even knows we are talking furniture.

At least I have a preview of the treats to come. I study the empty folding chairs, the long table lined up against a wall with an empty punch bowl on one end. Enough of the media feeding frenzy in the other conference room, folks! I have had my hour in the spotlight, and am now ready to eat, drink and be merry, for tomorrow we vie. Again.

"Now, Dasher! Now, Dancer! Now, Prancer and Vixen! On, Comet! On Cupid! On Donner and Blitzen!"

I can hardly wait to meet those naughty-but-nice girls, Dancer and Prancer and Vixen, and having Cupid in there does not hurt a bit when it comes to Christmas merriment. Then we can all get Blitzened.

But for now I slip back into the darkened conference room, where all present are gazing raptly at my onscreen pirouettes, unaware that I was not merely performing but running for my very life from a lurking assassin . . . and have likely just done so again!

What they do not know will not hurt them, or my film career. What a pro I am! At both of my professions. I pussyfoot up to the familiar form, scent and foot of Miss Temple Barr. *She* was not loitering anonymously in any closets, and she will have no notion of my recent close encounter. When the lights come on, I will be sitting meekly beside her, ready for shoveling into whatever distasteful means of confinement and transport she finds necessary in the Big Apple.

But inside I am a free spirit.

Party on!

Chapter 15

Claus for Alarm

Deck the Halls with . . . pigtails and coveralls.

Everyone escaped the conference room at six-something that evening. Despite the massive quantities of coffee consumed, they lurched blinking like zombies from the still-dark room into the well-lit halls.

While they'd been closeted within their media cocoon, the outer world of Colby, Janos and Renaldi had altered dramatically. The exiting people couldn't evade it, since they all nearly tripped over the major change in personnel. An unlikely addition.

Toddlers, tots, tykes and preteens ran, roared and raised heck up and down the halls, all dressed like Santa's elves in green and red (some rebels in green *or* red), imps clothed in plaids, paisleys, velvet, corduroy and velour, in holly and cat-angel Christmas prints.

Halfheartedly chasing the escapees were harried parents from knots of chatting wives or joking husbands.

Andrew Janos, obviously coveting a Golden Globe award, never stopped running his camcorder, but came charging from the dark, the camera's light blaring like a steam locomotive's single warning headlight.

The din, of course, was many times the normal hubbub of hyped-up ad people stepping on each other's sentences and building mole-hill notions into media-campaign mountains through a round robin of creative one-upmanship.

Temple hadn't bothered donning Louie's CatAboard in the dark, so she toted him and it before her, no hand free to shelter her ears from the shocking howls, squeals, giggles, bleats, bellowed orders, whines and assorted, and mostly ineffective, parental pleadings.

"Duck into my office," Kendall suggested in Temple's ear. "You can change there. I don't think you or Louie would much care for the rest room at the moment."

Temple watched a young mother squat before an adorably dressed little girl, struggling to comb a tangled ponytail. The child's protesting screech would have deafened a bat, or Batman.

Temple nodded yes to the suggestion, clutched Midnight Louie as close as his girth would permit and made for Kendall's crowded office.

"Did your father really mean that the cats were not to be confined for the party?" Temple asked Kendall as they arrived at her office door. "I mean, all those strange kids wandering around. Uh, not that the kids are strange, inherently, only that they're unknown to the cats and the cats are unknown to them and someone could step on someone's toes or tail and someone could claw or bite someone."

"Colby, Janos and Renaldi kids don't claw or bite," Kendall said with a firm smile. "I think Dad's looking for how the cats react to crowds, unleashed. There'll be pet store openings to attend, and the spokescat has to be mellow enough to roll with the punches."

Temple eyed Midnight Louie, lolling with flattened ears in the bosom of his cradle. "Mellow" was not a word she would use to describe him.

"But . . . if there is an incident, and kids can tease animals without meaning to—"

"We want to know *if* there will be an incident. If one occurs here, our employees are less likely to sue for a cat scratch than the public at large. Better to know now. What's the matter, are you afraid that Louie will be ninja cat outside his carrier? He was a pussycat on the conference table."

"But the people sitting around it were adults, not kids."

"Don't be too sure about that," Kendall said sardonically, shutting the door.

The message was clear: the Christmas party was another "test" for the animals as well as the people. "Don't hiss, scratch or bite," Temple admonished Louie. "And don't snag my velvet dress or anybody else's."

She swished her black stretch-velvet turtleneck dress from the door hook, and changed clothes with a nervous eye on some still-lit offices in the opposite skyscraper—a cleaning guy waved. Once the dress was on, she waved back, then topped her velvet neck and shoulders with a red-beaded openwork shawl. Trust Las Vegas for the latest experiment in instant, portable glitz. Her plain black Stuart Weitzman pumps sported red Austrian-crystal lips that were either cheeky or surreal, depending on interpretation. They certainly looked Christmasy. She was afraid to trust the fully spangled Midnight Louie Austrian-crystal shoes to such a big, toe-stepping, punch-spilling crowd.

"Too bad you're fussy about wearing anything off camera, Louie. That flamingo fedora you wore in the Las Vegas ad footage was *très chic,* but would be sadly out of season here and now. And I guess you'd snarl at a red bow tie on a collar."

Louie, who had leaped atop Kendall's desk to bat the red fringe that draped from Temple's bodice, withheld comment. But not his claws.

"I hope you used your conference-room box recently," Temple admonished her bored darling, wishing she'd had the foresight herself to manage a rest-room visit earlier.

In minutes she had extracted her small purse from the bottom of Louie's carrier, a great place to carry valuables like credit cards, and slung it over one shoulder. She picked up Louie, sans carrier, and managed to open the office door. First, she peeked into the hall.

The Tiny Tot Parade had assembled elsewhere by now, but the Children's Chorus came loud and muffled from deeper within the suite of offices.

As if following a latter-day Pied Piper's audible trail, Temple found herself passing the darkened conference room. Something moved within. Someone. Someone wearing red. The motion stopped the moment it attracted her sideways glance.

Louie chose that instant to decide that he was no longer a carry-cat.

Four dangling legs flailed. Temple, fearing snags in her expensive new velvet dress, held his weight away from her. She had an invisible opponent. Gravity grabbed Louie's leaden mid section and pulled until it pooled like mercury in his tail section. Louie ended up falling/jumping to the floor.

Being a cat and instinctively recognizing the least convenient place for him to go at any given moment, he immediately darted though the ajar door into the darkened conference room.

"Lou-ie!"

Temple felt like the harried mother of a delinquent tot. She dove into the dark after him, her hand slapping the wall inside for light switches.

Her palm found only smooth flannel paneling. Such oversized rooms as this usually featured multi-switch installations, not near the door like a normal switch plate, but someplace discreet and unexpected . . . and far away. Still, Temple thought, one guiding light switch must be near.

She fumbled in the dark, wondering whom she had seen lurking in here. "Lurking" was the only word to describe the darting, shy almost-motion that she had glimpsed. Now, the vast dark room was silent except for her own clumsy thumps and shuffles. Louie, naturally, could navigate this dim expanse as quietly as a snowfall.

Temple's fingers finally found a single light switch four feet from the door, and flipped up the lever. One wan light winked on, revealing Louie in Halloween-cat pose, back arched, on the conference table, facing off with . . . Santa Claus.

Then Temple remembered. Brent Colby, Jr., always played Santa at these company Christmas parties. He had to change and hide out somewhere until he made his entrance. Thanks to Louie, she had stumbled into his dressing room. Great move.

Louie clearly nonplussed Santa, and he seemed equally startled to see Temple. He had backed away from the open door's sight line. His mouth remained frozen into a round, jolly little O, as if he wanted to speak to her but had thought better of it.

She wondered if, like the tin woodman, he needed a little oil at the jaw joints. Then she noticed a costly crystal lowball glass beside him on the table.

Performance anxiety. And she wasn't helping by barging into his preappearance retreat.

She hotfooted over to collect Louie. By then Santa had found a traditional twinkle for his eye and had raised a forefinger to his lips.

Temple nodded, happy to comply with the holiday deception she had almost messed up. Santa glanced down to her shoes, frowned, and then winked.

Temple tucked Louie under her arm, despite velvet-raking possibilities. Cost of doing business.

"No claws!" She hissed the command to him under her breath. She shrugged apologetically at Santa Claus and hefted Louie higher. "You know the kind of claws I mean," she told the man in red.

Then she rushed out without a backward look.

Down the hall thirty feet she stopped beside an identical door, also ajar. This door leaked light and noise like a festive sieve. Entering, Temple found herself the last guest to arrive. Everyone from the conference room was in-stalled here now, along with triple their number in children and significant others.

Even Yvette's pink and Solange's chartreuse carriers had made the relocation, sitting side by side and looking like anemic holiday decorations. All the cats were free to roam, except Maurice, who was on a leash.

Temple didn't know what would happen if she let the felines mix it up, but Louie weighed a ton. Though he had not flailed since they had left the other conference room, he had steadily slipped down her side. He now hung at hip level. One notch lower, and he'd be on the floor again.

She let him drop, realizing that the cats had wonderful chaperones anyway: kids of all sizes and ages, eager to sur-round them with curiosity and affection. The kitties, per-haps, would not welcome pats from sticky hands attached to high-pitched voices and sudden, jerky movements.

Temple was in the same beautiful pea-green boat with her one pussycat as every other woman in this room was with her one-plus offspring: she had a charge to watch every minute so that no one did it damage and it did dam-age to no one. All Temple really longed for was a long, hot soak in a bathtub somewhere quiet.

"Thought that went well."

A Colby cousin, a blond guy her age that Temple would have thought handsome if she had never seen Matt Devine, had edged over with a cup of ruddy wine punch. Since his other hand held a glass of harder stuff, Temple took the wine.

"Thanks. I actually needed this. Did the audition session really go well?"

"Absolutely. Vote's not in, and The Client hasn't spo-ken, but, ah, you certainly have my vote. That's off the record."

"Of course. And thanks for the support."

"I'm behind your alley cat one hundred percent too. Not that they haven't done well with Maurice, but your Louie combines streetwise charm with a certain elegance."

"I think so too. And the lucky lady cat?"

His flaxen head shook. "Pity about the petite silver. Bad break. Still, no client wants a tabloid appearance, not even for a cat. Besides, that sister of hers is a standout filly. Never even heard of the breed, but she films like a brandy Alexander goes down. Don't you think?"

"I do. Perhaps Yvette could have a cameo role."

His pale head shook. "In this business, you're either top cat, or no cat."

"So Maurice's career is—?"

"You've heard of the dodo?"

"As in . . . dead as a doornail?"

He nodded. "I must mingle. No one should suspect a preference."

With that he ambled away . . . to the side of Savannah Ashleigh.

No doubt, Temple thought, too weary to temper her newly acquired Las Vegas cynicism, he would tell Savannah that *she* had an edge in his opinion. But he didn't carry her any libations. Perhaps he preferred her hands free.

The wine punch was too strong for Temple's burgeoning headache, but nothing from the bar interested her, and the kids were all drinking something dark green, which would probably be supersweet and sticky.

Midnight Louie, she noticed, wasted not a second in sprinting away from the kiddie corner, where Solange and Yvette were cornered back to back, ears flattening as dozens of sticky fingers patted them right on that prize-winning doming.

Savannah Ashleigh was doing nothing to protect the Persian siblings, having changed into something less comfortable but more befitting the season—a white leather jumpsuit festooned with star-shaped silver studs. No doubt the superlarge star rather lewdly studding her right breast was supposed to represent the one that had led the Wise Men to the manger.

Temple trailed Louie, nervous about the havoc his alley-cat habits might wreak among such delicacies as a Christmas tree decorated with Venetian glass ornaments with a minimountain of exquisitely wrapped presents beneath it. This was Louie's first Christmas indoors, as far as Temple knew, and she had no idea how civilized he would be.

Much to her surprise, he avoided this tempting pile of twinkling lights, fragile decorations and beribboned, bright papers begging to be pounced on, torn, crushed and then pursued.

"Worried about your pal?" Kendall asked.

Temple's statuesque guide looked truly elegant in burgundy velvet, much more the yuppie boss's daughter that she was.

"Just watching. He seems fascinated by the chimney. Maybe it's those eight tiny reindeer atop the roof. They look kind of mousy from here."

"Don't let our art director hear you! That's his creation."

Kendall smiled fondly, and Temple realized that she must have attended these parties as a child herself.

"Daddy adores these hokey events. Sophisticated New York adman, and yet he insists on playing Santa Claus every year. I shouldn't give the surprise away, but pretty soon Santa will come sliding down the chimney—there's a little hatch into the kitchen next door—and it's ho-ho-ho time and presents for all. Then Santa goes back up the chimney and the party's over for another year."

Kendall sighed. "We've all told Daddy it's not necessary any more, and rather undignified, at his age and weight, to keep donning cotton batting and less padding every year to go wriggling up and down that chimney. He could just appear at the door like every other homemade Santa in town.

"But it's a tradition, and Daddy just loves family traditions. They all do, Colbys, Janoses, Renaldis." Kendall's nostalgic look soured.

She sipped her martini, a big-enough sip that the floating olive barged into those perfectly aligned Scarsdale teeth. "That's probably why so many of us intermarry; as kids we see each other early and often. Not always a good idea. That's my ex over there. Carlo. He prefers Carl."

Her nod singled out an attractive, dark-haired man in round, horn-rimmed glasses, a Renaldi who was neither olive nor Lombardy poplar tree. "Even after a divorce, there's no getting away from one another."

"Did you have children?"

"Not us. Not married long enough. But we would have, I suppose, if Carl could have torn himself away from his sports cars long enough."

Louie had paused before the faux fireplace, sizing up the wallboard chimney. Temple kept an eye on him, but her mind was meandering elsewhere.

"You know, Kendall, what you say reminds me of the Rothschild family."

"The Rothschild family? You know them?"

"Not the current generation, or their ancestors. But that's how they became the premiere banking family of Europe, despite being Jewish at a time when most Jews were confined to ghettos. The Rothschilds had lots of sons and daughters, and those had lots more sons and daughters. So the first cousins married each other when they grew up to keep the business in the family. Outsider sons-in-law were drafted into banking too."

"We're not that bad!" Kendall looked alarmed. "The Colbys, Janoses and Renaldis are hardly related. It's quite a tribute to Daddy, setting up shop, so to speak, with army buddies from a very different side of the social street way back in the sixties."

"I can understand it. Common military service forges strong bonds. Were they stationed overseas, or what?"

"Vietnam," Kendall said ominously, in low tones. "The older generation doesn't like to talk about it. We weren't around then, but I understand the worst trauma was afterward, coming home, when the peaceniks had turned the country around and returning vets were called baby-killers to their faces."

"Really!" Temple, shocked, recalled her aunt Kit telling

her how much she didn't know about the sixties just last night. She'd have to check some books out of the library.

Kendall nodded. "Not that Daddy served in an enlisted man's unit. He was attached somewhere else, but he must have crossed paths with the other men at some point. All the older men in that war were scarred somehow. Dad and Tony and Victor never talk about it. That must have been especially hard on Victor and Tony, they were second-generation Americans, gung ho to serve their country. Then they come home and they're treated like criminals. Nobody in your family was involved in Vietnam?"

Temple frowned. "I'm the youngest of five. I guess Dad was a family man. Were men actually being drafted then?"

"Oh, yes. Daddy's generation doesn't talk about it, but they were so hush-hush we kids actually got curious enough to look it up. The demonstrators were hippies who claimed that the draftees were all poor guys, while kids from wealthy families got college exemptions. When I heard about that, I became even prouder of Dad. He's never said it, but he didn't *have* to go to Vietnam. That's why Victor and Tony are so loyal to him. Apparently, he was higher in rank, but he stood by them."

Temple nodded. All this was Greek to her. It was scary what you didn't know about your parents' pasts, as if you assumed they began when you did and you both accumulated only common memories. Was one of her brothers or sisters a Vietnam baby, conceived simply to get a deferment? She didn't know what the rules were then, but they could have shaped her entire life, and she would never even know it. The sixties was such a crucial decade. She did know that. What were her parents like then? Maybe nothing like she thought.

"Your cat's gone," Kendall said.

Temple looked again at the chimney. Not even the dangling stockings were stirring, and Louie was nowhere in sight.

"Look!" a childish voice halloed. "Lookie. Kit-ty, Mom-my!"

The real "Mommy" looked up. Temple followed her example. Oh, Great Marley's Ghost! Louie wasn't gone. He had just sprouted wings. He now perched atop the cotton-batting simulated snow edging the chimneytop, black as a lump of coal dropped from the cardboard Santa's pocket as he sat laughing in his sleigh above it all.

The eight tiny reindeer looked much bigger now in comparison to Louie's silhouette, and their glitter-dusted hooves seemed ready to kick Louie off Santa's territory.

"Louie! Get down."

An adult chuckle sounded in the quiet room at Temple's command. "That cat is just a natural center of attention."

The speaker was Gerald, the senior member of The Client, but Temple's business instincts had decamped for the moment. How was Louie going to get down? And would he? Cats were notorious for scaling neighborhood Mount Everests like Sherpa guides, then stalling at the top until the fire department sent a ladder unit to get them, which most fire departments wouldn't do nowadays.

No firemen were in attendance here, and admen did not strike Temple as a particularly athletic breed.

"Louie, you come down," Temple ordered, fire in her eyes and voice.

He looked at her, then considered the assembled humans staring up at him and found the size and awestruck quality of the audience good. So, he promptly obeyed her.

"Amazing!" The Client, all four, spoke as one the moment Louie vanished down the chimney.

All eyes now fixed on the painted black hearth. The room was so still, despite the children, that everyone heard a discreet *thump* as Louie's four feet touched floor. He ambled out, looking right and left, as if noting the presence of subjects.

He finally stopped at Temple's feet, looked up with sober green eyes, and meowed plaintively.

"Aaaah," said the crowd.

She wanted to strangle him, but there were too many witnesses. So she picked him up and patted his head, which probably suffered from mediocre doming, but neither Temple nor Louie would know, and neither would care.

"You could have fallen," she said, infected by the maternal concern radiating like winter heat all around her.

He responded with his most contemptuous look. So much for the power of parental love. Now she knew how mothers of teenagers felt, especially in public.

The din and festivities were resuming. Glasses clinked, children whined for Santa and every third one seemed to be dropping a glass. Luckily, the glasses were all made of plastic, but the green stuff was as sticky as Temple had surmised when she joined some other women in bending down to blot it up with cocktail napkins.

As soon as she was done, she collected Louie again, who had remained beside her. She shifted his weight to glance at her watch. Only two more hours to go before this command performance was over. Two hours!

Louie watched her with a wrinkled brow. Then he glanced back to the scene of his most recent attention-getting device.

"You've done chimneys before, Louie," Temple whispered. "I'm surprised at you, repeating an effect. That's hardly professional. Max would never do it."

Louie growled softly and pushed away with all four feet, effecting his release. He stalked to the corner where the Ashleigh cats were still attracting too much attention. Louie's arrival diverted their fans. While Solange and Yvette repaired mauled ruffs and tails, Louie sat like an offended sea cow and allowed the children to run their sticky fingers over his shoulders and pull his tail. He flashed Temple a wounded look.

Now what was that all about? she wondered. But not for long. The Client was descending on her en masse, begging to hear about Louie's reputed crime-fighting exploits.

Temple wanted to be at Aunt Kit's. She wanted a bubble bath and peace and quiet. She actually wanted to be home in Las Vegas, where it was warm and where the only hubbub to interrupt tranquil days of desert sun and forty million tourists breezing through town was the occasional nearby murder . . .

But this was Showbiz and Louie was her baby. She gritted her teeth and recounted his adventures, embroidering shamelessly.

Midway through a riveting account of the Houdini séance during which Louie had performed his first chimney trick, the room's lights flickered, then dimmed.

A buzz of speculation interrupted Temple's tale. She looked around. Louie was nowhere to be seen, but of course there was a crowd of wall-to-wall people in the room.

On the Santa wall, a spotlight illuminated the painted hearth and mantel. Bells rang out, not deep-throated church bells, but the tinselly jingle of horse-bridle bells. Poe's bells of "crystalline delight" that "tinkle, tinkle, tinkle in the icy air of night." Kind of reminded Temple of Yvette out for an evening on a New York sidewalk.

For a moment it did feel cooler in the room, then a bent, red-garbed figure came bounding out of the fireplace, his false basso laugh booming good cheer.

"Well! What a fine convention for Santa! And what a splendid tree. Shall we see who's been naughty and nice this year? Have you got a chair for these old bones . . . and a cup of cocoa and maybe a cookie?"

"Oh, yes, Santa," crooned the children, running to the buffet table to scoop up fistfuls of cookies.

Santa sprang, most lively, to the stuffed armchair positioned near the tree.

"Now, girls and boys, I need an elf, or maybe several, to bring me the booty under yonder tree, aye, my hearties?"

Temple blinked. The line had begun as if intoned in the biblical richness of John Huston being particularly hammy and had ended on a note of Long John Silver.

Amateur actors! She was surprised that a man as dignified and aristocratic as Brent Colby, Jr., had secreted so much ham under that French-bread baguette exterior of his.

She began to agree with his daughter Kendall that he

was a remarkable man. Courageous enough to ignore the considerations of class and enter into business with men from blue-collar backgrounds: hard-working, bright men no doubt, but in the sixties, of which she realized she knew nothing, were such alliances that common? Maybe they were after the chasms in custom the Vietnam protests had created.

Hadn't a movie star whose image then wasn't much different from Savannah Ashleigh's now—Temple knew old movies, if nothing else—become a lightning rod for in-your-face Vietnam War protest? Jane Fonda, now a corporate wife.

Temple shook her head. She would need to read a lot of contemporary history books to understand the earliest of the three decades of her lifetime.

Meanwhile, the party went on without her, and Louie. Names were called, beguiling little elves handing out presents with childish self-importance—how nice that the kids were not just the getters, but the givers. Temple was jolted from her reverie only when her own name rang out. Shortly after, a waif in baggy red tights and a Rudolph the Reindeer jumper toddled up to offer her a package, after being directed all the way by helpful adults.

Temple opened the wrapping, aware of everybody watching for a few seconds . . . Inside the signature-blue Tiffany box (that oddly insipid pale blue that verged on turquoise), she found a vermeil black-cat pin with emerald eyes.

She smiled a thank-you toward Santa on his homely throne. And saw something odd about his eyes behind a mask of good cheer and spirit-gum wrinkles, beneath cotton-batting eyebrows, eyes that held a nagging question in them that only she could answer . . .

What question could Brent Colby, Jr., have for her, a humble maybe-employee under consideration?

Another name was called, Savannah Ashleigh. Another tyke proffered a gift, another pin in the saccharine-blue box, age-old sign of elegance. Two cats, two sets of gem-stone eyes winking topaz and aquamarine in the light.

And then, before the guests of honor could get their minds on current events, Santa was done. He sprang up, energy incarnate, red and white, larger than life, bluffer, heartier, to the fireplace.

"A Happy Christmas to all, and to all a good night!"

Up Dancer, up Dasher! Up Donner and Blitzen and Louie and Vixen—! The figure lifted stubby arms in the single spotlight, then vanished upward.

Spotlights brightened on the cardboard cutout of Santa and his eight reindeer atop the chimney, but they seemed what they were, cardboard, even Rudolph's rhythmically blinking nose.

For a moment, Temple knew the ache of a child who could no longer believe in Santa Claus, no matter what she held in her hand.

She looked around. Children were gazing up, to the pale sky of a whitewashed ceiling, believing in fairies, ready to clap for Tinkerbell. They expected Santa to emerge up top from the chimney and dash off behind his eight tiny reindeer.

The hearth spotlight dimmed and went out.

Above the cardboard Santa and sleigh and reindeer glowed an ever-increasing light.

"This," said Kendall's breathless voice beside Temple, "is when he appears at the chimneytop, blends with the Santa in the sleigh, and then all the lights go out . . ."

But Santa never exited the chimney.

And the deer did not disappear in a triumphant flash of glitter-strewn hooves.

And the children who had seen this before were silent as the night.

And the children who had not seen this before were puzzled, thinking something was missing.

And the adults who had seen this before were as still as death.

And the adults who had *not* seen this before were . . . worried.

Finally, before the lights had dimmed on the cardboard Santa in his cardboard sleigh drawn by his cardboard deer with one red-lit nose, something appeared at the chimney mouth.

This was no North Pole apparition, but a coal-black cat. Here he had stood before and here he stood now and yowled, long and loud, so that finally, someone . . . everyone . . . understood that something was very wrong.

And all the lights went out.

Chapter 16

Virgin Mary Blues

A baby-pink spotlight aimed a direct hit on the Blue Mermaid's tail fins, making her look more like a blue whale, or a '59 Cadillac.

The figure was huge, maybe twenty feet high. The Blue Mermaid had stylized curly yellow hair, and wore a strapless dress that resembled jersey more than scales. Matt recognized that it was exactly the shade of blue that the bartender at the Brass Rail had tried to describe.

Matt stared past the overblown figure into the starless night. Las Vegas outshone mere starlight. The sky showed no constellations, only a flat black velvet backdrop for the neon aurora borealis haloing the Strip.

He had recognized George's despised shade instantly: VMB. Virgin Mary Blue, a bright, cloying blue sweeter than denim and darker than baby blue. Mary, the Mother of God's, signature color, duplicated on millions of gilt-edged holy cards and thousands of plaster statues now relegated to church attics.

Sometimes it shows up in strange places. An elderly devout Catholic, usually of eastern European descent, will suddenly paint his entire house blue, or will slather VMB on the inside of an upended claw-foot bathtub-shrine, place within a statue of the Virgin wearing VMB, and become the talk of the town.

Matt wondered what the paint-makers called the color.

This VMB, though, was chipped in places down to dirty white plaster. And if the Blue Mermaid was not a vamp in the modern style, like the bold women in assorted harnesses he'd recently seen pictured outside the sexually oriented businesses, she did remind him of Mae West. A larger-than-life female fertility idol, all dressed up with nowhere wet to go within four hundred miles, except Lake Mead.

Matt knew one thing: the man who painted this effigy sixty years ago had been Roman Catholic. Only Catholics like VMB, out of lifelong conditioning.

He passed the motel's vestigial front office, where a faint incandescent light gleamed and a scent of stale sweet-and-sour hung on like olfactory heartburn. He supposed he could ask after Effinger there, but what man who moved from casino to casino ahead of the jaw-breakers of the world would register under his own name?

And what if this man he held in his hand in a sketch he couldn't quite see in the dark, what if this man was only an Effinger look-alike? It happened. Maybe Effinger was really a-moldering in the grave, in whatever public three-by-six the city had dumped him. And, if not, which dead-end room here was his?

Matt stuck his hands, and the sketch, into the pockets of his faux sheepskin jacket and slowly toured the motel's interior U-shape. A sign by the office offered rooms by the day, the week or the month. That made the Blue Mermaid a next-door neighbor to a flophouse, one that bled the helpless, unwanted poor of enough money to pay for a far more decent rental unit in a better neighborhood. But they'd never be accepted there.

Few units had vehicles parked outside. Either the renters

were out, or too broke for wheels in this mandatory-mobile society. The figured curtains in the quaint, narrow windows were all drawn as tight as their sagging folds would permit. Some were safety-pinned shut. Raucous voices rose as Matt passed, reaching that point of futility when they're too loud to understand. Once he whiffed the pungent sour breath of marijuana smoke. His shoe brushed something on the asphalt . . . a used hypodermic needle. Discarded condoms shone sickly pale among the blown-in refuse like stranded, dead jellyfish.

He knew about all these things as an academic knew about gin-drinking in eighteenth-century England. The Blue Ruin, gin was called then, and it mostly ruined the already discarded, the penniless, the poor. Why was it easier to consider impoverished people as one great unwashed mass, no capital letters necessary? The poor. Too large, undifferentiated and inhuman a problem to address. As "the rich" were too faceless to envy and overthrow, "the poor" were too vague to do anything for or about.

But the tenants at this motel under its mantle of Virgin Mary Blue weren't only unfortunates. Some were criminals. Molina could probably spot signs of a lot more than drugs and sex, were she here. Drugs and sex happened in the best of parishes nowadays, and priests weren't quite the unworldly shepherds that they had been a couple generations ago. If some priests and preachers had abused children in the recent past, they had done it in the Iron Age. Still, holy innocents had abounded in the good old days. Matt had known and admired many of them, who would be shocked and saddened by his presence here, by his purpose here.

And what was that purpose? If he found Effinger, he would find out. *When* he found Effinger, he would find himself.

In the dim light, he paused to jot down what numbers remained on the doors. Some rooms were obviously unrented. Some were just empty, occupants out, or only there for a couple of the twenty-four hours paid for. Some units sounded like whole slums in a bottle, fussing children, whining adults, whimpering animals competing with the scratchy blare of a television set tuned to some show as unhappily hyperactive as they were.

Matt settled against a dim doorway near the street with a view of the entire U. One thing. Effinger's western getup made him a silhouette to remember. Maybe another urban cowboy or two roomed here, but not a whole herd of them.

The night wasn't cold for a Chicago native, thirty-something degrees. He braced a hip against the doorjamb, kept his hands in his empty pockets and blended into the ambience. He remembered glimpsing his face in the smoky bar mirrors. Why the mirrors, anyway? To see other people come in, or to make sure one's self was there?

He couldn't deny his outer aspect now, his conventional good looks. But what should he do about them? He recalled T. S. Eliot's famous poem about J. Alfred Prufrock, a man as indecisive as his era. Like Prufrock, Matt found himself dwelling on minor decisions more than major ones.

Should he do something different with his hair? Grow it longer, cut it shorter in the monk-cut so popular among the trendy but ignorant young punks? Spend his hundred bucks on a haircut rather than a bribe for a bartender in a sleazy joint? Should he buy motorcycle boots to go with the Hesketh Vampire? Maybe enroll in a photography class. Subscribe to a magazine, but which one? Go into group therapy? He had preached enough to Temple about group therapy, and there was one for ex-priests, called Corpus. The next word that came to mind nowadays was "delecti." And how should he accessorize his new red couch the length of Long Island?

In his old life, he had few personal choices. He worried about values, not minutiae.

What did he hope for from Effinger? Because, no matter how much young Matt still hated the man's guts, not-so-young Matt must still need something from him. Confirmation of his worthlessness? Whose? Effinger's or

Matt's, the failed priest so unfit for a secular world? Closure. The truth.

Just plain revenge?

Matt winced as the cold sank into his bones, and wished for a boiler-maker. It didn't matter which part you drank first, he decided. They both would be bitter medicine.

Something shuffled over the refuse. Crushed aluminum cans scraped along the concrete. Papers hissed as they were scuffed along.

Matt's head drooped, his eyes were shut. He was the next thing to sleeping upright, but the sound had awakened a memory from the past. A fact seen and heard then, and not noted.

But now . . . That loping walk, the hip, affected shuffle of a fifties high-school hoodlum with cleats on his shoes. Click, shuffle, click, click. Ducktail greased. Short T-shirt sleeves (and they were white messageless undershirts then) rolled around a soft cellophane-wrapped pack of Camel cigarettes. Jeans tight and sagging low. Engineer boots with cleats. Click, shuffle, clickety-click.

Matt could still hear Cliff Effinger coming home, no cleats in the seventies, but the gait always threatened cleats, moving past the living-room rug and then echoing dully on the pitted kitchen linoleum. Matt had stared at that linoleum a lot, a graphic tenement of little windows, a Mondrian pattern boiled down to its cheapest, ugliest incarnation, only Matt hadn't known Mondrian from Matisse then.

His head lifted. His breath held.

A figure shambled toward a dark door across the way.

It wore a hat.

Hats were still worn in the sixties, by some. Fedoras shaded Sinatra's lean and cunning cinematic face. Age had filled in Sinatra's hungry angles, softened his flesh into a moon of Dutch cheese, all runny and forgetful. Like Brando's godfather, about as benign as a tumor. Las Vegas had been his beat, he ran with the Rat Pack here. The mob ran Las Vegas then. Not now. But *somebody* was dumping dead men in the ceilings of major hotel-casinos. If not that old-time religion, who?

Maybe he should ask Effinger.

Matt lurched away from the wall like a drunk. His ankle had gone to sleep.

He had to stop and wait for the pins and needles to jab the bloodless flesh to life. Waiting on pins and needles. And above, the Blue Mermaid, watching in her saccharine-blue gown.

Blessed Virgin Mary, star of the sea. Matt moved slowly so he didn't shamble like the man he was following. It was all too easy to turn into what you hunted.

Effinger fumbled at a door midway up the U's opposite upright.

Holy Virgin Mary, rose of memory.

Matt was catching up. Quietly for a lame man.

The door creaked ajar.

Most Holy Virgin Mary, rose of forgetfulness.

A light weaker than a drink at the Gilded Lily pulsed on.

Blessed art thou.

The man in the Western hat pushed the door open farther, paused, lit a cigarette. A spark cursed the darkness and went out.

Full of grace . . .

Smoke, acrid and pure nicotine.

Now and at the hour of our death . . .

The door was shutting, the room closing, the Bible falling shut, the confessional door unlocked but inescapable.

Matt's hand and foot wedged between door and frame.

"What?" someone asked irritably. "I don't owe you a thing."

Amen.

Matt was shutting the door behind him, searching for the light.

"Who the hell are you?"

"Who the hell are you?" Matt demanded in turn.

The face under the wide western shadow said nothing.

Matt took the hat off.

"You're crazy, man! You're on something. I ain't got no dough, no way."

The voice was . . . not loud and roaring. Matt tilted his head to see the face at a different angle.

The skin wasn't so much wrinkled as scored. Too much sun and sin in Las Vegas.

And he seemed . . . shrunken. Small. So small.

"Oh, Lord! Holy shit! What're *you* doin' here? You're gone. You're as good as dead."

"I'm not dead, and I'm not as good as I used to be."

"Look. I was a prisoner in that damn town. Damn icebox. I hada get outa there, all right? I did, didn't I? Didn't I go? Like a lamb when you got ugly. What's your gripe after all this time? You're supposed to be in some Holy Roller place, wearin' black like a damn nun. You're not here. Naw. Can't be here. Who the hell are you?"

"Who do you think, Cliff?"

"That's not my name. I'm Clint Edwards. Got that?"

"Yeah, I got it."

Matt moved around the cramped room, turning on every light switch he could find. Under its tilted shade, the table lamp by the door had only a forty-watt bulb. A bathroom cubicle tiled in stained white shone sickly under a buzzing fluorescent bulb that flickered like a strobe light above the tiny mirrored medicine chest. The outer room boasted only one more light, whatever would leach from the screen of a battered black-and-white TV opposite the lumpy double bed.

Matt turned the TV on too, and turned up the sound knob, so the passionate late-movie voices argued in the room like real people. A woman crying and pleading. A man yelling. It sounded just like home.

"Whatcha doin', you goddamn little freak, always lookin' at me with those big googly eyes! Always watching me. I told you to keep that TV down or off! This is my place—"

"No, it was our place. And then you came."

"Why shouldn't I have? Your ma thought it was a-okay. Don't like that, do you, kid? Your ma wanted more than a squalling brat to look after. I fit in real good."

"Why aren't you dead?"

"What—? What the hell you talkin' about? You want me dead, is that it?"

"No, Mr. Effinger. I can't want you dead. I'm a good guy in a black skirt, remember? I'm just wondering why you aren't dead when your ID was cramming the pockets of the dead guy they found at the Crystal Phoenix a few weeks back."

Effinger backed toward the bathroom, his face as white as the streaked tile. "I don't know nothin' about that."

"You have to. It was your ID."

"I lost that. At the bus station."

"And the dead guy looked a lot like you. Same age, same general physiognomy, same build."

"I don't care what his physiogomectomy said, I don't know some dead guy at the Phoenix from Adam."

"They think they buried you, Effinger. Doesn't that make you feel safe? The police think they buried you, but I don't."

"You're nuts. A priest shouldn't act like this. I knew you were a bad one when you knocked me down on the kitchen floor. You were just a punk. I could have wiped up the linoleum with you, but I didn't want to hurt your ma."

"But you did! You hurt her a lot. I heard it. I saw it. And I'm not a priest any more."

"You can't quit that. They don't let you."

"A little like the . . . mob, isn't it?"

"What mob? No mob in Vegas these days. You're nuts. I'm gettin' outa here."

He ran like a rat for every exit.

The door, but Matt was there first. The window, where

he tore at the torn curtains and slammed his palms on the glass.

Matt pushed him back.

Effinger looked for something to hurl at Matt, but the TV was bolted down, the lamp was a flimsy joke and . . . he ran for the bathroom.

Matt thought of a high narrow window like Midnight Louie's escape hatch from the Circle Ritz, and of a narrow, ratty man shinnying through another window like that.

He made the bathroom in four giant steps, and slammed the door behind him.

The fluorescent light buzzed warning like an angry hornet.

"Get away from me," Effinger squealed, retreating into the tub edge, the tiles bouncing back his voice.

Once his voice had been thunder, Matt recalled, and his footsteps earthquakes. Clickety-click, stomp!

Cleats. Clint. Wanting to be somebody, and always being Cliff.

Effinger was standing in the tub, clawing at the tiny frosted glass window above it.

"They'll kill me, you stupid kid! All that old stuff was nothing compared to what I'm into now. For now, they like me alive, but later, who knows? You're gonna be the death of me."

Matt seized Effinger's cheesy western jacket by the shoulders, and dragged him back from the window.

Effinger reached up behind him, fingers clawing for Matt's face. Matt jumped into the ancient bathtub and kicked Effinger's foot from under him. The man folded onto his knees on the yellowed porcelain. Rust trailed down from the ancient water spigot like old, dry blood.

"You're gonna kill me!" Effinger's voice ran hot and hysterical.

Matt yanked the right faucet until the pipes screeched, and pulled up the porcelain lever in the wall. Cold water trickled from the tinny shower head. Effinger was screaming as if under boiling steam as Matt hauled him up into the icy baptism of rusty water.

"Blood. You're killing me. I don't deserve it. I'm a victim. They got me by the short hairs. You stupid, stupid punk—"

The water spat on Matt's face and ran down his forearms. It was going to ruin his faux suede jacket.

Finally, Cliff Effinger sagged in his hands like wet wool. His water-soaked clothes reeked of unlaundered urine and hard liquor.

Matt pulled the guy up again until the ragged stream of water from the shower head ran down Effinger's face like spittle, into his closed eyes and chattering teeth. He was small, so terribly small, after all.

"Listen," Matt said. "You aren't worth hurting back. Calm down. I'm not going to touch a hair on your mostly bald head." That was why the hat, not disguise. Vanity.

"You're . . . not?" Effinger hiccoughed like a spent, hysterical kid.

Matt jerked him out of the piddling shower stream and shook him until the water beaded off his clothes.

"No." Matt held Effinger against the cracked tile with one hand while he turned off the water.

"What you gonna do?"

"Nothing personal."

"Huh?"

"Brace yourself for a touch of cold air."

"What? We going outside? I'll freeze in that night air."

"It's nothing like the Chicago air that January you locked me out all night."

"Hey, I was hot-tempered then. Young and hair-trigger, you know?"

"No, I don't know." Matt had him at the unit door. He opened it and looked out. Deceptively deserted.

"Where we going?"

"There's a public phone outside the office. If you keep your mouth shut, the manager won't even know we're there, and that you messed up his bathroom."

"Huh? Who you gonna call?"

Matt's smile was grim.

"Ghostbusters."

Above them, the Mermaid loomed like a Virgin Mary Blue blimp.

Raising Saint Nick

Sometimes I live up to my reputation. I am one unlucky black cat for somebody.

Here I stand, the focus of all eyes (which is as it should be), but my presence on this ersatz roof is very bad news for somebody. Not that anybody puts two and two together.

I have not liked the layout of that chimney since I first saw it. I liked it even less when I took a second look only minutes before and saw that what I did not like before, I liked even less now that somebody had changed it.

Now there is somebody in the chimney, and nobody knows but eight cardboard reindeer and me.

Are you getting tired of all these "bodys"? Somebody, anybody, nobody . . .

Well, get used to it, because there is a body in the chimney and it is not me.

"Where is Santa?" somebody yells out.

Good question, dude. Why do you not take a look up the flue?

Finally somebody is smart enough to examine Santa's escape route. The woman named Kendall who has been shepherding Miss Temple Barr about walks over on brisk heels, bends down to look up the chimney and screams.

The first one is a scream pure and simple, and works pretty well. The second one is a word, and it finally gives all the dumb-bunnie nobodies an idea of what is up, in this case up the chimney.

"Dad-dy," she screams.

Now I am a daddy myself (though not intentionally, but that is never taken into account). It does give me a chill to hear that note of panic and disbelief in Miss Kendall's wail.

Miss Temple, upon hearing it, rushes over. Now we are in good hands.

She does not have to bend far to peer up the chimney.

"Lights," she orders. "Bring the camcorder. It has a light that will fit up this chute. We need some slight men who aren't afraid of heights or close quarters, fast! From what I can see, it might not be too late to get him down."

Janos Senior is the first to respond. He and the cameraman son arrive at the same time. Andrew Janos, who has been tirelessly shooting the party as he has tirelessly shot banal events all day, points the lens up the flue.

"Colby?" Janos Senior calls up the dark tunnel.

I look down, my eyes slitting to the width of a straight pin at the direct light. That way I can see perfectly, and it is as I expected. Just below me, Santa twists slightly in the chimney, creating an eerie scraping sound. His booted feet hang loose of the wooden ladder nailed to one side of the chimney. A golden snake shines in the fractured light from below, circling the uppermost rung of the ladder. It extends down to lose itself in Santa's curled white beard, beneath which it has no doubt tightened on his neck.

A chain of gold. My own fur brushed against it on exiting the chimney the second time tonight, when my ladder was not wooden rungs, but a red velveteen suit.

I watch Janos senior's harried face block the light as he scrambles up the ladder. "Oh, my God."

He must shimmy past the dangling Santa suit, and it was not an easy task for me. But he is a wiry little guy. Somehow he manages it and wriggles out onto the narrow roof ledge near me. I do not expect him to balance on the two-by-four chimney rim like the footsure dude I am.

"Tony!" Victor Janos yells to Renaldi senior in a voice that would start a parade. "Get in the chimney and lift up his feet. He's . . . caught on something. I'll try to release him here."

The watching crowd whispers and rustles. Some hang-up, they think. Some glitch. A few men head for the bar and mothers bend to rub paper napkins over sticky chins.

Miss Temple does nothing of the sort. She keeps her place at the crowd's forefront, needing to be there just to see, and keeps a steady eye on the action. Tall, uneasy Kendall follows her, glancing at my little doll nervously.

The men are grim, shouting and grunting only at each other. Brent Colby, Jr., was no lightweight. Or do I give something away? Surely no one of any brains who has been modestly attentive, like my little doll, can have failed to realize that what we have here is no overweight Santa wedged in his escape route, but a dead man hanging in a chimney by a golden chain.

I give that Janos senior credit. You can tell he has been in a war zone. That plucky fellow manages to pull up Santa by his suit shoulders enough to loosen the chain. It thuds against wood.

"Tony!" Janos senior shouts sharply.

And below Tony grunts, but catches the freed weight. The chimney is narrow enough that it will brace the corpse if Tony can keep it from crashing to the floor, which he does. Beside me, Janos senior lets himself over the chimney side, hanging by his hands, and jumps lightly to the carpet below.

I do not follow his derring-do example. Not that I could not, you understand, but I wish to examine the inside of the chimney now that the unfortunate victim is not obscuring the murder weapon. The police will not like having Janos senior's fingerprints on it, but did they expect me to make like a Russian sailor and yo-ho heave-ho to the "Volga Boat Song"? Manual labor is not something I am made for.

"Did he pass out?"

I watch Miss Kendall hurry to the supine Santa the two partners pull from the blackened hearth. Even I wince before I turn and jump down onto the first tell-tale rung. The police will not like my padprints on the wood, nor my claw marks, but tough tooters.

The chain hangs in a long straight golden tail, like a plumb line.

When last I saw it, and the last that Brent Colby, Jr., saw it, the chain was arranged in an open coil like a basketball hoop from the second-to-top rung. I think back to my alley-running days to figure how it happened. Probably much as my pal Mumblety-peg met his end on a loop of jump rope left hanging from a jungle gym. As this dude Colby climbed, the victim tripped some mechanism that released the gold chain to fall on his shoulders. Startled by the unexpected weight, he backed down, too late. The chain tightened and choked, and his hasty retreat only caused his feet to miss the narrow rungs. He swung free, to his death.

Below me I hear the piercing cries of Miss Kendall, who now knows the obvious and the worst.

But I am not quite ready to desert my observation post. Yes, something is still here, and even stronger now, although it is disembodied: the faint whiff of a relative of my favorite stimulant, catnip.

Some call it cannabis, but I have more often heard people call it marijuana.

Is it possible that Mr. Brent Colby, Jr., was dying for a smoke?

Chapter 18

"... Hung by the Chimney with Care"

Temple was amazed by how fast the festive conference room had cleared of all but essential personnel.

Gone were the children in their gay attire. Gone were the mothers with their hankies and Handiwipes in hand. Gone were most of the Colby, Janos and Renaldi copywriters and junior account executives.

They would all have been banished to the other conference room, but Temple had reported seeing Santa waiting to make his entrance in there. The police might want to examine the room without it having been trampled by dislocated Christmas party émigrés.

"What *won't* the police want to examine?" Victor Janos burst out, running arthritis-swollen fingers through his hair. He winced at the gesture, and pulled his hands away. "I must have strained my hands." His face was almost as flushed as the corpse's.

Tony Renaldi no longer looked lithe and dapper. He even stooped a little to show his fifty-some years. But he laid a hand on the smaller man's shoulder.

"You did good," he said, lapsing into the talk of the barracks, the polished overlay of the boardroom lost for the moment. "You got in there quick and we got him out as fast as we could. It was just too late, Victor. You know what that's like."

Victor shook his head. With his suit jacket gone, and his white shirtsleeves rolled up, he looked younger despite the strain on his face.

"And you, young lady." Renaldi summoned a shred of charm for Temple. "You thought pretty fast. You and your . . . terrifying cat."

Renaldi had been the first to pull himself together and summon the police. "I'll call the precinct," he had said, rushing out. "Too bad it's a weekend," he had added.

Now Temple wondered what a holiday death by misadventure meant in New York. Fewer police on duty, slower response? Las Vegas was the opposite case. She glanced again at the supine Santa. He resembled a department-store mannequin abandoned on the chic gray industrial carpeting.

She understood what Tony Renaldi was saying. Louie had tried to draw their attention to the chimney. When he had perched up there the second time, he seemed to be saying: why didn't you listen when I tried to tell you something was wrong?

It was too close to the parody of the Lassie films: "I think she's trying to tell us something." Animals often are trying to tell us something: that they're lost or homeless, or hungry or want affection. Why couldn't they try to tell you something more subtle as well?

Brent Colby would never know that a cat had played a key role in the discovery of his death.

He looked disturbingly alive even now. His face was flushed and swollen beneath the thick white whisker-frosting, a look in keeping with the popular representation of Santa Claus, but hideously altered from the pale, blandly patrician features of Brent Colby, Jr.

Kendall sat alone on a folding chair, her body angled away from the gruesome scene by the chimney.

Savannah Ashleigh and cats, as well as Maurice and handler, had vanished along with the party-goers.

Temple had not been allowed to leave, not since The Client had pointed out her experience in what they called "the murder line."

Midnight Louie remained by default, and because his pawprints were probably all over the crime scene. Temple wondered what Lieutenant C. R. Molina would say about that, happy that she and Louie had no history as suspicious characters in Manhattan. Yet.

Janos and Renaldi had shown their executive mettle, though, from the tense moments of rescue to the realization that came when they laid the body on the floor and stared down at the scarlet face of their dead partner in its gruesomely jolly guise.

"Was it a freak accident?" Renaldi asked again.

"Coulda been." Janos's cigarette, lit minutes before and forgotten, did a slow burn between his first two fingers, building a precarious smokestack of ash.

"The chain?" Janos again.

"Maybe Brent wanted an extra prop, wanted to make a jingling sound as he exited the chimney, I dunno. Coulda been a last-minute inspiration he concealed up there before the party got started."

The partners' wives and adult children occupied the first two rows of circled chairs, as ordered, their grim faces oddly contrasting with the rich colors of their expensive holiday best. Temple suspected that their role in the death investigation would be what it was in real life and the company brochure: photogenic but anonymous moral support.

Colby had been a single parent with one child, Kendall, the only member of her immediate family present. She sat alone, facing the back of the long room, sobbing quietly. Temple wondered why no one comforted her.

"Where are the goddamn police?" Janos's usual staccato style was seasoned with unusual profanity.

Despite his quick, cool action during the attempted rescue, he was clearly the overexcitable partner.

Renaldi shook his head. "I called only a couple minutes ago, Vic; it only seems longer. This *is* a weekend before a major holiday. We can't expect instant response."

"We are an important firm," Janos said, temper flaring. His tone implied that he cared less about the firm's high standing than its usefulness in getting speedy official response. "God. Poor Colby."

Among the accidental audience on the folding chairs, a woman smothered a sudden sob.

"Can't we . . . cover the body?" Renaldi asked Temple again.

She was used to being consulted about public relation policies, not police matters.

"Ah, I don't think so. Anything that disturbs the victim or the area hampers the crime-scene technicians. Remember, that was an issue at the Nicole Brown Simpson crime scene. Taking him down was a major disruption, but we had to try to revive him."

"Even in 'Nam we could cover the . . . bodies," Janos muttered.

Temple could guess what adjective he had edited out at the last minute, an adman to his bones now, but still a grunt in his soul.

"Nobody there cared about how or when; they knew," Janos went on. "I thought it was cruel then, but this is crueler."

Janos and Renaldi exchanged a mute glance of shared memory. A look that was also wary, Temple noticed. Cautionary. Like a Santa Claus putting a finger to his lips. Was she watching men who had fought in war together reverting to battlefield discipline? Or murderous partners putting on a good show for the survivors?

Louie lingered by the chimney. When she went to collect him, he was batting something around in an utterly cat-like way. She bent to find a small dark screw, wood fibers clinging to its curves.

"Leave that for the cops," she said as she hefted him into her arms.

The Client had taken the four front-row seats nearest the exit and farthest from the scene of the crime.

"Miss Barr," one of the women called softly.

Temple tiptoed across the carpet, not wanting to disturb those sober, drooping faces of family watchers in the front row. An instant had transformed the festive conference room into a bizarre funeral parlor: the corpse on display without the concealing grace of a coffin, the mourners dressed more for Mardi Gras than the Service for the Dead.

Temple slipped into a vacant seat alongside The Client, beside the woman with a graying bob whose name tag read MURIELLE KOSLOW, PROMOTION.

"Did your cat really sense something was wrong?" Murielle asked, patting his sagacious head.

"Possibly. Louie has a talent for that." Temple looked down to find a flake of white defacing her velvet skirt. Probably litter from Louie's paws. She picked it off. Then, not wanting to, uh, litter the floor, put it in her skirt pocket. If you wear black so black cat hairs won't show, trust the contrary species to leave a pale dandruff of litter as well. "Or," Temple continued in light of Louie's latest cat trick, "this big lug may have just been acting like a cat, climbing for the challenge of it or to serenade the lady kitties from the nearest thing to a rooftop. Why?"

Murielle sighed, a gesture that lifted each Client's chest in turn. "I wondered if we had paid attention . . . if that might have made a difference. Someone getting to him sooner."

Temple knew what bothered her, and almost everyone in the room who had taken time to think about it. A man had not only died before them, but had probably taken a while to do it, the entire struggle hidden by a painted chimney and abetted by a complacent audience anticipating the next "special effect."

"The fall and the tightening noose could have snapped his neck," Temple said. "Death might have been instant."

"Oh. I suppose that would have been better."

Down the line, the senior Client leaned his torso into Temple's view. "How will the police deal with so many witnesses? Can they do it without keeping us all here until tomorrow?"

"Maybe they can't." Temple watched four strained faces tighten. "Usually, in a crowd scene like this, they question everyone and let the least likely suspects go. That's why I suggested the others go to the other conference room. It'll speed things up."

"You mean we're suspects?"

Janette, the older woman next to Gerald, spoke with appalled realization.

Temple shrugged. "We're the current account on the docket. A death like this could be a freak accident, or murder with a motive ranging from soup to nuts."

"And we're the nuts?" The Client number three was named Arden Hoyt. She had a round figure with curly hair to match and looked like she'd be a lot of fun under better circumstances.

"More likely the appetizer," Temple reassured her, and them all. "We're out-of-towners. What are the chances of one of us blowing into Manhattan and deciding to commit Murder One?"

"You mean—" The Client, senior, leaned forward in his seat again, to speak in a stage whisper. "You mean that if the death wasn't accidental, the murderer has to be either family, or a business associate?"

Temple glanced around to ensure that no one else could hear her. "And this being a family business—"

"It could be both," The Client number four, Janette, added with a sober nod.

Temple shrugged again. The less she committed herself, the more her stock rose in their eyes. She began to understand why the police were so tight-lipped on a sensational case. Better to say nothing at all than to stick your neck out and be wrong.

Temple rose and went to Kendall. Louie was there too, nosing her slack, curled hand that hung near the floor. Kendall's other arm curved along the chair's metal back, that hand fisted as well, and her face rested on the wrist's wet surface.

Her eyes lifted to follow Temple's arrival. "Daddy was so disappointed about our divorce. We never really tried, he said. In his day, people tried." She blinked, not to disperse tears, but in an attempt to refocus her entire point of view, to see the past in the light of this dramatically different future. "Maybe he was right. We kids never did understand why the partners were so tight. A war we hardly heard of didn't seem to be enough reason. But that was his generation. They were loyal. We're yuppies, young urban have-it-alls . . . fast-faders."

"Maybe." Temple sat wearily on the next chair, facing the front of the room. "It's hard for women to understand men and war. Guys have a love-hate relationship with conflict. Maybe, like sports, it's one of the few places men can form deep friendships without the fear of being labeled homosexual."

"Why does it take violence to make men friends?"

Temple shook her head. She didn't feel like analyzing anything right now. She got up and plodded to the wake at the front of the room. Where were the police? Granted, New York City had a tad more traffic and a few thousand more streets than Las Vegas, but. . . .

The conference door opened, making a mousy creak that hit the silent huddle of people like a shotgun blast.

Someone filled the opening, haloed in the hall light.

Behind them all, Kendall wailed. "It's D-D-Daddy!"

As the only surviving relative, she bravely had stood to greet the officials, yet all she could blurt out was the victim's name, a poignantly childish call for Daddy.

Temple braced herself, ready to take over at this difficult time. That was what public relations people were for, even if the relations were with the police.

The male silhouette stood framed in the doorway, its form lumpy and bloated. As the man stepped forward, the room's perimeter down lights resolved the visual ambiguities. He was not what they had expected: a New York City uniformed officer or detective. Not unless the officer had gone undercover for the holidays in . . . a Santa suit.

Everybody stared, speechless, at the dead man's macabre twin.

Santa realized that something was very wrong. His hands lifted to peel off his jolly bearded disguise. The puzzled, smooth-shaven face beneath was frowning, frowning at the room, at Kendall Colby Renaldi. Santa's cap, hair and beard wilted from his hands like Spanish moss.

"What's wrong? Where is everybody? I couldn't pass through the kitchen without grabbing a cup of coffee to revive me for the end of the evening. Sorry I kept you all waiting. What's going on here? Kendall, baby?"

At that, Kendall Colby Renaldi burst into hysterical laughter.

The newcomer was Brent Colby, Jr., in the flesh.

Chapter 19

No Way Out

Matt kept his fingers rolled in the greasy scruff of Effinger's jacket collar while he patted himself down for the quarter that would kick-start his captive down the road to justice. Maybe.

Nine-one-one didn't seem appropriate, so Matt dialed nearby police headquarters. He didn't expect to find Molina in, not this late and this close to Christmas, but he knew domestic violence boiled over at such socially heated times of year. The department's number was easy to remember.

Effinger fidgeted in Matt's grip but didn't try to bolt. Must be a shock to see a pip-squeak kid from your past come back like Eliott Ness.

"Molina available?" he asked the first human voice that answered.

"That depends. What's the problem?"

"I've got someone she's very interested in getting ahold of." Effinger weaseled out of his jacket some, so Matt slammed him up against the motel wall and dug an elbow into his stomach.

"Call tomorrow."

"Can't. I literally have the guy in custody, and I can't hang on to him all night."

"What did you say your name was?"

Matt gave it, fearful of being taken for a crank caller otherwise. Lord knows he got enough of that breed at ConTact. And so did the police.

"I don't see what I can do for you, Mr. Devine."

"Look. The guy in my hands right now is supposed to be dead and buried on Clark County's tab. He may be involved in a couple of murders."

"I'll call Molina, but she won't be crazy about this. Citizen's arrest isn't what people think it is. I assume your socalled suspect is not sticking with you voluntarily. He could press charges against you."

"The only thing he's going to be pressing in the near future is his jailhouse baggies."

"Okay, okay, desperado; where can the lieutenant reach you?"

Matt sighed. That meant they'd have to hang by the outside phone, freezing and looking obvious. He strained to read and repeat the pay-phone number in the faint light, absently twisting one of Effinger's arms tight when Matt sensed a break for freedom in the making.

"You can't do this! I'll sue."

Matt hung up. "It's a friendly family misunderstanding. Holiday tensions and all."

"What're you gonna do? Who'd you talk to just now?"

"Someone who wants to see you in the worst way."

"She ain't here in Vegas?" Fear touched Effinger's sullen voice.

"She?"

"I ain't telling you nothing. I ain't telling the police nothing, and I certainly ain't gonna tell a defrocked priest nothing."

"I'm not defrocked. I left with blessings and a small stipend."

"Stipend. Blessing. I ain't heard nice-nelly words like that since I got the hell out of that Polack neighborhood in Chicago. Worst place I ever been in."

"We agree on that. Why'd you stay, then?"

Effinger's shrug loosened Matt's clutching fingers. They were starting to go numb.

"I got smokes in my pocket. Okay if I dig 'em out?"

"Which pocket?"

"I sure don't want your fingers in 'em."

"If you want a smoke, you're going to get them."

"Left front jacket. You was such a wimpy kid. How'd you grow up to be so hard-nosed? They don't teach that in the seminary."

"I was never wimpy. I was just a whole lot smaller than you were. I thought about killing you every day, back in Chicago."

Effinger held still as Matt jammed an unfiltered cigarette into his hand in the near dark. "I'll keep the matches," Matt said.

"Sure did practice those Jap moves, though. You caught me by surprise that day. I'da never gone down if you hadn't jumped me."

"But you did go down. And you're going to go down again. The cops in this town are mighty interested in you, dead or alive."

Effinger laughed as Matt struck a match head against the thin brown striker line. A Gilded Lily matchbook. The sulphur smell was warm and rich, like gourmet coffee grounds. Effinger's crumpled cigarette trembled as he inhaled, cupping his hands around the spark of red warmth.

That impromptu shower wasn't doing either of them any good in this cold night air, Matt thought, hating to share even discomfort with this man. And where was Molina, besides off trying to have a life?

"Why'd you move in on us?" Matt asked.

Effinger inhaled, letting the wall hold him up, either resigned or waiting for a chance.

"Your ma wasn't bad-looking in those days. And I wasn't such a poor specimen myself. She had a house, and you were just a little kid. I figured you were like a pet rat or something. No trouble." His upper lip curled over the cigarette moving up and down with his mumbling lips.

"She wouldn't leave the old neighborhood," Effinger went on, blowing out memories with his cigarette smoke. "They treated her like shit, but she wouldn't leave. Didn't want you to grow up without 'family.' Family! Big dumb Polacks who disowned her the second you were born, a stye in God's eye. I was raised Cath'lic. I know the drill. You're a bastard, Matthias. Fact is, I'm the only legitimate father you've ever had, or ever will have. And she wouldn't say word one about the guy that done the deed. Oh, my, no. That got to me. Like he was too good to mention to the likes of me. I needed to get out of the family stuff, sneerin' but not lettin' go. Sneerin'. Even she and you started sneerin'. So . . . I took off for Vegas. Lived my own life. Finally left for good when the little yellow-haired ingrate jumped on me like he was playing Godzilla."

"You didn't just leave. You hung around for years, yelling and cursing, drinking and hitting. You only left when I made you."

"Yeah, you'd think that." Effinger blew smoke out his lower lip, so it streamed upward like the ghost of a burnt offering.

"Face it, kid. You makin' me kiss linoleum wasn't why I left. I was more'n ready to go. I'd made connections here in Vegas. The chorus girls were younger and gamier than your ma had ever been. So I split, and if you wanta think you was man enough to make me, well, I guess the last fifteen years have shown you you're not even man enough to be a skirt-swishing priest."

Matt almost wished he could smoke. Could inhale acrid air and spit it back out as toxic fumes. But he wasn't angry, not now.

"You know why you're standing here talking to me, Effinger? Even though you don't know who I called and who might be coming, and that makes you nervous? Because, finally, you can't get away. You can't hide behind a corpse, or my mother, or the years. I saw it in the motel room. You're such a little man. In every way. You're not worth my anger. I'll never forgive you for what you did to my mother, and I'll see you in prison or in hell, that I know. But I don't have to be there. I don't have to pull the plug or hit the switch. I just have to know how really insignificant you are. I think the people you're working for now know that too. I think they're waiting until your usefulness fuse fizzles out. And then you'll be another truly unidentified body that dropped out of nowhere on the way to home, sweet hell."

"You hate me, kid. You still hate me as bad as you did then. And you can mumble all the 'Hail Marys' you want to, but hate's a big sin. If that's all I did, show you that hate and hurt make the world go round, then I'll take the final drop to whatever, satisfied. Why should you have a life, Mister fair-haired pretty boy that mama dotes on and daddy left behind to bug some poor guy who ain't no relation to no fussing kid?"

Matt was starting to see what a pawn and an anchor one small child could be, that *he* had been, when the phone squealed beside them. He collared Effinger again, jerking the cigarette butt from his mouth and crushing it out on the damp asphalt, as if tidying up the school scum for an appointment with the principal.

"You're developing a gift for timing that rivals that of our Miss Barr." Molina's dead beat voice hummed over the line at its most sardonic, but a glimmer of genuine curiosity leaked through. "So you got him. The real live Cliff Effinger. Why the heck during Christmas week? I'm supposed to be making illuminaria tonight out of lunch bags, not doing paperwork on a guy everybody'd rather see dead. He still in one piece?"

"And talkative too."

"Damn. Okay. I'll have to stop by the office first. Might be half an hour. You can baby-sit him until then without committing a misdemeanor or a felony, right, kemosabe?"

"Yes Ma'am," Matt said, adding the name of the motel and the room number.

"Not your kind of people there, padre. Watch them, if not Effinger. I'll be as fast as I can be."

He marched Effinger, like a truant kid, down the line of battered doors to Door Number Three, feeling the unexpected bliss of total control. For all his spit and bluster, Effinger had been no physical threat since Matt had fought back and knocked him to the floor in Chicago. Too bad it had taken Matt a wrong vocational turn and sixteen-some years to see that.

"She coming too?" Effinger asked nervously.

"In a while. Meantime, you and I can reminisce in your room."

"What kind of room you ever had?" Effinger asked when they returned to his ugly little unit. "You priests like to put on a show that you're holier than us, with your second-hand cars and your first hands on the altar boys and girls."

"You know, Cliff, first you say priests are sissies, then you say they're satyrs. Which is it going to be?"

"Satires? Yeah, they're a joke, except it ain't funny. They're everything bad, and the old women listen to them like crazy, the mothers and the grandmothers, and the young babes with their knees Superglued together. I bet you didn't see a lot of that. A guy with your looks. You grew up real pretty, I'll give you that. I shoulda fixed that better."

Matt laughed, surprising himself as much as Effinger. "I bet you're really dying to know. I should realize by now that meanness always comes from envy. You really are a sorry excuse for a human being. I bet whoever's using you to cover up what's going on wished that could have been you hitting the craps table at the Crystal Phoenix. Don't worry, you'll get your turn in the spotlight. I'm sure of it."

"I wanta watch TV." Effinger stared straight ahead at the now-dark, dusty rectangle.

"Sure. Whatever station you want, Cliffie."

A sly smile crossed the wizened face. "Channel forty-eight."

Matt went to the TV to tune out the interference. A blizzard of snow whitened the screen and its electrical howl muffled dialogue.

"I could use a drink too. It's in the bottom bureau drawer."

Calling the busted piece of furniture a "bureau" was a gentility Matt couldn't endorse. A bottle half full of smoked amber liquid rolled over like a corpse when Matt jerked open the stiff drawer.

Effinger slumped on the rumpled bedspread, gazing slack-mouthed at the sleazy snow. Not about to run. Then Matt tuned in on what the television was trying to show them. Porn movies. A woman with grotesquely large breasts blurred in and out of view, and a man was pleading and promising . . .

Matt lifted the bottle from the drawer. He'd never seen a pornographic movie. Maybe it was about time, and besides, the reception was virtually a shield against sin. And the Blue Lady guarded above.

Keeping an eye on Effinger, he went to the bathroom, where the showerhead still dripped mournfully. A glass white with a wake of toothpaste sat on the old-fashioned pedestal sink. Matt ran the left faucet until hot water came. Then he washed the glass with his fingers in the boiling water, until it was clean and clear again.

He poured three fingers into it and joined the rapt Effinger in the other room.

The on-screen lovers were grunting now, like pigs in pig heaven, if that happened to be a blizzard. Matt leaned against one wall, between Effinger and the door, and watched the interference perform its acrobatics to what sounded like the "Anvil Chorus."

Effinger glanced at him resentfully. "That's my booze."

"Thank you." Matt toasted with the glass and drank. Rotgut was rotgut; he was beginning to appreciate the wonders of brand-name liquor. Still, this was a celebration. He was free, finally free. He didn't even care if Molina could hold Effinger on any charge. It was enough to know he finally had to answer to something. The past was just the past, and needed to be settled somewhere other than here, at some future date. Future. Matt had a future.

Matt's thoughts unrolled, drowning out the television sound effects. He glimpsed bodies in conjunction now and then, but he felt no sense of sin, only of liberation. The Halloween monster had taken off his mask, and he was just Jack Nicholson. The joker. The joke.

Matt drank again, feeling the fire chase down to his stomach and hang there like an internal vigil light. What had Effinger said? About Matt being a bastard? Matt had never thought of him, the other father, the real father, the faceless sire who had paled after the arrival of his substitute. Temple had implied once that the identity of that man was the true corrosive secret in Matt's personal nonhistory.

Temple. Wait until she heard—!

The knock at the door was so discreet that Matt feared one of Effinger's friends, or at least an associate, had arrived.

Effinger grasped at that wild hope too, sitting up and tearing his eyes from the dubious on-screen action.

"Huh-huh-huh," someone grunted in muzzy living sound.

Matt went to the door. No peephole, like in respectable motels, and little light outside to see anyone by in any case. At the Blue Mermaid, you took your chances.

He took his for the last time that night and cracked the door.

"Police," came Molina's jaded contralto.

He opened the door wide, noticing her hand came away from beneath her open jacket. At the Blue Mermaid, Lieutenant C. R. Molina took no chances.

Effinger tensed on the bed, then sagged again as he took in Molina. He looked back at the TV.

Molina approached him. She looked to Matt like she always did, a blank slate in a tailored pantsuit. A competent career woman who carried no briefcase, and no purse. Who wore no shoes worth noticing. And a gun even more low-profile. She stood between Effinger and the TV screen and looked him over.

"Yup, this is the guy. I guess congratulations are in order. You'll have to tell me how you did it sometime." Not tonight. "You check his ID?"

"Uh, no. I mean, I knew who he was."

"But who does he *say* he is now?" Molina pulled Effinger upright. She was a physically impressive woman, almost six feet tall in low heels, but Effinger didn't look that small in contrast. Matt frowned. Was the smallness he sensed in the man purely spiritual? He had felt like Goliath hauling around an unworthy David all night. But Effinger was his size really. Why had Matt felt so confident? Why had Effinger caved so easily, besides the fact that all bullies are cowards?

Molina glanced at the liquor glass. "Better put that on the bedside table, if you can call it that. Don't want our John Citizen to look like a lush."

He obeyed as Molina went to the ajar door and called someone outside. "This is the right guy. Come on in and play patty-cake. I don't want to get lice under my manicure."

Matt glanced at her fingertips, startled. The same short, unpolished blunt fingernails as always.

"Professional joke," Molina said, quick to catch his glance. "Lieutenants don't have to don latex except at crime scenes."

The plainclothes detective came in, hands ghostly in surgical gloves.

Matt still wasn't used to masked and gloved dentists. He'd never thought about the police having to dress more formally for the job in this age of AIDS.

The detective had Effinger lean his hands against the wall, and soon was tossing a few belongings on the bed-spread.

Molina picked through them with a ballpoint pen from her coat pocket. "Look at this AARP card. Harvey Kittel-man. Poor old Harvey's probably missing a lot more too. Las Vegas is a candy store to you guys, isn't it, Effinger?"

"I'm not answering to that name. I'm not answering anything."

"Why not? Didn't I hear him volunteering to come in for a polite police interrogation?" Molina asked her partner.

"Absolutely."

Matt watched, a fascinated observer of a television cop-show scene. Effinger performed like a trained seal who knew the routine by heart.

"Mind if we cut off your reception?" Molina asked iron-ically.

Matt didn't realize she was talking to him until the si-lence grew awkward.

"Huh?" He glanced at the television set, which had responded to fresh body heat in the room by resolving into perfect focus. He saw . . . knees, elbows, buttocks, breasts in impossible juxtaposition, threes and sixes of everything . . . no wonder— "No. I mean, yes. Please."

Molina's tall form already blocked the screen. The sound died abruptly.

"It wasn't tuned in and I wasn't watching," Matt added lamely in the sudden silence.

"This motel is mainly a passion pit these days," she said with academic dispassion. "Perfect hideout for Mr. Effinger."

"You have nothing on me." The guy was still truculent.

"Probable cause for a lot of things," she answered, tak-ing a slow turn through the room. "Starting with a citizen's arrest."

For a confusing moment, Carmen Molina reminded Matt of Kitty O'Connor. Or maybe the actress on the TV had, the brunette on the bottom with—

"You can go now." Molina was peering into the bathroom. "Kinda messy in here." She stopped by Matt as her partner hustled Effinger outside. "Looks like he'll have a bruise or contusion or two. Nothing serious, or actionable. How are you doing?"

"Fine." Matt started for the door. His joints resisted movement. Maybe his struggle with Effinger had been more strenuous than he felt at the time.

"I'll call later with any news," Molina added, "but don't cancel Christmas on my account. By the way, where's your cohort?"

Matt turned, a question on his face.

"Las Vegas's Nancy Drew. I was sure she'd be in on this."

"Temple's out of town for the holidays, until New Year's."

Molina nodded. "Out-of-state relatives. I'm surprised she'd leave you languishing over the holidays. And look what you got yourself as a present!"

"She's visiting *a* relative," Matt corrected. He resented Molina's put-downs of Temple. "I think you met her aunt, Kit Carlson, during the romance-convention fracas."

"New York? She's visiting her aunt in New York? Just for fun?"

"Some people do have that, Lieutenant."

Her cobalt eyes, definitely too dark for Virgin Mary Blue, glimmered with unsaid response to his gentle gibe.

"And," Matt added, rubbing salt into the wound for the absent Temple, "it isn't just a family visit. Temple is meeting with a Madison Avenue advertising agency. She and Midnight Louie are under consideration for an assignment as spokes . . . people, I guess, for a major pet products company."

"You mean I might be able to turn on my TV and get the dynamic duo live and in color in my off hours too? I'd rather watch bowling."

"If this came through, I imagine Temple—and Louie, of course—would be doing a lot more traveling."

"Thank God for small favors." Molina came abreast of Matt at the door. "Speaking of which, thanks for the collar. You did a good job finding Effinger. Did you enjoy it?"

"Not as much as I thought I would."

Molina nodded. "That's good. Because you don't ever want to try a vigilante act like that in this town again."

"Unless I happen to run into Max Kinsella."

"That would be worth seeing; you making a citizen's arrest on Kinsella. Better keep your hands off him; I want that collar. As for Effinger's arrest, remember: just one to a customer, and only because you're such good friends with Miss Temple Barr."

Molina grinned and left, leaving Matt to close down the motel room. He did it slowly, methodically, searching the tiny square closet with a few crinkled garments slumping on wire hangers, checking under the bed and finding only dust, food stamps and parking chits, and a business card for a private-dancer service.

Matt dusted off his hands when he was done, and killed the buzzing light in the bathroom. He shut off the table lamp just before pulling the door closed.

Sighing, he pushed his hands into his pockets again. So long to get here, so little to show for it, not even the indulgence of a fit of anger. He couldn't believe he hadn't made mincemeat out of Effinger.

He had a long walk back to the Showboat parking lot for the Hesketh Vampire. Like reputedly real vampires, revenge was turning out to be mostly a pain in the neck.

Chapter 20

The Ghost of ☠mas Past

First came the Seventeenth Precinct squad, two uniformed police officers who saw immediately the unfortunate facts: this was a complicated death scene at a high-profile location with a nobody-victim. Before they began interviewing the sixty-some witnesses, they called for reinforcements.

She arrived in ten minutes, with a male detective in tow. It seemed the lead cop on the Santa Claus case would be a female detective-lieutenant who had done weekend duty as all good workaholic up-and-coming women should. Her last name was Hansen.

Lieutenant Hansen stood about five feet one, was as blond as Scandinavian furniture, had delft-blue eyes, a winter-red nose like Rudolph and spoke with a LaVerne and Shoirley accent. You know, New Joisey.

She also kept looking at Temple, because Temple kept looking at her.

As soon as Lieutenant Hansen had sized up the situation—and the population in both conference rooms—

she had called for reinforcements. She tossed her long black wool coat on a chair back, along with the yellow angora muffler, beret and matching gloves, then strode to the front of the room on her low-heeled red boots that exactly matched her nose.

Were it not for the nose, which she was blowing into a wad of tissue at the moment, she would have been pretty. Her black suit was indeterminate beyond that.

"Is there anyplace else that could hold this many people besides the other conference room?"

"My office?" Brent Colby offered the suggestion from where he sat, beside his relieved but emotionally burned-out daughter.

"And you are—?" She eyed the Santa suit with disbelief.

"Brent Colby, Junior. The Colby in the partnership Colby, Janos and Renaldi."

"And the erroneously supposed victim?"

He nodded gruffly.

"Where did you wait out this second Santa-appearance thing?"

"My office."

Her flaxen head shook its disapproval. "Nope. We'll want to inspect that scene too."

"My office is a 'scene'?"

"Anyplace is that a major player was, or was supposed to be, at the time of the death. Other suggestions for relocation?"

"*My* office," Tony Renaldi said quietly. "It's almost as big as his. I'm Tony, the Renaldi of Colby, Janos and Renaldi."

"Is Mister Janos here too?"

Victor Janos held up a hand.

"Good. Let's go."

Everyone in the room rose, then paused like third-graders in search of a class leader. Colby, Janos and Renaldi headed for the door, Colby sweeping his daughter along as if she were in their protective custody.

As they filed out, Temple made sure she was last by fussing with Louie and his carrier. Lieutenant Hansen was marshaling her forces at the door, a trio of intent men, two in uniform. She pointed to the Christmas scene and its sad centerpiece, dead Santa Claus.

"If we don't want to be here all night, we'll have to separate the sheep from the goats fast. I'll take the nearest and dearest. You handle the extras and see if you can get any leads on who really died here. Unless he arrived in the red long johns, the victim's gotta have street clothes somewhere. You lose something, miss?"

Her tone was unchanged as she whirled on Temple, well aware of her eavesdropping. This one-woman-computer-of-crime's outer casing was 180-degrees different in style, but the operating system was SGM—Solid Gold Molina.

"Just getting the cat back into the bag," Temple said. "He's the one who discovered that something was wrong, you know."

"No!" Hansen didn't even look at Louie, or heed Temple's words. "Quite a Christmas tale. You know where Mr. Renaldi's office is?"

"No."

"Follow the yellow brick road." She pointed to the hall, and Temple hastened to duck out the door.

Behind her the lieutenant's ratchet-rough voice resumed, outlining and assigning procedures. "How many kids? First, we have to get the youngest ones off-scene. I'm afraid our on-call clown has other holiday engagements. Any other ideas?"

Temple found the right office by following the low thrum of speculation that emanated from it like the drone of bees from a hive. Now that their leader was not the victim, the employees and associates of Colby, Janos and Renaldi busily buzzed with speculation about the possible murder—and possible murderer—in their midst.

As Temple entered the standing-room-only event, Colby was attempting to calm them down, his well-manicured hands sketching a conductor's grave gestures on the smoky air.

"I know this has been an emotionally trying night," he was saying, soothing. "I'm pretty bowled over myself. I'm sorry if I misled you. But, look; I'd finally listened to my daughter, and others, and decided to forgo scaling a cramped chimney this year. So I hired a pro. How he happened to get himself killed, I don't know. One thing I do know: I was never in that chimney, or going to be in that chimney, so I was never in any danger."

"But no one *knew* you *weren't* going to be there, Brent," Janos's dark baritone put in. "You miss the point." A small chrome implement Janos was using to groom under his fingernails slipped. He cursed silently and shook his hand.

"The point is," Colby explained with paternal patience, addressing everyone in the crowded office, "that because it happened here, everyone assumes I was the intended victim. It's far more likely the Santa substitute was. I mean, we know nothing about him."

"You must," Temple noted as she took a vacant spot along the wall. "You hired him."

"I interviewed him, briefly. Not a very substantial-looking man. A bit rough-edged, frankly. But he'd done this Santa gig often before, even at Macy's, and insisted he could handle the chimney-climbing bit."

"Where'd you find him?" Janos asked sullenly, still digging at the invisible dirt under his nails.

"One of the employment agencies, where else? But, ah . . . I hired him on the side."

"Why?" Renaldi sipped a demitasse of coffee from his office espresso machine. The fine china cup was as translucent as the half-moon on one of his perfect fingernails.

Colby shifted in Renaldi's white leather executive chair. Renaldi and Janos sat in the comfy visitor's chairs. The others crowded on the couch or held up the walls.

"Why hire someone under the table?" Colby asked back. He loosened the thick black belt holding his stuffing in place. "I finally bought the arguments that I was too old for the stunt, but I didn't want to make the fact public. The ersatz Santa was supposed to disappear as I always did, come and tell me the act was up, leave, and then I'd appear in my regular Santa suit to accept the usual congratulations for my feat."

"Where did he change?" This question came from the Little Dutch Girl look-alike in the office door, in brisk tones.

"Executive washroom." Colby glanced quickly at his partners. "I couldn't have him seen in the men's room, now could I?"

"We need the key." The lieutenant held out a small, pale palm.

All three partners dug uneasily through their pockets. Only one produced a key. Renaldi.

"I gave him my spare," Colby said, "to keep the switch secret."

Lieutenant Hansen walked over for the key. "He hung out in the executive washroom for how long?"

"He arrived at seven P.M. as agreed. I got him set up."

"He bring his own costume?"

"As I said, he'd done this before. That was the deal. A ready-to-go Santa."

Silence filled the room as the ironic implications of "ready-to-go" reverberated among this word-oriented advertising crowd.

"And he appeared in the chimney at—?"

"Eight," Kendall said. "I was always anxious about Daddy doing this, so I was very time conscious."

Lieutenant Hansen nodded. A bun of blond braid big enough to choke a Central Park horse coiled at the back of her head. Her fine, embroidery-thread-satin hair, Temple thought, must be long enough to reach her fingertips. Not exactly Molina's style. Fascinating.

"He wasn't always in the bathroom," Temple put in.

All eyes switched from Kendall to her.

Lieutenant Hansen swaggered Temple's way. "You saw him someplace else?"

"Lurking in the media conference room. Hey, he did lurk. The room was dark and I was passing when Louie ran in, so I had to go in and retrieve him."

"Louie?"

Temple patted the black cat head protruding from the carrier hitched to her torso. "Midnight Louie."

This time Hansen took in the entire setup. "What's a cat doing on the premises?"

"He's auditioning for a cat-food commercial contract."

"I see." Lieutenant Hansen clearly did not see, but she wasn't going to admit it. "So you saw a Santa Claus in the conference room. When was this?"

"I was the last one to enter the party room, so I'd say about seven forty-five."

"What was he doing there?"

"Not much. Never said a word. Just put a finger to his lips like a jolly old elf. I see in retrospect that he was hiding out until it was time to make his entrance."

"And how did he do that?" Hansen turned back to Colby.

"A small kitchen adjoins the conference-room wall where the Santa chimney is installed. There's a heating vent we modified to lead into the 'chimney' years ago, when this tradition began."

"How many years ago?"

"I don't know, Lieutenant. It's something I've done so long I've forgotten when it began."

"When I was six," Kendall piped up with an odd, childish eagerness.

Colby nodded. "She's twenty-six now. So it was twenty years ago."

"All right." The lieutenant eyed the crowd scene until she spotted Victor Janos. "You have an office? Where?"

"Next door."

"Fine. We'll interview you there, separately, starting with those least related to the incident."

The process took two hours, occurring simultaneously in the big conference room down the hall and in Tony Renaldi's office. The Client was the first group to be dismissed, en masse, as befitted their unified front. Wives and children, except for Kendall, left next. Employees trickled out one by one.

By the end of an hour, Temple's turn came.

Victor Janos's office was a model of masculine simplicity: brown, leather-accoutered and uncluttered.

Lieutenant Hansen, seated behind the massive mahogany desk, gestured Temple to a chair, but Temple declined.

"With the cat attached, standing is easier."

"It must be rather like being pregnant," Hansen agreed, already jotting disconcerting notes in her book.

First came the deadly predictable routine questions. Temple recited name, address, phone number both in Las Vegas and here in New York City, when she had arrived for the party, where she was between then and the Santa Claus appearance. She also explained her relationship to the partners of the firm.

Then Hansen got down to the nitty-gritty.

"Apparently you're the one who split the onlookers into the group sent to Renaldi's office and the crowd kept on the crime scene. Why?"

"To get the children out, number one, before Santa's death traumatized them, or before they milled around enough to mess up the death scene."

"Good thinking." The New York lieutenant said it the way Molina would, as if she meant the exact opposite. "Nothing like saving the police time and trouble on a major crime scene. Why were you playing traffic cop?"

"I have . . . experience."

"As a school crossing guard, or what?"

"I've been present at other crime scenes," Temple said. "By accident."

"Most people present at crime scenes are usually there by accident. Unless they're accessories to the murder. Are you?"

"No. I'm just an experienced witness. You can ask the Las Vegas police."

"We will. Who?" Pen was poised.

"Lieutenant C. R. Molina, crimes against persons unit."

"Molina. One *l,* one *n?*"

"And one *o,* one *i,* one *a.*"

Hansen glowered up at her. *Up* at her. Yes! And Temple bowed over by a twenty-pound cat.

"I should get the cat's name, I suppose."

"Midnight Louie. That's 'midnight' with a capital *m,* and Louie—"

"As in 'Louie, Louie'?"

Temple nodded, and then she was free to go. For now, Hansen added with a dire flourish.

Temple paused at the office door to read an elegant blue-enameled clock on the bookshelf: 11 P.M. Only 8 P.M. in Las Vegas. Lieutenant Hansen might actually reach Molina if she called soon. That would be a conversation worth eavesdropping on.

Temple wondered if she should call Molina to warn her. No. The minute she hit Aunt Kit's, she was going to be in a warm bath and Louie would be whisker-deep in a big dish of milk with a little shot of creme de cocoa.

Gosh . . . Kit! She had expected Temple home at least an hour earlier. Was a cab catchable at this late hour? Probably, but maybe she should train Louie to run them down like mice, to leap on their hoods and hang on. That would get their attention, even if she couldn't.

Temple collected her clothes in Kendall's empty office, dumped them in the tote bag and trudged to the hall elevators in her high heels, too weary to change.

Going down the hall, Temple remembered the sinister, cadaverous figure she and Louie had followed only yesterday morning, on their first visit to Colby, Janos and Renaldi. He had vanished down the hall like the ghost of Jersey Joe Jackson at the Crystal Phoenix Hotel in Las Vegas. Maybe he had been an omen of bad things to come. Truly the Ghost of Christmas Past.

Watching the elevator floor-indicator inch toward her position, Temple yawned and shivered at the same time.

The head he-Client had hinted that she and Louie had his vote for the job, if the three clones didn't vote otherwise, she assumed. Maybe that was good news, but now it seemed trivial compared to what had happened.

Even Old Saint Nick wasn't safe when Temple, the bad-luck bearer, was on the scene. Wait until Kit heard that Santa Claus had been the death of the party!

Chapter 21

Thanks for the Memories

Matt had barely got home to the Circle Ritz when Molina called.

"Something happen?" Matt knew he sounded anxious.

"Not yet. But I'm inviting you to the interrogation, after all, as an unseen observer. From what little conversation we've had with Mr. Effinger so far, he's got a whole smorgasbord of answers. I thought you might be able to detect some of the smoked sham-on-rye he's handing out."

"I'm . . . honored."

"Don't be. It's my way of saying thanks for keeping me on overtime during my kid's Christmas break. Seriously, this is my one free crack at him—yours, too, unless you want to push a deep personal interest over the legal line into stalking, and I don't think you do. I want this round to count."

"Ditto."

"Get here as fast as Max Kinsella's motorcycle will take

you. Don't speed, though, not noticeably, and don't expect too much."

Matt hung up, understanding that one low-level interrogation was small stuff. Still, he and Molina had a big stake in what Effinger would say, would give away. What was Effinger to her, and she to Effinger, that it mattered so much? Maybe a promotion. Maybe a bigger crime to be uncovered. Maybe Max Kinsella to hound and hunt down for something concrete, instead of just nagging suspicions.

Help Molina, help himself and help Max Kinsella right out of Temple's life. Molina would tell him that was in Temple's best interests, but Matt had always found doing things for people's own good a form of dictatorship. He could only think of Temple's searing disappointment if Max proved to be criminally involved.

Effinger.

Trapped. In a room. With Matt behind a one-way mirror, watching him for lies. Justice? Or for just another foolish attempt at erasing a painful past with a vengeful present?

Matt checked his watch. Not even 8 P.M. Lucky he had the night off.

At 8:30 a uniformed officer escorted Matt by elevator to the proper floor. The young, stoic guy gave no indication of what he thought of Matt's presence or mission. Probably nothing.

Molina met him in her long, narrow office, as cramped and dysfunctionally functional as usual, and led him to a string of small, nondescript empty rooms.

"We're interviewing him in there. We gave him a coffee break." She led Matt through a different door to another room as antiseptically devoid of decoration as the one indicated. "You'll look and listen from here. I'll leave the interrogation room if I want to confirm what he says with you. Just sit down and get comfortable."

Matt eyed the oak armchair that belonged in a courthouse anteroom. It was no red suede sofa. He couldn't help smiling.

"Coffee?" Molina's tone was as warm as the Stewardess from Hell's.

"Yeah. I brought a notepad and pen."

"Aren't you the Boy Scout, always prepared?"

She shut the door, giving him an instant tinge of claustrophobia, which was ridiculous in the face of the huge picture window framing the adjoining room. She returned soon, butting the ajar door open to enter carrying two plastic cup holders and their filled cups.

Matt accepted one and sat down, watching the blank window. Imagine, viewing Cliff Effinger like a specimen bug in a plastic box. If only he had glimpsed this day years ago.

Matt felt like someone watching an ill-produced early TV show. The Spartan setting—a wooden table and metal folding chairs—was as stark as *The Honeymooners'* apartment in the Jackie Gleason classic skits, and remained empty.

Could people live with so little as the Kramdens had in New York City of the fifties? Matt had wondered that the first time he'd viewed retrospectives of the early TV show. Now he wondered, could the police do much with so little? A bare room and a few questions, with a peephole-turned-picture-window that everyone recognized for what it was.

Finally the door with the chicken-wire-sandwiched window glass opened into the next room. A mustached man in a beige shirt and pants showed in Effinger. Molina came last, coffee cup in hand. Every click and rustle and scrape of their motions transmitted to the room Matt occupied.

Molina spoke. It was her show. "You know your rights," she told Effinger and the tape recorder. "You've waived the presence of your attorney."

"What's to wave at?" Effinger's upper lip writhed in

an Elvis-curl. He waved at the window, and Matt flinched. "I don't have an attorney and I'm not going to answer much."

With his hat off, he looked worn and seedy, but his age-seamed face still had the mean underbite of a junkyard dog.

"Just wanted to know your whereabouts on September twenty-ninth of last year."

"Like I keep a Day Runner."

"Think."

"I wasn't even in Las Vegas around then."

"Where do you go?"

"Places. L.A. Chicago."

Molina nodded. "Any witnesses see you there?"

"No! I visit places, not people."

"In L.A.?"

"The track."

"In Chicago?"

"The dogs."

"Always gambling. Why travel for it when it's all here?"

"Variety."

"What do you know about this man?"

From his observation post, Matt could see a black-and-white photo of the corpse that fell from the Crystal Phoenix ceiling last fall, the corpse that had carried Cliff Effinger's ID, but not his fingerprints. What had anyone hoped to gain from that?

"What do I know about this guy? He's dead?" Effinger offered with a shrug.

"Why did he have your ID on him?"

"Was it my ID? Probably he stole it."

"What about the ID you're carrying now?"

"What about it?"

"It's not yours."

"Prove it."

Molina got up, walked to Matt's window, folded her arms and kept her back to Effinger. "We don't have to prove it. We can get your fingerprints. The inkpad tells all."

"Not all. People can have their fingerprints altered."

"To match yours! Why on earth would anyone want to be taken for a petty crook like you?"

Effinger shrugged.

Molina turned back to the table and skated two more photos from the folder toward him. "Know these guys?"

Effinger's glance was cursory, but Matt saw something tighten in that indifferent face. He'd always done that when he was preparing to lash out, or to lie to someone's face.

"Nope. Never saw them."

Molina eyed the photos with a certain ruefulness. "Well, that doesn't surprise me, Cliff. Seems no one's seen these two Vegas eyesores for a few months. My guess is that someone quietly took them out."

Effinger grew even stiller.

"You have any idea who might want to do that, hmm? They're ugly customers, as they used to say, but small fry, really. What do you think? Did someone run or buy them out of town, or just drive them out on the desert?"

"Like you said, Lieutenant. They're not worth the cash or the gas. I say they took off for greener pastures."

"Like L.A.? Or Chicago?"

Effinger shrugged.

Molina packed her folder and picked up her empty coffee cup. "Coffee anyone?" she inquired in a tone that didn't encourage a yes, not even from her so-far-silent interrogation partner.

She left the room and Matt braced himself.

A moment later his door opened.

She slapped the folder down on the table, then leaned on the table edge.

"We'll get zilch from him. At least directly. What did you notice?"

"He was lying about the two photos you showed him."

"Of course."

"Were they the hoods who assaulted Temple?"

"What do you think?"

"Are they really missing?"

She nodded.

"He knew them, Effinger did."

She nodded.

"Then—" Matt realized where he was going, and stopped.

"Say it." Molina smiled grimly. "You're not protecting anyone or anything but your own shadow-sense of honor. Effinger lied about knowing those two thugs, who are—?"

Somehow he had become the one being interrogated. Seeing Molina's cleverness in using one to prod the other, he understood—almost sympathized with—Effinger's weary reluctance to speak. But there was no escape for anyone who still pretended to honesty.

Matt opened the folder to pull the two photos into the light. "If this is the pair who assaulted Temple, that means that—"

"That means that their intense interest in Max Kinsella's whereabouts, and their unadmitted recognition by Cliff Effinger, ties Kinsella into the recent casino killings."

"You're not saying Kinsella killed these absent creeps? If they're dead."

"I'm saying that he's one of the few people in Las Vegas I can think of who could, and would. If you have any idea where he's gone to ground—"

"I don't."

"If you have any idea that Miss Temple knows where he's gone to ground—"

"I don't, I hope she doesn't and I wouldn't say even if she did."

Molina swept the photos back into the folder. "But you do see what—and who—Effinger knows? You know anybody in Chicago who might provide an alibi for him?"

"I'll ask the next time I get there," Matt said, as blankly as she.

"Do that. And don't forget to tell me what you find out." Molina pushed herself free of the table's hard-edged support. "You can go now. The coffee isn't that good here."

Matt left, aware that Molina had always hoped to get

more out of him than Effinger during this double-edged interrogation.

He began to wish he had throttled Effinger before the
man could destroy Matt's present life as thoroughly as he
had his past one.

Chapter 22

Santa Who?

Temple awoke feeling she should be someplace else.

But this was Sunday, her muzzy brain finally figured out
as it took in the tall windows covered with drawn white
miniblinds.

She wasn't scheduled to return to the advertising agency
offices until Monday, even without the intervention of a
death.

She patted the bedcovers, in search of either Midnight
Louie's big furry body annexing the comforter, or her
glasses, which weren't on the bedside table. The glasses
materialized under her hand. She'd fallen asleep reading
the Colby, Janos and Renaldi promotional booklet she had
shown Kit.

Her dreams came back, a jumbled "Christmas Carol"
production with Colby, Janos and Renaldi as the three
ghosts and old Ebenezer Scrooge the cadaverous figure
that had ridden up on the elevator with her that first
day. Or did Scrooge symbolize the Old Year, the bent,

paper-thin, robed figure with the scythe . . . Death himself?

Heavy. Temple donned her glasses and let her toes do the walking along the bedside as they felt for the fat, fuzzy bedroom slippers Kit had lent her. Knit wool slippers packed easily, but they were no protection against bare wood floors in a cold climate.

When she was properly shod in her borrowed mukluks, she skated over the polished oak to the windows to slit open the blinds. A white overcast sky blazed in, shaking down powdered sugar against the window glass.

A great day to stay in, curl up by the coffeemaker and attack the *New York Times*'s hugely nasty Sunday crossword puzzle . . . or the more relevant puzzle of a death by hanging from a golden chain.

Kit was in the living room, already immersed in the four-inch-thick paper, a mug of coffee on the sofa table in front of her, and Midnight Louie sprawled on the classified ads section, carefully cleaning his fingernails, i.e., claws. He reminded Temple of Victor Janos in Colby junior's office last night. A strange, compulsive reaction to a sudden death in the area.

" 'Morning, Temple." Kit barely looked up from the paper. "Coffee's on in the kitchen. Box of bagels, box of sticky buns, box of croissants. Grab a mug, a thousand calories, and come back in."

Temple shuffled off to the triangle of kitchen around the corner. The coffee smelled of cinnamon and nuts. She kept it black instead of adding her usual whitewash of skim milk and joined her aunt on the couch.

"There it is." Kit slapped a fat section of newsprint onto Temple's flannel lap. "That looks like a Minnesota nightgown, granny. How did you come by it?"

"Honestly. I brought it with me when I moved to Vegas. For when I had a cold."

Kit nodded. "Nothing like floor-length flannel to soothe the savaged respiratory system. I thought I detected a faint perfume of Vick's VapoRub. Good thing we're both single at the moment. Check out page thirty-eight."

Temple paged through the ink-laden sheets, trying to contain a sneeze. How long would messy, heavy, tree-slaying newsprint last, she wondered, now that cyberspace was here?

"I don't see anything, Kit."

"Lower right. Two inches."

"MURDER MUST ADVERTISE. Cute. That *New York Times* staff certainly has a wide background."

"Dorothy Sayers title, isn't it?"

"Did you read her too?"

"Ages ago. Probably when she was still alive. Too bad they never found anybody to play the part who could live up to the Wimsey in her mind, the way that Jeremy Brett went over the top to reinvent Holmes."

"Some characters are meant to live only on the page. I can't believe this. An item in the morning paper. How—?"

"New York may look inefficient to outlanders, but we do just fine here. Get a lot done, well done."

"This is odd. It says the street clothes of the 'slain Santa' carried no identification."

"What's odd? The 'slain Santa' or the no ID bit?"

"Both, as a matter of fact. Lieutenant Katrina must have told a reporter that the death was not an accident. Kind of soon to make that judgment."

"I told you. We don't waste time here. Besides, how many golden chains end up in a booby trap at the top of a pressed-wood chimney?"

"At Christmastime a lot of golden bric-a-brac ends up lying around. Maybe Marley's ghost was set to make a later appearance."

"That's interesting." Kit looked up through the mottled-indigo metallic of her eyeglass frames. "Marley was a *business* partner, wasn't he? Maybe the chain was sending a message."

Temple stopped considering the fact that she'd probably look just like Kit in thirty years; in fact, she looked a lot like her now—maybe she should try contact lenses again soon.

"You mean that the means of death, the golden chain, was symbolic, not just handy?"

"How many golden chains you got hanging around your place?" Kit's skeptical eyebrows overshot her eyeglass frames. "Of course, I may be discounting any leftover props—personal or professional—from your erstwhile boyfriend the magician."

"Just handcuffs and silk scarves," Temple rushed to assure her aunt, then realized that she had done nothing of the kind.

"What I can't figure out," Kit said after a truly pregnant pause and a sip of coffee, "is why the dead man was taken for this Brent Colby, Junior, for so long, even by his own daughter, not to mention partners and employees."

"Any homicide cop would tell you that strangulation does not produce a pretty corpse, and I can testify to the fact. Talk about a dark red and swollen face. Besides, he was still wearing the Santa getup, and all that shows is eyes and nostrils."

Temple sipped her coffee, then squinted at the gray canyons of Manhattan out the windows. "After the death, when I was thinking everything over, I realized that when I blundered into the wrong conference room, I'd swear that the Santa guy looked startled and then *guilty* to see me. I figured I'd caught the dignified Colby lurking with intent to surprise. But *he* seemed more surprised by *my* presence than vice versa. Anyway, that's the kicker. A face full of permanent-waved cotton batting totally distorts the features underneath. I keep trying to imagine what the Santa I saw would look like without the whiskers and mustache and fur-trimmed cap down to his frosty eyebrows, but it's impossible."

Kit nodded dolefully. "Now I get the picture. If I were a crook trying to pass as somebody else, a Santa suit disguise would be my number one choice. It distorts face and figure, yet it's so familiar to people from their earliest childhood that we never try to look beneath it; that ruins the whole point of Santa."

"Then the likeliest scenario is that the golden chain was meant for the custom-shirted neck of Brent Colby, Junior, but only Colby knew he was using a substitute this year. That opens up oodles of motives, especially among Colby's closest associates."

"And family."

Temple frowned. "I'd hate to think Kendall did it."

"Why?"

"Well, she's his only daughter, and she's been nice to me."

"Temple. Judas was 'nice' to Jesus in the Garden of Gethsemane. Those who will betray you with a kiss are the most dangerous of all. What about Mrs. Colby?"

"A long-gone ex, I'd assume. Nobody even brought her up. Guess I should. I'll delicately ask Kendall about her family background first thing Monday."

"Don't you imagine the police are doing plenty of that today? Maybe they'll crack the case by Monday."

Temple shook her head and tapped the tiny article at the back of the huge newspaper section. "Not if the dead Santa had no ID. Someone doesn't want him identified, and that makes it look like he was the target."

"You did say that Colby had learned about him from an agency?"

Temple nodded her head.

"I know some agency people. I could call around this afternoon, see if they remember Colby calling."

"On Sunday?"

"The Naked City never sleeps," Kit intoned as flatly as a true-crime television-show announcer. "And inquiring New Yorkers want to know who's been killing Santa Claus."

"I can't believe I traveled three thousand miles to run into another murder. I wonder if the lady lieutenant here called the lady lieutenant in Las Vegas about me yet."

"Don't look so glum. It never hurts to have people talking about you."

"Not homicide detectives. Molina might tell Katrina who-knows-what. She's not fond of amateur anythings."

Kit leaned against the couch back, forgetting about Midnight Louie, who growled.

"Goodness! We are grouchy this morning." She sighed. "You think you saw Santa's eyes before. I'd bet you did. You've had theatrical experience. Actors never forget eyes. Did he seem uneasy to recognize you?"

"No. More surprised. You don't suppose it was suicide?"

"Now there's a notion. This is intriguing. What if this poor nameless soul wanted to cause a little stir as he left the world, perhaps more than he merited while alive? A public hanging at a Christmas party would do the trick. Sad what some people will do for attention."

"Or . . ." Temple sat up. "What if the golden chain wasn't making a statement, but the dead man was? What if he blamed someone at Colby, Janos and Renaldi for something, and wanted to embarrass the firm? Bad publicity like this is poison to an advertising firm. It upsets clients."

"Corporate revenge. I like it. All we have to do is find out who he is . . . was . . . and what he might have against a big advertising agency like CJR."

"All? Kit, he could be someone who . . . lost a loved one to a faulty product for which CJR handled an advertising campaign. He could have no overt connection whatsoever and still could have that kind of a motive. What do you really think 'we' can do about it?"

"We can start with what we know, and I know those agency people who hand out most of the Santa assignments around this town. And Rudy might have some ideas." Her fading red hair trembled as her head nodded firmly. " 'Every journey to a thousand parts always starts with a single phone call.' Article One of the Actor's Creed."

Chapter 23

Moby Couch

The evening of the morning after the day before.

Matt stood in the glare of his apartment lights, sweating like a stevedore and gazing at a white elephant. At a bloody Moby Dick of the landlubbing world.

A long, sinuous S of red suede sofa snaked diagonally across the parquet floor in an otherwise almost-empty room.

"Temple—" he threatened the emptiness, or the sofa, aloud.

His wallet was lighter by another hundred and fifty dollars. Movers that could muscle an eight-foot-long sofa up three floors of a building built in the fifties with narrow-everything didn't come cheap. Getting it out would probably be best accomplished by wrestling it to the patio railing and dumping it overboard, after shouting suitable warning, like "Timmmmmm-ber!"

He walked around it, hands on hips, shaking his head. "Temmm-ple," he repeated softly.

He had to admit that in nighttime lighting the behemoth

looked pretty good. The flagrant red had a holiday dash. But his brick-and-board bookshelves looked like escapees from a prison for makeshift furniture now. What did he need a living room for, anyway? He had no visitors, and wasn't likely to have any, not with the transient company he kept at the hot line.

Matt decided to give himself a talking-to, since Temple wasn't here to do it for him. All right, Devine. This is a pretty cool sofa, after all. And you paid enough for it. Could have had some nondescript yuppie cotton-duck-covered love seat for the price, and a floor lamp.

He sat down smack in the sofa's middle and stared at the brandy-colored wood floor. Well, he supposed he could get one of those white, hairy goat rugs like Temple had, and stick it in the sofa's front curve. Only it wouldn't be genuine. Nothing living would die (or decorate) for his sins. Synthetic. Come to think of it, Temple had said "suede."

Matt stroked the smooth fabric. Not as soft as velvet, but not as harsh as cotton duck either. Except for one stain on the back, the sofa was in perfect condition. Someone must have taken good care of it for a long time.

Suede, though. At least the suede-bearers had probably served humankind in a dozen different ways. Matt leaned his elbows on his knees to study his empty white walls. One of Rouault's Christ-figure paintings would look nice on that wall, and crucifixion scenes always have a dash of red in them, especially Rouault's deceptively prettified stained-glass style . . .

Christ! He wasn't furnishing a convent. This was a bachelor pad. Why did everything he thought of come up churchy? What other artists' work had he seen? Van Gogh. Not much red there, except in his self-portrait sans ear. Aha! Renoir. He nodded. Plump bourgeois women and children in quaint late-nineteenth-century dress. Lots of reds.

Didn't exactly go with a sofa that was just two long curves: shorter back support, and long, long seat. Of suede.

How many suedes had died so his rear could cushion it-self on this soft surface?

Georgia O'Keefe, maybe. Modern. Innocuous subjects, flowers. Big like the sofa, lots of lush reds. All pretty erotic, of course. He had heard. Didn't want to send that message any more than the one behind Rouault's jewel-tone meditations on sin, suffering and death.

Oh, Jesus. He meant it as a prayer, not an epithet. Is this my forty days in the desert? My temptation? A long red suede sofa?

Matt put his face in his hands. How could he know who he could love, when he didn't even know what he could like?

So it came back to Temple. He missed her. And he was actually glad the ridiculous sofa had arrived today and dis-tracted him from the encounter with Cliff Effinger last night.

He hadn't slept all night, but then he was used to being up, working, those hours. That wasn't it. The triumph was rolling around inside of him, bumping into all his tender spots. And he'd discovered what Molina probably already knew. He had banged himself up right royally with Effin-ger, and vice versa. Funny, he'd hadn't felt a thing at the time. Adrenaline?

So he was aching all over today, and of course he had to help the two beefy guys with beer guts that would choke a horse manhandle the sofa upstairs. Couldn't take the el-evator. Too small. Why would such a little woman like Temple fall in love with such a big sofa? Uh-oh, Matt's inner voice warned. She fell in love with Max Kinsella, and he ain't exactly small. Opposites attract, dummy. Rule number one of the secular, coeducational world.

He'd had a headache all day too. Probably from those partially tasted cheap drinks. Impersonating a gumshoe of the old school was hazardous to clean nineties lifestyles.

He glanced around, surprised at being encompassed by a curving palette of pure red. This sofa certainly didn't let you forget about it.

The phone sat on its shaky-legged table. He should . . . call Temple. Tell her the unsinkable thrift-shop sofa had arrived safely. Tell her—

She had left the number, and he had left it right by the phone.

Matt slid about six feet down his new sofa to the end and punched numbers. About 2 P.M. in New York, his wristwatch told him. Might be home between meetings and eatings out.

The phone rang exactly twice before it was answered.

"Hello." Perky. Familiar. Like smelling fresh espresso.

"Temple?"

"No, her aunt. Kit."

"Oh. I'm calling from Las Vegas—"

She cut him off before he could give a reason. "Which one are you—the blond or the brunet?"

He didn't like being reminded of *that*. "The blond." He said it coolly, like a natural blond should.

"Good." Her slightly raspy voice lowered to conspirator-level. "I liked you best."

"I'm sorry, Miss Carlson, but we've never met. I heard about you, of course—"

"Same here. And . . . I glimpsed you both in the casino. Temple really shouldn't reduce the man pool by *two*, given the male-female ratio among the aging population."

"Temple shouldn't do a lot of things she does, but I do think she should talk to me, if she's there, and if you don't mind."

"I do, but I am a good, if heartbroken, hostess. Nice talking to you, Matt."

He rolled his eyes. *Now* what was Temple saying? About him, about Kinsella?

"Matt!"

Her voice was so vibrant, so nearby, despite the long-distance line that he forgot his list of annoyances. "Hi. Glad I caught you in."

"How goes everything?"

"The sofa came."

"Really?"

"It was pretty difficult, and expensive, to get up all these stairs. The movers said a baby grand would be easier."

"Stairs? Why not the elevator . . . oh, too big. Too bad. Listen, my aunt's place is down in the Village, where they have a lot of upscale vintage stores and I think, I *think* your sofa is a Vladimir Kagan."

Suddenly it really was *his* sofa. "A Vladimir Kagan? No wonder it's red."

"Fun-ny. Kagan is German. I spotted his stuff when Kit and I window-shopped the pricey vintage places. Kagan is a fabulous custom designer who was avant-hot in the fifties; now his pieces are undergoing a huge revival. You need to tip up your—what did the brochure call it?— 'extravagantly biomorphic' sofa and check the bottom for any signatures or labels."

"Temple. Three men could barely get this thing here upright. How am I going to tip it over solo, and look for labels?"

"I'll do the label part when I get back."

"Thanks."

"You sound kind of terse. Everything okay? If it's a Kagan it's worth four thousand dollars, easy, in New York or L.A."

"Yeah, but it'd take five thousand dollars to get it there. Besides, I kind of like it here, I decided."

"You do? I'm so glad. I worried during the whole plane flight that I'd buffaloed you into something you'd hate. I get carried away sometimes."

"I noticed. I like it. The sofa, I mean. Not you getting carried away. But I like that too. I doubt I'd have the nerve not to like something you liked."

"Awww."

"How are things going there?"

"All right, but it's New York and it's noisy all night, sirens and garbage trucks from Hades, and crowded all day, and they have split elevator banks and don't tell you, but Louie is being a lamb. Isn't it a little early for you to be up?"

"I had last night off."

"And—"

"What do you mean, 'And—'?"

"Matt. I can hear the strain in your voice. I heard it from the first. It can't be just from hustling collectible sofas up three flights of stairs."

"You're scary sometimes."

"Thanks."

"Temple." He gathered himself to hurl headfirst into a topic that was a lot more volatile than a flaming red sofa, or a flaming redhead. "I found him."

Her words stalled for the first time. "Effinger?" she said finally.

"Effinger."

"How?"

"One of the little sketches you suggested. A . . . woman contacted me and said he was hanging out at an off-Strip casino."

"Well, what happened?"

"A lot. But it's not suitable for long distance. I'll tell you when you get back. I'm working New Year's Eve, but maybe we can have New Year's Day dinner."

"You never take the rough nights off, do you?"

"I don't have a family, and the others do."

"Maybe you do too, and you just don't know it yet."

He found another dead silence growing. "I have the sofa now for quite a clan."

"Hey, you can't let just anybody sit on an extravagantly biomorphic collector's item like a Kagan couch."

"Just you, then. And me."

"That sounds pretty good."

"Did you have that in mind when you made me get it?"

"Maybe. But what happened to Effinger? Surely you can give me a hint."

"I found him at his motel, which you know well."

"Yes, Nostradamus. Which one?"

"Did I rhyme the last sentence? Must have been the boilermaker I didn't have while bribing half the bartenders in town."

"You, hitting the streets and the bottle like Sam Spade? Wish I'd been there. You were going to tell me where 'there' was."

"The Blue Mermaid Motel. No, you wouldn't really have wanted to be there."

"Ooh, sleazy. What did you do when you caught up with him?"

"I didn't kill him. I just collared him. Called Molina and handed him over later. She was peeved I hadn't forewarned her, but I didn't exactly know that was gonna be the night."

"So. You okay with it?"

"Better than okay. I didn't kill him."

"I didn't think you would."

"How come I wasn't so sure of that?"

"Because you're the Hamlet of the Circle Ritz. You're so busy debating the right thing to do, and if you'll do it, that you sometimes miss the obvious."

"So what was so obvious?"

"You're not like him, Matt. Never were, never will be. You'd never kill him."

"But I hate him."

"You're entitled, and besides, you make yourself so guilty about *that*, that killing him would ruin your fun."

"Temple, if you ever die, you'll go to heaven, or—if there's a form of sanctioned reincarnation—you're going to come back as a very long red sofa and bedevil the life out of somebody for forty more years."

"I hope so," she said. "You can sit on me anytime you like."

He didn't answer that one, especially with weird fragments of porno film dancing in his head along with the usual seasonal snowflakes and sugarplums. She went on without pause, anyway.

"What are you doing for Christmas? Working?"

"No. Not this year. I called the supervisor today. I'm going to take a few days off. Go up to Chicago."

"Sounds like a good idea." She spoke so cautiously that he could almost see the red light in her mind.

"Maybe, maybe not. I think you were right, though. There are more issues than Effinger."

"I am? I said that? When?"

"In one of your usual glancing moments of brilliant insight too dazzling for you to see yourself."

"You mock me, Hamlet."

"You need it."

"I don't like men with too many secrets."

"Oh, I think you know that mine are pretty pedestrian. But you *are* having a good time there, despite urban blight, and Louie's fine?"

"In his element! Speaking of ham. And—"

Now *she* hesitated. Saving the worst till last, Matt thought. *What could have gone wrong—?*

"There's been a murder. At the advertising agency. But don't worry. Louie and Kit and I are on the case. Gotta go now; Kit and I are having brunch at the Russian Tea Room, and if you don't get there on time they send you to Siberia or something. Have a Merry Christmas despite yourself, Matt, please! I miss you."

And she hung up.

Sometimes he thought that Kinsella should have her. Would serve him right.

Chapter 24

Rudy, the Red-nosed Pothead

Kit hung up from calling a string of names in her personal phone directory, a volume so fat and crammed with odd bits of paper that it was held together by a rubber band.

"I'd much rather have chatted on the phone half the morning with the darling Mister Devine in Las Vegas, than do this."

"He called; not me. Besides, our conversation didn't last that long. You still exhausted your list, didn't you?"

Kit nodded, then took off her jazzy metallic-framed glasses to rub her eyes.

"Don't you do this," she warned Temple. "Rubbing is bound to give you premature bags under the eyes. Will knock you right out of parts you're too old for. But I am burnt out. All those tiny little numbers to read and dial, and not a bit of useful information."

"You still think like a professional actress, Auntie. You can always have your author photo digitally retouched, so who cares how many bags you have?"

"I do," her aunt said so sharply that the dozing Louie beside Temple growled.

Kit growled right back, then redonned her glasses to scan the disorganized book's contents.

"I might have to take up the stage again," she added. "What with the publishing fallout."

"There's a publishing fallout?"

"Yes. Kind of like the Age of Aquarius for book people. Major realignment of all the communication media to see what form of word and picture will survive the millennium. Why? You plan on breaking into publishing anytime soon?"

"No . . . but I have a friend who might have a book to market soon."

"Fiction?"

"No. Exposé, I guess."

"Of anybody famous?"

"No. Only slightly notorious."

"Notorious is almost as good as famous these days. A notorious former Vegas mobster, perhaps? I'm available to ghostwrite the right project."

"No gangsters. Just . . . international terrorism."

"Wow." Kit took off her glasses again to rest her eyes, which looked only reasonably baggy for her age. "Any chance you'll name names? Subject? Writer?"

Temple shook her head. "I shouldn't have mentioned it."

"Probably not. Get my hopes up, will you? I'd hate being a detective! This is so boring and it got us nowhere."

"You say you know every employment agency in New York that would handle holiday Santas?"

"Well, the ones worth knowing about. There may be some outfit down in the Bowery . . . ."

Temple stroked Louie's satin ears. "Then we know *some*thing. The dead Santa wasn't hired through a legitimate agency."

"Colby, Janos and Renaldi wouldn't know of any other kind of agency. They are big time, Temple. A major agency in this town, and that is something to crow from the chimneytops."

"Chimney. A fatal chimney. A fake, fatal chimney. What a bizarre way to kill somebody! Why that way?"

"It's dramatic."

"Life is not a cabaret, Kit, contrary to the song. Most killers don't look for an innovative way out that would thrill the heart of the Bard of Avon, or even Andrew Lloyd Webber. The last thing a killer wants is a murder that calls attention to itself."

"Why not? Maybe that was the point. I certainly wouldn't push someone I wanted to kill in front of a cab. So . . . shoddy and unimaginative. Nobody would ever suspect anything, especially with the traffic in New York. And look at this scenario. It's perfect. A roomful of witnesses, nobody near the body, the whole thing concealed behind painted bricks. It's like a magic show. Except that at the end of an act, the corpse would jump up and we'd all shout, 'It's alive!' "

Temple sat forward, causing Louie to slide into the space at her back. "But he did jump up, didn't he? The supposed corpse, I mean? He wasn't dead. He made a dramatic resurrection in front of everybody."

"Colby, you mean."

Temple nodded. "I'm beginning to wonder about Louie's behavior too."

"You should." Kit's narrowed eyes drilled through the sleeping cat's Rubenesque form.

"He's so perceptive," Temple said. "When I think about it, he was remarkably friendly to the Santa Claus we found in the empty conference room. I thought he had dashed in there on some quirky feline mission, but now I wonder."

"You think Louie knew someone was in there?"

"Probably. I sensed some movement, and he's a cat. Cats survive by sensing movement. But I think it was more than that."

"More than cat and mouse?"

"I think that Louie knew the guy in the Santa suit too."

"Louie knew him! Right. Our chief witness is a cat. An out-of-town cat, whose chief experience of Manhattan is being toted to and fro in a purple parachute. Who would Louie know in the Big Apple?"

Temple was stumped. "Only you."

"On-ly youuuuu," Kit crooned back, trouper that she was. "Only . . . rouuuuuu."

"Rouuu? Oh. Rouuuu-dy! Your friend who answered the door. No!"

"Maybe he saw Mommy kissing Santa Claus."

"You mean, at the advertising agency. He . . . saw something he shouldn't have when he came early for the gig, and got killed for it?"

Kit was paging through her address book, her agile fingers scattering slips of paper right and left like huge snowflakes. "Shiii-shi-ite. Rudy doesn't have a phone listing. Can't afford a phone."

"Can't afford a phone, in New York? That's like being deaf and blind in Macy's."

Kit nodded solemnly. "Poor Rudy. That's why we all helped him. He had some dump farther down in the East Village, where it hasn't become fashionable yet. A rent-controlled place he qualified for years ago." Kit shut her book, like a Bible she had suddenly realized was a bad translation. "A lot of people live like that in New York. On the verge. The edge. You never notice them, until they die."

"Rudy is not dead, Kit! He was a Macy's Santa just a couple nights ago. High-profile Santas like that don't go jelly-belly up. They come back to ho-ho-ho again. Have you got a street address on him?"

"Yeah, but it's no place you and I would care to go after dark."

"We'll bring Louie. People seem to give me a wide berth when I'm loaded with Louie." Temple held out a hand. "The book, please."

The cab driver kept wanting to take them to Houston—not pronounced Hue-ston, like the very big city in Texas, but House-ton, like the very bad street in New York City.

Temple knew enough to quail at the street name, but Kit was implacable. She repeated the address, and ended up directing the cabby.

The street the cab stopped on was narrow, shadowed, empty, lined with tall trucks and scary as hell.

The cab driver managed to convey that he was loath to leave the ladies off here, even though he did not speak English.

Temple worried when a New York City cab driver had an attack of conscience about letting a passenger off.

They exited the vehicle, the driver begging and pleading with them until they broached the building's iron-railed door.

No security system was in place to make entrance difficult.

Kit breezed in ahead of Temple, her long faux-fur coat brushing the peeling woodwork.

"Sixth floor," she said with brio, marching over a carpet of smashed trash to a paint-pocked metal elevator door scratched with incomprehensible obscenities.

"Kit—"

"Hush. In New York, attitude is everything."

The lobby felt as icy as the outside air. Temple clutched Louie to her bosom in his carrier, glad to have some concealed weapons nearby even if they were only claws.

When the elevator creaked open the scarred outer doors, an odor of cat box nearly knocked them off their feet. Actually, the odor was not cat box, but—Louie forgive her!— it was better to think of it as an animal odor rather than human.

Kit swept onto the putrid car like a czarina in sable and pushed the button for the sixth floor with the tip of her leather glove.

Her head was high.

"Think of England, dear," she advised.

"Why the Hades should I think of England when I'm

in the heart of Hell's Kitchen or someplace? I will think of . . . *Boys' Town*."

"Spencer Tracy," Kit said soothingly. "In a Roman collar."

"A blond Spencer Tracy in a Roman collar," Temple corrected as the rickety elevator lurched upward with suspicious fits and starts.

"Spencer Tracy was silver-haired in that movie," Kit corrected.

"You have your Sthpen-ther Tra-thy, and I'll have mine," Temple said between gritted teeth. It was hard to speak clearly while breathing through your mouth.

Midnight Louie cried in protest, but then, he had no holy figures to invoke for protection.

Then Louie hissed. It sounded remarkably like "Baaasst!"

"I think that Louie's saying that Spencer Tracy was a bastard," Temple said.

"Louie knows nothing about it," Kit replied. "Tracy couldn't divorce his wife to marry Katharine Hepburn because he was a devout Catholic. One of Hollywood's few off-screen tragedies."

"Devout Catholics are the pits," Temple said.

"I happen to admire Spencer Tracy. He was a fabulous actor."

"But I bet he wouldn't be caught dead in this dump."

"That was Bette Davis. Now, please, constrain yourself. We're almost there."

Kit was right. The elevator soon stopped. The ruined doors took their time about deciding to open.

Temple streaked out, Louie in her arms. Kit followed, glasses perched on her nose.

"We should have brought a flashlight," she noted.

The hall lay before them, more smelled than seen, a stew of hot-plate cookery, unclean corridors and bathrooms too far from rooms.

"I suppose you don't have vintage buildings of this age in Las Vegas," Kit said.

"Only the Blue Mermaid Motel."

"The Blue Mermaid. What an evocative name. It should be used in a play."

"Where are we going?"

"To Rudy's flat."

"How will we find it?"

Kit sighed. Her faux fur brushed Temple's wrist. "I have a number, which I cannot see. Perhaps we will meet a kindly guide on the way."

"Perhaps we will meet a housing inspector."

"Not in New York City! Onward."

Finally, finding no sense to the numbering system, by dint of approaching innumerable doors and by process of elimination and the curt direction of disturbed residents, Kit and Temple stood before one narrow door.

"What if he's home?" Temple asked. "Won't he be mortified that we hunted him down?"

"He may be, but *we* will not be." Kit was still doing her Empress of all the Russias impersonation. "We are merely visiting an old friend for the holidays. We'll take him out for cheese blintzes or something. Look, Temple. If rent control ever phases out, this place will be snapped up, rehabbed like my building and become one of the finest addresses in lower Manhattan. Consider our visit . . . premature."

"Consider poor Rudy the renter an endangered species."

"Rent control has allowed a fringe person like him to have a home all these years. At least he'll have a couple years to look for new accommodations."

"If he isn't dead already."

"Temple, please! I've been trying not to think of that. I guess we have to knock. There's no doorbell."

"You're wearing the leather gloves."

Kit lifted her chin again, and her fist, and rapped three times.

Knock three times . . . no answer.

Several more attempts were answered only by silence.

Louie had, by then, had it. He meowed in an angry tone,

then wriggled his head and forelegs free of the bag. Two black cat paws pushed on the door.

And it opened.

"What a natural!" Kit slipped past Louie into the dark beyond. "Remember to say the cat did it, if anyone should ask."

Inside they were accosted by a pair of assertive odors: ancient, brittle newsprint and mildew. Temple and Louie sneezed in tandem. Somewhere in the dark, Kit scrabbled for a light switch.

"This reminds me of the conference room," Temple whispered, rather than whistled, in the dark. "And look what happened there."

Her answer was a soft click. A wan puddle of light spread on the ceiling like a stain.

Kit was a huge, humped figure vanishing into her own shadow down a dim hallway. "Wait here, Temple. Rudy! It's Kit Carlson. Merry Christmas! Are you home?"

Temple waited. "Louie, it's so cold in here. Don't they have heat?"

Midnight Louie wriggled in his carrier, but he didn't try to leap to the floor. Temple figured his nose told him what had been on that floor, and he wasn't going to follow an act like that!

"Temple!" Kit's voice from far down the hall sounded clogged. "I've found a flashlight."

Temple ventured down the dark hallway, cheered by a wavering comet of light at the end of the tunnel. The odor of stale Oriental food grew. She figured a tiny kitchenette lurked behind an ajar door. Another open door floated by; beyond it, she glimpsed piles of papers and books.

Kit's flashlight took wild stabs at illuminating parts of a tiny room at the hall's very end.

"This place is laid out like a classic railroad flat," Kit said. "Narrow and cubbyholed and homely. I don't suppose you're old enough to remember the Box-car Kids books?"

Temple couldn't respond before Kit answered herself. "No, of course not. Too young. Railroad flats. A boon from an indifferent housing authority and time itself. A rent-controlled throwback, a hidden refuse heap, but its residents' own. Rudy lived here. Smell the stale pot."

"Lived?"

"He's not here now, and I haven't seen any sign of a Santa suit about the place. I know he had his own outfit. Look at those baskets." Her flashlight sketched a mattress on the floor surrounded by wicker laundry baskets full of papers. "You wonder if he collected them for warmth, or content. We had no idea how he lived, we old actors lending him the occasional hand. We remembered him tall and slender and as limber as a weeping willow. He had a fantastic talent for mime. That made him a great street beggar later. Looked so pathetic. When we got him cleaned up a few years ago, and lined up regular jobs, he always showed up. And always came back to here, the place he'd gotten years ago. Do you think he's really dead, Temple? Or just . . . out on the town in his Santa suit doing another gig?"

"I don't know. Maybe we should come back by daylight to find out if he's come back here. Or maybe we should call the precinct and ask to see the body, sans everything."

Kit snapped off the flashlight. "I was afraid of that."

For a long moment, in the utter dark, she thought of Rudy.

Chapter 25

A Very Bad Joint

I have not been in a down-at-the-heels dive like this in ages.

I am sorry to report that people live in places across this great land in which I would not kennel a dog . . . and my opinion of dogs is well known. I am also sorry to report that there were times in my not-so-recent past when I would have been happy to have such a joint to cut the wind.

Speaking of joints, I am surprised that my two lady friends have not commented on the roaches around this place. I refer both to the six-legged variety, which skitter away from the flashlight beam as if it were a laser-sword from *Star Wars* and they were Darth Vader (given some people's belief in reincarnation, they could be), and the shriveled brown butt-ends of marijuana cigarettes. I would think that Miss Kit Carlson, given her vaunted flower-child lifestyle in the decade of the sixties, would have more than a passing acquaintance with such storied leftovers of the era.

In fact, I pat one atop a dresser so it rolls on the floor. Miss Temple gives the object the distracted frown of one who is concentrating so hard on holding her breath so as to avoid noxious odors that all her other senses are on vacation. Miss Kit favors me with a dirty look, and casually kicks the roach out of sight under the dresser.

Maybe she does not wish to further scandalize her niece, or is worried about Rudy's reputation, which is like locking the barn door after Native Dancer is out and has gone cantering on to greater glory. So while the ersatz Snoop Sisters debate the state of the missing resident's health, I am pretty convinced that he was the dead guy in the sky at the advertising agency's Christmas party.

What a way to go! Strung up like a stocking and cut down like a lump of coal. At least the condemned man had a last cigarette, from the odor my nose detected going up the chimney. He had a lot of previous ones in this place here, although the butts are cold and dead as a smoked mackerel.

Of course, if I now know for sure who met his Maker in a chimney, I do not know why. A guy from this side of Skid Row would hardly be worth killing for love or money. So it comes down to the current theory among the amateur set: Rudy was an unintended victim. Brent Colby, Jr., had been so successfully mum about using a shill in a Santa suit this year that this poor dude swung in his stead.

I wonder how the perpetrator feels about slaying the wrong Santa, but mostly I am not too interested in the state of his—or her—conscience.

The question is, will the murderer make another attempt on Colby before Christmas Day rolls around?

Chapter 26

Home for the Holidays

"Your cousin Bo will meet you at the airport."

His mother's voice had been expressionless when he had called her back with his flight times. He found himself mirroring her apparent indifference.

"That's fine, if I can recognize him. He hasn't gone bald and grown a goatee, has he?"

"Bo, oh no. He'll be at the gate."

Matt nodded, though she couldn't see him.

"I don't like to drive in traffic like that," she added. "At night. And the airport is so big and busy."

"That's fine, Mom. I don't expect you to chauffeur the ex-priest home in triumph."

A pause as flat as their dialogue. "I didn't tell them yet."

"Yet? It's been almost eight months."

"Yes. Well. An opportunity didn't come up."

"Great. That leaves it to come up at the holidays."

"I didn't think you were coming back."

Not "home." Back. Not "this year." Ever.

"It's true I didn't get home much from the seminary, or

later, when I was changing assignments. A priest's life is pretty demanding."

"I know that. It's quiet here at Christmas." He could picture her looking around the small, boxy rooms with their pillared forest of dark, unpainted woodwork between main rooms, a legacy of the twenties. "I haven't gotten a tree in years."

"I don't need a Christmas tree."

"We—the family—usually celebrate at Wanda and Stach's place Christmas Eve and then come back into town for midnight mass at St. Stan's."

"I know that, Mom. I used to live there, remember?"

"Not for a long time. I don't understand what you're doing in Las Vegas."

"You know why."

"No I don't, Matt. I know what you *think* you're doing there, but . . . it doesn't matter. It was so long ago. I've forgotten about it, and I'm glad that I have."

"I haven't forgotten. Maybe I couldn't until now."

"Until now?"

He grasped the speaker end of the telephone receiver, hard, and stared at the immensity of red sofa slashing across the shiny wooden floor.

"I found him."

"Oh, dear God! No, Matt."

"I know you don't want to be reminded. I don't blame you. But I was just a kid then. I need to understand."

"To understand what, at this late date? To drag out my disgrace before the family like a Christmas present? Again? And now you're not ever—"

His mother's emotions rarely stirred. Now she was angry. Not at the past, not at the man who'd beat and deserted her. But at *him,* her son, the only one who'd stood up for her.

"I discovered that it's not Effinger I don't understand," he told her, matching her agitation, as if she had summoned it. "I tracked him down, grabbed him, handed him over to the authorities. Then I realized what I really wanted to know was the other side of it. In Chicago."

"Cousin Bo will pick you up," she repeated in her deadest voice, the voice that he had heard for most of his three decades and counting.

He thanked her, wished her good night and hung up.

The closer he got to the center of the family web, the more he stood to lose. His mother disowned his quest, and his cousin Bo was a hearty Polish chauvinist who'd never left Sandburg's Chicago of hog-butchering, meat-packing plants that produced a lot of bologna to feed its teeming immigrant-spawn yearning to breathe free at ice-hockey games, over hot-dog vendors' fat-laden, steaming franks. And beer. Don't leave out the inalienable right to casks of beer for the boys, with the kitchen and coffeepot reserved for the girls and gossip.

It suddenly occurred to Matt that he was glad the hunt for Effinger had drawn him to Las Vegas, where almost everyone he passed on the Strip was a transient, where Milady Sleaze dressed up in denim and diamonds, where even the Statue of Liberty boogied at the ersatz concrete canyon of New York–New York—the theme hotel and casino, that is.

He looked at the red sofa, which might be a Kagan, and nodded his head. Nobody in the old neighborhood would have a wild and foxy sofa like that.

Matt carried his duffel bag up the connecting ramp to the gate at O'Hare International Airport. His left cheek was still icy, as if numbed by a dentist, from leaning against the window for the entire three-hour flight, watching the land change underneath him.

First sand and the rugged red-rock canyons of the West. A spilled sunset on the earth's dirt floor. The Rockies, magnificent in mobcaps of snow, skiers' delight. Then farmers' fields, flat and rolling, scribed as if by a giant compass into concentric circles of dirt and drifted snow. 'Twas not the season to grow even holly. Or mistletoe. There was never mistletoe at family Christmases; too pagan a custom.

He'd had a drink on the plane, despite being stunned by the four-dollar price tag for the dollhouse bottle of scotch whisky. His hands still shook a little. Facing the old folks at home would be worse than sparring with Cliff Effinger at a tacky motel.

He blundered into the mirage of faces looking toward the connecting tunnel like an audience in search of a star, blue eyes and blond hair in natural profusion. What did cousin Bo look like now? Six years older than Matt, almost forty, and never left Chicago in his life. Dutiful to family errands, even for his aunt Mira, who didn't exactly sit at the center of family affairs. But then a Pole will do almost anything for a priest; the Polish Spring had really begun when one became Pope one day.

The faces were expectant, but not for him. As soon as the press of departing passengers behind him eased, Matt stepped out of the flow and looked around. Maybe he had changed too.

The circle of waiting faces lit up in turn, and looked beyond him. People rushed together like colliding atoms, combined, and formed a new unit that walked as one down the long, echoing concourse toward the baggage-claim area.

He'd wait ten minutes, then head for the ground transportation area, though he'd hate to pay for a cab all the way to St. Stan's. He was couch-poor now, thanks to Temple.

"Matthi—" The voice began a greeting, then edited itself to a rule laid down by a firm teenager years before. "Matt. Over here."

Matt watched a form bob through a ring of waiting people. He tried to fit the lanky, cherub-cheeked teenager he had always thought so tall to the Santa-size roly-poly guy crashing through the circle of waiting people.

"You haven't changed a bit," Cousin Bo said as he pulled off a sheepskin-lined glove to shake Matt's bare hand. "Say, that sissy sheepskin jacket is okay for a

Chicago autumn, but it won't cut no ice now. It's the dead of winter here. Got any bags I can carry?"

Matt was mesmerized by Bo's bulky, quilted yellow nylon jacket and massive boots. His girth had expanded, but his flaxen hair had dwindled to a few slick strands across a baby-pink scalp. His cheeks were still plump and rosy, and the cold had singed his ears scarlet. A knitted cap peeked out of a jacket pocket like an elf's cap.

"No bags," Matt said, slinging his carry-on strap over a shoulder. "I can handle this."

"I don't know what you were thinking of, Father Matt." Bo swung into step beside him, reverting to the familiar form of address. Becoming a priest had made even indifferent older cousins respectful. "This is Chicago, you know. We have a reputation to keep up as the biggest, the baddest, the coldest, the windiest city west of Lake Erie."

"I've got gloves in my carry-on. I almost didn't recognize you, Bo."

"Put on a little lakefront property in the last few years." His gloveless hand circled on the quilted stomach, while his other hand touched the top of his head.

Matt almost expected Bo to start patting his pate in the children's game where the left hand can't differentiate from what the right hand is doing. Matt felt a little guilty about letting Bo stay behind the times on the state of Matt's vocation, but he wasn't about to enlighten him. Why blow the only respect you've had in your life from a bigger, burlier older cousin? The only time Matt had really felt a part of the extended family of Belofskis, Zabinskis and Geniuszes that surrounded his mother and himself in their isolation like the Pacific Ocean an atoll, was when he had announced he was leaving their transplanted Polish island for the seminary.

"How is everybody?"

"Yeah, you haven't been up here in a while, and not for Christmas for . . . well, I don't think you ever celebrated Christmas here since seminary."

"I don't think I celebrated it much before then either."

Bo cleared his throat and started stuffing fat pink fingers into the stiff glove. "You sure look good, though. Sis always said it was one of God's incomprehensible wonders that you . . . well, you know what women say, a lot of ado about nothing. She called you the Incomprehensible Wonder all the time you were off in seminary, but she got over that when you took final vows, or whatever."

Matt smiled to himself. Incomprehensible Wonder almost competed with the Mystifying Max. "Sis," he recalled, had been a placid, brown-haired girl with a wicked tongue that belied her buxom self-satisfaction.

Overhead signs warned of upcoming REST ROOMS, NEWSSTANDS, COCKTAILS and FOOD.

"They sure make you walk for your supper around here," Bo complained, as if his dinner had been slow in coming. "I got a parking spot close in, at least."

"Close" proved to be another long hike. The vehicle was a perfect icon for the Windy City, a pumped-up, four-wheel-drive machine rimed with snow and salt around the wheel wells.

"This'll do it," Matt commented as he swung his bag and himself aboard.

"Darn right. You got to give this climate something to fight with."

The vehicle lurched down the exit, while the passengers bounced on the upholstered captain's chairs covered in stiff vinyl. Matt wondered what a thing like this cost. More, he thought, than a red sofa.

Pustules of yellow light pocked the dark streets. Simple street lamps and headlights seemed sinister. Matt didn't bother to anticipate the route: he dug his lined gloves from the duffel bag and donned them, his fingers already stiff with cold. Despite having been run within the half hour, the Isuzu was cold, inside and out, on every surface: seat, window, dashboard. A heat-blower puffed chill air like the North Wind personified, while their white breath broke on the windshield like surf.

"You forget," Matt said.

"Especially in sunny Nevada." Bo grinned, knowing exactly what he meant, and glanced at him. "You got a new church there?"

"It's an old parish. Our Lady of Guadalupe. Hispanic, predominantly."

Matt judged his carefully evasive half-truths with the contempt of a disgruntled critic. He was beginning to realize that there were worse things than confronting Effinger. There was always that anchor of American life until now, that holy trinity of Mother Church, the family . . .

"How's my mother?"

"You know her, pretty unexcitable, not boisterous like the rest of us Polacks." Bo's eyes slid to Matt's face. "Of course, you're not a total Polack."

Matt looked at Bo's profile, at his blue eyes slightly bulging from their sockets, as if the fragile light blue were too delicate to see through without great strain.

Matt's brown eyes were unusual with blond hair, but he knew that blue is the recessive trait. Perhaps his father had not been pure Polish, or possibly Polish at all. He wondered which aunts and uncles knew the true story. They used to speak Polish in front of the kids, and would never reveal what they had been saying. Among the children of immigrants, adults had the secret language, not the kids. Matt knew even less of the language now than he had then. Sounds and syllables were familiar, but white noise. He had never felt Polish in the naïvely chauvinistic way they had. He had always felt different. Maybe he was half Hispanic. Maybe that was the secret that kept his father a mystery. Or maybe the son of an Italian or a Greek. Immigrants, even unto the third or fourth generation, remained clannish and close-minded, determined to keep their heritage undiluted. The Old Country lived on in the new, even as ancient peasant genes thrived in them all as they all strived to escape their humble heritage.

"Too bad more of the kids aren't home this Christmas." Bo's comment reminded Matt to ask after them.

"How old now?" Bo was a happy man, on solid ice.

"Stan, the oldest boy, is off at the University of Syracuse on a hockey scholarship. Big fella, you can bet. Stefania went to secretary school, only it's computers and word processors and such these days. She's got a job in Florida, of all places. And a boyfriend. She's visiting his folks in Nebraska for Christmas, and they'll be comin' here for Easter. Name is Torrence, her boyfriend. Good Catholic boy, though. No ecumenical wedding needed there."

"There might be one in the family someday. How old are the rest?"

"Krystyna, she's, uh, seventeen. And Colette's thirteen, gettin' tall. Scott's almost twelve, and little Heather is, gollee, eight now. Time goes by."

Matt nodded, trying not to smile at how the children's given names became more yuppie the younger the offspring. Old Father Slowik wouldn't have liked those more recent baptisms.

"Slowik still pastor?"

"No, Father Matt. He got a little . . . confused. Oh, he's still assigned here, but he doesn't do much but lead the rosary at funeral visitations. I hear they're going to send him somewhere warm pretty soon. Sad. We got a young guy now for pastor. Younger than you even. From Krakow. Says mass in Polish. One each Sunday, for the old folks. Gotta admit even I don't remember it like I used to."

"I think I'll avoid the Polish mass myself," Matt said, laughing.

"You should ask Father Czerwonka to let you celebrate a mass while you're in town. Be a treat for the family."

Matt only nodded, not wanting to make momentous revelations here and now. Not when they were heading to a bigger confrontation on the old battlegrounds, the house on Sofia Street.

"Man," he remarked, "that's a lot of snow. Funny how you forget about the realities of places you leave."

"Got a whole winter's worth by Thanksgiving. Five feet. Remember shoveling all that shit? I mean, stuff."

"No you don't. I bet old Father Slowik lets out some earthy strings every now and again."

"Well, yeah. How'd you know?"

"Priests are as likely to blow off steam in small bad habits as anyone. Now that his mind is playing tricks on him, he won't be as careful not to scandalize the parishioners, that's all."

"Really? Priests cuss?"

"Really. And Father O'Reilly in Tucson was in the habit of cheating at golf."

Bo laughed. "Yeah. But I don't remember you getting into jams when you were a kid. Mr. A Plus all through school. Mr. Clean."

Matt nodded. "Kinda abnormal, when you think about it, isn't it?" He kept his eyes—and smile—on Bo's profile until he got a return look.

His cousin's face went slack with confusion, uncertainty, a brief glimmer of something. His thick gloves lifted from the wheel as he flexed his fingers.

"I guess you learn things about human nature in the religious life. I dunno. We working stiffs with families, we kinda rush through life, wondering where the time and the money went."

"I never had much of either," Matt said, wondering if that were a blessing or a handicap.

He looked out the window at the huge, pale mounds of snow by the roadside, lit intermittently by streetlights so they seemed to be an endless exhibit of snow dunes, dimpled with brown sprays of slush.

"How long you staying?" Bo asked.

"Just past Christmas. I decided I owed myself a holiday vacation for once."

"Yeah, being the celebrant doesn't allow much time for celebrating. I hope you can tilt a stein or two while you're here."

"I hope I can do more than just tilt it."

Bo's blue eyes crinkled with humor. He laughed like a bear, hearty as all outdoors, and punched Matt lightly on the knee. "That's a good one. Caught me there. You know, having a relative that's a priest makes you kinda step careful."

"I know. You shouldn't do that, not with any priest. It's an isolated life, in many ways. Let them be a little human now and again."

Bo nodded, serious. "Yeah. There aren't that many priests left any more. That's why we had to go all the way to Poland." He frowned. " 'Course, they're a little old-fashioned there. Want to put the foot down on earrings on schoolgirls, and you know the howl you'll raise if the girls can't visit the Piercing Pagoda in the mall, even little Heather— Heck, I seen babies in earrings. And the boys are startin' in, like they're not *men* unless they got a pearl stud in one ear." He glanced apologetically at Matt. "Didn't mean to complain; we're lucky to have Father Czer-wonka."

"I doubt the state of people's ears has much to do with their state of grace. Seventy years ago the taboo was see-through stockings on flappers' legs."

"Now they have see-through swimsuits! Honest to God. Not that I seen-through one, or even seen one, but you read about these things in the paper."

"You should see Las Vegas."

"Yeah, Father Matt. I wonder about you being there. Pretty eye-opening, ain't it?"

"It's a city, like anywhere. Most of the people there live ordinary lives."

"What about living off gambling? Used to be we could all point at Las Vegas and shake our fingers, but now the lottery and the Indian casinos and bingo games are every-where. My very own mother visits the bingo hall once a month."

"I don't know, Bo. I'm younger than you. I don't have to worry about anybody's taste in earrings but my own, I—"

"Father Matt—you don't . . . I mean—Jesus!" Bo

wrenched his eyes from the freeway, trying to glimpse the other side of Matt's face.

"No, no. Not me. Don't worry. Some inconsequential things hold. I shall not wear my trousers rolled." The reference was lost on Bo, but Matt smiled to hear an imagined Temple twitting him: "another Nostradamus line, Divine."

Back to Bo. "I promise you I'll go to my grave without an earring. Remember that later."

"Whew. Everything's changing, you know. Hardly can figure out what to think or do any more. Unless you go to one of young Father Czerwonka's sermons. It's inspiring, to hear someone that sure."

"He's younger than I am, you say."

Bo nodded.

"Give him a few more years in America. He won't be so irritatingly sure any more."

"Yeah. It is irritating. I mean, what does he know about Mary Margaret and me never hearing anything at home but the kids squabbling and the dogs barking, and we're supposed to— Oh, God, that crazy fool Buttinsky! Did you see how he cut in front of me? And nothing but ice slick right here. Look at him, tooling along like he's in the right."

Bo's vehicle swept by the offending minivan, his fist punching a horn blast. "Damn asshole . . . By God, it's a woman!" His invective sputtered out from sheer shock.

Matt had tuned out the plaint of the middle-aged blue-collar-guy-who-meant-well, but-the-world-was-making-it-hard-for-him-to-understand-it.

Places had an attitude their people reflected, Matt thought. Bo's was pure Chicago Sandburg, brash and decent and worried he might not be. He would never have trousers to wear rolled or unrolled, only jeans or pants. He would never have a red suede vintage sofa. He would never have any rest until he died, confused but hopeful that it was all true, the bit about heavenly reward and what ye sow ye shall reap, and what he had mostly sown had been kids, and he was mostly pretty damn proud of how they had turned out, earrings or not.

Matt kept his face to the window and the dark. He was beginning to half recognize intersections and storefronts. He was getting closer. He was coming home.

Chapter 27

"Cold and White and Even . . ."

"You're making a big mistake," Temple told Kit when they were back at Cornelia Street, safe and warm and tired from hiking six blocks for a cab.

"Nonsense. I'm reporting possible evidence to the police."

"I'm telling you, you'll be sorry."

"I'm doing my duty as a citizen. I will have no regrets."

Tossing her head and assuming a Sidney Carton-going-to-the-guillotine pose, Kit dialed the precinct station number on the card that Lieutenant Hansen had handed around generously.

No one on the case was available, but, Kit said later, "A very nice desk sergeant took down my name and number and the fact that I might know who the dead man is."

Temple shook her head and went to gaze out the living room's glassy prow. What a view! If only New York had a touch more neon, like Las Vegas, that would be a show! Every building here was so . . . gray and staid. Not a neon flamingo in sight. And if some backstreet storefront windows offered a clutter of sleaze, you had to be passing by to notice it.

True, the city glittered in a starry sprinkle of little yellow light bulbs, the ones Temple called fairy lights. But the buildings were so high, the main avenues so wide and the other streets so narrow, that this modest dusting of glitz paled against the cold, wet-asphalt-gray of a December day in the Big Apple.

If so many yellow cabs didn't populate the streets, New York would be positively gloomy. She wondered if Matt would have a good Christmas in Chicago, where it might be colder, but at least it would be a white Christmas.

"Aren't you changing for bed?" Kit asked as she breezed by, lowering the blinds on the windows. "We don't have to retire right away, but we can at least get into our comfy jammies."

"Auntie, that is a loathsome scenario. Here I stand in the most sophisticated city in the world, and I am being urged to get into my jammies at only three-something P.M. by a female aunt. Couldn't we at least go listen to Bobby Short at the Carlyle Hotel?"

"One does not just crash that kind of venue. But why don't you want to change out of your street clothes?"

"Because we're going to need our street clothes very soon."

"I just told you; we're not going out this evening."

The phone wheedled for attention.

"Yes we are," Temple said dourly, "and it won't be a hot spot like the Carlyle Hotel."

"Yes?" Kit crooned to the phone. She always answered it as if she were in a play, and Noël Coward might be on the line's other end. "Yes, Lieutenant."

Kit turned and nodded significantly to Temple, one of those *"You see?"* nods that Hardy was so expert at bestowing on Laurel.

Hardy's smugness, of course, always meant a great fall.

"This afternoon?" Kit's limber voice stretched the three syllables into an incredulous four.

"Now? But—I see. Yes, I am very certain that I know the Santa Claus victim. He was a poor soul with no living family that we know of. A few of us looked after him, and he was at my place just four days ago. Well, I don't know. I've never seen a corpse before that wasn't still alive. I mean, my previous corpses have all been onstage. Yes, I've been to a funeral home or two, but those corpses are made up to look like someone else much better looking than the deceased. All right."

Kit hung up. "What a rude man. Can you imagine hauling us out on instant notice like this to the city morgue?"

Temple nodded. "I was trying to tell you. You can't call a police station saying you think you know who an unidentified corpse is. They get very interested, even if it is Sunday afternoon. And I think most morgues are called medical examiner's offices nowadays."

"Blast!" Kit began to look worried. "I don't really want to see Rudy in . . . that condition."

"Dead?"

"Dead and not prettied up. Have you ever seen a corpse on a police slab?"

"I doubt the process is that crude. Matt saw his corpse in a special viewing room."

"Matt Devine *saw his own corpse*?"

"No. His stepfather's corpse. The one he was looking for."

"The stepfather . . . or the corpse?"

"The stepfather. The stepfather just happened to be a corpse by the time Matt found him. Supposedly. Anyway, the morgue had a viewing room, so Matt was standing somewhat above it—"

"Like in a theater balcony?"

"Not that high, and not nearly that distant. He described a picture window with a curtain. When the curtain was drawn, he looked down on the body of his supposed stepfather, lying on a gurney."

"Euuuh. Not much showmanship there. Yank and gawk."

"Matt couldn't make a positive identification."

"Whoa! You just said the corpse was his stepfather."

"I said maybe. Matt said that death had . . . changed everything. The muscles relax, you know."

"Well, of course I know! I'm an ex-actress, we are used to visualizing. How relaxed? Jaw agape and all? Or bandaged shut like Marley's ghost?"

"I don't know. I guess you'll just have to find out."

"We'll just have to find out."

"I don't know what Rudy looks like."

"Of course you know what Rudy looks like. You met him right here at the front door."

"In Santa guise, remember? You're the only one who can identify the unadorned body."

"If I can . . . identify the body. Temple! Why did you let me call the stupid precinct?"

"I tried to warn you."

Kit gazed at her half-closed blinds. "It's so cold and damp out, and we've already been tramping through a substandard housing arrangement."

"You mean the romance of a railroad flat?"

"Oh, do shut up. I know this bossy lady lieutenant you talk about is going to be some savage, six-foot-tall amazon from Brooklyn, whose father was a pipe fitter or a stevedore or something."

Temple kept mum. Lady cops weren't all cut from the same mold, that was for sure.

"You will go with me, won't you, dear? I mean, you're the expert in these matters."

"Lieutenant Hansen would not be happy to hear that. I'll go, but you had better keep your mouth shut about my brushes with homicide in Las Vegas. I suspect that Hansen got enough dirt from Molina without your chiming in."

Kit nodded meekly. Even her hair seemed paler in the

lamplight. Going to see your first body was never a great pre-Christmas experience.

For once Temple blessed New York City's native attributes. The continuous rush of traffic through the overcast afternoon was like a mountain stream that is heard but not seen, distracting and even refreshing.

She and Kit arrived at an anonymously blockish sixties-built building at Thirtieth Street and First Avenue right off the East River. Tall, anorexic aluminum letters announced this as the "Office of the Chief Medical Examiner." Up the few steps they glided, under an entrance accented with blue tile work. In other words, they would hardly know they were entering a morgue, if they hadn't known it.

The reception area was empty due to the imminent closing. A man in a dark green-brown all-weather coat was hunched over the reception desk, arguing about them with someone they couldn't see. Kit and Temple retreated quietly to some chairs to wait.

"They're not relatives, but they saw the guy only three days ago. They say he has no known family. Listen. I know it's almost closing time. I'm on OT myself. But it's worth a shot. If the photo isn't a positive, I'll have to take them downstairs. Lieutenant Hansen is very anxious for a break in this case. It involves some highly placed citizens. You know the neighborhood; it isn't exactly the Bronx."

Apparently, the petitioner won, for the man turned and looked toward the entrance.

"Here we are!" Kit could never stand not being the center of attention. She waved and scooted over to him. Temple, mortified, followed.

"You're Miss Carlson?"

The man sounded surprised, but he couldn't have been more surprised than they were. Standing straight, he loomed well over six feet, making Temple and her aunt feel like pygmies.

"Detective Ciampi." He eyed them with equal dismay. His dark eyes hesitated on Temple. "And this is—?"

"My visiting niece, Temple Barr."

"She saw the deceased as well?"

"Oh, yes." Kit's eyes were disingenuous behind her enlarging lenses. She wanted an escort into the heart of darkness that she knew better than this looming, gloomy detective who had the face of a kindly bloodhound.

Temple could feel Kit's tightening fingernails through the ribbed cuff of her jacket. Kit was worse than toting Louie around!

"Better fill these out." He handed them clipboards with a form. "Since you're not relatives, you won't need two pieces of ID, but I'll want to see one from each. You can sit down, if you like."

He looked at his watch and then at the thin-lipped woman he had persuaded to admit them.

"Golly, Temple," Kit said as they hurried to the chairs. "I don't need to see Rudy's body *that* bad."

Temple checked her wristwatch. "Twenty-five to four. Plenty of time to do our civic duty."

Detective Ciampi tried not to hover, but he was too big to avoid it. He collected their forms and Temple's driver's license. Kit was humiliated to discover that she had no photo ID but her AARP credit card.

"I don't like to flash *that*," she confided to Temple when he had left them.

"But you can get one of those when you turn *fifty*. You're much older than that."

"Shhhh! Even the dead have ears."

"Having ears doesn't mean hearing anything."

The detective returned their IDs and something else: a Polaroid photo of the deceased.

He handed it to Kit. "This do it for you?"

"Is it good enough for identification, you mean?" She stared at the small, ruddy face. "It looks like him, but I usually saw him standing up."

"That's no longer possible, ma'am."

Kit cast Temple a pleading glance.

"You'll have to decide for yourself if that's enough to go on."

"No. No, it isn't possibly. I'm sorry."

Ciampi smiled sadly. Temple had a feeling New York cops had a lot of reason for that. "Don't be sorry, but you will have to see the body in person. She necessary for a second opinion?"

His eyebrows indicated Temple.

"No." Kit clutched Temple's wrist harder. "For moral support. She's done this before."

"Oh, she has." Ciampi sounded like he was humoring a four-year-old. "All right, ladies, let's get this show on the road."

He headed for the admissions desk, Temple and Kit following like orphans of the storm.

"That's interesting," Temple said. "I assumed visitor's badges would be required, but apparently not."

"We're not really *visiting* anyone," Kit complained, her voice low but vehement. "Not anyone who can talk back, anyway."

"No, but it is a restricted facility. This will be a new experience."

"I thought you'd done it before?"

"No, I've heard about it, from Matt."

Kit dropped her arm. "What kind of moral support are you, then?"

For answer, Temple thrust a tube of lip balm at her aunt.

"I don't want a breath mint."

"It's not a breath mint. It's a medicinal lip balm."

"I don't need a lip balm. My knees may be shaking, but my lips aren't chapped."

"Put some on your nose."

"Why should I put smelly Vaseline on my nose? I may be seeing the dead, but I don't wish to look like a kook while doing it."

"The medicinal smell will deaden the . . . dead smell."

"You think we'll be close enough to smell a dead smell?"

"I think it's pretty pervasive around these places, even if they have a viewing room."

"Oh. Is there a ladies' room—?"

"I don't think you want to linger here."

"But I can't sniff anything here."

"Good. Keep up the good work when we go inside and 'downstairs.' "

Kit only had time to give her niece a horrified look before Ciampi came to escort them past the reception room and into the bowels of the ME's office.

Everything was businesslike and sterile. Temple had a feeling their route avoided such areas of prurient interest as autopsy rooms.

The elevator to the basement was nondescript and silent. Detective Ciampi took the lead as they left it.

"I still don't smell anything," Kit whispered to Temple, having commandeered her wrist again.

"Good. Try not to detect any undertones."

"Undertones. Like with perfume?" Kit defied all advice and sniffed madly, bunny-rabbit-style, until her nose twitched. "Oh!" She reached for the lip balm in Temple's hand and jammed the open tube into her nostrils like an addict sniffing cocaine. "Sorry. Want some?"

"I used it in the cab."

"My. You do know a trick or two. I'm sure the corpse won't care that I reek of Mentholatum, and I don't have a significant other at the moment . . . nor am I likely to if the odor lingers as you say."

The room to which they were led at last was not empty. A stiff figure was waiting for them, but it was upright and reasonably alive.

"You're on duty? I've got an identification to make." Detective Ciampi pulled out a notebook to give the figure clad in the gruesome green baggies of an operating room some numbers.

The trio were led to a row of huge metal file drawers.

"Just like on TV," Kit whispered.

"Open the locker," Ciampi said.

And just like on TV, the attendant pulled one out. The unveiling was an eerie, silent process, revealing a body inch by inch.

Kit knew her role in all this and edged in front of Detective Ciampi's great bulk to see better. Temple did too. The skin was still highly colored; at least they were spared a ghastly pallor. Temple looked carefully. With the beard and accouterments removed, Santa had lost all his inflated good cheer. He was a thin, red-faced man, and the body beneath the fabric was slight.

"Oh, yes," Kit said. "I knew him."

Temple kept waiting for the "Horatio" that should end that line from *Hamlet,* but for once Kit was unaware of the theatrical antecedents of her words.

Her head tilted to a different angle, as if by altering her perspective, she might alter the inescapable fact. "Rudy Lasko. He was at my apartment only . . . three? . . . nights ago. He was doing Macy's."

"You're sure?" Ciampi's voice was an official monotone.

Kit nodded as bravely as any widow. In the overbearing light, her nostrils gleamed.

"Yes. Oh, yes. I don't know if the redness is from his Santa makeup or . . . what happened, but other than that, it looks just like Rudy."

"You have an address?"

She gave it in a firm, clear voice, adding, "I can refer you to several other people around town who dealt with Rudy recently. He was sort of our cause. We tried to look out for him. I guess we didn't do a good job."

Ciampi nodded at the attendant. The drawer slid shut with the ball-bearing efficiency of a greatly burdened file drawer, gave a final click and stayed shut; the man on the unseen tray stayed dead.

Detective Ciampi took Kit's arm to guide her from the room. "You ladies did all right. The reason most IDs are handled by Polaroid from the reception desk is that we had too many relatives screaming and fainting and the ME's office doesn't have the staff or space to tend to them." He glanced at Temple as they reached the door to the entry area. "Good trick with the VapoRub, or whatever. Tried it myself the first time."

Temple felt a certain undergraduate glow, but Kit was silent as they left. She even let Temple—Temple!—hail a cab.

They got the B-movie-variety driver, the veteran Brooklynite who not only spoke English, but spoke it continuously.

"Downtown? You sure you wanta go downtown? Lucky it's Sunday. And youse ladies know where you were standin' in front of? City morgue. Back up a few steps and you woulda been right in there with all the stiffs. Not a good place to end up on a Sunday afternoon, huh? All the way down in the Village, you want to go? O-kay. Open a window if this cigar bothers you. Drivin' a hack is a heart-attack special, I get what relaxation I can. You been to any good places in town? The Met? Guggenheim's pretty interestin'. What about the Statue-a-Liberty?"

And so it went. Temple was beginning to regard Cornelia Street as Home, Safe Home. She and Kit sighed in unison when they were back inside her condominium.

Kit spoke first. "I could use . . . a better grade of perfume. Quick! Where are the tissues?"

"On the kitchen counter where you keep them."

"Golly, Temple, you look silly with your nose all shiny." Kit slumped against the countertop. "I hate to admit it, but I've never been inside a morgue before. It's a trip."

"This is my first time too, and we barely penetrated the facility."

"You, a newbie? Can't believe it. Where'd you get that lip-balm trick?"

"I read somewhere that police officers use it when they have to visit the morgue."

"Yeah. Even those big, burly pros like Ciampi. I don't feel like such a wimp."

" 'Those big, burly pros' include Lieutenant Hansen. I wish you could have met her."

"Why should I want to? From what you've said she's Sonja Henie on acid-etching skates."

"You should see Lieutenant C. R. Molina of the Las Vegas Metropolitan Police Department. She's almost six feet tall."

"No! I guess women go to all lengths nowadays when it comes to career choices."

Temple giggled, and leaned against the counter alongside her aunt. "It wasn't as totally horrible as I feared. When Matt did it, he seemed really torn up."

"Men! They can't take the realities of life, like death. We women are tougher. Men don't have menstrual cramps. Speaking of which, I feel a figurative siege coming on. You want some brandy before bedtime?"

Temple nodded, now ready for an early retirement. "So that was Rudy?"

"Unfortunately, yes. Why do you think I need the brandy?" Kit kicked off her ankle boots and hopped atop the counter, then she stood on it to open the highest cupboard.

Temple babied the bottle of Courvoisier Kit handed down until her aunt jumped to the floor again.

"Damn!" Kit hopped from one stinging sole to the other. "I wish they wouldn't design kitchens for giants, or men. Yup. It was Rudy, all right."

Temple nodded, accepting the juice glass of brandy her aunt poured without comment. Kit was really shaken up if she was serving brandy in juice glasses.

"I think I recognized him too."

"You? How?"

"The eyes. Not that the corpse's had any expression, but they were the right color. He recognized me from your place the earlier night, and wanted to say hello, but didn't want to blow his act. That's why he seemed surprised to see me. Why should your niece be at the site of his next job? Wild coincidence, huh?"

"Happens all the time in New York City. You get this many millions of people together, and the coincidences will knock your socks off. It's uncanny. I noticed it when I first moved here. In fact, not noticing any coincidences is the exception to the rule."

They repaired to the living room, where Midnight Louie had beat them to the prow-facing leather couch. He was sprawled full-length, slantwise, so no human could sit comfortably on either side of him.

"Greedy guts," Temple said.

"Oh, but he's tired out. All those hard hours of work at the advertising agency, and then we drag him out to the seamier side of the city. Let him rest."

"Louie has dragged himself to the seamier side of the city many a time, believe me." Temple shook her head.

Before she could rearrange the big oaf, Kit had sat happily on the area rug and leaned her head against the couch seat.

"Let the big guy rest, Temple. I don't feel like sitting up straight right now anyway."

"I suppose sitting on the floor with a juice glass full of brandy reminds you of those wild parties you went to when you first came to New York."

Temple imitated her aunt in stretching out her legs and leaning against the couch seat. Between them, on the couch itself, Louie stirred. A big black tail slapped across Temple's face, then was still.

"*There's* somebody who's feeling no pain," Kit said.

Temple brushed his tail aside. Of course it didn't stay swept aside, but swung back to tickle her cheek.

"I don't know how cats can relax so completely," Temple said, moving away. "When it's people who could use a break. Especially after this afternoon."

"Indeed. Between visiting Rudy's flat and seeing Rudy himself flat at the medical examiner's, I feel like I've got apple jelly for joints."

"You do sound tired. It must be awful to see someone you knew pretty well laid out like that."

"That's the rub. I saw Rudy fairly often, but I didn't really know him well. None of us did. In fact, none of us knew him at all after he came back from Vietnam in . . . oh, must have been sixty-five."

"I wasn't even in preschool yet."

"*Pre*school! How baby boomer of you, Temple. We didn't have such decadencies in my youth."

"Apparently you made up for it later."

Kit frowned. "What everybody remembers from my salad days is *Hair*, the musical, and hair, shoulder-length or more, on guys, and psychedelic Volkswagen vans. That's the funny, freaky stuff. The rest of it was pretty bad. Race riots and war protests. I guess we were a wild bunch because we really thought it was 'eat, drink and be hairy, for tomorrow we die.' "

"So how was Rudy different when he came back from Vietnam?"

"Addicted to everything in sight, for one thing. Cigarettes, booze, pot, whatever they were smoking or sniffing or injecting in Alice's Restaurant, or is it Alice's Wonderland magical-mushroom medicine cabinet?"

"But wasn't everybody into changing consciousness then?"

"No! I never used drugs. Didn't like what I saw it did to people. I had plenty of imagination on my own. All the Vietnam vets were pretty wasted. It made you feel guilty for not having been there, even if you were a girl and couldn't get drafted. So you provided a shoulder for some sad war stories. Most of the vets stabilized and disappeared into real life, but Rudy never made the transition."

"So he leaned on you and your friends for thirty years?"

Kit nodded. "You had to have been there. We were all in the sixties together, no matter what role we played. They were violent, unsettling times that turned our values upside down. There hasn't been a watershed generation like ours since the Depression. We're all vets, in a way."

"But . . . here you are, perched in your cozy condominium, and there was Rudy, down in that rat hole."

"I didn't know. We knew he had a 'place,' and that's comfort enough in New York City. So the guys bailed him out when he got picked up for drinking and I found him jobs. He didn't strike you as an unhappy man, did he?"

"No. Quite the contrary. When I ran into him in the conference room, he seemed quite cheerful, like it was our little secret. Of course, to him the secret was bigger than finding Santa in the wings before his 'surprise' appearance. He knew who I was, and that made it even funnier."

"Rudy was great at getting into character, as long as he didn't have to keep it up too long. And he was so good with kids."

"I saw that."

"Maybe that's not such a bad way to die, playing Santa Claus."

"I've seen worse. A lot worse."

For a moment Temple saw Darren Cooke, a gun poised at his temple, and a forefinger laid over his on the trigger.

Louie lashed out with his tail, striking her face again, and she jumped as if shot.

This was it. No more messing with murder. It was invariably messier than it looked.

Chapter 28

Mother and Child Reunion

Strings of exterior Christmas bulbs outlined the eaves and many doors and windows on the street in southeast Chicago where Matt had lived as a boy.

The thousand points of lights emphasized the gridwork sameness of these nineteen-twenties remnants, four-square two- and three-story flats with basements, the upper stories for rental residents. The interiors would offer cramped bedrooms with odd angles, inconvenient doors and windows that broke up any wall space that had a prayer of hosting a couch or a bed, furniture jammed against long ranks of radiators painted in an attempt to disguise their homeliness. Dry heat would bake nosebleeds, split ends, static hair and cracked fingernails into your very DNA.

And outside during the winter, wet cold creeping up your sleeves and down your jacket neck.

Matt sat in the idling truck, reluctant to leave Bo's rough warmth. His kids were lucky.

"Thanks for the ride," Matt said.

"See you at my house Christmas Eve." Bo ripped off a

glove in the now-heated interior, seized Matt's hand in his hot pink fingers, shook it. "Nice seeing you again. Shoulda been sooner. Can't wait for you to see those little hellions of mine. You're looking to be the only priest in this and the next generation of the family."

Bo's last words helped spur Matt to depress the door latch and tumble into the subzero chill. Wind whipped a few flakes of snow into a pseudostorm around him.

"Thanks," he muttered into the frigid north wind, feeling his nostrils pinch shut on every icy inhalation. He slammed the door quickly to preserve the truck's hard-won interior heat.

"Say hi to Aunt Mira—!" Bo shouted in farewell.

The closing door cut off her name. Matt stuffed his right hand back into its inadequate glove. Acrylic-lined leather didn't cut it in this climate.

He stared at the two-story house, dark among its brighter brethren, lightless, only a faintly perceived glow warming the first-floor windows behind the drawn curtains. Still shuttered, still secret in a hushed, unspoken way.

"Holy Mother, be with us now . . ."

For some reason, he pictured a blue mermaid.

". . . and at the hour of our death."

The shoveled walk made a crooked, narrow, slovenly path, fit for playing a kid's game like "Pie," not for walking on. Snow pressed past the feeble modacrylic barrier of J. C. Penney pants and thin Sun Belt socks into the sides of Matt's suede shoes, encasing his feet in ice packs. Motorcycle boots. That was the way to come home to Chicago in winter. Ready to kick aspirations in the behind.

Matt mounted the five steps to the porch door. Screens had been exchanged for glass storm windows, and fine, dry snow had drifted against their corners, erecting lattices of frost.

Matt tried the aluminum storm door. Locked, as he had expected. Security was important to Chicagoans, worth a trek through the small porch's icy air to inspect the caller. Matt punched the old button-model doorbell, wondering if it still worked, or if he'd have to bang on the glass and metal door like a tramp.

Near the front door on the left (a second door led to the upstairs tenants' quarters), a light switched on, pouring through the square porthole of glass.

The brass lock and knob shook, then turned as the front door opened. Someone stood silhouetted by the warm interior light, eyeing his snow-swirled figure, deciding.

She minced across the indoor-outdoor carpet like an old lady in her heavy, lined slippers.

Matt felt panic attack. Why had he come? Who was this stranger? He had found Effinger, hadn't he? Who else mattered?

Rose of Memory, Mother of Forgetfulness . . . now and at the hour of our birth . . .

Now!

She unlocked the door, told him to watch the last, high step up (as if his muscles hadn't memorized it decades ago), led him into the light and the warmth, suggested he take his shoes off and leave them by the radiator.

Matt didn't want his shoes off in this house. Not yet. He did wrestle off the gloves and the sheepskin jacket. A Midwestern winter made sure that when you weren't fighting the weather outside, you were fighting free of your outerwear inside.

"What do you think this is, the Riviera?" she was asking, lecturing. "Those things wouldn't keep a polar bear warm. Here. Put your gloves and jacket on the radiator. They'll be warm when you leave, remember?"

"I've just gotten here and you're already thinking of when I'll be leaving?" he joked. Maybe.

"No! I thought you'd forgotten, that's all. Haven't been anywhere with a decent wind-chill factor for years."

"That's true. My assignments since the seminary have all been below the Sun Belt."

"Somebody up there must like you. In the seminary in Indiana, I mean."

He smiled at his mother's conciliatory joke and sat in

the first nearby chair. It had always been there by the door, the sprawling, square forties maroon-mohair model.

"Coffee?" his mother asked.

"Not this late."

"You? Getting older? Cocoa, then."

Cocoa. That cup of chocolate haven/heaven in a cruelly cold world. Matt nodded, relaxing suddenly. Mothers made things, tended things, made people comfortable. Sometimes even their own children.

She came back from putting on the makings and sat opposite him on the slightly sagging cocoa-brown sofa he remembered. His mother wore no makeup but a little lipstick. In winter it was colorless lip balm. Her monotone skin deadened the delicate color of her blue eyes and turned her hair, a compromise between blond and silver, into dingy yellow-gray. She wore it straight back from her face, in a clip at the nape, as she always had. It was just long enough to flare into pale barbed tufts, like porcupine bristles.

"Plain" would be the word to describe her, yet it was that untouchable plainness of Wyeth's Helga paintings. Frankly middle-aged and Old World, and still a girl hidden there somewhere.

Matt wondered how scandalous anyone would consider it if a senile painter from the Chicago School of Art painted his mother nude, in all her pleated, fading plainness. Compared to the glimpses of the pornographic film in Cliff Effinger's room, the Helga paintings were Madonnas of the Old School. He'd never looked at his mother as simply a woman before.

"Your ears and nose are as red as when you were in fifth grade," she noted, pleased. Something about him had not changed, some autonomic reflexes even he could not control.

"Fair Polish skin," Matt said. "But I got a little tan in Las Vegas."

"That'll be bad for you."

Eternal policewoman, Our Lady of Perpetual Health and Hygiene . . .

"Not too bad."

Something *ting*'d in the kitchen.

Matt let her go for it. He wasn't ready to see how little the kitchen had changed. But he studied the room when she was gone, as he had studied her when she was present.

First he saw the usual picture of the Black Madonna, that Polish icon, that iron doll in gilt and lace, in inadvertent black face. A Valentine Barbie with a soul of steel.

The same brown and yellow floral wallpaper climbed the little wallspace not covered by wide oak woodwork. Yuppie couples would kill for this unspoiled house, he suspected, as they flocked to old Catholic neighborhoods to rehab two- and three-flats into spacious single-family homes and enroll their precious few children in the few remaining Catholic grade schools. Safer, you know. Fewer drugs and gangs. An ethical commitment. Not perfect, but better. Not as good as prep schools, of course, and still dear, but perhaps more democratic for the twenty-first century . . .

"Here." His mother wafted the mug of cocoa before him like a domestic magician. Miniature marshmallows floated, pure-sugar icebergs, in a cinnamon-brown sea. Soon the heat would melt them into a supersweet, gooey cream that would coat his wind-chapped lips.

Food was the eternal panacea in dysfunctional families. Eat. Swallow whatever must be. Say nothing. Eat.

Matt sipped the hot chocolate.

"Divine," he said.

And she stiffened.

They were sparring partners, trapped in a ring from long ago, never daring to reveal weaknesses or strengths, fated only to keep dancing, dancing away from one another . . .

"Why did you come back, Matt? This year in particular?"

"Maybe I wanted a pat on the head. A 'thanks' for bringing Effinger to some kind of justice."

"He's been out of our lives for years, thanks to you. Maybe I didn't pat you on the head for that." Her hands were empty. She had made nothing for herself. That was the problem. "It scared me. The violence in you."

"Violence? Mine? All those years absorbing his violence . . ."

She waved a hand, dismissing the past. "I was glad to have the house to myself again. To ourselves again. In a couple years you were off to seminary, and I was alone. You won, and then you left me alone."

"You can't mean that Effinger was better than loneliness?"

"Not at the end. But, in the beginning . . . why do you think I married him?"

"I can't imagine why. Is loneliness why you put up with . . . that for so long?"

"No." She folded plain hands, no rings, undecorated by anything but the more prominent veins of middle age. "You're why I put up with it."

"Me!"

She refolded her hands, to keep them warm. "I didn't like your pursuing Effinger at this late date because he was the effect, not the cause. But I didn't want to go into all the old whys."

"Why not?"

She smiled. "Still asking like a child. Because some of them are inexplicable, even to me now, and will be inexplicable to you now as well. A mother doesn't like looking like a fool to her child. She's supposed to know everything. I knew nothing. You've always known Effinger wasn't your father, Matt. I don't understand why he was so important to you."

"Because he was the only father I knew. Because he was this stranger who had appeared out of nowhere when I had lived quite contentedly without a father, because he brought noise and fear and pain to you and us and to this house." Matt looked around, sure the walls and floors would creak in agreement with him. "I never knew why one day he wasn't there, and the next he was."

"He was not your father. He never acted as a father to

you, certainly not a good one. He was my husband, that's all. He was a necessary evil."

"Why? Why on earth was a lazy, ill-tempered, ultimately violent man who wasn't worth the bones in your little finger necessary to us? To you?"

"Because he would marry me."

"That's it? Everyone knew about us. It's not like we weren't news. I was about to enter kindergarten. We were stable, until he came."

She shook her head. "We were not. You thought we were, but we were not. We were nothing. We were a blot on the parish, a stain on the family, an embarrassment, and as you went through school, fatherless, the shame would have been rubbed in worse and worse.

"I was nineteen when you were born. In age. I was . . . fifteen, the way Polish girls are raised, kept away from the boys, hearing stories of Saint Maria Goretti, the patroness of virginity, the little Italian girl who was raped and stabbed but lived long enough to forgive her attacker. That's what made her a saint, not her pain, not her death, but her forgiveness of her despoiler."

"We agree. That kind of standard lessens women. It implies that they'd be better off dead than to be tainted forever by rape. It makes them property, not people."

"You think that? A priest?"

"An ex-priest. But I've always thought that. The seminary was strict; it was doctrinaire, but ten percent of the seminarians were women in my day, and more are enrolled now that so few men are joining the priesthood. The instructors didn't quite dare hold the double standard as high as they might have, and they were never as Old World as we were at St. Stan's. Actually, the seminary was very liberating for me."

His mother sat back, underneath the Black Madonna, an expression on her face he'd never seen before.

"Perhaps this will not be so difficult," she muttered. "Or perhaps it will be even more difficult, to make you see how it was then."

"I want to see," Matt said. "You don't have to make me. Just let me in." He set the empty cup of cocoa on the low table next to the chair, with its cheap, ringproof, baked-on finish.

"There's no point getting into your real father. I was eighteen with the mind and heart of a child. We met only once. I can't say what happened. I was too ignorant to know. There was chemistry. It felt like a miracle. He was very handsome. I can't say I loved him, or he loved me, but we were both dazzled for the moment. I never saw him again."

Matt absorbed the story, vague as it was. "Once, and I—?"

She nodded. "As if the angels were laughing at me. I'd heard the tougher girls in school, the ones who rolled their uniform skirts higher than the rest and who smoked cigarettes and worse in the rest room. They were . . . taking chances all the time, and trusting to shaken bottles of Coca-Cola to protect them. Apparently it worked, for I was the only one who didn't graduate."

"You didn't graduate? Not even . . . privately?"

She shook her head. "No. Everything changed. I was sent away to a very cold, hard place for girls like me to wait. We worked like drudges, cleaned up the delivery room even when the morning sickness made us vomit. Twice a week we were walked into 'town' for 'recreation.' The recreation was the townspeople's. They gawked and pointed at us. When our times came it was like torture. Comfort seemed to be too good for us. Most were persuaded to give up their children to couples who could have none. I was stubborn."

"My God, Mother, that was only . . . thirty-some years ago. What you're describing is some medieval penitentiary for fallen women."

"It was only thirty-some years ago, but it was like that. In far northern Wisconsin. I think the place is a hospice for the terminally ill now."

"Why did you keep me?"

"Are you complaining?"

"No, I just want to know. It would have been easier the other way."

Again she shook her head. "No. I've seen some of those girls since. They've had easier lives, but they're haunted harder. I can look at you now. Despite the past, you are healthy, well educated, you have spent most of your life serving others. I only mourn your priesthood because I saw it as a sanctuary for you. If now you want to live another life, go ahead. I just . . . don't like the past. Look forward, not back."

He nodded. "Then you don't disapprove?"

"No, never that. But I'm fearful. I don't want you feeling what I've felt for so long. An outcast in your own family. Your priesthood redeemed us, and especially you, as my marriage to that man redeemed us. In the family, in the church."

"But . . . he was worthless."

"He was a husband, and he was willing to marry in the church. As bad as things became in this house later, beyond it they were much, much better. I was able to go out and get work—"

"And needed to, with that lout around."

"Matt!"

He shrugged. She felt she had made the right choice, the only choice. She would never admit otherwise, but he wondered if she understood the effect of that unhappy domestic life on him, or the fears of himself it had raised.

"What about my real father?"

She straightened nonexistent folds in her gray wool skirt. His mother had never worn pants; in her youth, the fifties, Polish girls wore skirts and were not allowed to don trousers. Much less blue jeans . . . ! Surely, those rules were long gone now?

"I never heard from him again." When Matt would have spoken, she went on, raising a hand. "This you must never tell anyone. When you were just past two, a man came from the City. Downtown Chicago. A man in a very fine suit. He said he was a lawyer, and that . . . the family had learned of our existence because their son had died. In Vietnam. I was to have a settlement. A one-time settlement, and then I would have nothing more to do with them. It could be child support, paid on a certain schedule, or something else I wanted."

She smiled and looked around. "I asked for a house, just a two-flat. With a house I would have the security of rental income from upstairs, and whatever small wages I earned would be sufficient. The lawyer agreed, and handled everything."

"But you bought it here, in the old neighborhood, that was going the way of all old neighborhoods, into decay. No new start. No escape."

"There was no escape for me anywhere. And you were better off knowing the family. Bo and Mary Margaret hadn't moved out to the suburbs yet. The house was why Cliff married me. He had big plans in those days. I think he was sincere in his way. Only when his big ideas didn't work out, he drank and then he gambled, hoping to win a fortune, and finally he became . . . But he left. You left. The Latinos moved in, some of them, but the yuppies want to move in more. Real-estate values have escalated. You'd be surprised. I have the house."

She was the daughter of people who had been through the Depression. The house was everything. And it had given them stability, even as it had attracted the worst element in their life together. Matt nodded. He couldn't argue with her choice of so long ago.

"Was Devine really my father's name?"

She shook her head. "I never knew his last name, and the lawyer wasn't about to tell me. Devine is a name I got from my favorite Christmas hymn, not spelled that way, but I changed it."

"Christmas hymn?" Matt's memory pulled up no phrase containing the word "divine."

" 'O Holy Night. O night divine.' " She was smiling.

Matt, knee-jerk shrink that he had become, wondered if

she realized she had named him for a night, a single night, on which another infant was born, if not conceived. Or was Matt conceived on that night? His birthday was in September . . . ?

"What was his first name?"

"Who?"

"My father."

She hesitated. "If you don't mind, I'd rather not say. I . . . can't say it. He was from a well-educated, well-to-do family. It's not only the settlement that makes me think that. It's how I met him. In church, lighting two full rows of candles before the Virgin. I guess he came to St. Stan's because it was old-fashioned enough to have the plaster statues with the tiers of candles before them, and the poor box. He was going to war. He didn't have to, he said, but he thought it was the right thing to do, even though he had an easy out. I suppose that was college."

"And that was the night when . . . ?"

She looked down, to the bare, entwined hands on her lap. "I've said enough. I was another person then. You see why that man in Las Vegas doesn't matter at all any more?"

Matt nodded again. She would never understand that while she could suffer Effinger's abuse for the long-term good, a male child in that household could never be reconciled with it.

The blood feud went on, not over Matt's mother any more, but between Matt and Cliff Effinger. Over what had happened between them. Some wars you can't opt out of, as Matt's real father had apparently known before him. Those are the wars you fight with yourself before and after you fight them with—or for—someone else. Maybe turning Effinger over to the authorities would end this conflict. Matt would see how he felt when he got back.

"What are you going to do when you get back?" his mother asked, eerily echoing his thoughts.

"I don't know. I've got some major decisions to make. About my job. About other things."

"Have you made friends in Las Vegas?"

"Yes. Yes, I have. The volunteers at the hot line are quite interesting, quite admirable. And I have the wildest landlady; she's loaned me her motorcycle to get around on."

"Motorcycle!"

"Don't worry. Electra's in her sixties. Yeah, she rode that motorcycle before she lent it to me. And . . . I'm sort of friends with a police lieutenant."

"Any girlfriends?"

"Well, the police lieutenant's a woman, but I wouldn't exactly call her a girlfriend. My neighbor, Temple, is pretty incredible, though."

His mother nodded, smiling, politely inquiring, trying. "Temple." The name probably struck her as odd, if not blasphemous. "Is she a nice girl?"

Matt doubted that Temple would object to the term "girl" under the circumstances. "A very nice girl."

"Catholic?"

"Not . . . quite."

His mother nodded cautiously, smiling, but said nothing.

Chapter 29

"Chestnuts Roasting on an Open Fire . . ."

Temple returned to Colby, Janos and Renaldi Monday morning fully loaded for Louie (CatAboard, Allpetco cat food, cat minilitterbox), wondering what they would do today after the disaster Saturday night. Would it be business as usual?

Not if Kendall Colby Renaldi was involved.

While Temple had spent her time off tracking the sad life and sadder dead body of Rudy Lasko, Kendall had been doing something very different.

She met Temple and Louie as soon as the receptionist announced them. Her face was pale and her eye makeup merged with the dark circles around her eyes, but a bundle of manila folders lay in the crook of one arm, and her voice was brisk.

"Temple. I'm so glad you're early. We need to talk."

Temple trudged after her clicking heels to the tiny office. Kendall didn't even offer to help her unfasten Louie's carrier or take her coat. She shut the door as soon as Temple was inside the cubicle and began speaking.

"It's incredible that I didn't think of you sooner. Daddy has been playing the stoic, trying to dismiss what happened. He insists that the victim, whoever he was, was really the intended victim, or else the victim of some outré accident. But who would want to kill some nameless Santa Claus nobody knew was going to be there, except for Daddy and the man himself?"

"Well, the Santa substitute could have mentioned the assignment to a friend. But I happen to know he didn't have many. So, really? Your father believes the actor was the target?"

"He's just trying to reassure me. He knows what a shock this has been. First, my divorce. Now this." Kendall sat at her desk and tapped her pile of folders. "Daddy is simply too confident a man for his own good. If someone tried to kill him once, and missed, that someone will try again. We've got to find the killer."

"*We*'ve?"

Temple was feeling overheated and slightly sick in her outdoor clothes, so she unlatched straps and began to struggle out of Louie, Inc.

"It's so obvious!" Kendall was oblivious to surrounding distractions. "Who's right here, with plenty of experience with murder? You!"

"Don't forget Louie."

Kendall glanced at the cat, now struggling out of the unfastened bag. How symbolic, Temple thought.

"I don't know what the cat can do here, or what he did anywhere else. Certainly, he was impressive in alerting us to the . . . hanging. Daddy keeps saying, who would want to kill him, but he isn't looking at things as I am."

"And what are you looking at?" Temple was interested despite herself.

Even Louie leaped atop Kendall's desk and began pawing the file folders in an eerily purposeful manner.

"I'll tell you soon enough." Kendall clapped a hand over the folders and gave Louie a narrow look. Then she leaned closer to Temple and lowered her voice. "Daddy may not know it, but when Carl and I were discussing divorce, it came out that Carl can't count on his daddy to tide him over in the manner to which he has become accustomed, because poor old Tony's private investments have taken a fatal turn for the worse."

"How would that motivate the elder Renaldi to want your father dead?"

"Daddy is the head and heart of this agency. With him gone, the remaining two partners could sell it for a bundle and divide the spoils. Of course I would get Daddy's portion—if they don't kill me too—but each surviving partner's share would be plenty. This is a report on the agency's worth."

"What makes you think that Victor Janos would give up the business without a fight?"

Kendall clenched the fat file she was about to hand to Temple. "Because Victor Janos commissioned this report on the state of the agency on today's market. I got it out of the personal files in his office."

"Why would he want to bow out?"

"I'm not sure, but both these guys are in their fifties. Maybe they crave an early retirement. Daddy will work until he drops. Or *is* dropped."

"Wouldn't it be simpler for your father to buy out his partners if they wanted to retire early?"

"Both of them? At his age, it'd hardly be feasible for him to continue on solo, and solid new partners are hard to find. Besides, the name means something. Colby, Wilcox and Whatzit would be meaningless. Unfortunately, the partners are like the Three Musketeers. They've always been in lockstep."

"Why would Victor Janos want to sell?"

"I don't know. But I've never trusted the man, not since I was a tiny child. I always wondered why Daddy associated with someone so . . . rough. You can see his edges still need filing down; he's not adapted as Tony Renaldi has."

"What about the grand sixties experiment? Men from different levels of society united by an ugly war into a friendship that overleaped social barriers. You know: the sixties, everybody get together and love one another. Sometimes literally, from what I hear."

"Listen. The partners have been inseparable, but it's always been business underneath the socializing." Kendall's eyes narrowed again. She looked older and harder. "I was awake all Saturday and Sunday nights, thinking. That was a clever, difficult way to murder someone? Whoever did it had to know how traps and snares work. Weren't there tunnels and traps in Vietnam?"

"I'm only a few years older than you, Kendall. Don't look at me. I don't know." This time Temple narrowed her eyes. Narrowing one's eyes felt so Humphrey Bogart. "I do know that the victim was also a Vietnam vet."

"There! You see?"

"What do I see?"

"That it *can't* be just a coincidence. Maybe . . . maybe the dead Santa was hired to do in Daddy and somehow got caught in his own trap."

Now Temple understood how Lieutenant C. R. Molina felt about amateurs.

"That doesn't make sense. Your father was not going to be anywhere near that chimney Saturday night, and no one knew that better than the guy who played Santa Claus in his stead."

"The actor could have feigned being sick, then asked Father to do the chimney routine for him."

"Great idea. But he didn't. He went up the chimney and hung himself."

"Maybe he had a change of conscience. Maybe he had war flashbacks or something and decided to commit suicide."

"Thirty years later in somebody else's chimney?"

Kendall shrugged. Her haggard desperation both tugged at Temple's sympathies and exasperated her. Kendall had seen her father "die" before her eyes. The fact that the victim wasn't really him didn't lessen the emotional damage. A man had died by another's hand. Now Kendall sat shuffling files and papers, hunting for a motive and a killer and suspecting everyone around her.

"Could it be someone from the younger generation?" Temple asked.

Kendall looked up from pawing through the papers, and froze. "You mean . . . someone like Carl, my ex-husband?"

Temple nodded.

"No. Oh, we've all lived our lives under the umbrella of the firm, and I'll work here as long as Daddy's at the helm, but none of my peers really are that interested in taking on the agency once their fathers retire. I guess advertising was exciting back in the sixties. Television was still pretty new and there were a lot more daily newspapers. But everybody's into the Internet now. I can't think who else would want something, something about the firm, badly enough to kill my father. Except one of his partners. They were in a war, weren't they? They killed people then. Why not now?"

"What's on for me and Louie today?"

The abrupt change of subject startled Kendall into answering. "More mock interviews, lunch here with The Client. Nobody's heart is much in it, but Daddy won't let this account slide away because someone went nuts."

"I suppose I could get better acquainted with Victor and Tony. Anything you can think of to get me some private moments with them?"

"Oh, thank you!" Kendall grinned. "I can think up something." She pulled another file from a drawer. Temple glimpsed her own name on it.

"Improvisation is the name of the game in advertising." Kendall flipped through Temple's vitae as blithely as if it were wrapping paper. "Aha. Says here you're consulting with a major Las Vegas hotel on a new multimedia attraction."

"The Crystal Phoenix."

"Huh?"

"That's the hotel's name."

"Oh. Too bad it isn't something big like Caesars Palace or the MGM Grand. Anyway, new attraction equals promotional campaign. Who better than Colby, Janos and Renaldi for the job? We'll both look good if I bring you in as a potential client."

Temple shook her head, meaning agreement, but also conveying a certain skepticism. "Okay. I'm undercover for now. Bring on the murdering partners."

Temple learned a lot just from the way Kendall approached each man.

She began with Tony Renaldi, which indicated she suspected him less and liked him better. At his office door, she poked her head through, smiled and asked, "Got some espresso for a couple of weary survivors?"

"Kendall! Of course. And Miss Barr is the other customer?"

As smooth as extra virgin olive oil. Women in, coffee prepared, cushy guest chairs drawn up to the massive desk and Tony himself installed in the white leather chair that Brent Colby had commandeered Friday night.

The only snag in the scenario was Midnight Louie, who marched in on quiet cat feet and leaped atop Renaldi's black Lucite desktop.

"Why would he want to be here?" Renaldi asked in jest. "Black on black is no advantage to either." He stroked Louie from head to tail-tip, earning a thrum of purr and a further exploration of his desk.

There was nothing like a toddler or animal for bringing out the true temper of a man or woman. Temple settled into her chair to watch Louie put Tony Renaldi through his paces. But first she studied their common prey.

Tony Renaldi, with his commanding stature and silver-edged dark hair, fit the slightly effete chair much better than Brent Colby, the graying blond Yale graduate, who would show to better advantage against clubby hunter-green or burgundy leather. The tufted pale chair provided a theatrical frame for Renaldi's feline masculinity. Temple tried to picture him as a young man, a private in Vietnam. She could do it best by casting him in some theatrical part she knew, say a gang member of the Jets in *West Side Story*. A twenty-year-old Tony Renaldi would have the lean and hungry look of "yon Cassius," who lusted after Caesar's power. His edges would be sharper, rawer, the immigrant heritage more obvious and more truculent. He might get into barroom brawls with fellow soldiers, debate whose hometown was better, or who got the bar girl . . .

The Tony Renaldi of today steepled his manicured hands and smiled at Temple. "I assume you wanted more than coffee, Miss Barr, or Kendall wouldn't have brought you here. Some questions about the cat-food promotion?"

Temple could be a velvet glove too. "Not at all. As a matter of fact, Kendall suggested I see you about an upcoming project I'm involved with. I'm consulting for a Las Vegas hotel that's planning an update. We'll introduce a theme park and interactive ride. Does your firm ever handle that kind of showbiz thing?"

Midnight Louie leaped from the desk to the long narrow table crowded with memorabilia along the window. He threaded through the costly office art objects and framed photographs like a wirewalker, disturbing nothing but the dust, and there was probably damn little of that.

"Handle Las Vegas hoopla? Not yet," Renaldi answered Temple, "but we'd like to. Rather, I would. Kendall brought you to precisely the right office. Las Vegas has become very sophisticated about marketing its unique attractions in the past decade. A major New York agency like CJR could position your hotel project to shine in the international focus needed today. We have a strong Internet section as well as top staff in such traditional arenas as television and print media. I thought your field was public relations as well."

"Yes, but I'm a solo act. A mere freelancer. I'm functioning as idea person for the project, but new approaches are always welcome."

"Good. CJR likes to get in on a project from the bottom up. Who are your principals?"

"The owners of the hotel, the Crystal Phoenix."

"Ah. 'The classiest hotel in Vegas.' Clever positioning for a smaller hotel. Snob appeal amidst a blizzard of hype. Am I guessing wrong to say that the Crystal Phoenix will be upping the hype ante, all in the best of taste, of course?"

"Exactly. We want to keep our reputation, but expand to a new clientele."

Renaldi nodded. "First, we'll settle this cat-account question. Then we can investigate other matters. You wouldn't count us out if the client chooses a representative other than yourself . . . or your impressive cat?"

"Business is business. The two matters are entirely separate."

Renaldi nodded. "A mature attitude. But I don't think you have anything to worry about."

Temple truly hoped so as she rose to shake hands with him and follow Kendall out of the office.

"That was *good!*" Kendall whispered as they went down the hallway. "You're a real con woman. Where's Louie?"

"He stayed behind to investigate," Temple said airily.

Victor Janos, feet on his cluttered desktop, was hurling darts at a board on the back of his office door when Kendall knocked. He stopped when they entered.

"Come in!"

They did, and faced a man with a raised dart in one hand, ready to arc it right toward one or the other of their eyes.

Janos was not a needlessly cordial man.

"What is it?"

"Um. I brought Miss Barr to see you. About a possible Las Vegas commission for the firm."

"Las Vegas. Surface without substance. The perfect product for CJR. Show her in, Kendall, and then get thee to a nunnery, or wherever it is that young Carlo Renaldi would prefer you were, other than here."

Janos's crooked grin tried to be self-deprecating, but the attitude wasn't in him. Temple was suddenly aware that this was a man who had killed, and who could kill again, no matter how many decades had passed since Vietnam.

Kendall retreated without a farewell glance to Temple. She thought Janos was the murderer. She was leaving Temple to confront him alone.

Janos looked Temple up and down as if she were a commodity. "Sit."

Temple sat. "I was wondering," she began.

"Yes?" He expected a schoolgirl subject.

"Why you're number two in the firm name, and Tony Renaldi isn't."

He sailed a dart past her head. She heard it sink into the soft cork of the target.

"Good question." Victor Janos grabbed a fistful of shelled peanuts from a chrome bowl on his desk and began crunching. "Ever hear of a 'point man'?"

Temple shook her head. Damn Kendall! What had she gotten Temple into? Janos was a different man since the Santa Claus death: abstracted, bitter, mean.

"Point man. Guy who sticks his neck out. Goes first into a booby-trapped tunnel, a field of buried bombs. It takes guts. It takes stupidity. Sometimes, it takes a hero. But most of the time, it takes a shmuck. You know what they're gonna do?"

Temple shook her head.

"They're gonna leave me on point, and fade out. They forget where we came from. They forget where we were gonna get to. They forget everything but me, the guy on point. Perpetually on point."

"I guess I do know what a point man is," Temple said.

Janos's molasses-dark eyes dared her to be worthy of his time and attention.

"I guess I was on point when those two thugs jumped me in a parking garage, or when the guy who wanted to bring a whole neighborhood down had me trapped on the second floor of a burning house. Or when Savannah Ashleigh tried to have my cat falsely accused of impregnating her precious Persian."

"Come on." But the dart he held was poised, drawn back behind his head.

"I guess there are a lot of ways of being 'on point,' for a lot of different people," Temple said. "We all take risks. Maybe it's cigarettes. Or drugs. Or drink. Or AIDS. But you have the medals to prove it."

She nodded at the small wooden frames pocking his wall, each centered by a small metal object.

He swung his chair to face them. A regiment of medals from a war that many considered shameful and that was hardly dignified by the term.

"You know," Temple said, "when they keep referring to what happens in a war as an 'engagement,' you can hardly tell if it's a battle or a social event."

"Or a business arrangement." Janos spoke past the back of his chair, as the dart zinged home to a target halfway between two framed medals.

The chair spun around, and Janos dived into a desk drawer.

Temple stiffened, expecting to be confronted by a pearl-handled revolver at least, shades of Patton and World War II.

Janos pulled a bottle from the bottom drawer, and slammed it to the desktop.

"You don't know nothin' about war or medals or Vietnam, but I guess you got guts or you wouldn't be here. You wouldn't be talking to me like you think you know me." His eyes blurred. "All the women we saw in Vietnam were whores or grandmas with grenades in their hands or little tiny kids with strategic parts missing. Which one are you?"

"I'm not in Vietnam. I'm in Manhattan, and it's Christmas and Santa is dead."

"God is dead. So what?"

"Mr. Janos." He glanced at her with those tormented eyes so capable of dishing out what they had gotten, and given, thirty years ago. "Why are you second on the company logo?"

"Because I always did the grunt work, and the worst work, the dirtiest and the deadliest work. I wasn't smooth, not like Mr. CIA Colby. I didn't have the imported-oil potential of Mr. Renaldi. I'm not any good at the advertising game, because it's a crooked game, and it takes a crooked man. I was a lot of things, but I was never that."

"I believe you."

"Why? Why does it matter? Too bad Colby didn't swing."

"Do you know anything about the man who died?"

Janos shook his head, tilting the bottle into a glass he pulled from behind a fake set of gilded leather-bound books.

"Rudy was a Vietnam veteran too," Temple said. "Not a very successful one. He couldn't even pass as a success, like you. I hear he was in and out of a lot of VA hospitals, and was a panhandler for a while. Friends from before the war got together and tried to keep him together, but they couldn't do much."

"Rudy?" Janos leaned forward as if he were deaf. "Did you say Rudy?" For the first time he was really listening to her.

"Yes. Does the name mean something to you?"

Janos was looking beyond her, maybe at the dart board, maybe at the ghost of Christmas past. He shrugged, taciturn again. *All is calm, all is bright.*

"Kinda ironic, I guess. With Christmas so near. The dead man being named Rudy, like Rudolph the Red-nosed Reindeer. Funny, huh?"

But Temple didn't believe for one jingle-bell moment that Victor Janos would know irony from an ironing board.

Her mind modified the carol's words to fit her suspicions as she left his office. *All is calm, all is dark.*

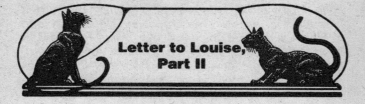

Being the Meditations of Midnight Louie in New York City

"Well, here I am again, maybe-daughter-dearest, watching the snowflakes fizzle against the window glass while my mitts hit the old keyboard like it was a bottle of the best, heaviest cream eggnog, fresh from Elsie the cow herself and her good bovine buddy of clan Glenlivet.

"Perhaps you would cut me a little slack if you could see how I have been wined, dined, and whisked around the Big Apple recently. I have had so many uniformed chauffeurs in the past few days, many of foreign extraction, that I am inclined to salute rather than make condescending small talk with them.

"Miss Temple Barr will not let me out of her vicinity, perhaps acting under the mistaken impression that this mother of all cities might intimidate me. Anyway, she keeps me in tender custody so I do not dirty *my pads on any dog droppings that have been un-collected by rude parties when I pass from the curbed limousine to the solid-gold revolving doors that lead to Madison Avenue office buildings. Miss Temple Barr is so impressed by what she calls the 'Art Deco ambience' of the gilt elevator doors here that she pauses every time we enter to offer contemplation and worship. Did I mention that the streets are paved with solid granite?*

"Despite the unrelentingly posh surroundings we enjoy, the only place these privileged tootsies of mine are allowed to land are atop the high-gloss mahogany conference table at the high-powered advertising firm of Colby, Janos and Renaldi, CJR to the cognoscenti.

"Even in this haven of affluence befitting a media spokescat, murder will out.

"Yes, your old man—I mean, your possible nearkin—is once again the first on the scene of a crime. In fact, I saw the murder weapon before it was sprung, but of course no one would listen to me. Somehow the taint of those street days will not wear off, and I am still regarded as an unreliable witness.

"This was a bizarre death by hanging, from a golden chain, no less. Although one can concoct a likely scenario for a freak accident, I lean toward the freak murder. I not only suspected something of this nature, I served as town crier in this case, scaling a steep roof to halloo the horrible news from the chimney tops.

"Those present, being human and naturally obtuse, mistook my alarm for a cute cat trick.

"I actually heard mention of the David Letterman Show as I stood there in full cry, my coat fluffed to emergency fullness.

"Needless to say, the imbeciles present soon discovered the error of their assumptions, led by Miss Temple Barr. (I do not mean to include Miss Temple Barr among the imbeciles present, which the previ-

ous sentence structure might imply, but I am not about to strain my mitts by backwards-deleting my entire previous sentence.) I am not to the keyboard born, you know, even if I am swaddled in royal-purple velvet to keep the cruel northern wind and snow from my precious hide when borne outdoors.

"Anyway, my investigations have taken me from the cushy seats of power and influence in midtown Manhattan to the Lower Depths of the Village, where the sad domicile of a wasted life offered insight and a bad smell.

"So I am quite the celebrity on both the advertising and crime fronts. I cannot say that the female lieutenant in charge of the case is giving my opinions the proper hearing. But my Miss Temple is there, and I can usually make her see reason eventually.

"As for the competition for the top spokescat position, I have had an edge over the 'other' candidate all along, even though the loathsome Maurice has had a fully effective politically correct operation since his indiscretion with the Divine Yvette.

"I have been gently twitting him by calling him 'one-ball' and more recently 'none-ball' in street patois. Oh, he snarls and hisses and growls, but he only undermines his chances at being selected as the most civilized, suave and sophisticated spokescat in the country. He is so predictable.

"I will not go into the new blonde in town. I realize that as a working woman you spurn females whose pulchritude is their ladder to luxury, fame and lazy days. But the Sublime Solange is a sweet, modest individual, and so shy she hardly seems aware of her stunning beauty. The Divine Yvette, Maurice's cast-off, is sadly disillusioned, but she is a wonderful mother to her scraggly quartet of yellow-bellied kits. I fear her unwed pregnancy will result in the loss of her fat television contract, but her heartless mistress, Miss Savannah Ashleigh, the same vicious bitch—

that is purely a scientific term for a female dog, so I am not using bad language here, only comparing the hussy to the species she most resembles, which is certainly not thine nor mine—who hoped to end my masculine career, has forsaken Yvette for the rising star of her unsullied sister Solange.

"I assume that among humans the word 'unsullied' equates with 'cannot be proved,' so am doing my politically correct best to see that Solange becomes a wiser but still winsome pussycat.

"Thus I prepare myself for an exotic Manhattan Yuletide, one brimming over with merriment, money and murder. If I have a minute, I will try to round up a trinket to bring home for you. We are, after all, possibly related, though such things are always difficult to prove, especially when there are residuals in question.

"Yours in mice, vice and lice on the run,

Midnight Louie, Esq."

Chapter 30

Christmas Spree

"Should I call you 'Father Matt' or 'Cousin Matt?' "

Matt eyed his driver, who was wheeling the lumbering minivan in and out of freeway traffic as if it were a bumper car in an arcade.

"Just Matt will do."

"Okay." She flashed him a nervous, yet fascinated look. "I'm not sure if your cousin's kid is a second cousin or a first cousin once removed, but I gotta admit I wasn't too happy about getting assigned chauffeur duty during Christmas break. At least you aren't the usual outa-town-relative type. You know, the fidgety spinster aunt who tries to tell you how short your skirts are, and how to drive."

She swerved the wallowing vehicle across two lanes of bumper-to-bumper cars to avoid slowing down behind an old Volkswagen bug that was only doing the speed limit.

Matt had to clench his teeth to keep his mouth shut. Now was the moment to distract himself with an ejaculation to a favorite saint, such as *Blessed Saint Christopher, keep us alive for the next ten minutes!*

"I must admit," Matt said, vainly feeling for a handhold on the van door, "that when I asked Bo if anyone could be spared to take me around, I didn't expect a teenage chauffeur."

"*Teenage,* how gross. I'm almost out of high school, for God's sake. I can't wait to turn twenty, then nobody can refer to me by that disgusting term."

"Sorry."

"Oh, I didn't mean *you!* You've been off with all those priests in the rectory. It's not your fault you don't know what drives people my age nuts."

Seventeen, Matt thought. This was going to be a long afternoon.

"What do I call you?" he said.

"Thanks for asking. Not Krystyna with all the *y*'s! Too groady! Krys is fine. Some people think it's short for Krystal, which is cool. So what do you want to do at the mall?" she asked, switching lanes to beat a huge black pickup truck to the exit lane. "Dumb redneck!" Her eyes flashed venom into the rearview mirror. "These Southerners can't drive on ice and snow worth spit. What do you drive at home? And where is home?"

"Las Vegas."

"Really? Cool. Do they have churches there?"

"More than most cities. And a whole flock of wedding chapels."

"They hardly count as churches."

"They do for the couples who get married there."

The mall, a Monopoly-block array of massive beige rectangles, loomed like bunkers on the minivan's right. Matt didn't know why anyone called these motorized behemoths "minivans"; they were roomy enough to host camping parties of Cub Scout packs.

"So you drive a Civic or something in Las Vegas?" Krys asked as she turned into the parking lot.

"No. A motorcycle."

"A motorcycle?" She jerked her head to see if he was kidding.

"Watch out for that Blazer!"

"Oh. Yeah."

Ignoring the blare of an angry horn, she scooted the van down an aisle lined with parked cars, then suddenly swerved into an empty space that had been hidden by a massive custom van until they were practically past it.

"Do you really drive . . . ride a motorcycle?" she asked.

Matt nodded, pulling his gloves out of his jacket pockets, and amused by what it took to impress the almost-postteenager these days. "It's on loan from a friend."

"What kind? A Harley? Hardly."

"It's a British make you wouldn't know. Hesketh."

She shook her head. "What color is it?"

"Silver."

"Cool." Krys tossed the van keys into the tiny purse she wore slung slantwise over her bulky jacket and hopped out of the vehicle.

Matt climbed out in his own good time, beginning to appreciate the ease of getting onto a motorcycle versus entering and exiting one of these sliding-door rolling warehouses.

"Does it go fast?" she asked over the van rooftop.

"The motorcycle? Sure, if I let it."

"Oh, that's too cool. You're the only priest I know who rides a motorcycle."

Matt had come around to the driver's side. Bo's daughter was a deceptive five feet eight inches tall, a big girl with a mature look way beyond her behavior. Her easy energy and naïve enthusiasms were going to wear him out in an hour, but he couldn't spend the entire afternoon lying to her by omission.

"Listen, Krys. Nobody else knows this yet, but I left the priesthood several months ago. And although I'm sure some priests do ride motorcycles, I'm not one of them and they don't ride Hesketh Vampires."

"Vampires? Your bike is called a Vampire? Why?"

"It, um, howls when the engine gets up to speed."

"Oh, I want one! Too cool. So."

She clicked the control to lock the van's many doors, then slid him a wary glance. In it, Matt could read speculation about the stir his news would cause in their thoroughly Catholic family.

"I never heard much about you when I was growing up," she said, turning and maneuvering over the ice-rutted parking lot with mountain-goat delicacy. Matt fell into the same surefooted step with her. "Just that you were a priest, the only priest the whole darn family has produced. They kept looking at my brothers and sisters and me like one of us should be a sacrificial virgin or something." Krys glanced down, then the toe of her flimsy ankle boot stamped flat a ruffled rut of snow. "I'm getting read the riot act just for thinking I might not want to go to a Catholic college."

At the mall entrance, Matt opened one of a rank of glass doors for her. "That's not exactly written into the Council of Trent. There are other good schools. Still, you can't beat the quality of education."

He had forgotten about store vestibules in the north. Here, out of the wind, everyone paused to stamp snow clods off their boots, and stuff their pockets with the gloves and scarfs that would soon become suffocatingly hot inside the mall, then advance through a second barrier of glass doors.

"What exactly do you want here?" Krys asked as he ushered her through a second door.

For a moment, Matt paused, interpreting her question in the global sense. What *did* he want here in Chicago, among this family of strangers? Then he realized that her world was the here and now, and at this moment, that was the mall.

"Presents for my mother. I brought the usual boxes of candy, but I wanted to get her something more personal. It's been a long time since I was home for Christmas." He smiled at Krys. "Actually, I'm kind of glad you're my escort today. I could use a personal shopper."

"You got it! I adore shopping, especially when it isn't with my money, which there's darn little of." She studied him again. "I thought the minute I saw you that you didn't look like a priest. You don't even look like the rest of the family."

He wasn't going to touch that one. "I look like my mom, don't I?"

"A little, maybe, but she's so—" Krys visibly reined in her tongue.

They paused in front of a huge, two-sided display of the mall's layout of stores.

"I know what you mean about Mom. That's what struck me," Matt said. "The old house is so plain and dreary, all the colors faded to the same nothing tone. I'd forgotten how it looked here in winter, not like the Christmas cards with fresh snow mounding over everything. Old snow gets packed with dirt and cinders and turns into ice, like a comet."

"All the houses in our old neighborhood are like that. They're old and everything in them is old-fashioned. But I just don't like the winter, period. That's why I'd like to go to school someplace on the West Coast."

"That kind of atmosphere can get old in its own way," he warned her. "Anyway, I was thinking about getting Mom something pretty to wear, but you know her better than I do, and you know what women would like way better than I would."

"Yeah." She eyed him, laughed, blushed, then met his glance again. "I can do it. Personal shopping, I mean. But your mom's a tough case. Aunt Mira doesn't seem to have any preferences, for anything."

"Well, I know what we can't get her: nothing . . . too radical. Too bright, or what she'd consider too young. With a restaurant hostess job I'd think clothes would be more of a concern, but—"

"Look at where she's a hostess! A neighborhood family-style place that's been there for years. Nobody under forty goes in there," Krys added with intense disdain.

"Well, then take me to where people under forty go to buy nice things for people over forty."

"Gee, I don't know that territory either. Matt." Obviously, using the first name of an older cousin, and older ex-priest cousin, was a kick. Krys (maybe short for Krystal) frowned at the colorful blocks representing various stores. "I guess I'll just take you where I never go! What's your budget?"

"I have no idea. But I do have a credit card."

"I *love* credit cards!"

"With a very modest credit limit. You don't build up an impressive financial history in my former line of work."

"No, I guess not."

They joined the streaming aggregates of people cruising the mall's brightly lit but still vast and institutional corridors, despite the plastic fir boughs and Christmas lights frosting shopfronts, escalators and the high glass atrium ceilings.

A medley of Christmas music filled the air above them, and overpowering bursts of scented candles exhaled from shop entrances.

"Crazy, huh?" Krys obviously didn't expect an answer. "Okay. Here's Chessey's. Let me do the talking. I'm sure these witchy old bats will jump on us the minute we enter, they're so anxious to make a sale."

Krys angled toward a shop whose windows featured mannequins in expensive dressy suits, quite different from the merchandise-crowded, glitzy shops bristling with holographic accessories and lots of imitation black leather that drew her like a magnet.

In her taut black tights—leggings, Matt had seen them called now—and the short bronze vinyl anorak, Krys resembled a gilded pumpkin on stilts, a kind of Cinderella's coach before the fairy godmother had gotten to it.

The middle-aged saleswoman who headed toward them with lacquered hair and heavy gold jewelry clanking like Marley's chains would probably have glowered Krys out of the shop, had she not been accompanied by that moving target in any mall: a man who needed to buy something for a woman for Christmas. In other words, a man who had money and needed help spending it.

"May I assist you?" the saleswoman crooned in the impeccable grammar that always seemed so phony.

Matt wasn't used to such catering, but Krys acted as if she'd been thirsting for it all of her life.

"Yes, please. We need something for an older lady. Nothing too frilly, too glitzy or too impractical, but pretty."

"A relative?" the saleswoman asked.

"My mother," Matt put in.

"Oh, good. Is her coloring similar?"

He nodded.

"And she *can't* be much over forty-five—" The woman's permanently smiling face was turned to Matt but her eyes wandered to Krys with a certain admonishment. "Older lady" was hardly the phrase for one of her and Matt's mother's age, the tone implied. "Had you any idea what you wanted? A dinner suit? A good blazer?"

Krys had been looking around like a kid in a whirligig factory. "A blouse!" she said triumphantly to Matt, lifting her eyebrows in search of approval.

He nodded. "Great idea."

"But nothing polyester," Krys declared sternly.

"We don't carry any polyester," the woman said. "This way."

They wove through racks and glass cases, Matt catching glimpses of foreign glitters. He felt like he was plunging deeper into a jungle of feminine snares, alien and intimidating.

"Her size?"

Matt and Krys exchanged a helpless glance. "Medium," he suggested.

Medium would never do for a salesperson at a finer store. "How tall is she?"

Matt nodded at Krys.

"And the same size?"

He was forced to consider his cousin's daughter as a womanly form. Given her sturdy frame, she probably played ice hockey as well as lusted after motorcycles and the mock-leather bustiers he'd seen highlighted in the teen-punk shop windows.

"Slighter build," he said.

The saleswoman eyed Krys significantly.

"I'm an eleven. Or sometimes a thirteen," she confessed as if forced to.

"Ten, then. For your mother, sir."

They were led to a rack of silky garments, and then the saleswoman left them to the private misery of selection and price comparison.

"Anything too fancy will turn her off," Matt said.

Krys nodded. "I'll try not to swoon over the cut velvet and laces, or the absolutely dishy snakeskin metallic print over there."

Matt eyed the reptilian blouse in question. "Thank you. Well, we know what *not* to get her now."

"I guess I'm useful as a warning sign: bad taste posted here."

"Not true. But you're younger and can get away with it. Besides, Mom seems too subdued. I want something that'll make her want to wear it."

Krys pulled out an ivory satin blouse dripping old-fashioned crocheted lace. She ran her fingers down the silky sleeve to the frilled cuff, then lifted a small white tag and wordlessly showed it to him. Ninety dollars.

Matt nodded. "For the right blouse." But secretly, he was shocked.

They made a round of the circular stand. "No prints," Matt said. He had read somewhere once, long ago, that Jackie Kennedy only wore solid colors. His mother, he figured, shared the same rigorous taste.

They debated at last between the ivory blouse and a gray one with white satin ribbon detailing. Still muted, neutral, recessive colors, Matt thought with dissatisfaction. She needed . . . he wanted . . . something that would lure her into the light of the present day. Something for rebirth, something she couldn't resist even as she suspected it was a trap.

His eyes paged through the fifty-some blouses circled like fashion soldiers with their backs to the wall. And then he spotted it . . . a swell of color like an ocean wave.

He reached in, drew the hanger off the rod.

"It's . . . pretty." Krys sounded surprised.

He held it up to the light. A modest, feminine article that no woman he knew would wear—not Temple, or Electra, or Sheila at work, or Carmen Molina . . . or especially the woman who called herself Kitty. Full sleeves, a tailored softness and yet a sense of feminine frill here and there, more felt than seen.

Krys held it up against herself, a question on her intent, girlish face. Then she frowned. "You have brown eyes. Your mother's are blue."

He nodded, took the blouse from her and smiled like a saint who had found salvation. For the particular blue of this blouse vaguely alternated between aqua and powder-blue, like pictures he'd seen of Caribbean waters. It was a rather indescribable blue, except that he had defined it long ago, and knew it was the one color his mother could not resist liking, from years of preconditioning.

Chessey's had surprised him, and itself, by carrying one

blouse, size ten, in true Virgin Mary Blue. His mother was lost.

Krys had been impressed. "A hundred and ten dollars," she whispered loud enough for every passerby to hear when they rejoined the mall traffic, a fancy paper shopping bag lined with colored tissue dangling from Matt's hand like a door prize. "You are a big spender for a religious guy."

"Where do you think all the bingo money went for all those years?"

Krys giggled, reveling in irreverence. The favorite priest was always the least priestly.

"Matt, this is wild, and I don't know if you can afford it, but I know something that would be a knockout on your mother, with this blouse and just plain anytime. I'd . . . forgotten somehow that she has those gorgeous pale-blue eyes." Krys pulled his free hand, as if he were a reluctant parent, to lead him into a fine jewelry chain store that occupied an entire corner space. "Can we go in here, huh?"

He nodded. It was fun to edge someone else, and himself, into the light. To be edged into the light, even if it was only the commercial spotlight of Christmas. He began to understand Temple's self-appointed mission.

His mother had been like this before he had loomed on her horizon like a nightmare, he realized. Every woman had. Temple had, and still kept a bit of it as a shield against the disappointments of time. Carmen Molina had been here, or had hoped to be, once when she was very young, but now she was busy interring that memory behind the perimeters of her profession. How would she deal with a growing daughter if she denied her inner sprite? Maybe he should write a self-help book: *Finding Your Inner Sprite.* Or was that just a secular pseudonym for the Holy Ghost? he wondered.

But inside the promising store, goods lay in dishearteningly similar ranks within their well-lit cases. Same designs, different strokes. Red stones in one, green in another, royal blue in yet another.

Krys skipped the precious rubies, emeralds and sapphires whether genuine or "man-made," leading him to a case displaying jewelry set with purple, amber and blue stones.

"I can help you? Sir. Miss?"

The clerk here was male and from the Indian subcontinent, but his smile was as genuine as the man-made diamonds' glitter was false.

Krys nodded, pointing to the blue side of the display case. "Can we see some earrings, clip style?" Her hazel eyes rapidly consulted Matt, then she continued. "Something elegant."

The salesman didn't hesitate, but pulled out velvet case after velvet case, until six were lined up on the glass countertop.

"The finest blue topaz, in vermeil." His hand presented them as one would introduce a visiting dignitary to a head of state. The clerk ebbed away to a decent distance, so they could discuss prices in private.

"Ver-meal?" Matt asked.

"Gold wash over silver," Krys replied with expert intensity. "Great look, cheaper price. See! Only seventy-eight dollars."

Matt loved the way she threw the word "only" around at a shopping mall. He was feeling like a weird cross between a harried father and a sugar daddy. But he had the credit card, and the clerks were only too happy to press it between the carbon-backed pages of a sales slip as if it were a memento from the high school prom.

Krys tried on each earring, describing merits and flaws. "Pinches." "Too overbearing." "I'd adore these, but your mother—?" "Very classy." "Too *matron*ly." Whether for herself or his mother she never said.

The earrings they selected were large blue topaz teardrops surrounded by silver with gold accents.

As they—*he* was.paying for it, or rather, the card was, Matt noticed a Plexiglas stand by the register displaying cards of sterling silver earrings and pins. He glanced at Krys's ears with their discreet, for nowadays, earrings in triplicate.

He turned the display piece until an amethyst-set ornate cross came to the fore. "You want a souvenir?"

Her eyes widened, then emptied in wonder. "Souvenir?"

Matt took down the cross and put it on the counter. "Add this in," he told the clerk. It was only twenty-eight dollars. His sense of proportion had magnified.

Krys was all eyes. "For me, really?"

"I appreciate your help today. Besides, you can tell your friends you got the cross from an ex-priest who rides a Vampire motorcycle."

"Oh, cool. Oh, way, way, way too cool. Can I wear it now?"

Since no one disagreed, she left the shop with the amethyst cross swinging in her right ear.

"Does it bother you," she asked breathlessly, "crosses being such popular jewelry now? Are we being too shallow?"

"Those 'Y-shaped' necklaces in the Sunday-paper department-store ads are nothing but rosaries. Maybe it's a religious renaissance, huh?"

"I don't know. They're just . . . cool." She fingered the small box in the tiny bag she carried, with the blue topaz earrings. "She can wear these with gold or silver," Krys explained as they melded with the still-milling shoppers. "Did you see how the Indian guy at the shop thought these were for me when I tried them on? He took us for a couple, can you believe it?"

"No. I'm too old for you."

"Hey. You can't be over . . . twenty-seven, right?"

"Wrong."

"What are we, anyway? We never did decide. First cousins or what?"

"In any case, it doesn't matter."

She stopped to pout.

"Stop flirting with me."

"I *am not!*"

"Catholic girls always want to flirt with a priest, or an ex-priest. It's a stage."

"A stage! You act like I'm a teenager, or something. Hey, it's almost three o'clock. Can we eat? I'm beat and I'm starving!"

"Me too. Sure."

She ordered a chili burger, jumbo fries and fried jalapeño cheese sticks. Matt almost got indigestion from watching her shovel every bit of it down.

The fast-food restaurant rang with the noise of raised voices, the cash register, transitory dishes and silverware, and the passing bustle in the mall traffic lanes alongside it.

Matt nursed a beer after nibbling on a club sandwich and watched her eat.

"This has been fun, after all!" Krys said, chewing happily. "You're way cooler than I thought you'd be. And I know your mother will love her stuff."

She knew more than he did, but he smiled anyway.

"My family's so stuffy! We don't even put up a mistletoe sprig for Christmas at our house."

"I remember. But I also remember your family having a beautifully carved, old-country crèche scene."

She made a disparaging face. "I'm going to get a mistletoe sprig this year and nail it up and then I'm gonna catch you under it." She had a glob of ketchup on her chin.

"I don't think so."

"Can I have a sip of your beer?"

"No."

"Come on. It's not like I've never drunk it before."

"I'm sure you have, and I'm sure you will again, but it's illegal here."

She finished her fries and finally wiped her mouth, inadvertently fixing the ketchup chin. "I want to find something for a friend of mine. Have we got time?"

"Sure. You're the one who's giving up her Christmas break."

She shrugged modestly and looked pleased.

This time they wandered into the anchor department stores' menswear sections. Matt, used to shopping discount chains for the cheapest of everything, was amazed again by the profusion of unusual and costly things. Sueded silk flight jackets, leather vests and dusters, designer suits.

"I know ten guys who would wear this," he noted, indicating an iridescent sharkskin suit that retailed for close to a thousand dollars.

"How do you know guys like that?"

"They're brothers, sharp dressers, and good Italian Roman Catholics except at confession time, and they live in Las Vegas."

"Wow. What are you going to wear for Christmas at my house?"

"What I brought." He glanced around the crowded area. "Maybe I could use a heavier sweater. It's colder here than I remembered, and I didn't have much notice that I was coming up."

But the sweaters were close to two hundred dollars a pop, and all had pictures woven into their patterns, ski chalets or St. Bernards or something Matt didn't care for.

Krys appeared from behind a rack of London Fog raincoats, apparently a perennial gift item.

"Look at this!"

She held up a brown velvet blazer.

"Depends who you're getting it for."

"You!"

"I'd never wear a thing like that. And you don't have the money."

"But you do. And I'm a personal shopper, right? You're giving your mother all that fancy stuff. She might go for it more if you were dressed for the occasion."

"A velvet coat? I'm not a . . . huntsman or whatever."

"Listen. Brown is the new neutral and velvet is very In. And it's on special. Only one forty-eight. What's your size?"

"Not one forty-eight. Put it back."

"Oh, please. I think it'd look divine on you."

"Where would I wear a thing like that?"

"Las Vegas? Use your imagination."

A salesman had overheard the classic male/female fashion debate and had scuttled over faster than a sharkskin leech.

"Marvelous new fabric, sir. Stain-resistant. The young lady is correct; brown is the must-have neutral of the year for both genders. A forty regular, I see. It also comes in eggplant, navy and moss green."

All versions were produced and before Matt knew it he was forced before a full-length mirror in the brown one, eggplant having turned out to be purple, navy too "harsh" and moss green too "decadent," by which Matt thought the salesman meant it reminded him of a fungus.

The brandy-colored brown velvet one, however, had subtle golden highlights, and even Matt could see it was sinfully flattering. First a red suede sofa, then a brandy velvet coat. These women were exactly as the church had represented them for centuries: seductive, frivolous creatures who knew the meaning of self-acceptance and emotional expression, not repression. He liked them very much.

And he had a cream turtleneck sweater that would go nicely underneath.

"Done," he said, producing the credit card again. The jacket didn't even need alteration.

"We're through here," Krys said as they moved briskly through the mall.

"What about your present for a friend?"

"He already got it for himself." Her eyelashes batted flirtatiously at Matt. "But I am definitely still in the market for mistletoe."

"Dream on. Where's the . . . vehicle."

"In the Wooki lot, why?"

"You've had your way. Now I have mine. I drive on the return trip."

"You don't like my driving?"

"It stinks. But your shopping is A-plus."

Chapter 31

CATNYP *for Literary Lions*

What is the sleuth out of water, the investigator out of time, the snoop out of suppositions to do when she, or he, hits a brick wall?

Hie thyself, not to a nunnery or a monastery, but to a public library.

Haven owed to rare Ben Franklin, a free retreat to which Emma Lazarus's poor, homeless and huddled tempest-tossed immigrants could turn in illiterate masses yearning to breathe free, to read all about it. In due time they did, unto the *Washington Star* and the *National Enquirer.*

Now, it was time that Temple caught up on her reading.

The cab dropped her off right in front of the place. (A Christmas miracle.)

Surely the New York Public Library on Fifth Avenue resided eternally in some national racial-memory data bank.

Temple had seen these ranks of serious gray stone steps, with the gigantic and lordly lions on either side, in maga-zines, books and probably cyberspace. But here and now, for Christmas, they wore bow ties! Red bow ties. If only Midnight Louie could see them now! Perhaps he would be less uppity about the simple red velvet collar Temple had bought with the holidays in mind.

Of course, the library lions' red bow ties were affixed to the bottoms of huge Christmas wreaths. The entire arrangement gave their fiercely feline meins (manes?) a humorous, holiday air, like seeing Charlton Heston wearing a beanie with a propeller on top.

Temple tripped up the stairs (in the light, airy sense of the verb, not as in tangling in her own feet) and entered a large interior as substantial as she had imagined—light gray limestone, marble and granite combining into a basso choir of stones and surfaces. She chose to walk up the wide staircase suitable for the entrance of a Cleopatra instead of taking the discreet elevator tucked down a corridor.

On the third floor, wood was added to the architectural orchestration, shining, smooth wood, a choir of coloratura sopranos in counterpoint to the solid stone basses of the building's ribs.

A mural-swathed rotunda awaited outside the book section. Temple gravitated to the Public Catalog Room. She was a member of the public. She had a cat, and perhaps even a log, if her diary counted.

First she had to scour the catalog. She discovered that the New York Public Library computerized catalog was called CATNYP, a good sign. Lions and tigers and bears, oh my. The subject matter of the Vietnam War scattered far and wide, and she wanted more recent summaries, summations written in the distant third person, overviews that might serve as a map.

Finally, after whole quarter hours of grazing, Temple brought her blue and white call slips to the reference desk.

Now the stern, substantial environment went to war with itself. She was to hie to the South Hall Main Reading Room to wait for her number to appear on a lighted board.

Was this hypertext heaven, or automated hell? She felt as if she were in an intellectual cafeteria, a fast-food-for-the-mind McDonald's. Except that the ceilings were so soaring she thought of cathedrals and shrines and the magical, mystical elevations of the Himalayas. Was anything as satisfying as knowledge? Maybe chocolate. And (shhhh, this is a library) sex with the proper not-stranger.

The Delivery Desk brought her babies to her with twenty-first-century efficiency. Temple finally settled down at a mundane table with her books and notes. She was trying to absorb ugliness in the midst of beauty. She read about officer fraggings and the freak-show talents of Vietnamese prostitutes and the treatment of napalm burns. She read about pot and Pol Pot, and how the world had delved into an adolescent self-mutilating phase before she could speak or walk. She read about CIA schemes and Asian immigrant dreams and an endless cycle of cynicism and self-indulgence and sin in Saigon and San Francisco.

All of which led to motives for murder. Two themes struck her innocent post-sixties mind: the Vietnam War's unprecedented divisive dissension at home: flag-burners versus flag-wavers, American against American, citizen against soldier, and how that ended in veterans coming home to be reviled, rather than honored. The Gulf War, comparatively brief as it was, hadn't been like that, though veteran charges of exposure to chemical weaponry were eerily similar in both wars, a PR ballet of accusation, denial, suspicion and investigation.

The other thing that struck her was drugs, how pervasive they were both at home and abroad, a unifying factor among protesters and protested, both the nihilist's and the idealist's painkiller of preference. Drugs that made dealing death bearable, drugs that made fighting death something one could deal with day after day.

Everyone worried about kids using drugs, in her own generation and the ones before and after it, but she had never seen anything like the drug-nirvana of that part of the sixties that she had lived as an infant, toddler and child.

People—young adults—who had lived through that intense period, that paroxysm of flirtation and fatal engagement with death and drugs, here and abroad, could be capable of anything. Any time. Any where.

Chapter 32

Christmas Party

"I don't know what to say," Matt's mother said in the car on the way to Bo and Mary Margaret's house in the sub-urbs.

"Now, or later?"

Matt had left the slushy freeway at the proper exit and now drove carefully through the early-dim, snow-packed streets. His mother's older model Honda Civic might be as unpredictable as she.

"Are you going to tell them?" she asked.

"Unless you want to do it."

"Do they have to know?"

"No, but I have to tell them."

"They really were proud of you."

"And won't be any more, because I'm not a priest any more? How have I changed? Really?"

"Oh, Matt." Like a lot of women, she thought that suf-ficed.

"Oh, Mother."

"When did it become so terrible?"

"When having a baby was a price a woman paid. And only a woman. You tell me."

"If I'd given you up, we wouldn't have this agony."

"Maybe. Maybe not. I've counseled adoptive children who were sexually abused in their new homes."

"Oh, God! I didn't think it could be worse."

"It can. It is. We really didn't have it that bad; you're right about that, if I put it in context. But I can't put it in context when it's a secret. Secrets kill. They kill love, and hope, and family unity. That's why victims of sexual abuse are advised to admit the abuse, to name the abuser. Frankness frees. Secrets imprison."

"If you say so."

His mother had withdrawn to that inner world that was defined by her own worries and shrunken sense of self-worth. Matt sighed as he drove, wearing the brandy velvet blazer under his sheepskin jacket. It felt tight and confining, unlike the casual clothes he wore in Las Vegas.

Cold climates encouraged confinement and withdrawal. He ached for the wide-open warmth of Sin City. For snow-clear streets, and sun-god days. For neon nights. For Temple and Electra and the Circle Ritz. For Midnight Louie. For Bennie and Sheila. Even for George and Verle. But he was with his mother, and he ached most of all for her.

Thinking of the presents wrapped and tucked into a shopping bag in the backseat gave him colder feet than the poor heat circulation this old car could manage. Thinking of telling the extended family about his new status brought the cold to the level of his heart. This was the most difficult thing he had ever done, except for leaving the priesthood.

"The young people nowadays," his mother said, as if answering his unsaid thought, "don't go into the religious life like they used to. Now the church recruits old, used-up people like me; widows and widowers, people whose children are gone, who can become lay assistants."

"Wouldn't it be simpler to just let women be priests?

They're eager to do it, like all of those excluded from something for centuries."

"Women priests? I don't know if women . . ."

"Mom, you are one. You ought to know."

"I've never liked being one. It's brought nothing but heartache. You can hunt Cliff and track him down. What can I do for revenge? I never want to see him again. I never wanted to hear of him again. Your salvation comes at my cost."

"Your solution is self-abrogating avoidance."

"Your solution is confrontation and violence, just as his was."

"There must be a middle ground."

"It isn't here, in Chicago, at Bo and Mary Margaret's house."

He was silent for a bit. "I think I remember the way. That's pretty remarkable. Maybe what I should do is just enjoy myself. Celebrate Christmas. Would that make you happy?"

"Oh, yes, Matt. No more pain and accusation. I've had enough to last a lifetime."

And it had, Matt thought.

The Belofski house was bigger, higher, peakier than Matt's mother's old southside place in town, which had been bought with the secret wages of sin and guilt. Unshuttered windows brimmed with light and shadow figures moving on the accidental stage of a well-illuminated house on a dark December evening.

The broad walks had been scraped clean to the concrete. Matt helped his mother navigate the frost-slicked path, but she didn't really need assistance in her loafer shoes. He carried the shopping bag overflowing with presents: hers for her family, his for her.

Moving from the ear-crisping cold outside onto the steamy front porch and then through the thronging main rooms felt like a spiritual journey, each step meditated upon many times before being taken in real life.

Matt smelled cinnamon and apples, strongly spiced sausage, beer and eggnog.

The Christmas tree, seven feel tall, commandeered a hall corner. Bo came to collect their coats, then directed Matt and his mother into the living room.

They had just passed under the oaken arch when Krys materialized before them like a rather large elf in a short red velvet skirt, a black leather vest dangling hardware, a white blouse dripping ruffles and the cross earring, among others much less refined. Tonight her lips were painted purple to match her nails.

"Goodness, Krystyna!" Mira Devine said. "You've grown so much this last year; you've grown right out of that skirt."

"No, ma'am, I haven't." Krys grinned and pointed up at the center of the archway.

Matt turned to bump into a cluster of white berries hanging there. No way, he thought. Not with the family politics here tonight. He was a walking catalyst for a lot of people's unacknowledged crises; he understood that.

Bo came back, jovial as a jelly-bellied Santa, his face florid. He clapped Matt on the brandy velvet shoulder and drew him away from the two women. "Let me introduce you around, cousin. Lots of folks here haven't seen you since you were a little shaver or your . . . ah, induction."

"Fine. But don't introduce me as Father anything. I've left the priesthood."

Bo froze in amazement. "You didn't say that at the airport."

"It didn't seem the right time."

"What'll I say here, like to relatives and neighbors?"

"Say I'm your cousin, Mira's boy. Matt Devine."

"They know what you were."

"I want them to know what I am."

"What is that now, if you're not a priest anymore?"

"I'm a hot-line counselor. A mostly honest man. A good neighbor. A bad enemy. A friend. A son. A cousin. A reluctant motorcycle rider. A pretty good martial-arts expert.

And, lately, a natty dresser. I could be a ladies' man, but I haven't got the heart for it. Ask your daughter. And I'm a Don Quixote, looking for answers where there are only questions. This family is one of the hideouts."

Bo had paled with every new description on Matt's list. Now he said numbly, "My daughter?"

Matt pointed at the mistletoe drooping from the arch's central post. "She's a great kid. You have to show her that you trust her before she needs to prove to you that you can't. Let her go where she wants to college. She'll learn. That's what it's all about."

"Matt, I . . . I don't know what to say."

"Say nothing, then. Just think about it all."

"Jeez. Mary Margaret . . ." Shaking his head, Bo went in search of his better half to share his shock.

Matt retreated to the appetizer table near the fireplace and poured himself a cup of punch. He watched the dynamic of the rooms alter as guests arrived. Couples came in, bundled to the eyeteeth in mufflers and turned-up collars. Coats went upstairs to a bedroom depository. The guests, stripped down to their warmest festive clothes, gravitated to their separate spheres.

Men gathered at the fireplace or the informal bar, talking duck- and deer-hunting, sports and stocks.

Women, dressed in their best and looking their most attractive, clustered around the younger children or hied to the kitchen to "help."

Matt circulated, eavesdropping as only an outsider can. Women discussed recipes and infant care, although a younger cadre gathered in front of the blank TV set and dissected workplace politics with a will. Krys and her age group met in corners to whisper and snicker, unlikely objects gleaming at their ears in symbolic rebellion. He smiled to see Krys sporting his gift cross like it was a tattoo from a punk-rock band.

His mother, he noticed, drifted unnoticed from women's group to women's group. As the only woman among them unaccompanied by a husband, and as once the most beautiful, he could imagine what a threat she had been in her youth. And he had begun to see beauty as a force to be acknowledged, as well as reckoned with. His mother's current drabness, her cultivated invisibility, were the result of decades of abuse, not just from a man named Cliff Effinger, but from her own family and culture and church.

He himself had been inclined to carry on that tradition. And now look at him: tracking a man down on the mean streets of Vegas, flirting with underage semicousins in big-city malls, trying to do unto his mother as Temple had done unto him, trying to awaken the sleeping beauty in everyone, including himself, for without self-love, there was only self-hate, and self-hate always looked outward for others to share the burden.

"Matt! I remember you!"

A guy Matt didn't remember had come by, flushed with good cheer and Polish beer.

"Larry. Aunt Marya's boy. Bo said you've rejoined us poor sinners 'washing and sweeping' in this vale of tears, as my four-year-old says. I don't blame you for leaving. The church is pretty messed up these days. I tell you, I'll think twice before I let my little Ashley become an altar girl someday after all the admissions that have come down. No wonder you left."

"Your little Ashley is pretty smart. Washing and sweeping is better than 'wailing and weeping in this vale of tears,' but it's still women's work. Maybe your little Ashley should skip parish work and go straight to seminary after high school. She'll find a lot of women there."

"You're kidding."

"I'm not. Women really want to learn theology. They respect it more because it's been denied them. Maybe they're latecomers, but they're better ministry candidates than most men nowadays."

"But the Pope—"

"There'll be another Pope. And another. In the meantime, I'm really enjoying counseling work."

"Oh, good. You're in California now?"

"Close. Las Vegas."

"Say, what about that place? I'm taking the family there for Easter. I'll look you up. Gotta see that New York–New York skyline hotel. And there's a water park, I'm told by the three water spaniels the fairies switched for my real kids."

"What are you doing?"

"Not much. Wage slave. The economy keeps dipping every time I get a little ahead. Wife's working now. Hey, the kids are almost all in grade school—Catholic grade school—and there isn't enough for her to do at home, now that she's got me and the boys on her chore-doing list." He shrugged. "I thought we'd be traditional, like the old folks." He glanced to Bo and his compatriots across the room. "But things change, huh? Hope you like life in civvies. You know, you could get a job as a model. The family's never been a slouch on good looks, especially the women."

"Thanks. I owe it all to my mother."

"Your mother? Oh, yeah. You're Mira's kid." He nodded. "A nice lady. Kinda quiet."

That was just it. His mother had no reason to be a nice lady. He considered her confession: he had resulted from one night of unconsidered youthful infatuation. Maybe that was more than most people had in their whole lives. Maybe human passion had its own reason and right for being. But was the price always a denial of any passion, then? For work, for what was right, for each other?

Finally the crowded kitchen countertops were fully loaded, covered with turkey and ham, hot dishes and creamed vegetables (which seemed a contradiction in nutrition), and potatoes of every variety in every form: whipped, mashed, stuffed and sliced.

People shuffled past to fill their plates and settled on any available seat to chow down.

Matt spotted a figure dressed in black like an aging gunfighter, and wasn't surprised when the corner of his eye caught it settling near him, wearing the twin to the formal black suit Matt still kept in his closet at the Circle Ritz.

The old man's eyes were the color of water, faded by age to near translucency, but his handshake was as punishing as ever. Matt recognized that grip as common priestly compensation: an intensity born of little physical contact with others except through these social rituals. Celibacy could be a lonely avocation, spreading beyond the avoidance of one gender to an alienation from everyone.

"Good to see you again, Father Slowik. Do you need anything more? Silverware? Napkins?"

"Only a memory update. But I recall you, Matthias. Quite a squaller at your baptism."

"Maybe I had something to protest."

Father Slowik might be losing his short-term memory, but his instincts were as honed as ever.

"I know you've left, young man. They told me just now. I grieve for you, whatever your reasons. It's hard to get in, hell to get out, and sheer purgatory to have been, and be no more. You haven't left the church, though?"

"Left the church? No. I was released from my vows, that's all."

"That was enough in my day." Father Slowik pushed his ebbing glasses back against the bridge of his nose. "From what I've heard you were a good enough priest, Matthias. I hope you'll be a good whatever-else you choose. Your mother's glad to see you, I'm sure."

Matt wasn't sure, but he didn't say that, any more than he would point out the old man's mistake with his name. Matt had switched to coffee, and studied the brown liquid staining the inside of Mary Margaret's best china cups. The old habits had broken down with the old neighborhoods. Bo had married Irish.

"I'd like to visit you at the rectory, Father, before I leave."

"Me? No one wants to see me any more."

"I do. I have some questions about, oh, the old days. You might remember some things. About my . . . origins."

"Old days." He nodded almost happily. "Those I remember, and, believe me, Matthias, skirts were never as short as *that*, not even in the sixties, and I do remember them quite clearly."

Matt turned to catch Krys watching them. "Short skirts won't destroy the world; shortsightedness might."

"I've got that too. Well, ring me up. I'm almost always there, unless they let me out to give extreme unction. Don't trust me with the words and music any more, boy. Not even at mass."

"After Christmas Day, I will," Matt said. He stood to shake hands with the old man again, despite the risk of instant carpel-tunnel problems.

The priest's stiff, wrinkled hand brushed the forearm of Matt's sleeve. "Nice fabric."

So much nicer than a lifetime sentence of black serge. For a few moments, Matt watched the old man move stiffly from group to group, mangling names and hands, always welcomed but then ignored, like an aging family dog, a black Labrador retriever.

Finally it was time to begin the Christmas Eve present exchange.

Matt found memories of this event as blank as Father Slowik's mental notebook. Had he ever enjoyed Christmases here? He sat quietly on the sidelines as gifts were handed out and exclaimed over.

He and his mother were invisible, mere onlookers to the others' connections and interactions. He felt his anger growing like a cancer. Had his illegitimacy relegated them to the family fringes? He had always blamed Cliff Effinger for everything wrong with their lives, but now he saw a more benign enemy at work. Simple denial. A tacit group resolve to ignore the unsavory facts of Matt's birth that incidentally added up to ignoring Matt and his mother.

Matt vaguely remembered being in this house at Christmas, but the memories weren't vivid, weren't warm. The rage that had refused to tear Effinger limb from limb was building here, on this supposedly safe ground of family. He felt like Samson, eager to pull the pillars down on the Belofskis and Zabinskis and all their houses, not a blinded Samson seeking blind revenge, but a Samson blinded by an ugly truth he suddenly could see.

Then, his own name was called. Startled, he accepted a wrapped package.

Inside were a Chicago-warm muffler and gloves, and a card from Bo and Mary Margaret. He nodded his thanks across the room, saw them mellow and beaming. Maybe keeping up traditions was a kind of safety net. Maybe they accepted him and wanted him back. Maybe they'd bought too many muffler/glove sets for too many children.

When his last name was called again, it was for his mother. Matt watched the blouse box pass from hand to hand to her lap. It caused quite a buzz. Apparently, she was seldom in attendance, and seldom remembered.

She opened the box delicately, ribbon and tape dismantled, not torn. When the lid lifted, everyone strained forward to see, even Matt, and he knew what was inside.

The color converted them all on first sight. Women sighed and men nodded. His mother actually held it up to her shoulders and stroked a silky sleeve. But would she ever wear it? There was no question about the earrings, which, being much smaller, were presented unheralded, although Krys hovered to make sure they worked.

"These are . . . so expensive," his mother whispered. They lay in one open palm like Christmas candies too decorative to eat.

"Try them on," Krys urged. "I want to see. I helped pick them out."

"Oh, you did?" Mira glanced with open alarm at the pewter implements dangling from Krys's ears, but clipped first one, then the other earring on.

"I'm not used to having something stuck on my ears," she said.

Matt noticed that her every comment was an objection or a subtle criticism. This house reeked with people telling other people what to do, even if the only victim was themselves.

"You'll get used to that," Krys said. "And they look gorgeous with your eyes."

His mother cast those eyes down. Compliments were anathema, and "gorgeous" wasn't in her vocabulary. "Too expensive," she murmured.

But she didn't take them off.

Halfway through the present-opening, the giant box of Ethel M chocolates Matt had brought as a hostess gift was passed to them, half of the brown frilled paper cups empty. Too expensive, Matt thought ironically, mentally toting up his holiday spending spree.

His gift from his mother arrived in a medium-size jewelry box. Inside was a dress watch, department-store designer brand, with a sleek, fashionably unreadable dial and a black leather band.

"You talk about 'too expensive.' " His gentle chiding made her smile at their role reversal. Matt swiftly exchanged the new watch for the clunky twenty-dollar model he wore. "Looks much better than my old one. Thanks, Mom."

He put his arm around her shoulder and kissed her cheek. She smiled as shyly as a teenager, or as a teenager should in olden days, before purple lipstick made shy smiles an impossibility.

Matt wondered if the watch represented Christmases past, and time lost, or Christmases future and time yet to be squandered or savored.

Somehow, with the present-passing ritual, the news about him had become common species too. More people approached him, fascinated as much by what he would do now as by what he had done before.

Matt recognized so many facial types, even in the younger generation. His old neighborhood was inbred, static. But it wasn't just that he was of the rare younger generation who had become a priest, he realized, he was of interest because he had *left*. Left the neighborhood, the city, the state. And now he had left again, left the priesthood.

Then people he had almost forgotten, puzzle people whose adult faces hid traces of the familiar childish ones, came up to shake his hand and remind him who they were and who he had been in their memories and to ask how he was doing now.

"Phone counseling, huh? Must be tense work, especially in Las Vegas," said an overweight woman with coarse gray hair corkscrewing to her shoulders.

He was horrified to recall her as a grade-school class-mate. Time was already sorting people into parodies of their childhood selves, and his generation was only in their early thirties.

"Like endless confessions," she went on, "but with more interesting sins than in your ordinary parish."

"Sins are the same everywhere. What's your line?" Matt had recognized the hearty, no-nonsense manner of a work-ing woman.

"I got a law degree after the kids were in school, and now I run a low-cost legal-aid pool for anybody that really needs it—the poor, the handicapped, single mothers, any-body the system is used to stomping all over."

"Now you're the one with a hundred stories to tell, I bet."

"Sure can tell you live in Las Vegas, Matt, but I won't take that bet."

He was amazed by how they remembered him from school: good on the swim team, always studious. Several said they had been surprised when he entered the seminary. They sounded so benign in retrospect, his school days. These people had seen the surface he had wanted them to see. He had always been successful at misrepresenting himself, even to himself.

When the crowd had dwindled to immediate family, Matt checked his new watch, surprised to find it was after eleven.

Mary Margaret, Bo's Irish wife, paused in picking up

empty dessert plates and glasses. "We always go to midnight mass at St. Stan's. Want to join us?"

He turned to consult his mother, but she wasn't in the chair she had occupied all evening.

"Kitchen." Mary Margaret's graying head nodded in that direction.

Matt grabbed some empty plates—he knew from several rectory housekeepers that a man entering a women-at-work zone had better bear a token gesture of pitching in—and wended through disarranged chairs to the house's crisis center.

Now the countertops were piled with the disorderly remains of the feast; there was hardly a place to put more plates. The women's duties were winding down; dishes would be done in the morning. So they clustered around the battered kitchen table. Matt was surprised to see his mother there, the new blue topaz earrings twinkling like the exotic eyes of some hidden persona just behind her everyday self.

They were talking hairstyles.

Matt interrupted long enough to find out if she wanted to attend midnight mass, while the other women gazed on him with the fond, interrupted attention he was used to evoking from older women.

She did, and he left, bemused. He had a feeling that she had never been swept into female holiday circles before, that she had been like him, the utter outsider.

Returning to the now-deserted living room, he was waylaid by a purple-lipped vixen.

"You've been ducking that archway all night," she said.

"Darn right. Did you trap anybody else?"

"Only Uncle Stach. This family may eat like the Russian army, but otherwise it's very repressed."

"Maybe that's why everybody eats like the Russian army. Thanks for your help at the mall. Your gift ideas were a hit."

"I had no idea your mother was so . . . shy."

It wasn't shyness, but he saw no need to correct her. She

herself was shy, under that brash exterior. Everybody developed a second skin in high school, to keep the first one from being flayed to shreds, he decided.

"You going to come back?" she asked, leaning against the heavy oaken post at the end of the archway.

"My mother lives here."

"She's always lived here, and you didn't come back."

"I will more often now that I have a personal shopper here."

"Hey, that's what I'm good at. I guess I should major in nursing, or something that pays well, but I'd really like to do art."

"Do both."

"That's a tough load."

"It'll pay off when you graduate and can go either way. The time to bear down is when you're young and have the energy. It doesn't last forever."

"Does never knowing what you should do last forever?"

He laughed. "Yeah. That does. Forever."

"I bet this was hard for you. Tonight, I mean."

He nodded. "But easier than I thought. Things we fear are always like that."

"Like the superbig roller coaster at a theme park?"

"Roller coasters aren't on my Ten Worst Things list."

"No, you're all grown-up."

She sounded despondent, so mired in Jekyll/Hyde indecision about who she was and what everybody else was. Matt felt a wave of tenderness for her, for himself too, when he had been there.

He put his hands on her arms and kissed the black lips that wanted so desperately to be recognized without being betrayed. It was a high school kiss, sweet and utterly unsexual on his part, just deeply affectionate.

Her eyes were shining. She was bedazzled by her own power in making what she wanted to happen more than by the kiss. An older guy had recognized her. A man who wasn't supposed to like girls that much.

"Can I write you?" The words blurted out, unpremeditated.

He hesitated, not wanting to turn a fleeting moment into an unhealthy obsession.

"Never mind." Her eyes were shifting away, thinking about becoming ashamed.

Matt hated that look more than anything in the world, his mother's look, which he had grown up with.

"Sure you can write me. I just haven't been at my place long enough to remember the address right off. I live at the Circle Ritz."

"That sounds like a dude ranch."

"It's this wild four-story apartment building with condominiums too. Built in the fifties. Round. There's a wedding chapel out front."

"That is wild."

"That's Las Vegas." He gave her the address. "Don't you want to write this down?"

"I'll remember it." Her eyes were shining again.

The women started drifting in from the kitchen.

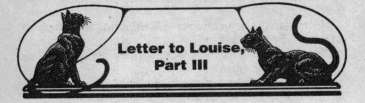
Being the Meditations of Midnight Louie in New York City

"I am about to impart to you some priceless wisdom, just in case you are my daughter and could use some guidance. Being priceless, wisdom is no doubt undervalued, but here I go anyway: the best place to be on Christmas Eve, I have discovered, is the kitchen. That is where all the eats are, and where the noise level is the least.

"I have unwittingly spent many a Christmas holiday out-of-doors, aware only that there were a good many more turkey leavings outside my favorite restaurants during the season to be merry. Also, the handouts came with a tad more mercy, but not noticeably so.

"Now I have seen the light. Or, rather, I have seen lots of lights. It is fitting that I am spending my first indoor Christmas in Manhattan, which becomes an island of illumination for the period. The small twinkling lights Miss Temple Barr adores (perhaps because she is more than somewhat small and twinkling herself) bedeck the city's stern gray-granite face like electrified fleas on a dignified Russian Blue grand champion. (I pity these purebreds; they are never allowed to have any fun. There is something to be said for being relatively worthless in the scheme of things.)

"I understood that humans became merry and bright at such a time, but admit that either quality is in short supply around Miss Kit Carlson's domicile this Yuletide. I should report my progress in investigating murder most foul, in the high-rise atmosphere of a Madison Avenue advertising agency, the very place where I am a VIP (Very Important Pussycat). A man playing Santa Claus (he of the red long johns and white curly whiskers) became entangled in a length of golden chain while exiting the traditional chimney at the company Christmas party. It turns out the Santa who was hung by the chimney with care was an actor-type acquaintance of Miss Kit Carlson.

"So she has decided to move her Christmas Eve party to the day after the holiday in deference to Rudy's death, as he was known to most of her acquaintanceship as well. The festivity will instead be a farewell party for Miss Temple—for myself and Miss Temple, I might point out, were there anybody sensible to point it out to. By then, Miss Kit says, there may be something to really celebrate, such as Miss Temple's and my elevation to feline spokespersons. Or the solution to Rudy's bizarre death.

"Still, Christmas cannot go unheralded. Food is casual but in ample supply, and often left out on the countertop for a little Midnight noshing. Miss Kit has installed a small fir tree atop a living room table and twined it with fairy lights and other glittery folderol.

Certain packages wrapped in gaudy paper and ribbon lie beneath it. I even detect an odor of exotic catnip beneath the pervasive stench of pine tree, but try to ignore it, as surprise seems to be a highly valued commodity at these Christmas festivities. (Although the suspense of Santa never emerging from the chimney was not one of those valued surprises.)

"Needless to say, the spokescat search at said advertising agency has ground to a halt, not only for the holiday itself, but until your old man . . . I mean your elder maybe-relative . . . solves the manner, motive and mastermind of Rudy's death, which of course is murder in the first degree. So there is no rest for the hunter of wickedness, not even on Christmas Eve. I suspect I will join my ladies in lounging around and sighing, although I will not be joining them on their Christmas Day outing to St. Patrick's Cathedral, where something known as high mass is to be celebrated.

" 'I am not even Catholic,' " I hear Miss Temple protest lukewarmly.

" 'You never know,' Miss Kit responds with that mock severity she is so good at. 'And it never hurts to be well rounded, just in case. Besides, sectarian religious concerns aside, it is glorious theater, and the music makes the latest Andrew Lloyd Webber Broadway smash seem modest.'

"So I will be alone by the phone on Christmas Day, at least for a while, twiddling my shivs while waiting impatiently for my gift weed to cure for a few days longer. It seems present-opening is to be delayed by Rudy's death as well. I do not think the dead dude would begrudge me a little holiday nip, given his own lifelong proclivities, but must abide by others' sense of propriety, which is never as liberal as my own. Since I do not drink . . . wine, I have plenty of time to leave the ladies to their holiday blues and

French reds in the living room and retreat to the computer.

"I find myself in a contemplative mood as I face great changes in my lifestyle and the specter of future fame and fortune (though my fortune will be tied up with the affairs of others and certainly cannot be lavished willy-nilly on remote relatives). Perhaps it is time to let bygones by bygones. I see now that my job as house detective at the Crystal Phoenix hotel was a mere stepping stone to greater things, so it is your world now, and welcome to it.

"Now that I have been altered beyond my wildest dreams (and also have seen dozens of human offspring in mass holiday revelry at the advertising agency), I must admit that your headstrong hieing to the veterinarian for spaying was perhaps not a bad decision for a career woman like yourself. From what I hear, you are doing a good job at keeping the ruder elements in line at the Crystal Phoenix. All in all, you are not a bad kit—though by no means mine beyond a shadow of a doubt; I am no deadbeat dad, only cautious—and in the spirit of this season that seems to mean so much to humans, I offer you an olive branch (or even some of my imported nip, should I ever get it).

"And you could do worse than to consult now and again with your esteemed grand—er, grand friend, Three O'Clock Louie, who has traveled widely and seen much of the world that even I might be a tad ignorant of.

"So let us hope that Bastet blesses all of catkind this season, every one, and even a few deserving humans.

"I am sending this whole E-mail file to Miss Van Von Rhine's office, trusting that she will see it gets to the proper party. She is pretty smart for a human. I am in such a mood of reconciliation that I even send Chi-

nese New Year greetings to Chef Song, and fond wishes that his koi remain in the best of health until I get back.

     "Yours in news, nip and nostalgia,

     Midnight Louie, Esq."

>

Chapter 33

"O Night Devine . . ."

Two in the morning was a strange time of day to be out with your mother.

At 2 A.M., mothers were usually safe and warm at home, waiting for delinquent kids to show up.

Matt's mother sat beside him in the frosty car interior, waiting for the car to warm up enough to drive. Their ears still rang with the magnificent choir music that had filled St. Stan's to the top of the stained-glass windows. The holiday mass been long and taxing in its way, but inspiring as well. And fighting the cold to get there and back added an element of value that Matt knew he would never find in a Las Vegas church or a warm climate.

Clouds of auto exhaust bounced against the frost-etched windows, while the cold motor throbbed as if its combustible heart would break from the strain of starting in below-zero weather.

Matt grabbed the windshield scraper, left the warm spot his body heat had thawed into the driver's seat and got out.

Snow squeaked under his shoes as he circled the Civic,

scraping portholes of view into all the windows. Matt only remembered now that he hated that particular squeak more than anything, even more than chalk squealing across a blackboard. At least he'd never be near a blackboard again.

Cold chased him back into the car, then made itself at home. Matt's teeth were chattering, but he didn't dare turn on the fan yet. It would still waft in the arctic cold.

The car ties squeaked on the snow too, as they fought free of the side ruts and spun onto the glazed central skating rink of hard-packed snow called a street.

For the first couple of minutes, neither one spoke. Too cold to take large gulps of air into your mouth. The house was only ten minutes away, at normal speed.

Finally his mother broke the silence.

"We can have some hot cocoa when we get home."

After the rich mix of foods at the Belofsky buffet table in the suburbs, something sticky-sweet, milky and marshmallow-topped was the last thing Matt craved. But he didn't say that.

"Sounds good," he said instead.

Silence.

"The choir was lovely tonight."

"Everything was perfect."

Another silence, the silence of socially exhausted people. His mother apparently felt obligated to make small talk.

"I don't know what Bo's middle girl is thinking of."

"Krys?"

"Those clothes! So short and dark and strange. Purple nails and mouth. And those awful earrings, if you can call them that. She looks as if a porcupine had thrown its quills at her. Wearing a cross, of all things."

"All the young girls wear that stuff. And worse."

"Not in my day. I don't understand why you encourage it."

"I don't encourage it. I tolerate it. There's a difference."

"You tolerate too much."

"Are we still talking about Krys, or about something else?"

His mother sighed. Sighs were potent maternal weapons, mute accusations of offspring misbehavior.

"The girl obviously has a crush on you, and you seem to encourage it. You may have left the priesthood, but it's still scandalizing. To the others, I mean."

"Mom, girls got crushes on me when I was *in* the priesthood. It goes with the territory. Only now I know how to handle it. I used to take it too seriously, like you do. Most teenage girls develop crushes on older unattainable men. To Krys, I'm still pretty unattainable. I used to blame the phenomenon on my looks, but this time I realized that something more serious and less shallow was going on. Krys wants to be an artist; she wants to do something different from the rest of her family, maybe go to college out of town. Heresy for a Belofsky. She is desperately seeking a role model, someone in the family who did something different, and then I showed up, the prodigal ex-priest. Maybe a crush on me far away in Las Vegas will keep her safe from the all-too-attainable guys who can short-circuit her plans to become somebody."

"There are lots of women she could use as a role model."

"In the family? Who?"

"I work."

"At something you love?"

"I work for money, not love. I always have. Even that was looked down on, that I wasn't home all the time. For you."

"Who was to look down on you? Your family? If you hadn't worked, we wouldn't have eaten. Not with Cliff spending all his money on gambling."

Bars of light from the overhead lamps rhythmically rolled up the hood and across the windshield, bathing them in fleeting stripes of light. In one of those rolling lightning slices, Matt saw his mother's expression. Bitter.

By criticizing Krys's blithe immaturity, she castigated herself by proxy. She'd been Krys's age when she'd become pregnant. She'd had one crush, a lightning strike that had been both quick and fatal to those involved.

"I used to draw," she said finally. "In school. I won some prizes."

Matt realized then that he had pasted her bitter expression on his own preconceptions. Krys's burgeoning sexuality didn't bother his mother as much as the younger woman's possibilities, her independence, her *choice*.

"Sounds like artistic talent runs in the family," Matt said casually. "Except for me. I just doodle when I'm on the phone."

"A man in Cincinnati is famous for his doodles. Makes good money for them."

"No, that's not going to be my line, I'm afraid. You'll have to take it up again if you want an artist in the family."

"Do you . . . really 'blame' things on your looks?"

"Why?"

"I did too."

Matt was silent, navigating the narrow and rutted alley that ran behind his mother's house, passing wooden garages with double sets of sagging single doors that looked exactly like hers, looking for a landmark that would say they had arrived.

He finally spotted the bare snowball bush by the garbage can and turned into the short driveway. The headlights dramatized a blank pale yellow canvas of peeling paint.

Matt got out to pull the door open. Snowflakes falling again danced in the headlights. Like celestial dandruff, it punctuated his coat sleeves with dozens of white periods.

For the next few minutes they emptied the car of presents and leftovers, then navigated the foot-wide path through two feet of piled snow to the back door.

Inside, the house was dark and silent, except for the occasional *ping* of a radiator. Then the glaring kitchen light snapped on, and by the time the food was put away, the idea of making or consuming anything else had died.

"You know," Matt said as they moved into the living room, his mother going ahead to turn lights on, he following to turn them off behind them, "I've never seen any photos of you when you were young."

"There aren't many." She paused to jerk on the front doorknob to make sure the door was locked, then headed for the back hall to the bedrooms.

"But there are some."

She looked back over one shoulder, the earrings he had given her glistening like her eye whites. The overhead hall light made her face a black-and-white patchwork of planes and angles.

"Some. I can look them up in the morning, if you like."

He nodded and followed her down the hall.

Chapter 34

Back to Base Camp

By Thursday, the day after Christmas, Temple had developed a battle plan.

It was based on hidden suspicions, deception and treachery, but it fit the situation pretty well.

First, she called Colby, Janos and Renaldi and got Kendall on the phone.

"Temple! I'm so glad you called." Kendall sounded feverish. "There was such a blowup after you left before Christmas. The partners were going at it hammer and tong. They were even throwing their awards at each other.

"But I have a new theory. This is a second-generation scheme. It's Carl. Carlo. My rat ex-husband. He needs money. Daddy hasn't got it. Or . . . is that *my* daddy? No! I'm getting confused. It's so awful here. Everybody hates everybody else. I guess they always did. Can you come over, Temple? It's a real dogfight."

Temple was not surprised.

Kit watched her bundle up with suspicion, especially when Temple hitched on Louie and his CatAboard with the grim intent of an Old West gunslinger tying on the double holster of Colt revolvers.

"Temple, first you go to the library, which almost no one in New York does at Christmastime, except kids, and now you're going back to the weird advertising agency on Madison Avenue. I feel terrible that I've got an appointment and can't go with you. Do you need my Mace spray?"

"I need a flak jacket, Kit. Or maybe that should be 'flack' jacket, since I am one. But I have finally seen the light, and it isn't pretty."

"Temple." Kit hurled herself again the front door, like a protester. "Is this about poor Rudy?"

"It was never about poor Rudy. It was about rich man, poor man, beggarman, thief."

"You need backup," Kit said, squinting without her glasses.

"I have Midnight Louie."

"He's no protection."

"His absence is, for your computer. With you gone, and me gone, think what he might get up to."

"I can't be sure the little devil deleted half of my new novel. Thank God I have a backup on diskette."

"You can't be sure he didn't. Besides, the Shadow knows."

"The Shadow. He's black all right, but what can a cat know?"

"What the nose God gave him can smell. You can call Lieutenant Hansen, if you want."

"I'll call the paramedics—for myself!—if you keep me in the dark like this."

"I don't think anyone's dangerous any more, Kit. Rudy's death was a . . . flashback. The whole thing's falling apart anyway. I just want to be there when a very sad person learns the bitter truth."

"Cut the clichés, okay? Truth is always bitter. Listen. Rudy wouldn't want anyone else hurt, honest. Don't take this further than Rudy would."

"Kit." Temple encased her aunt's hands in her nylon-

and-down mittens. "Rudy wouldn't be dead if he had been willing to take this as far as it would go. He died because he really didn't mean any harm. And that's such a dangerous position to take, with the guilty."

Kit put her head in her hands. "What will I tell your mother if anything horrible happens?"

"Tell her I had a good time in New York."

Temple yanked the door open and headed for the elevator.

Louie sneezed once, then growled.

"Keep that sniffer in prime working order," Temple instructed him. "I saw what you did at Rudy's place, and I'm counting on you, and on old habits dying hard."

Temple hailed and got the first cab that she spotted. Kit was right. It was all attitude. She'd found that out when she had tried to outmacho Victor Janos.

She got to Madison Avenue in mid-afternoon. No cat people were scheduled. That whole matter would be settled with phone calls, telegrams and letters after the New Year. Would she and Louie win the endorsement sweepstakes? Temple could not care less. She was really angry. They were lying about Vietnam before she was born, and they were lying about it right now at Colby, Janos and Renaldi.

A few snowflakes were flying, but not enough to cling. The street people huddled over heating grates, trying to be invisible when the police were forced to come and kick them away from the only outside warmth the city of New York offered.

Temple paid the cabbie and walked into the bustling lobby, heading straight for the correct elevator bank. She couldn't believe she had been so ignorant just a week ago.

The elevators were as handsome as ever, but reminded her of escorts whose true selves have shown through the façade, who pale by comparison with reality, who show the skull beneath the skin.

She could see the entire steel spine of the building as the

elevator shot her up its empty shaft to the thirty-second floor. Another skeleton was ghosting down the hall on clattering anklebones. Just out of sight.

Louie lifted his nose in the empty hall, and sniffed, nostrils and whiskers trembling.

"Good boy."

The outer office was deserted, the receptionist surprised to see her. "We're about to close; we normally close early all through the holidays," she said, her jet-black braids glossed into the sheen of India ink. Her nails were shiny, and painted the color of ripe pomegranates.

Temple wondered if they celebrated the Asian New Year of Tet.

"You must be here to see Miss Kendall Renaldi—"

"No, I'm here to see Mister Brent Colby."

The receptionist's kamikaze nails hit buttons. Temple was instructed to sit for a while, but was finally buzzed in.

She and Louie passed the almost-closed door of Kendall's office. They headed straight for the corner office, where Brent Colby worked.

You could think Colby, Janos and Renaldi's name was decided according to alphabetical order. Or you could wonder about just what was the underlying order.

"Miss Barr."

He stood when she entered the room, as a gentleman should, but he seemed oddly detached.

"I don't understand why you're here. The trials . . . that's what we call this audition period, not that it's a dog obedience show. Sorry, Louie. A cat obedience show, although that seems a contradiction in terms. Not as if the trials, er, auditions, are over."

"I'm sorry too." Temple sat on a cushy visitors' chair and unfastened Louie. "I may have given you the wrong impression. This visit has nothing to do with the cat-product auditions."

"No?" He leaned back in his swivel chair, tilted his head, waited.

"I'm afraid it's about Kendall."

"My daughter?"

"She has been distraught about what almost happened to you."

"No, no! She's been distraught over what she thought *might* happen to me."

"I see. Anyway, I didn't want to leave you out."

"Leave me out?"

"Kendall was excited about my role as advisor to a Las Vegas hotel on an upgraded facility. She trotted me around to meet the partners and make my pitch. But she neglected to include you."

"Daughters. They think you're God, and they sometimes forget you for that very reason. So you wish to make up for her daughterly oversight. Commendable."

"No. In my own interest. My employers would be impressed if I were able to intrigue a major New York advertising agency with their account."

"One hand washes the other."

"Always."

He nodded. "You were right to persist and come to me. Have you seen . . . the others?"

"Oh, yes. Kendall saw to that."

"Kendall?" He looked disturbed now.

"She is such an adoring daughter, and so fearful that your trusted partners wanted to kill you. She wanted me to see if either of them were unduly greedy over the Las Vegas account."

His steepled fingers had stopped tapping one another. "And were they?"

"Not in my opinion. I'm afraid your daughter has been seriously disturbed by the recent events here. I wanted to warn you, so you could attend to her."

"Are you saying Kendall is crazy?"

"Well, she's been kept in the dark; what else is she to think?"

"Kept in the dark? How?"

"Vietnam," Temple mentioned, bending over to release Louie. "Do you mind? He's getting restless."

"I'm getting restless. You're saying that Kendall isn't . . . normal. Now you're bringing up Vietnam, which was a long time ago."

"Not in your generation's lifetime. Did you know that the murdered Santa Claus was a Vietnam vet?"

"Murdered? I can't agree to that. I still think that some bit of carelessness . . . he must have brought in that chain as a sound effect, only it backfired on him."

"First he came to see you. The day Louie and I arrived."

"It's amazing, Miss Barr. The way you keep referring to that cat. Almost as if he were human. Certainly it's a good recommendation for you to get the job. Yes, I think I can strongly advise Allpetco to take on you and your stunningly smart Louie."

"How wonderful. Were you as enthusiastic when you hired Rudy?"

"Rudy?"

"Oh, I'm sorry. That was the name of the Santa Claus."

"I don't remember."

"No. No more than you would recall a certain Air America flight out of South Vietnam during the war. I found an obscure story at the public library. 'Vietnam mystery.' The plane loaded with illegal drugs, that was diverted to China. Wasn't Rudy the pilot?"

"Rudy? I don't know any Rudy. As for this Air America—"

"An infamous arm of the CIA, according to library sources, which no one would question if it carried contraband. Drugs. Marijuana? A feeble base for a killing, both financial and—years later—physical, but you were all there: I've seen the memorabilia on all your office walls and can picture the rest. The two lowly but heroic draftees, the nobody pilot and the CIA man who wanted to make a financial killing out of Vietnam, to start a business his blue-blooded father abhorred. The library had an article on your Yale-man father, but you weren't like him. You wanted to be an advertising man. A hypester. A manufacturer of smoke and mirrors. The other two men you black-mailed to go along. They became your partners. The third man you lost track of, a pot-smoking zoned-out pilot who hardly knew where he was, much less what he was doing.

"I saw it on Janos's and Renaldi's walls: the Golden Hemp Award. No real trophy, except from the pot-smoking brotherhood. You are the only partner who keeps no war memorabilia on your walls. You didn't want to advertise it, savvy spin-master that you always were. You were a shadow-player. But you played crooked and had to consort with the underlings."

"Who told you this? Who betrayed me? Janos? He always agonized over the deaths."

"No," said Temple. "Your daughter did, because she was searching so frantically for whoever would want to harm her beloved father. Oh!" Temple lifted a leg. "That Louie has snagged my hose. I think he's found something, under your desk."

She bent down and rose with her thumb and forefinger pinched around a tissue paper. "Oh, look, Louie! It's a nasty brown cigarette butt. Do you suppose that it has anything to do with poor Rudy, who could never outgrow sixties habits? Do you suppose the police department will be able to find just this mixture of weed and paper in Rudy's place? No, it's not catnip, old fellow, it's cannabis, as in 'I'd walk a mile for a Camel.' Would your war partners walk a mile for you, Mister Colby?"

Temple felt them gathering over her shoulder, drawn here by the rising voices. Janos and Renaldi, not innocents, but not murderers three decades after an old war.

"Poor Rudy. You never told your partners he had come here. Your deskside chats were uneasy explorations. You read blackmail into everything he left unsaid. But he never meant to tell, Mr. Colby. He never even remembered that there was anything fishy about one particular CIA drug run, I would bet. Only you remembered."

Colby watched Temple loosen the tissue, and the marijuana butt rolled onto his pristine desk surface like a rat turd.

Behind her, Janos spoke, and he spoke to her.

"You can do point for me anytime. You and that roach-sniffin', rat-rousin' cat of yours."

Chapter 35

The Last Twist of Hemp

"I . . . I don't know what to say."

Colby looked beseechingly from one partner to the other, but they were looking at Temple.

"So Rudy came here," Renaldi asked, "to interview for a Santa Claus job and that started it all?"

Temple eyed her prey, still genteelly sweating behind his desk.

"You recognized Rudy," she said, "and Rudy recognized you."

"I . . . suppose so."

"You talked about old times."

"Rudy talked about old times. I've never been sentimental."

"Rudy wasn't sentimental, he just didn't get it. Easygoing Rudy, who paid the biggest price, just didn't get it. That's why he had been the perfect pawn."

Janos cut in without asking to dance. "I always figured he'd been paid off."

Temple shook her head. "Only in weed, right, Mr.

Colby? Feed his head and he was happy. Story of his life. Story of his death."

"Listen!" Colby half-rose from his desk. "I didn't kill him."

"Are you sure you want to say that?" Temple was stern, and the partners kept quiet. They recognized a prosecuting attorney when they heard one.

Colby collapsed back in his chair. "I . . . don't know what you mean. Rudy was affable, as always. Grayer, thinner, but affable. He seemed to regard the coincidence as some kind of reunion."

"A reunion. What did he say?"

"Only how amazing it was that we should hook up like this, after all these years. How he couldn't wait to see Vic and Tony again. Imagine us three, big shots on Madison Avenue, and he was just an itinerant Santa Claus."

"You thought he was blackmailing you, didn't you?"

"Blackmailing?"

"All those genial comments, loaded with unspoken darts. Rudy tell you where he lived? Down in the Village in a rent-controlled railroad flat."

"He . . . mentioned it. Him downtown. Us uptown. Him still dealing in rats and roaches. Us dealing in the varieties of both that wore Brooks Brothers suits."

"So you hired him on the sly, outside the agency."

Colby nodded unhappily. "That way I could pay him more."

"Aw, how magnanimous." Janos had grown quiet with rage. "How much more, Brent?"

"A couple thou."

"A couple thou." Janos's voice dripped sarcasm. "We each cleared a couple hundred thou from the drug deal and that was big-time lettuce in the sixties. Why were Tony and me honored with partnerships, and not Rudy?"

"Maybe you had better memories," Temple said. "Maybe you'd have been harder to get rid of."

Renaldi nodded, and beneath the stainless steel exterior Temple glimpsed yesterday's pig-iron. "We weren't nobody's stooges, Vic and me. Not in 'Nam, not anywhere."

"So you killed the poor asshole." Janos had taken on the role of prosecuting attorney now. "You booby-trapped the chimney, like the gook tunnels that undermined the whole damn country. You set it up so he'd hang himself. Out of sight, out of mind."

Colby was silent, and sweating profusely.

"It's worse than that." Temple stroked Louie, who sat on her lap with a prickly suggestion of slightly protruded claws. His entire body was thrumming, not with a purr, but with tension, as if he understood the seriousness of this confrontation. "After his death, you destroyed his ID. Erased him. If my aunt hadn't known Rudy, he'd still be listed as missing in action.

"The innocent died for the wrong reasons, and the innocent killed for the wrong reasons," she went on. "Just like in 'Nam. Just like everywhere else."

"No!" Colby burst out, half-standing. "I plead guilty, not innocent. I was . . . afraid. I had so much to lose now. Everything I had built."

"We built it too," Renaldi put in. "Just because you were CIA didn't mean you were the mastermind. You were just ambitious beyond the pipe-dreams of us grunts, so we followed you."

"We could have as easily fragged you," Janos put in. "Maybe we should have. This whole . . . scam . . . up here on the thirty-second floor isn't worth Rudy's life. He was innocent, man, you know? He was the most innocent guy among us. We owed him. We owed him more than a rathole in the Village."

"I've seen Rudy's rat-hole in the Village," Temple said. "Louie has too. Pretty grim. Even so, he played Santa Claus for a living. Ho-ho-hoed at children for hours. He never meant to blackmail anybody, he was just glad to run into old war buddies. Wasn't he, Mister Colby?"

Colby put his face in his hands. "No," he said. "He had to have had an angle. Everybody has an angle."

"You killed him for nothing." Janos's rage was white-hot by now.

"No," Colby murmured to his own sweaty palms.

"No." Temple agreed with him. "Mister Colby meant to pay him off, to buy him off. If two thousand didn't do it, twenty would. Maybe even the original two hundred thousand. But he didn't get a chance. Neither did Rudy."

"What are you sayin'?" Now Renaldi was hot. "That our trusted partner isn't a murderer? One of *us* other guys is? Do you really think we'd turn in another grunt over money? Rudy was a pothead from Day One. We figured Rudy had been offered the partnership gig, but we weren't surprised when he didn't go for it."

"But the deal kept you quiet, didn't it?" Temple asked.

"Sure." Janos was calmer, more dangerous. "That's why we were brought in. We knew too much. But . . . this don't make sense. Colby here put up with our rough edges, babied us along, found places where we could contribute to the firm in our own ways. Why would he suddenly turn to cold-blooded murder after all these years? Especially when Rudy, poor bastard, could have been bought off with a song? Or, as you say, a lunch with war buddies?"

Temple looked at Brent Colby, Jr., who, after a long, focused silence, finally parted his fingers and lifted reddened eyes to face the room.

He shook his head.

Temple had mercy on him. "I don't think *he* did turn to murder. But someone overheard Rudy talking to him and jumped to the wrong conclusion. Assumed the worst. Blackmail. Someone else killed Rudy so Colby and the firm wouldn't suffer."

"Not me!" Janos was truculent. "By God, not me."

"Not me," Renaldi was as fast to swear. "We would have known Rudy. We would have known he was harmless, but, of course, we hadn't screwed him out of a share all those years ago, so we wouldn't have that guilt on our backs."

"That guilt is nothing like Mr. Colby will have to bear

now," Temple warned. "Let the punishment fit the crime, old as it was. It does."

"What punishment?" Janos, confused, was now ready to turn his wrath on the messenger, Temple. "This stuff is pretty tough to prove. All based on supposition."

"Maybe you three could tough it out, like you did in the old days. But I doubt the killer can. The killer is cracking already, madly trying to point even an amateur like me in the wrong direction. It was a spur-of-the-moment murder, a desperate move. I'm sure the police will find supporting evidence once they know where to look."

"Where? Not here! You finally admitted yourself that Colby's clear." Renaldi was fighting back too, for the cause, for the ill-gotten gains, for the firm. They were still the three musketeers from the sixties.

" 'A' Colby's clear. And 'a' Renaldi's clear, as is 'a' Janos. But Kendall Colby Renaldi is not clear, and I doubt she ever will be."

"Kendall?" Renaldi sounded incredulous, even contemptuous.

"Are you surprised a woman masterminded this? Don't be. Kendall was a rock-climber in college. She could have rigged the trap easily."

"But she was devastated when the body was found and everyone assumed the victim was her father," Janos put in eagerly, too stunned to stay furious.

Temple nodded. "She acted out the fears that drove her to destroy Rudy. Those same fears made it easy to point hysterically in directions away from her father when she was aghast to realize that the very man she had killed to protect might be suspected of killing Rudy himself."

"But—" Colby had found his voice again, and a measure of authority. "It was all a mistake, a misapprehension, if it happened that way you said. Janos is right. It's going to be hard to prove."

"Maybe. But this roach under your desk isn't the only piece of evidence Midnight Louie found."

"What else is there?" Colby sounded defiant.

"Something he found on the floor of the chimney and batted around. I picked it up, but I didn't realize what it was until yesterday when I dug it out and turned it over: a broken-off fingernail, a ragged, pretty big hunk. That's one thing I noticed about you gentlemen after the death: your fingernails. None were missing, and rigging that step and chain in the narrow dark chimney would probably have shown on the culprit's hands. When my aunt and I went to the ME's office to identify Rudy's body, none of his nails were broken, not that he had much fingernail to lose; they were chewed down.

"Kendall's fingernails, though, are perfect salon models, exquisite. It's her trademark."

"So?" Janos was unimpressed. "She's always beautifully groomed. So what?"

"Yes, but women get to don false claws. I keep seeing her that night, so distraught, her fingers tightly curled over each other, only the thumbs visible. I took it for a sign of extreme stress, and it was, but it was also a form of concealment until she could repair the broken nail, which has traces of the same bronze enamel she wears."

"But Kendall—" Renaldi was still unconvinced. "Granted the death-trap was a simple rigging job. A loosened rung on the way-up, the chain anchored to the top brace. Rudy could have slipped and the noose could have failed to have tightened on his neck. He could have grabbed it to save himself. The whole scheme might have failed."

"But it didn't. If it had, the chain could have been dismissed as it almost was: a jingly prop someone had added to the traditional routine without mentioning it to anybody. A miss wouldn't have been significant enough to investigate."

"And then?"

"I don't know. I don't know if Kendall would have tried again. Maybe the delay would have encouraged her to talk to her father."

Janos sighed and Renaldi echoed him, but Renaldi spoke first. "I think Kendall should talk to her father now."

Colby didn't disagree, but he glared at his two partners. "She's been taking her divorce from Carl hard, feeling she let down the firm and the family. I guess I'm all the family she's got left, and when she thought I was in trouble . . . if my daughter's involvement in this comes out, so will our self-serving drug deal in Vietnam."

"That was only money, Brent, money made off a killing ground." Janos shook his head. "This is murder."

"Rudy didn't have much of a life."

"It was his life," Renaldi said. "You know, Brent, it's pretty ironic. We all killed in Vietnam, and tried not to put faces on the dead. You did your share, and I bet we could all kill again, given extreme enough circumstances, but I never thought a kid of ours would ever grow up to do the same thing. I thought that's what we all went through 'Nam for . . . for the future. Nothing we bought, or stole or made of ourselves afterwards is worth protecting the past at the cost of one goddamn more death."

And that was that.

They rose and went into the hall, the men's feet dragging as they neared the ajar door of Kendall's office. They could hear her on the phone, her voice animated with the unflagging energy of an advertising account exec making a call.

Temple began hooking up the CatAboard for Louie.

"Aren't you coming in?" Renaldi asked.

She shook her head. "Too many people for a small office. Besides, it's not my job; this is private firm and family business."

Chapter 36

Louie's Last Laugh

Well, I never expected to be renowned for my superior snout.

That is such a canine characteristic.

Nevertheless, I am carried in triumph back to Miss Kit Carlson's digs, where she is much gratified to see Miss Temple and me return no worse for wear.

Rudy is revenged, and Colby, Janos and Renaldi are facing a troublesome reorganization.

Unless, as Miss Temple tells her aunt, the surviving partners can conceal the ancient skullduggery.

"Poor Kendall," Miss Temple sighs.

"Poor Rudy," sighs Miss Kit.

They are a devoted pair of sighers. I wish we sniffers would get more credit.

"How did Louie know that there was a roach . . . I mean an unfortunate remnant of an old habit . . . under Brent Colby's desk?" Miss Kit Carlson asks in all innocence. "I did not think that cats were sensitive to that sort of thing."

"Oh," says Miss Temple in reply. "Cats are sensitive to all sorts of things. I noticed that Louie was well aware of roaches of both the insect and vegetable variety when we visited Rudy's apartment."

"You did not say anything."

"I did not wish to embarrass you about the circumstances of your friend's lifestyle," Miss Temple concedes.

Miss Kit nods with heavy head. "You are right. Especially in regard to Midnight Louie's inestimable nose. Cats are indeed sensitive to all sorts of things."

"Except the human heart." Miss Temple sighs again. "I can solve everyone else's problems, except my own."

Well, I would cry buckets over that, but I do not see how nailing another murderer is going to have a quelling effect on my Miss Temple's love life. Mr. Max Kinsella is still in the same business, so to speak, and Mr. Matt Devine is hardly one to criticize her penchant for crime and punishment, being off on peculiar missions of his own half the time.

"Well," says Miss Kit, with great energy. "We girls will have a fine time on our own celebrating the coming New Year at my party tomorrow night and toasting Louie and your forthcoming media career—"

"You really think we have a chance in hell of snagging the Allpetco assignment after our role in exposing the advertising agency by solving the Santa slaying?"

"Well," Miss Kit begins gamely, "It does establish that you both have exceptional crime-solving tendencies . . . oh, Temple!"

"Oh, Kit! What?"

Miss Kit Carlson is laughing so hard she is sliding to the floor. Again. I look around for wine bottles, but none are visible. "I know I should be sober and saddened into the New Year, but . . . what you just said!"

"What did I just say? Tell me!"

"Santa . . . slaying."

"So?"

"Santa *sleigh*-ing."

"Is nothing sacred?" Miss Temple demands as she comprehends Miss Kit's meaning and begins laughing hysterically and sliding to the floor as well. I sense that I am in for one of those girl-talk evenings again.

Is nothing sacred? Obviously not. How sad to see the state into which two grown single women can descend when the only male influence on the premises is feline. I plan an early retirement to the bedroom and the word processor. Hey! Maybe I can write a happy ending to Miss Temple's love life.

Chapter 37

Merry Maximus Christmas

"A mouse must be stirring," Temple called to Kit as she raced for the apartment door. "No one else would still be out and about this soon after Christmas."

She swung the door open wide, infected by the season and perhaps a bit too won over by the idea that New York City was a village.

What was out and about wasn't a mouse; it was a man. And not just any man, like a milkman or a rent collector or an IRS agent; it was Max Kinsella.

Temple felt her face freeze in astonishment. With a red muffler, a fake-fur-lined brown duster, arms full of packages and melting snowflakes dewing his sleek dark hair, Max looked like a recent escapee from Minnesota—or a Dickens tale—not from Las Vegas.

"Ma-ax—" Before Temple's inflection had committed to ending in either an exclamation point or a question mark, Max had swept her into the warmth within on an invisible current of icy outdoor air. Temple shivered as she was enveloped in coat, packages and a cold-lipped kiss of greeting that quickly turned subtropical.

.She might have stayed in this cozy, tented atmosphere indefinitely, except that a parrot high in a balmy palm tree atop snow-capped Mount Everest was screaming for attention.

"Temple!" Kit's voice was a delighted screech. She loved surprises, and this looked like a good one. "You're being assaulted by outerwear on my very doorstep. Desist, you rogue London Fog!"

Max's encumbered arms (Temple still in one's custody) spread wide in a show of innocence and greeting. "Merry Christmas! You must be the cousin Temple is visiting."

"Flatterer," Temple growled beneath her breath, trying to elbow out from under cover of the voluminous coat.

Max's smile never faltered as Kit closed in to inspect him.

"You must be——" Of course she knew; she had glimpsed him and Matt Devine at the Crystal Phoenix casino, and an ex-actress never forgot an interesting face, let alone two.

"A bottle of Dom Pérignon for the charming hostess." From his bottomless folds of coat Max produced the usual oversize bowling-pin shape wrapped in silver foil and tied with scarlet ribbon.

"The Mystifying Max," Kit pronounced after unwrapping the gift and eyeing the bottle's ornate label.

The label must have impressed her, for she found her widest, warmest smile and added her blessing to the obvious.

"Come in, and don't import any more of that icebox air than necessary." She peered at Temple still lurking in custody with intent to dither. "So nice of you to keep my niece warm on the threshold. If you close the door behind you, I believe you will find her nicely thawed."

Temple glared at Kit. "Don't promise anything you can't deliver personally."

But her aunt was already floating down the long gallery,

bearing the champagne to the kitchen. "She'll hang up your coat."

Temple had already sprung open the almost-hidden door in the foyer wall.

"White cliffs of Dover, with a secret door. Interesting." Max, eyeing the lofty rooms, shrugged off the heavy coat.

" 'Cousin.' " Temple shook her head.

"Never hurts to ingratiate oneself with the relatives. Especially when one comes bearing immoral propositions."

"They look like ordinary Christmas presents to me."

"Very ordinary. No magic tonight."

"You? Resist the casual sleight of hand? Hah. What are you doing here, anyway?"

"It's Christmas. We're both out of town. I thought a formal call wouldn't be out of order."

"I meant in New York. I know *how* you found me here. You asked Electra where I was staying."

"My trade secrets—useless." He sobered. "I had business . . ."

Temple, silent, stretched to push the bulky coat onto the lone unoccupied wooden hanger. Max, who was good about helping with small struggles like that, didn't.

He did lean a hand on the closet wall, penning Temple into a tête-à-tête. "Almost New Year's. I think it's time we discussed the future."

She backed into the huddled coats.

"I don't."

"Champagne-cracker needed!" Kit's impressive stage projection called from the living room. "Raffles, are you available?"

Max, unlike himself, snapped to attention to obey the call of masculine social duty, leaving Temple stuffing his coattails into the clustered mass of dangling outerwear.

"I hate winter," she muttered to the abused coats, punching them into place.

By the time she emerged, red-faced but calm, Kit and Max were in the living room holding flutes of champagne in which bubbles twined upward like crystal strands of DNA.

A lone flute sat atop the Lucite coffee table for Temple to claim.

Midnight Louie reclined on the broad windowsill to the left, artistically arranged between two pots of pink poinsettias. On a side table, Kit's small gilded Christmas tree twinkled against the silent night's billions and billions of kilowatts making a private light show of upper Manhattan.

"Killer location." Max turned to lift his untouched glass to Temple's. "To the New Year."

Temple stood numbly by as he and Kit chimed glass rims in turn.

At last she understood what had seemed different about Max, what had made him an almost-stranger, and had turned her strangely shy—and even abrupt.

He wasn't wearing his ever-green contact lenses. His eyes were paler, and their true color, which she had never glimpsed before, blue.

She turned to confirm this astounding fact with another witness to the preblue Max: Midnight Louie, who was tonguing a forefoot while giving Max an evil eye of authentic emerald-green. He looked as dubious as she felt, but then, he always did. That "Oh, yeah? You and what other Doberman?" look was a patented feline expression donned with the first fading of kittenish baby-blue eyes. Cats learned early, it seemed, that the world is mean and man uncouth.

"Temple? How do you like it?"

Her aunt's question reminded Temple to sip the champagne. Her opinion was pointless. She couldn't tell a bottle of Andre's from a Dom Pérignon. "Fine."

Max had sat on the low sofa at Kit's invitation, legs akimbo. His usual black had brightened for the holidays: he wore a cable-knit burgundy sweater over a black silk turtleneck and slacks. Temple smiled at this somber concession to the holidays and took the last seat left on the sofa, beside Max.

Kit's white walls, golden floors and black leather sofa felt harsh and coldly modern for the first time. The bare windows seemed as bleak as a factory's, and the light extravaganza beyond them a cheap trick, a chintzy set, a mere advertisement for the *real* New York–New York: the hotel and casino about to open January 3 in Las Vegas.

Temple had no reason to find Max's natural eye color unsettling, or significant, except that it was the sole thing about himself he had always controlled religiously. The one small secret that had seemed the biggest betrayal of all. The theatrical green eyes were a key part of his philosophy of "loud" being a better disguise than naked. Why had he discarded the contact lenses now? More disguise? Or was he making a statement, and, if so, what and to whom?

Ah, Max! Thy name is eternal question mark.

"I want to borrow Temple," Max told Kit. He sounded as if he were talking in a rain barrel. He turned and took Temple's hand, still addressing Kit. "Do you have anything planned that I'd interfere with?"

"Only a cocktail party tomorrow night at six. They're in again, even among the younger set. A farewell party for Temple. You must come."

"Of course. But this evening—?"

"Temple is as free as a rolling stone."

"Dinner?" he asked Temple directly at last. "I know a little restaurant."

Max always knew a little restaurant and now Temple knew why. Undiscovered, out-of-the-way places were the natural haunts of secret agents, counterspies and moonlighting magicians.

She nodded. Her right hand was warming nicely in his, and, in her left hand, the champagne tasted like ginger ale. She set it down on the thick plastic tabletop.

"Come on, I'll get you a good warm coat." Kit rose, took Temple's free hand and led the way to her bedroom, whispering all the way.

"Why on earth are you acting like a zombie? If *that* had

appeared on my doorstep as a post-Christmas surprise, I'd be doing the mazurka on the ice rink at Rockefeller Center. As a matter of fact, he just did. Heck, *I*'ll go out to dinner with him if you won't."

"There are buried issues," Temple said cautiously.

"There are always buried issues. But not between Christmas and New Year's, sweetie pie. Please! *Perk* up. Smile. It can't hurt that much to look at him. Try not to be crabby to the man, at least. It looks too eager."

"Too *eager*?"

"Here's my best holiday coat." Kit wrapped a circle of sheared acrylic around Temple like a mother dressing a child for the skating rink.

"Kit! It's *red*! I never wear red. My hair—"

" 'Tis the season to never say never. And wear these fluffy little earmuffs. Won't hide your hair. Nothing is less romantic than hidden hair. You have gloves, don't you? In that awful quilted down thing in the closet?"

"I didn't have much notice to buy anything warm, and the down thing isn't that bad."

"These gloves go with the earmuffs. See. The same white fake fur on the cuffs. Don't you look adorable. Little bunny rabbit! Too bad you have nothing but this monster tote bag to drag around. No matter. Have a great time. Don't worry about keeping me up too late. I'll have Monsieur Louie to keep me warm. Ooh-la-la!"

"Kit! I'll put the damn gloves on myself, thank you."

"Good. Snapping out of your malaise, I see. Be crabby with auntie. See if I care. But be kind to Max."

"I am always kind to animals."

"Grrrr. Off you go."

Kit propelled her back to the main room where Max was waiting at the prow of the view, blending into the night's black velvet backdrop, his back to them.

"Here she is. I'll get your coat."

He turned at Kit's voice, his expression still abstracted from thought. "I left a few things under the tree. House gifts."

"We'll open them tomorrow night." Kit shepherded her charges to the foyer, then whisked Max's heavy coat from the closet as if it were made of thistledown and held it up for him like a very short butler.

He dipped deeply at the knees to accept her unneeded assistance and straightened so quickly the coat whirled around him like a cape. "Shall we go?" he asked Temple, his eyes still blue.

So they went into the cold, snowy night. Temple was glad she was so bundled up that virtually nothing—and no one—could get to her. Not even a magician.

Nobody on wheels in New York City had ever noticed her when she stood six feet out in the slushy winter street and beckoned frantically for a cab. Max hesitated near the curb and lifted one arm like a rather lazy conductor. Six cabs topped by unlit signs sped toward them like a racing field of greyhounds exclusively clad in yellow.

Somehow one always sank *down* into New York City cabs. Down into a slick worn seating surface polished by rear ends covered in Givenchy fur coats and polyester pants and worn blue jeans and designer leather. Long-gone occupants had left an aura of stale, backstage fumes behind them, along with a mélange of Brut and Poison and Opium and the sweetly nauseating hint of the occasional double-malt scotch vomit.

Max didn't bother with gloves, even in winter, yet his hands never cooled. Maybe he didn't want to hamper the tools of his trade, those magically nimble fingers. Now they clasped Temple's icy, gloved hand.

"There's no place like New York," he said. "The energy, the crowds and the rush. It's the toughest audience on the planet."

"I didn't think you were performing anymore."

He leaned back in the lumpy seat. "I'm always performing. You know that."

"Yes, and you were very good tonight with Aunt Kit. She practically pushed me out the door into your clutches."

The mention was mother to the reality. Max's clutches tightened around her.

"Temple, don't pout. It doesn't become you. I've told you more about myself than anyone outside the network knows."

"Max, I'm afraid! Of what happened to you, of what could happen to you. I've never known a professional wire-walker before."

"Yes you have. We all are that at times. Molina, the deceptively ditsy Madame Electra, your friend the good father, even Midnight Louie."

"Deceptively—? The good father—? Max, what have you done now? That was privileged information."

"Nothing's privileged, only private for a time. I had him checked out. Needed to know."

"That's despicable. Unfair. Vile. I mean it!"

"That's my job, Temple, and part of my job is to protect you."

"Not at other people's cost."

"*Always* at other people's cost. If finding out happens to explain just why you're so protective of his past, why you can swear that 'nothing' happened, so much the better for me."

"Max. I don't know what to say."

"Don't say anything for a while. I came to New York to see some people, find out if there was any realistic possibility of my withdrawing safely."

"From your . . . situation?"

He nodded, glancing at the cab driver beyond the battered grille. "We'll talk about it later. For now, let's just enjoy the ride."

A more unenjoyable ride she could not imagine, but Max pulled her against him and she couldn't resist the pull he exercised on her whether it was literal or not.

Temple surrendered to jostling along in the back of the fender-brushing, barreling cab, her head on Max's chest, even through the earmuffs hearing the thrum of his heart. She thought about them, Max in winter, with no hat, no gloves and an open coat. Herself, booted and bundled and gloved and earmuffed, and still cold.

She examined the chasm between them, more than style or temperament, and tried to gauge whether its depth and width had changed now that the burden of Matt Devine's priestly past was not hers alone. Through no fault of her own. *Mea culpa. Mea Maxima culpa.* Look at how she mixed metaphors now: Max was showing up in the fragments of religious ritual she had learned from Matt. Max the Inevitable. Matt the . . . Unforgettable.

Enjoy, Max had said, and she finally decided, quite deliberately, to do just that.

Temple smiled as her head bounced on the hard-muscled pillow of Max. Now getting overheated by outerwear in inner angst, she was also getting sleepy, very, *very* sleepy. That old Max magic was at it again.

The cab had stopped and Max had paid before she stirred to her surroundings.

"I said enjoy." Max was teasing her. "I meant relax. I didn't mean go comatose. Some date. Come on, sleepyhead."

She didn't bother telling him that this was the first time she had felt utterly secure in New York, but let him pull her across the cracked leather seat and out onto the sidewalk. There, the night cold revived her like refrigerated smelling salts.

The restaurant was a picture window of plate glass with one word scrawled across it that she couldn't read. Max swept her in a narrow door beside the window into a broom closet of a place crammed with tables and chairs knocking legs. Temple had a sense of being yet lower in Greenwich Village, maybe in some discreetly hidden yuppie soup kitchen.

No reservations; the aproned waiter led them to a tiny table for two slammed against the wall between thronging tables for six, both full of animated, preppie diners.

"Drink?" asked the waiter without preamble.

Temple thought she should be careful not to order anything too heady. But she wanted something warming, and exotic. She almost wished this were a touristy Oriental place, where she could order a Tokyo Typhoon with three kinds of rum and two kinds of liqueur, which came flaming with skewered fruit and a combustible paper umbrella.

"Gin, scotch, vodka, wine or beer," the waiter clarified with impatience.

Max was waiting for her.

"A martini," she decided. The quintessential New York drink. "With an onion."

"No onions," the waiter pronounced with the same absolute indifference at being found lacking that all service people in New York share.

Temple shrugged good-naturedly and waited to see what exotica Max would come up with.

"Scotch on the rocks." He was not asked if he preferred something other than the house brand. Temple was sure that he did.

They had to hunch across the tiny table to hear each other because of the racket. The slight wooden chairs threatened to tip over under the burden of their heavy outerwear. Despite the crowding and the din of many voices percolating into the air, the restaurant seemed chilly. They kept their coats over their shoulders. Besides, where would they have put them?

Temple gazed around happily. She had expected a slick, upscale restaurant with "décor" and a wine list and "nouveau" plates of next-to-nothing in the food department. This was infinitely better. It felt like ducking into a neighborhood restaurant on Lyndale Avenue in Minneapolis, where they had met and courted, if people still called it that.

Their drinks only came after the table of six near them got their entrées, and then the waiter lingered, pencil poised, hungry for their food order. And there was a wine list. A wrinkled half-page listing surprisingly pricey by-the-glass offerings.

Temple asked for the shrimp alla something or other, a pasta dish.

Max requested the chicken Parmesan and was firmly told that he would much prefer something other of the chef's invention. He shrugged.

"That's so rude," Temple whispered across the foot of space separating them. "Who does he think he is?"

"The chef."

"The chef?"

"And the owner."

"He waits tables *and* cooks?"

"Not simultaneously."

"And for this we have to pay eight dollars for a glass of wine we never heard of before?"

"It's sure to be excellent."

"Sure!"

Temple toyed with the short stem of her widemouthed martini glass. The martini glass's very silhouette had been an icon of sophistication since the twenties. A dozen Art Deco graphics featuring its rigorous sculptural form, so geometric, flipped through her mind. And no onion, just the usual salty green olive. New York City, where they seemingly had everything, was the one place where they made a point of not giving it to you.

Max was reading her Midwestern mind, and laughing at her.

"It's called chutzpah, and it was invented here."

"Like the martini?"

"Not like the martini. Not in a bar. On the street and out the window and up your avenue."

Temple lifted her precariously filled glass in a toast. "To the unexpected joys of not getting what you want."

"I hope not," Max muttered into his scotch.

"Is it safe to tell me what kind of a deal you worked out with the network? Gosh, it sounds like you toil for CBS or something."

"Not a bad cover. Well, I saw Uncle Walter," he added with elaborate caution.

"The gray eminence."

"Retired, but still active. Our founder. He was quite sympathetic to my ultimate goal, and thought it possible, even though it's never been done before."

"Leaving the network."

"Not alive."

Temple winced and chugalugged gin as smooth as French perfume, and about as pungent. "God, Max— You're not kidding, are you?"

His eyes glittered across the table, bright as swords. "I never kid. We agree that the only way is to clear up these casino deaths. Mine, and your friend's."

"He's got a name."

"Matt. Sort of flat and predictable, isn't it?"

"Rather like Michael. An archangel. I'd think you two would have something in common."

"Yes, but she's a bone of contention. A rag and a bone to pick and a hank of red hair of contention."

"I hate that expression."

"Good. Now we're off the subject of the late Father Devine."

"He's not dead."

"To hear you tell it, he is, or weren't you being absolutely frank?"

"I was, and he isn't. Can we talk about . . . Uncle?" She giggled, thanks to the martini. "Remember that old show that's on in reruns, like Mary Tyler Moore. *The Man from U.N.C.L.E.* That's what we can call you. The man from Uncle Walter."

"Glad you're enjoying yourself." Max picked up the table knife, which was oddly oversize, like all the silverware. He cut along the padded white tablecloth, a phantom incision with a dull blade, but precise nevertheless.

"Uncle suggested that it may be necessary to work with . . . Matt. No full disclosure, of course. And he agreed that you will have to be kept informed, might even turn up something on your own, as a liaison between myself and Matt."

"Me, in the middle? And no full disclosure for me either, right?"

He nodded. "Can't be. Trust me."

"Ah, you must be working for the government, after all. In Max we trust."

His warm fingertips touched her cold ones on the foot of the martini glass. "Look into my eyes. What do you see?"

"They're so different. That color. You don't look like yourself."

"Sometimes the truth is less attractive than the illusion."

"It's not that blue doesn't become you . . . it hasn't *become you* yet. Do you know what I mean?"

His fingers tightened on hers. "That I'm a stranger, again. I'm trying to be as honest as the laws of survival allow me."

"If things are as dire as you say, then you shouldn't have anything to do with me, for my own sake."

"That's true. That's why I want you to keep going to the mat with Father Matt. Get good at self-defense, Temple. Take it seriously. I suggest a pistol range too."

"What do you want? A mini-Molina?"

"I want you as tough on the outside as you are on the inside. If we're to be together, you'll have to be."

"Together?"

"That's another thing I've tried to work out. We can't . . . live together as we did before, but we can come darn close. I want it back, Temple. I want back everything we had before I had to leave. I'd never had that before, and I don't want to give it up."

She sighed, and gazed at her half-empty martini glass. Or half-full, as the popular philosophy insisted on looking at it. The gin had slightly blurred the edges of her senses and sensibilities. A murmur of voices around, the warmth of the encroaching tables and chairs and sagging coats made Temple feel both oddly safe and oddly removed. Was this Max's immoral proposal? Clandestine cohabitation instead of openly living together, as before? Yet he was offering her more honesty in the truly closed portion of his life and past, where danger intersected desire at a perilous angle.

"I told you I was faithful all the months that I was gone," he said softly. Yet his voice carried all the way to her heart. "You don't seem to doubt that, and I thank you. But I have to admit that it wasn't as difficult for me to be true as for most men. I've lived whole stretches as celibate as a priest, an honest priest anyway. Too dangerous, for me and for the woman. Why do you think James Bond has his Bond girls, a new one for every novel? They don't last, Temple. And in real life, Bond wouldn't either. And if he did, he wouldn't keep seducing some pathetically gorgeous girl to her inevitable end. When I broke the rules and took you with me to Las Vegas, it was because what happened between us was so true and powerful, I finally couldn't say no. I'm weary of being on the edge alone. I want a partner. I've had it with performing solo. In my magic act, in my life and in my secret profession. You're involved, whether you wish it or not, whether you still love me or not. We might as well make it semiofficial, and fight for what we both want. If we still both want it."

His eyes were searching hers, not the hypnotic green eyes of a cat, but the clear blue eyes he was born with. *Changeling,* she thought, *how will I ever know the real colors of you?*

During the silence of that searching moment, the waiter-cum-chef appeared beside Temple, wafting heavy pasta dishes in front of them both. Steam curled up in waves, like heat from a chill wet street. It was a curtain, a tissue of illusion between them, but it would soon cool and dissipate. Did anyone really want to see too clearly?

The magician of the menu announced a roller coaster of Italian syllables, the name of each creation.

Temple sampled her dish, surprised by the perfect yet elusive taste. "And yours?" she asked Max.

"As sublime as he said. Chefs are the most eccentric of geniuses."

"No, just temperamental. We aren't used to that, so we think it's eccentric. Tell me about your life . . . before."

They concentrated on eating, while Max doled out details between bites. It added up to a lifestyle Temple could only imagine.

"The first eight years, when I was young and foolish, it was like living in a computer-game world designed just for me. I was like the Little Prince to them, in peril, but also invaluable. I traveled in Europe, free of charge. My interest in magic was heaven-sent for my new role. I saw and studied with the best magicians the Continent had to offer. I traveled off-Continent, eastward. I was taught . . . everything I wanted to know and a great deal that I didn't know enough to want to know."

That was when Temple's expression had grown skeptical.

"Yes, even that. I had my Mata Haris. I was a blank slate, possessed by guilt and vengeance. They shaped me into a perfect weapon."

"Did you kill people?"

"The whole point was to keep people from being killed. I saved hundreds, I know, from bomb plots and hijackings and more personal mayhem. What I learned and passed on might have resulted in people's deaths. But these were people who'd be facing death penalties if they were caught."

"Should you be talking about this here?" The table was so tiny that their faces practically met over their empty plates, but still, Temple thought.

"Too noisy, too small. Besides, I'm wearing a powerful listening device; I'd hear anyone who said anything suspicious, or who was suspiciously quiet. Instead they're all discussing the best preschool in Manhattan and their post-Christmas cruise. Hardly matters of international interest."

"You're wired?"

"I'm used to listening in two directions at once."

"I guess. Tell me more about the Mata Haris."

Max couldn't keep from grinning. "Pretty heady for a teenager. It took my mind off my dead cousin and the pretty colleen who had divided us. I had a field day, and then AIDS began creeping in from Africa, and I grew up and discovered that I was a kind of plague carrier myself, and lonely besides. The glamour was gone. I was no longer coddled, but expected to earn back the investment in me. It wasn't a game, after all, but life and death. My life and death too. I was cut off from everything I had known, my family, my country, my culture. I became what was necessary, a magical mystery machine, remote from everything and everybody, playing a role. Those were my monkish years, and a good thing too, or I'd have never passed those Minnesota AIDS tests."

Temple shivered. "What a weird, empty, excessive life."

"They sent me to the U.S. on sabbatical, figuring I was about to crack from the strain. I did, but not in the way they were worried about."

"I was the crack?"

He nodded. "Want dessert?"

"No, I couldn't—"

"We'll share," he decreed.

Max was very good at decreeing, the Little Prince grown up.

The surly chef appeared to collect their plates and promised to return with "some" dessert. Of some sort.

Temple threw up her hands. "I'm beginning to think mystery menus are natural."

"Only in New York. What else do you want to know?"

"More about the Mata Hari types."

"And yet you are the soul of discretion on one lone ex-priest."

"*I* don't have exotic bedroom habits."

"You remember."

"That is not your problem, Max. My memory."

"No. My problem is what it always was, the moment I decided that the IRA had to pay for my cousin's death."

He absently moved the empty drinking glasses aside, though that would no doubt infuriate the waiter/chef. "You know those two thugs who accosted you? The ones whose rap sheets I brought up on the computer at Gandalf's house?"

She nodded.

"I've been trying to track them down. They were known around Vegas, but they haven't been seen since. My out-of-state sources come up blank. I don't think they'll ever hurt anyone again."

"They're dead?"

"And buried out in the Mojave, I'd bet. Whatever is going on in Las Vegas, someone wants a lid kept on it, at any cost. Do you feel safer?"

"That those men are dead?" Temple looked around, but no one was wearing a spy trench coat. "I don't think so. I don't need them dead. I hope you didn't—"

"No. Execution is not my specialty. Information is."

"Max, that's, ummph, so cold."

He nodded.

An entity appeared between them, flaming, and landed as softly as a chocolate UFO on the tabletop. Drizzles of white chocolate and raspberry sauce latticed the central core of white-and-dark-chocolate-checkerboarded cheese-cake.

"I can't believe," Temple said, "that we're going to eat this exquisite gazebo of chocolate and discuss what we're discussing."

"We're not." Max's clenched fist on the table relaxed suddenly. Temple hadn't noticed it before, but as his fingers parted she spied a small black-velvet box beneath them.

"You said no magic." Her tone was accusatory, but just barely.

"No magic. I had it in my coat pocket and brought it out while you were distracted by Mata Haris."

Well, what woman, no matter how thoroughly modern,

no matter how un-Mata Hari–like, is going to ignore a small square jewelry box?

Temple's icy fingers edged it to her side of the tiny table, then she pressed the catch so the lid flipped up.

The lighting in this nameless (to her) restaurant left as much to be desired as the specificness of the menu, if not the skills of the chef.

Still, a ring is a ring and hard to mistake. But it was not just a ring. It was a free-form flow of pink gold guarding a low-profile opal of incredible fire and subtlety. Diamonds stood guard, flashing their own more obvious fire.

"Max, this is exquisite, but what is it?"

He understood that she wasn't asking about the ring's components, but its meaning, to him, to her.

"A friendship ring?" Mischievous. "A preengagement ring?" Testing. "A what-the-hell, it's-gorgeous, I'll-grab-it-and-let-the-guy-think-what-he-likes ring?" Cynical. "It's my ring, to you. I hope you like it. I hope you'll wear it. I hope it means we have a future." Bottom line.

Temple lifted it off the small velvet tab that held it upright. Although made like lace molded from hot lava, it was a strong, solid design, broader than she would think a small hand could carry off. The dying light of the cheesecake (or whatever) flambé made it into a glimmering raw vein of ore: fugitive, elusive, like Max himself.

She lifted it between the thumb and forefinger of her right hand. Which finger should she try it on? There was only one; even recognizing that was a commitment she hardly dared think about.

She slid the band over the first knuckle of her third finger, left hand.

It fit like magic. Not too tight or too loose. A Cinderella shoe of a ring. She would expect nothing less from Max. She showed him her hand, which he took, his face a textbook picture of anxious concentration. He hadn't been sure it would fit (though he knew better), he hadn't been sure she would like it (though he hoped so). He certainly hadn't been sure she would wear it.

He glanced up, and in this dim restaurant, his eyes were light, but of no color, as water nullifies the hue of whatever it reflects into a translucent memory.

"Will you come home with me tonight, Temple?"

She never even thought to ask where home was.

Chapter 38

Encore! Encore!

"It reminds me of the Algonquin," she observed as they moved past the cozy lobby to the old-fashioned front desk with its pigeonholes of room keys behind the clerk.

"So would a lot of small hotels of this age in New York," Max said. "This one is quieter than the Algonquin."

He asked for the room key, standing on her left, her bare, beringed hand in his, as it had been since they had left the restaurant in a cab.

Temple's fingers weren't cold any more, heated in the furnace of Max's grasp. He took the room key and its old-fashioned wooden plaque in his left hand as smoothly as if it had been his dominant right; eerily flexible, Max Kinsella, and in moments they were huddled before the gingerbread brass grille of the elevator, waiting for the single car to waft them upward.

"Still cold?" he asked, bending his head so she could hear him.

"Not exactly," Temple answered with admirable understatement.

The elevator grille, and then the doors, opened. A wizened old man in a uniform, a hunchback, a wizard, opened the inner grille for them.

Max filled the small elevator like a giant, and their separate and entwining emotions suffused it like an aphrodisiac. Max crushed her into a long, tortuous kiss against the back wall. The old man's neck was too stiff to turn and see, but Temple sensed him smiling into closed wooden doors.

Max thrust a tip into his hand as they left the car. Temple had never heard of anyone doing that, but the operator said "Thank you, sir and missus. Merry Christmas to you too," right out of Dickens's *A Christmas Carol.*

"Poor man thinks we're married," Temple said, feeling fraudulent and anxious to get reality on record.

"I don't think so."

The room wasn't far down the narrow hall with its ancient brocade-pattern paper in gilded trellises that gave a sense of greater vistas beyond, and yet of confinement.

"I've got to call Kit and tell her I won't be coming back tonight."

"She knows."

"How do you know she knows? Yes, she's pretty hip for an aunt, but she might worry."

"She might worry more if you *did* go back tonight."

"Oh, really. That sure of yourself?"

"Of me, maybe. Of you, never. Just of her."

"I'll call."

"Fine. Now do you want to come in, or not?"

"Of course I do." Temple turned around when she was in the room. Small, high ceiling, high bed, lots of mahogany furniture from the forties, once splendid, and still pretty spiffy. A narrow door to a closet. A narrow door to a bathroom. And probably a hundred and eighty dollars a night, as a single. Oh! She was an illegal guest. A smuggle-in. A New York wetback.

"Temple. We've been here before. This is nothing new. Calm down."

"Where's the phone?"

He pointed to the bedside table, and to one of the closed doors.

"A phone in the bathroom? In a place this small?"

"They pride themselves on modern conveniences."

"I'll dash in, then."

She dropped her tote bag on the floor, and her coat and earmuffs and gloves, or Kit's rather, and vanished through the indicated door.

All white tile, with that ancient octagon-of-white–tiled floor grouted with black. Twenties. The phone was a wall model. Brand-new. She punched in Kit's number, glancing at her watch. Almost midnight. Going to get the old girl up . . .

It was answered on the first ring. "Hello." Kit, no doubting that husky contralto.

"It's Temple."

"No kidding."

"I just wanted to let you know that I . . . we . . . wouldn't be making it back to your place tonight."

"No kidding."

"Kit! You're my aunt."

"That doesn't make me dumb, does it? Don't answer that."

"Oh, Kit. I . . . I don't know. I'm not ready . . . I just have the dopey clothes I had on at your place and—"

"Tut-tut. Look in that ludicrously large tote bag of yours, Cinderella."

"Tote bag?"

Temple opened the bathroom door an inch. "Max," she said sweetly, "can you just hand in my tote bag? Thank you." Temple grabbed it and kicked the door shut. "What do you mean 'look'?" she demanded of the phone.

"Just look."

Temple pawed through the usual flotsam of her bag and felt something filmy snag on her fingernails. She dredged out a great deal of sheer black chiffon.

"Kit! What is this?"

"An example of a postmenopausal woman's optimism. Don't do anything in it I wouldn't do. I expect a *full* report whenever. Within the bounds of good taste, and close relatives, of course. Bye, dear. Sweet dreams."

The phone droned at her. Temple pulled and pulled and pulled black chiffon out of her bag until she felt like a magician doing the scarf trick. Well, Kit and she were the same size, and this certainly had to be better than second-best undies . . . and who knows what those European Mata Haris had worn just to the beauty parlor?

She peeked out a few minutes later, relieved to hear the homely drone of the television set on low. Only one small bedside lamp lit the room besides the eerie glow of the TV screen.

She ankled out, casual, aiming a comment at the man in the bed. "It's all yours. The bathroom, I mean!"

Why did resuming a love affair after an interim feel so much like starting one all over again?

A hand stretched out from the bed. She took it, gratefully; this high, narrow, old-fashioned bedstead required mounting.

"Guess what's on?" Max's profile was directed toward the TV. How . . . domestic. How . . . easy.

"What's on?"

"Mary Tyler Moore reruns."

"Really? It must be weird to be an actor and see yourself as you were thirty years ago."

"Must be."

Max had one hand on the remote control, and one hand on her. Men! God bless 'em.

Temple snuggled down next to him, and sighed.

His free hand trailed through a stupendous excess of sheer black chiffon at her hip. "Must have caught something exotic in there."

"From the forties, probably."

"Forties noir."

"Exactly."

The remote control clicked, and the TV went black, forties noir black.

Temple woke up in the night, hearing the mechanical wail of an ambulance or a police car. For a moment she panicked, not recognizing the shape and shadows of the room. Everything was dark except for a blot of white shadow at the big old window. She reached out in the bedclothes, touched a figure, sleeping.

The white blot of window was a spotlight. Temple stretched in the comfortably rumpled covers, realized she was missing something, and finally found a heap of black chiffon on the floor.

She yawned.

The bathroom door was closed.

She stretched out an arm.

And stretched.

And stretched and found only empty bed linens.

Temple frowned for a moment, then relished her unexpected privacy. She felt wonderful, all over. Body, mind, soul. Like an unused instrument that had performed a very private concerto. In the muted daylight, the alien ring gleamed on her left hand. A band, winding like a road. A stone, glittering like a rainbow pond. Diamonds like dew. Everything was . . . like, groovy.

She bent over the bed's edge to fish up the fallen chiffon. Might as well see in daylight what this thing had looked like last night.

Max should be out of the bathroom soon. She didn't hear the shower spattering . . . She got up, wriggled into the nightgown and tiptoed to the bathroom door.

A small desk crouched against the wall beside the bathroom door. An oblong of stationery caught her eye. An oblong of written-upon stationery.

She stopped, braced her arms on the desk and read the bold, left-leaning script.

Temple darling,

The salutation stopped her heart. It could only lead to one thing.

I hate this, but the call came last night and you were dead asleep. Something's happened in Las Vegas I need to look into right away. I thought of taking you with me, but remembered you and Louie may still have business at the advertising agency. I'll tell you everything as soon as you get back, and call you at your aunt's this afternoon.

This isn't the way I planned to wake you up in the morning, believe me.

All my love,
Max

"Max!" Temple repeated aloud, making a fist and hitting the paper.

On her white-knuckled hand, the broad gold ring looked like a weapon.

She relaxed her fingers. What else could he have done? Max.

Chapter 39

The Billie Holiday Blues

"How did it go?" Kit wasted no time in greeting Temple at the door. She peered beyond her, hopefully, into the hall.

"Mixed reviews," Temple said shortly, barreling past her in the warm red coat and bunnie-cute earmuffs and gloves.

Inside, she ripped them off and tossed them on a chair.

"Mixed reviews?" Kit collapsed atop her discarded outerwear on the chair. "You surprise me. Max surprises me."

"Me too. Oh, the main event was fabulous. It's just that the encore was sadly lacking."

"Encore?"

"He's gone. Left last night. Sometime. I was sleeping. Called back to Vegas."

"A magician is on call?"

Temple cast her aunt a quelling look. "Oh, it's not his fault. I understand. It's just that it was a teeny bit anticlimatic, you might say." Her smile felt wan, even to her. "Thanks for the radical gown. I really needed that."

"But the performance was . . . adequate?"

"Auntie Kit, your best gown did not serve in vain, that

I can assure you. I just like to wake up next to the man I slept with the night before. Like I said, it's not Max's fault. He has . . . obligations."

"I went out with a fireman once. Don't laugh, I did. Sweet man, sexy man, but he did keep odd hours."

"Odd hours. That's the way to put it." Temple glanced down at her left hand. "My Christmas present."

"Oh, honey! That's gorgeous. And very promising."

Temple nodded. "You're right. I'm being immature. The evening was wonderful, the restaurant, the food, the hotel, Max. I needed every bit of it too." Temple leaned against the wall. "It all just happened so fast. My emotions feel like they've been on a roller coaster."

"I can understand that. How long since you and Max have been together?"

Temple calculated. "Almost ten months."

"Sounds like things went better than most people would expect after all that time."

"He's going to call this afternoon."

"But he won't be here for your party tonight?"

"No. What did you really think of him, Aunt Kit?"

"Oh, my. Don't ask the deprived. Of course, I've been smitten ever since you reported that he told you that going to bed again would resolve all your doubts. I do like a confident man. Did it?"

"Yes, and no."

"Hmm. You're wearing the ring."

"I loved him, and he loved me, but I don't know if we can work out what needs to be worked out."

"Past tense?"

"Past tense bleeding messily into present and future, especially now that we've tumbled into bed again. I can't really explain what stands between us, Kit. It's very serious, and not either one's fault. We're caught by past circumstances. Nobody to blame. But sad just the same. For now, there's hope. I guess that's what I should concentrate on."

Temple shrugged. "Do you want your, uh, thingama-jiggy back?"

"It's your memory now. Keep it and wear it in good health."

"It's *not* wearing it that's so good for one's health, Aunt."

"Whatever," Kit said coyly, looking pleased.

The day would have been anticlimactic, like any morning after the night before, except that at 4 P.M. Kit's phone rang.

She dashed to get it, then stretched the cord as far as it would uncoil to check on Temple's location: brooding at the Manhattan cityscape for one of the last times this trip, a slick magazine lying open and unread on her lap.

Kit laid down the receiver and ran to get Temple.

"It's a man," she whispered like any roommate.

"What man?"

"I didn't ask, but who do you suppose? Who said he was going to call from La Vegas?"

Temple checked her watch as she rose and clomped over to the phone in deliberate contrast to Kit's hush-hush manner.

"It's only one P.M. there." She was about to point out to her aunt, who like most Easterners had a very vague idea of where time zones changed and what that meant, that Max would barely have had time to get to Las Vegas and tend to whatever was so urgent by now, much less call her. But she was at the phone, so she picked it up and said a slightly less perky than usual "Hello."

"Yes?" she repeated, as if something was wrong with the line.

"Oh!" She went on, aware that her whole tone had changed. "I didn't recognize your voice at first. Must be the long-distance lines. No, I'm not disappointed. Just . . . tired."

Kit came racing over on her even noisier scuffs, primed for eavesdropping, even if the act was fated to be one-sided. She leaned against the window ledge and concentrated so much Temple feared she could hear through long-distance lines.

Temple sat slowly on one of the tall kitchen stools, feeling bemused.

"Not too tired to talk, no. You are? This afternoon. How did everything go?

"Oh, really.

"That's . . . good. I mean, wonderful!

"Yes, I am pretty tired out." Here Temple glanced at her aunt with a significant look. "Yes. Up late. Maybe that's why I sound a little . . . 'down.'

"Well, I can't wait to hear the details.

"Yes?

"Yes?

"No!

"All right. I'll be back about noon tomorrow. No, don't meet me at the airport. Really; I mean it. It's such a hop, skip and jump home, and my luggage arrangement worked great, even with Louie the pouch potato aboard.

"Think we got the job. Pretty solid. Yeah, I'm excited. Solved the murder too.

"I'm sure you are too. And I'm glad, I'm really glad that your trip was so productive.

"Yeah. That's wonderful."

Kit had come nearer with every answer, watching Temple's face contradict her words all the more the longer the conversation continued.

"I'm so happy for you. Can hardly wait.

"Yes.

"Yes, I do."

By now Temple's face looked as empty as a deserted parking lot, but her voice had increased enough in energy and an upbeat volume with every answer to fill a Broadway house. Then suddenly that booming optimism failed. Her face crumpled.

"Bye," she whispered into the phone at last, her voice starting to shatter like a crystal metronome.

"Honey!" Kit took the phone from Temple's limp fingers, and checked for a dial tone, which there indeed was.

She hung up the receiver, still warm from Temple's death grip.

"Temple, what's the matter? I've never heard such an inane half-conversation outside a post-modern play, but you look as if you'd gotten your own death notice."

Temple shook her head no, but let her aunt guide her back to the living room couch.

Kit sat her down, not releasing Temple's hand until she sat beside her.

"Tell me, Temple. Who was it? What was wrong?"

"Nothing's wrong." Temple sighed abruptly, as a dog will sometimes do for no reason. Temple had a reason. "It was Matt, calling from Chicago."

"Something must be wrong."

Temple shook her head in a dazed way. "No. His trip home was not a cakewalk, but he resolved a lot, learned a lot. Now he's ready to go back to Las Vegas and take care of a lot, including any leftover problems with his stepfather. He feels his phone-counseling job is a dead end, that he needs to find something more in keeping with his education level, even his earning level."

"That's sensible. That's great."

"Oh, yeah. Terrific. I hardly recognized his voice. It was so sure, so happy. He sounded like another . . . person. He has so much to tell me. He can hardly wait. He can hardly wait—well, I don't have to go into everything. But he can hardly wait to see me again. Tomorrow. Kit. I've never heard him so up, so high, so . . . committed."

"Committed to what?"

Temple swallowed and finally looked at her aunt with truly tragic eyes. "To . . . life. To . . . love. To . . . us."

"Oh, honey."

Kit just took her hands again, and held them.

Chapter 40

Stompin' at the Algonquin

I cannot explain it. Karma is not within three thousand miles of this place, yet my conscience is bothering me. Some may think that one of my ilk cannot have a conscience, but I assure you that mine is in exquisite working order.

Much as I am pleased that the Sublime Solange is likely to partner me in a continuing series of film endeavors, I am not pleased by the shabby treatment meted out to the Divine Yvette. Sisters they may be under the skin, but the Divine Yvette was there first, both in my heart and on the television screen. I cannot let her think that I am a party to the cowardly way she has been victimized, betrayed and cast aside in a maternal condition. A certain once-royal British princess comes to mind.

So I must leave the cozy nest Miss Kit Carlson has fashioned for herself down in the Village, and travel uptown (as far as midtown, anyway) to my love's current hostelry, the Algonquin Hotel. I have heard Miss

Savannah Ashleigh boasting of her address to the advertising personnel, though how one who is about as high-brow as a Barbie doll would appreciate staying at a joint famed for hosting the Mount Olympus—browed Round Table wits of the thirties is beyond my Ken.

Such puzzles of human misbehavior aside, this small jaunt uptown is sure to be no cakewalk on a catwalk. Yet I am an intrepid as well as an inventive soul, and I figure if I can do Las Vegas blindfolded, I can certainly manage Manhattan with my eyes wide open and all four sets of shivs on intruder-alert.

Frankly, I am more concerned about traffic plain and simple than such evil elements as drug traffickers, gangs, personal electronics salesmen and predatory street people (as opposed to just plain street people, who are usually in no condition to prey on so much as a stray cat, more's the pity). I decide to make my trek at dusk, when nature conspires—even in such an urban center as New York City—to render my natural coloring an advantage.

My escape from Miss Kit Carlson's Shangri-la in the Sky will be my first challenge.

Luckily, Miss Temple and her aunt are consumed by the problem *du jour:* which Las Vegas swain is the more promising for Miss Temple's future happiness? Miss Temple has also grown complacent after having successfully carted me to New York and about Madison Avenue. She now views me as a furry pouch potato. Something she can tote here and there. I can see that ground transportation in this town is hell, but I am not ready to give up locomotion for life.

So I work my way to the front door, sit down facing it, and contemplate my options.

They are "poor" and "none."

I have seen neither hide nor hair of the vaunted "super" for this building, and from what I have heard of building superintendents in New York City, they definitely have both hide *and* hair, and probably two-inch fangs to go with them.

Such an individual would not willingly help out one of my kind.

My entry to this residence was effected by a visitor opening the front door, an easy invitation for one of my subtle tendencies to eel in, or out, unnoticed. However, this poor bloke is as dead as Christmas's hottest gift item will be in return lines next week. I am forced to reinvent the wheel, or, in this case, the hinge.

I am so discouraged that I leap to the window ledge. I often do my best thinking while reclining artistically between two potted poinsettias. By "potted" I do not mean polluted in a liquid sense, although these two could use some watering. I gaze on the building across from me. If I could only dream up some little act that would alarm a friendly, voyeuristic neighbor and send him or her rushing over to warn the ladies of an impending danger.

Then I look up. This apartment is strangely made, with high pointed ceilings and high shelves underneath them fit only for gathering dust or holding ugly large-scale decorative objects and innumerable small spiders. In some ways Miss Kit Carlson is living in a fish bowl and I am on *Candid Camera*. What can I do to inspire a stranger to rush over and ring the doorbell?

Locking a leg behind my neck and conducting some delicate personal grooming in plain view might enrage a few envious pussycats, but I cannot see a human coming all unhinged at such a display.

I could knock the rather unfortunate Santa Fe vase off the upper shelf, but the noise would draw the attention of my darling ladies, the eventuality I most desire to avoid.

I study a small, star-shaped metal object embedded in the ceiling. I believe it is a sprinkler system, a precaution against fires. In my experience, that is, in Las Vegas, Nevada, such escapees from Asian martial arts films are usually to be found in major buildings, like offices or hotels, but apparently New Yorkers are unusually safety-conscious, especially in old buildings that have been renovated recently.

Is there any way Midnight Louie could start a fire other than by coming on to some new girl in town? I leap onto a countertop to paw open a drawer, though hardly anybody keeps matches around any more.

Pity. The humble matchbook cover used to solve many a crime in the olden days, especially when used as a memo pad. Now, hardly anybody at all even smokes, except oysters and herrings, of which I am exceptionally fond. Still, my groping limb overturns one of those short stubby votive candles. And where there is wax with a fuse, there is usually a matchstick to light it.

Finally I work out a matchbook, but it is not one of those cheapie, flip-cover, old-movie jobs, but a tiny little box with tiny little wooden matchsticks in it. How adorable! Nonetheless, I take this worthless object in my teeth and hop from counter to espresso-machine top to distant shelf.

Now. To add flames to the fire. It takes my sharpest shiv to break into the box, then mondo maneuvering to work out one crummy miniature match. My next problem: providing enough friction to ignite the match, and enough of the proper kindling to set off the fire alarm. The entire job might have been easier if I had cracked Miss Kit's pantry door and broken into a can of Texas chili. Power to the pepper and the pussycat!

I cannot think of anything useful to burn around the place . . . until I remember the pile of papers Miss Kit Carlson keeps beside her computer in the room Miss Temple is sleeping in, when she is not sleeping out. They are only typed on one side, so I figure Miss Kit keeps them there for scratch paper. Pleased, I hop down to the floor by stages to implement the next, and most tedious, part of my plan.

Anybody dumb enough to have trained their eagle eye or telescope on these windows will be getting a most mysterious eyeful over the next couple of hours. Like a bunny rabbit, I hop out of sight, and then I hop back into view and up to the high shelf. My return trips are notable for the roll of paper clutched in my incisors.

In due time I have a nicely mounded pile of pages, each one titled "Siege of Sighs."

Finally, I drop-kick a match to the pile and scratch kitty litter until something ignites. (You must understand that I am not literally scratching kitty litter. I only use the stuff when there is not so much as a potted plant around as a substitute. But I use the same friction-laden movements with my hind feet that would burn litter, were it at all combustible.)

Finally a lucky kick slides match head against striker. I hear a sound of many wings beating, but it is only the leaves of paper that are curling as a cutting edge of bright fire eats away at them.

I skedaddle before any random spark catches my heels, and hunker down by the front door.

Not long afterward, an ear-splitting beeping goes off, accompanied by inmate shrieking, frantic phone dialing, downward drifting clouds of smoke and an urgent knock at the door, followed by a scrabbling sound of a passkey in the lock.

Above it all, the sprinkler system hisses to life and a gentle chlorinated rain falls on everything within range. Now the Leo the Lion at the MGM Grand hotel in Las Vegas is not the only one with a spraying problem.

But despite the hullabaloo, I keep my post by the door, springing forward to freedom when it bursts open and an excitable super spouting a language of the Indian subcontinent rushes through into the rain and the shrieks.

I am on my way to the fire exits, which are being thronged by nervous folk in nightclothes. The doors bat open and shut as tenants seek safety below. I thread through their legs on the dark, steep stairwell and am soon in the small lower lobby.

From there I am an ankle away from the freedom of the city.

In the distance, another of those annoyingly frequent New York sirens carries on like a banshee.

Everyone on the ground floor and the sidewalk outside looks up, so when I leap out fur to femur with an oblivious human, no one tries to stop me.

I sniff the evening air, which is much brisker than it is in Las Vegas. A pity. Scents do poorly in colder climes. I will have to use my other senses to follow the map route I have lain upon all afternoon. Luckily, Cornelia Street walks right into the Avenue of the Americas, otherwise known as Sixth. I take off down the street at a brisk trot, glimpsing Washington Square a block away. These pads were made for walking, but I have a long way to go up the spine of Manhattan before I hit the hostelry I seek.

In no time at all I am passing Fourteenth Street. Only thirty more blocks to go, but they are shrimp appetizers compared with the whale-length extent of blocks in Las Vegas. I pass churches and bars and office buildings. I am almost scuttled at Thirty-first when a bag lady decides that I am worse off than she is and tries to run me down with her shopping cart in the name of saving my soul. I dodge the squeaky wheels and take my chances underfoot, pausing to catch my breath at the Empire State Building. I am tempted to join the lines snaking to the top for a look-see at the Big Apple from the worm-on-top's point of view, but decide a tourist jaunt could blow my cover.

By then I am in Herald Square, where Broadway

crosses Sixth on its way to the seamy environs of Times Square. I sigh and head for more respectable realms, straight north, past Macy's department store. There I pause to offer suitable honor to the late Rudy, with whom I share a certain weakness for a certain weed, although my kind is legal. While I am paying my respects to a dead veteran, wouldn't you know some dude emerges from a building with not one but two Russian wolfhounds in tow. Or rather, the Russian wolfhounds have him in tow.

They eye me as one, launch a keening duet and tangle their leashes as they streak after me. Their owner has just become a boat anchor with nothing to snag onto.

I take off flat out, ears flat, feet flat, hair slicked to my back for maximum speed. I zig and zag, targeting tourists and other slow-moving pedestrians. On an even, unpopulated playing field I would be black caviar for those ancient hunters, but this is dysfunctionally chaotic New York City, boys, and I do not have any fancy harness holding me back.

I leave them entwined with a fairy-light bestrewed tree and a lady walking a toy poodle behind the New York Public Library. I give a small roar of greeting and triumph to the unseen Big Cats keeping guard on the building's Fifth Avenue entrance and pussyfoot the last two blocks to Forty-fourth.

Unfortunately, people in this city are more used to dog doo-doo by the curb than to the sight of an independent feline (and waste-management expert) on the move. They cry out and point to me, but I keep trotting and do not look back. It is lucky that my national commercials for Allpetco are not yet reality. It would really slow me down if I had to stop and sign autographs.

By the time I get to the Algonquin at Sixth and Forty-fourth, I am pooped, but only in the sense of being tired. I have not littered once upon the streets of New York, despite the stress of the chase. However, my breath blows frosty smoke rings and my sides are heaving. I collect myself outside the Blue Bar next door before attempting the final stage of my mission.

The Algonquin doormen are attired in long, full winter coats like the Wizard's guards wore in Oz. But I can work with long full coats. My wits and stamina gathered, I dart under the longest model on the shortest doorman. Within seconds I am within inches of the opening double doors. It is nothing for an old Las Vegas hand like myself to calculate the odds down to a whisker's breadth. I leap between the closing pincers of glass and brass without losing a tail-hair, then sprint through the inner set unscathed.

I am spit out into a lobby of the old school . . . say the library of Princeton University.

Luckily, the lobby resembles Mr. Robert Frost's wood: lovely, dark and deep. Age-darkened wood looms all around, providing excellent camouflage for a swarthy fellow like me. The carpeting, tastefully worn to a dull red, is less amenable, but no one seems to find my feline presence remarkable.

"Oh, look," says a lady with a Southern accent. "The famous house cat."

I bow and stroll into the eighteenth-century ambiance of the lobby-bar, moving among wing chairs and tea tables, head and tail high. At last, no hubbub. No dogs. No doo-doo. Just the tranquility so dear to the feline soul, and a smidgen of respect.

I am so pleased to be recognized despite the fact that none of my ads have run yet, that I fail to scan the ambience with all of my senses. Imagine my surprise to scent an odor of the most delicate feline nature.

A female of my species is very near.

Naturally, I cannot resist discovering if the Divine Yvette has accompanied her mistress for a cocktail, yet the scent is . . . foreign, if no less intriguing. I reconnoiter, arriving finally near a mahogany niche, a bookcase with the doors removed, which has been remodeled into a cat accommodation.

"Matilda's Suite" reads a plain brass marker. I study the décor beyond the red-velvet curtain held back by a golden rope. For a moment, the golden rope reminds me of recent unpleasantness, then I focus on the charming scene: rose-striped wallpaper, four-poster bed, a handsome parquet floor covered with scattered throw rugs, including a Persian of impeccable pedigree, a hanging candelabra, and the piquant touch of sock toy with a bell affixed lying on the parquet.

This Matilda must be one pampered pussycat. I sniff around trouser legs and pantyhose-clad ankles until I find the missing minx of the house.

There she lies, curled fast asleep on a tapestry-upholstered chair, a petite gray and buff tabby clad in an aqua leather collar.

"Pardon me, miss," I say in my best out-of-town manner. "I hesitate to disturb you, but I am a stranger in town."

Her golden eyes slit open, then she sits up, yawns and widens her pupils to take in my appearance.

"Well, I do not meet many of my kind here. Are you just stopping in for a drink or thinking of registering at the hotel?"

"I am visiting guests."

"Oho," says she, settling on her haunches. "Those high-fashion models on the ninth floor, no doubt. I have only glimpsed them coming and going. I doubt that you will get an audience with such snooty celebrities."

"My dear lady, I am a sort of celebrity myself."

"Oh? You do not look like Maurice."

"Him. He is dead meat. The name is Louie, Midnight Louie, and you will see more of me."

"I would not think that could be possible," she says, surveying my girth.

Well, she is a scrawny thing, and no doubt jealous. So I take my leave, knowing at least what floor to seek. Still, I do not wish to attract untoward attention, and the bellmen, at least, would recognize me for an unauthorized interloper, even though I only need to stroll in this relatively feline-secure environment. So once again I am forced to duck behind potted palms and semipotted persons to make my way to the elevators.

Here I am served by my nose. Speaking of potted this and that, I am sorry to say that the Divine Yvette's many stresses have led to a relaxation of potty procedures. And one of Miss Savannah Ashleigh's spike heels has managed to step into the scene of the crime.

I would be ready, willing and able to follow my Fair One's scent over the far Himalayas.

Tracing it to the proper elevator and then up to the proper floor is merely a matter of dogged persistence. By the time I am sniffing along the ninth-floor hall carpeting, I am reeling a bit, but still game. Or is that gamey? Certainly the spoor has hardly become cold. Or dry. I wobble down the hall until my nose directs me to a certain doorway.

The French are great believers in Nose. A well-trained Nose can discriminate between various vintages. A persnickety nose can tell a rose from a radish. A fine old feline Nose can follow a queen to her castle.

Number 917 it is. I pause to give the accomplishment of my quest a proper moment of reverence. I pause another ten seconds to gird my loins for a delicate mission. Wherever the Divine Yvette goes these days, so go the scurrilous offspring of the now-fixed Maurice. And also so goes the Sublime Sister Solange.

The average nomadic hero usually has only twain terrors to survive, like Scylla and Charybdis. I get Solange and Yvette and unknown offspring. It will take all the diplomacy and experience at my command to avoid playing favorites.

I decide to cut the suspense down to a reasonable time limit, and paw the door.

True, I have in times not far enough past felt the wrath of She Who Must Be Dismayed. But I am ready to face anything in hopes of putting things right with the Ashleigh girls.

At last my pathetic pawings are answered, but by nothing human.

A petite paw slips under the door to play padsie with my own. I am much encouraged that this is a "claws-in" pursuit.

In time, our machinations are jiggling the door in its frame. Then there is a mighty crack! And the door pops open like a jack-in-the-box.

I enter, the lion king in basic black, to discover Miss Savannah Ashleigh out, and both ladies at my beck and call.

"Oh, Louie," cries the Divine Yvette, who is on a first-name basis. "We have been robbed."

Robbed? Have some little kittens lost their mittens? I look around for the beastly little rug rats. I spy the offspring of Maurice treading carpet toward me with their needle-sharp nails. Cowards breed cowards. I catch the one in the lead by the nape.

"Slow down there, Sport," I mutter between my clenched teeth. "Did you see the perp?"

A flat-eared little head turns to mine, and comes back spitting.

"I am only five weeks old," she squalls, "and no 'Sport.' I cannot see shinola, you big bullyboy. Now release me before I scream kit abuse."

Obviously, she is blind if not unprimed in politically

correct defensive systems. I drop her like a hot coal. Sheesh. What a grouch.

"I meant by 'robbed,'" the Divine Yvette explains, "that I fear that Maurice and my sister will be the Allpetco spokescats."

"Neither one should count their kittens before they, er, hatch. Chin and whiskers up, my lovely. It is not over until the fat lady sings."

"What fat lady? My mistress would have a fit if she heard you use that phrase. It is true that she has been hitting the chocolate bonbons lately, but—"

I extricate myself diplomatically to pay my respects to her sibling and my likely costar, but first I trip over an encroaching youngster. I am fast deciding that Miss Savannah Ashleigh deserves a medal rather than a law suit for her actions toward myself and my now-impossible progeny.

I spy these hellions' aunt taking refuge under a dressing table. So I shake them off and ankle over to the Sublime Solange on my belly, complimenting her with purrs and licks all the way. It takes a handy fellow to handle a female.

I explain that I look forward to many happy film shoots with her, but that my first loyalties must remain attached to the Divine Yvette.

"How sweet of you, Louie." The Sublime Solange opens her citrine-green eyes until they seem to be suns going nova. "I like loyalty in a tom. I understand that you have taken a brave position to avoid polluting the planet with excess kits of checkered background."

"Well, I would not consider myself checkered, or even slubbed silk. Let us say that I recognize that a time must come when even the tommiest of Toms must take a position of responsibility in the community."

"Is *that* your position of responsibility?"

I look back to ascertain my form. It is perfect, as always.

"Yes, ma'am," say I.

"Aye, aye," says she.

It might be the beginning of a beautiful friendship, except that one of the tiger-stripe kits lurches over at a critical moment. I am forced to halt all operations (would that I had been able to do so a couple of weeks ago!), to pick up the miscreant by the scruff of its neck, and deliver the little bastard (a friendly figure of speech, I am sure) to its mama.

"Oh, Uncle Louie!" cries the interloper. "How big and strong you are!"

Flattery will get them longevity.

And so it goes in cat heaven. My harem of houris (two in number) lounge and purr benignly, while I am sore beset by Maurice's castoffs.

Some days it is not worth busting out of or breaking into a hotel, much less a nursery. Uncle Louie indeed! And we are not even related. I can hardly wait to return to Las Vegas.

Midnight Louie Bites the Big Apple

Wait a minute! I was under the impression that my new, politically correct status would be a lot more fun than it is turning out to be. So far. And all I have done so far is cry Uncle! But I must admit that I was not able to get around in my usual devil-may-care manner in my latest adventure.

I was beginning to feel distinctly like Nero Wolfe during this episode.

Not that I have developed a taste for orchids, although I am always ready to sample any bit of wild greenery that may cross my path, even if it is the cultivated variety. (I prefer feral flowers, myself. Wild game has a better flavor.)

No, it is just that the vicissitudes of the Big City being what they are, I can see why the superintelligent Mr. Wolfe chose not to dirty his foot leather with the grit of Gotham.

Me, I like to do my own footwork, and I am still light enough on my tootsies to manage it, if allowed to.

So I sincerely hope that the purple sling is a thing of the past in my future. Although, if Miss Temple Barr and I do win the purrsonal-appearance contract, I will have to train her to walk on a leash. It does not suit a dude of my talents to be toted hither and yon, and once I demonstrate that I can lead Miss Temple in precisely the direction that is best for her, we should get along well, although she may find it a bit demeaning being attached to me by a latter-day umbilical cord for the sake of her own safety. Some might think that she would not know where to go without a guide-cat, and in certain cases, especially criminal, that is indeed so.

I am pleased, however, that my long fondness for a particular weed has justified itself by proving useful in a murder case.

I am also pleased to have been introduced to a new leading lady. This is pure indulgence on the part of the author—not on *my* part (which is doing just fine, thank you), but on the part of Miss Carole Nelson Douglas. The Sublime Solange is no more than a pale imitation of a cat of my collaborator's acquaintance, one Secret in real life.

Even the name is secondhand, appropriately so considering that Secret and her mother, Victoria, were adopted as adults. Queen V (and she does act every inch the role, down to her flashing fangs) is a shaded silver Persian of the Divine Yvette stripe, but Victoria's Secret (who should definitely be in a lingerie catalog) is one of these shaded-golden throwbacks. If this is a throwback, you can fling me right back to wherever that is. I guess these golden girls and guys are considered a separate but equal breed now, but for a while they were in the doghouse, which is a terrible place for a cat of any color to be.

Such surprises as luscious new ladyfriends are the few rewards in the otherwise dangerous game of cat and mouse as played on the streets of Las Vegas or Manhattan by us detective dudes. It is all in a day's work for your trusty gumshoe-with-spikes. So is a well-deserved nap. Happy Christmas to all and to all a good nighty-night!

Very best fishes,

Midnight Louie, Esq.

P.S. You can reach Midnight Louie on the Internet at: http://www.catwriter.com/cdouglas

To subscribe to *Midnight Louie's Scratching Post-Intelligencer* newsletter, write: P.O. Box 331555, Fort Worth, TX 76163

Carole Nelson Douglas ♥s New York

The first time I saw New York City was on the high-school class trip, which was probably when most Americans were introduced to this quintessential metropolis. We saw a Broadway show: *Camelot* with Roddy McDowell, Robert Goulet and Julie Andrews. Richard Burton had already left the cast to hie to Italy to make *Cleopatra* with what's-her-name.

We must have walked all over Manhattan, because I remember our exuberant group dining at a steakhouse. My feet were so hot, sore and swollen that I discreetly smuggled some of those square little ice cubes from my water glass into my gold suede shoes.

Yes, it was damp. We adjourned to Radio City Music Hall, and while the Rockettes kicked up their heels, I slipped my aching dogs out of my damp flats. At departure time, my feet would qualify as balloons in Macy's Thanksgiving Day parade. I couldn't put my shoes on again.

That was the first of many lessons learned traveling to

exotic places. Never, ever take off your shoes! Especially on an international flight, I learned later.

My second New York trip came two years later, a theater tour. We saw several Broadway shows (including the musical version of Noel Coward's *Blithe Spirit* with Tammy Grimes and the late, great Bea Lillie as Madame Arcati), and an Off-Broadway show. The highlight of that trip was sipping Manhattans in a Greenwich Village bar and being driven back uptown by a black-cape-clad but charming Khigh Dhiegh, the wonderfully villainous Yen Lo from *The Manchurian Candidate*.

I was back the next year, a stopover for a smaller class trip to Europe. Our girlish trio of Midwestern college girls were impressed to say "Hello, Dolly" to Carol Channing when she made a grand postshow entrance at Sardi's, and to spot attorney Melvin Belli (almost as silver-blond as Carol Channing) checking in at the Sheraton Russell. We went dancing at a Village disco and walked dozens of blocks at midnight back to our midtown hotel with our high heels dangling from our hands, cutting through Grand Central Station. Try that in the nasty nineties!

Now I'm a veteran New York visitor and the memories are far more mundane. Nothing compares to the Big Apple's bite, but each year the siren sound of the night's many emergency runs keeps me up longer and the cabs get harder to slide in and out of fast enough to keep traffic flowing at the usual manic rate. New York, New York: it's a nice place to visit, but I wouldn't want to lug a twenty-pound cat around midtown in a kitty knapsack. Sometimes reality is better than fiction.

Available by mail from

TOR FORGE

CHICAGO BLUES • Hugh Holton
Police Commander Larry Cole returns in his most dangerous case to date when he investigates the murders of two assassins that bear the same M.O. as long-ago, savage, vigilante cases.

KILLER.APP • Barbara D'Amato
"Dazzling in its complexity and chilling in its exposure of how little privacy anyone has...totally mesmerizing."—*Cleveland Plain Dealer*

CAT IN A DIAMOND DAZZLE • Carole Nelson Douglas
The fifth title in Carole Nelson Douglas's Midnight Louie series—"All ailurphiles addicted to Lilian Jackson Braun's "The Cat Who..." mysteries...can latch onto a new *pur*rivate eye: Midnight Louie—slinking and sleuthing on his own, a la Mike Hammer."—*Fort Worth Star Telegram*

STRONG AS DEATH • Sharan Newman
The fourth title in Sharan Newman's critically acclaimed Catherine LeVendeur mystery series pits Catherine and her husband in a bizarre game of chance—which may end in Catherine's death.

PLAY IT AGAIN • Stephen Humphrey Bogart
In the classic style of a Bogart and Bacall movie, Stephen Humphrey Bogart delivers a gripping, fast-paced mystery."—*Baltimore Sun*

BLACKENING SONG • Aimée and David Thurlo
The first novel in the Ella Clah series involving ex-FBI agent, Ella Clah, investigating murders on a Navajo Reservation.